THE FETISH FIGHTERS AND OTHER ADVENTURES: THE F.V.W. MASON FOREIGN LEGION STORIES OMNIBUS

THE FETISH FIGHTERS
AND OTHER ADVENTURES

THE F.V.W. MASON FOREIGN
LEGION STORIES OMNIBUS

F.V.W. MASON

ILLUSTRATED BY

ROGER B. MORRISON
& JOHN R. NEILL

COVER BY

PAUL STAHR

STEEGER BOOKS • 2020

TABLE OF CONTENTS

The Word of Adjutant Kent 1

The Renegade Caid. 87

The Fetish Fighters. 151

The Twenty Wicked People 249

About the Author 281

THE WORD OF ADJUTANT KENT

*Legionnaire Roger Kent, the wreck of a fine
soldier, faces his life's crisis when the lonely
Foreign Legion outpost in the African jungle
is menaced by the Arab Suleiman's army*

CHAPTER I

A LEGIONNAIRE IN DISGRACE

ANKLE-DEEP IN THE sluggish coffee-colored current of the Goruol River, some eight or ten haggard men toiled listlessly with crowbars and sledge hammers to bore three small holes in the brown rock that formed the bed of the stream. On the bank above the sweat-bathed workers sat a guard in the blue and white uniform of the Foreign Legion, a rifle lying across his knees. Though he sat as motionless as a figure of bronze the perspiration coursed down his leathery cheeks in minute shiny trickles.

"Allo! là! Un croc!" One of the laborers, a man with a massive frame and a thatch of sand-colored hair, straightened painfully from his work and pointed a dirty forefinger at a barely visible ripple that was moving steadily toward that part of the shore where the—*ième Compagnie* of the Legion was in the process of building a little stone pier.

With a somnolent grunt the guard deliberately raised his Lebel rifle, sighted a moment, then shot at the ripple; his duties of guarding the prisoners included driving off the marauding crocodiles that had more than once dragged unhappy legionnaires to an exceedingly painful death.

At the sound of the report, crashingly loud in the oppressive heat, the other prisoners apathetically straightened their backs and stared at the spurt of foam where the bullet struck. There was a sudden submarine flurry as the missile struck, glanced and

1

"Any other skunk that wants the same dose, step right up!"

ricocheted with a dismal whine off over the unhealthily green grass on the far shore.

From among the rushes arose clouds of frightened birds that circled high into the hot, humid sky, then settled again out of sight.

"Missed him," remarked the big man disgustedly. "That guy couldn't hit a flight o' barns if they were tied down—"

"Allez! Go on, you lazy swine!" growled the guard, stung by the prisoner's remark. "More work and less talk, camel of an Américain!" The guard slapped a vivid green fly that had lighted on his neck, prepared to resume his seat, but hesitated when along the shore appeared another legionnaire hurrying at top speed. The white skirt of his puggaree fluttered out behind like a white signal flag.

The prisoners in the water rested, thankful for an opportunity to halt before the dynamite should be inserted for the next blast.

"Look at the beggar 'urry," remarked an undersized wiry little man among the prisoners. "Tuppence old Laurier is abaht to peg out—tyke me, Kent?"

The American with a bitter curse passed the back of a hand over his bloated, bristle-covered cheeks to drive off the multitude of flies that attempted to congregate there, and studied the new arrival.

"No," said he as the messenger arrived and pantingly delivered his message. "More likely old Suleiman Tombohko's advance guard has finally showed up—God, I'm thirsty!"

"'Oo? Old Solomon, the Slave Raider?" The smaller man's eyes grew large in the deep tan of his sharp, reddish face. "I thought 'e were scuppered larst season down on the Gongola."

"As usual, Jerry, you thought wrong," observed the man addressed as Kent. "Old Suleiman's damned well alive and ornerier than a moose in November. Oh, God! What I'd give for a drink!" He glared fiercely at a bright-hued kingfisher that darted by, a gleaming azure jewel against the green of the tangled forest across the river.

THERE WAS more than a trace of bitterness in the little cockney's glance as he turned from observing the two excited legionnaires on the bank to look at the long, rugged face of his friend.

"You and yer drink!" he half snarled with a flash of gold teeth. "Yer mykes me fair sick! It`s yer damned guzzlin' wot's got us this trip to the *corvée* like it'as a 'undred times afore." He stirred and the current rippled oilily about his ankles and broke over the chain that linked them together as he moved away in deep disgust.

"Drink, drink, drink!" continued the cockney over his shoulder. "Carn't yer think of anythink else, yer big drunk? Cut it out, I tells yer, ye're only 'arf a jump from the funny farm via the *cafard** route."

At the cockney's shrill abuse, the big man's grip on the rusty crowbar tightened convulsively.

"Shut up, you little Limey whelp!" he cried, his coarsened features writhing. "Say another word and I'll smash yer damned head!"

Jerry retreated toward the shore. He knew that in moments

---

* Going insane from loneliness and monotony.

like this his bosom friend, Kent, was not far removed from a homicidal maniac; the craze for the drink that had been the blond giant's undoing was torturing, maddening him beyond control. The other prisoners, regarding the two speakers, moved aside, hopelessly, endlessly brushing off the swarms of stinging, humming insects that formed shimmering black halos about their heat-tortured brows.

"Allo là!" The guard had arisen and was beckoning the workers ashore. "Hurry up, you scrapings! Soldats Kent and Schwartz, take up the dynamite and march behind. *Allez!"*

With sudden energy the prisoners waded ashore, their ankle chains clanking softly, and with the green slime of the river clinging to their dirtied white trouser legs.

"Ah! The good Suleiman," murmured a lowering Greek with close-shaved head, "he will give us a nice little vacation."

Very quickly the detachment fell in with a guard on either side and commenced to ascend the long, low slope that led to the newly erected *poste* of Dori. Its walls of sun-baked brick were neither very high nor very thick, but they nevertheless formed an effective shelter against such crude weapons as the swarming Mamprusi and Damerghu war parties carried. These fierce tribesmen bitterly resented the efforts of Mme. la Republique to put an end to slave trading, and objected very strenuously to the French interference.

"Gawd, wot a 'ell 'ole," groaned Jerry as he eyed the post. "No food, no life, no sport, nothink but fever 'eat and stinks. Hi 'opes as 'ow Hi goes west in the next shindy."

The *poste* comprised a long, low group of whitish buildings on the top of a small hill commanding a ford and a bend in the river. A single tower was reared higher than the balance of the buildings and from its crenellated top sprouted a flagstaff. On this the tricolor of France drooped listlessly.

Under the visor of a stained and battered *képi* Jerry glanced sidewise at his comrade; the tall American was toiling up the slope, a small blue box of dynamite balanced on his naked shoulder.

"Blowin' like a bloody foundered 'orse," muttered the cockney to himself. "And 'e orter do it wiv never a sigh. 'E's fair rotten wiv the liquor."

Presently the little column of the disgraced passed through the heavy timbered gate and found themselves in the midst of feverish activity. Everywhere were legionnaires sweating and cursing wearily as though preparing to repel an attack in force. Case after case of ammunition was withdrawn from the white-walled magazine and placed in convenient corners. Pails of water, too, were produced and set beside the yellow ammunition boxes. Everywhere was orderly confusion and the bull voice of Manuel Espada, the sole remaining sergeant, rang over all the noise.

As the prisoners halted in a single ragged line, a corporal issued at a trot from the main barracks and approached the guard, his face quivering with heat and apprehension.

THERE WAS an expression of surprise on the guard's face as he took the message. Then he spat resoundingly as he faced the wretches before him.

"Prisoner Kent! Step out!"

Stupidly the big prisoner raised bleared and hollow gray eyes and shambled forward to the accompanying clatter of his ankle chains.

"Stand up, pig!" rasped the guard, irritably. "You are to report to the captain at once. Pray God, he removes your quarrelsome, devil-sired presence forever. Get along now! Take thy filthiness from my sight!"

"Aw, shut up!" Kent's broad hands opened and shut menacingly, but the Lebel's muzzle arose with swift, unmistakable intent into line with the American's chest, and the blond prisoner subsided, to follow the orderly out of the blinding glare of the courtyard and into the fetid dampness of the little barracks.

As Kent slunk along at the orderly's heels with a guard standing close behind, his right hand, trembling with the unsteadiness of the habitual drunkard, rose automatically, as though to feel whether the buttons of his blouse were fastened; he had been a smart young soldier once. A bitter grin twisted his darkened features as the groping fingers encountered bare, sweaty flesh instead of trim whipcord.

Tallest of the three, he bent his head as they progressed down the dim, hollowly resounding passage where the air grew thicker and became tinged with the smell of moldy leather and chloride of lime.

Then a low querulous murmur filled the passage.

Suddenly a single voice rose to an agonized scream. "Ah, *Dieu! Dieu!* I die of thirst!" Then it sank again to the level of those other smothered groans.

The orderly in front of Kent shivered visibly and his hand twisted the ends of his long black mustache in nervous anxiety as they passed the short corridor from down which came the moans.

"Lieber Gott!" murmured the orderly in a voice that quivered perceptibly. "If this accursed fever gets any worse—Three new cases to-day!" He shook his head dolefully and rapped at the door of the orderly room while Kent halted with the delirious wretch's despairing cry ringing endlessly in his ears.

He straightened automatically as the door opened and the German orderly gruffly told him to enter.

"Wonder what new punishment old Laurier's thought up?" wondered the American as, with wet trousers flapping about his ankles, he passed through the door. "He sure loves to ride me. Maybe he'll give me the works this time and finish it up right. Wonder where I can find a drink?"

He thought with grim pleasure of a certain legionnaire, Hans Nurmer by name, lying in the overcrowded hospital nursing a broken jaw. The fact that Corporal Nurmer had been bullying an unfortunate, slow-witted Dutch boy to the verge of suicide when Kent, drunkenly and forcefully interfered, had made no difference to that worried, hard-eyed officer known as Captain Laurier.

The American had struck an officer, and that, soliloquized Kent, was punishable by death in times of war. The approach of the slave-raiding chieftain, Suleiman, could very conveniently be construed as a state of war should the distracted, fever racked captain decide to remove a trouble-making drunkard. A vision of a white bullet-pitted wall with a firing squad standing rigidly ready in front of it arose in minute detail before Kent's bloodshot eyes.

AT A word from the guard Kent shuffled through the orderly room and halted with a clank of fetters before the thumb-marked door of the captain's quarters.

The guard presented arms and stepped back as the orderly waved Kent through the door.

"Shut the door," directed a feeble voice while Kent stood momentarily blinded in the glaring light from a window across the room.

Gradually the American was able to recognize the outline of a man sitting in a bent position over a desk which was littered with papers. Kent barely suppressed a cry as the face revealed itself at last. Kent's own features must have shown his amazement, for the captain stiffened.

"Your tact, *soldat* Kent, does you little credit," panted the officer in uncertain accents. "Am I really then so changed?"

"Why—why, no, sir," stammered Kent. "It was the light, sir."

"You lie, *soldat* Kent," stated the officer wearily. "I am changed—I am a dying man." His hand, as it rested among the papers, shook violently, as though with a palsy, and the deep-set gray eyes burned with an unnatural light. "It's the fever. Why do those fat idiots in Paris want this forsaken Territoire Militaire?"

For some moments he mumbled uncertainly under his breath and sat staring fixedly at his hands as though they were something he had never seen before.

"Beg your pardon, sir," croaked Kent—how his throat burned for just a little drink! "Hadn't you better be lying down, sir?"

Quite deliberately Captain Laurier looked the prisoner in the face as though he sought to see something behind those bloated, coarsened features, and he slowly shook his head.

"No, *mon enfant*," he murmured heavily. "I'm far gone, and there is much to do. Every second before I die"—he drew a shuddering breath—"is precious. I have this *poste*—stand still, *sacré nom du Diable!* You are at attention!" The yellow-faced officer blazed forth in a terrible feverish access of rage. "I ought to have you shot! Of all the worthless, drunken, trouble-making wretches I have ever been condemned to command, you are the worst! You lie, you steal, you're slack, you'd do anything for a drink, you're altogether rotten—" Captain Laurier's sunken eyes gleamed savagely in their sockets. "I ought to have had you shot months ago. You've done nothing but make trouble. Your drunken fights breed discord of the worst kind."

UNDER THAT blast of scorn Kent's head swayed forward and he passed the tip of his tongue over split, sunburned lips. He swallowed miserably as he realized every word of the indictment was true. A fine end for Roger Kent, cadet captain of his class at the Point!

"Bah!" snarled the figure in the hot, dark blue uniform coat. "I must be mad to think of—" He broke off suddenly and, supporting his weight on his hands, he leaned over the table. "You, Kent—tell me the truth. God knows it seems impossible, but were you an officer once?" Those gray eyes seemed like bayonet points glinting before Kent's eyes.

Something deep in Kent's alcohol-sodden being arose in rebellion at the biting contempt of that fine-featured Frenchman. His loose lips writhed back as he snarled: "Yes, damn you, I was a damned good one, too! I was on the staff of—"

Then he remembered, and his taut figure relaxed.

"As I thought," muttered Laurier, and he swayed where he sat. "Then I was right. And now, my friend, I'm going to settle you once and for all. Stand aside, Schonblum!" He shouted feebly toward the door. Instantly it was opened and the orderly appeared, an automatic gleaming in his sweaty, dripping hand. "Order a squad with ball ammunition to the wall of the granary."

Kent's heart gave a great leap as he heard the words; so he was to be shot after all. Then he sighed in not unpleasant resignation. Well, that solved the question once and for all; and he was not in the least afraid to die. But it was an inglorious end—not at all what Cadet Captain Kent had foreseen when, with his newly earned commission rustling pleasantly in his suitcase, he had started forth to the Staff School in Washington.

Here he was about to be executed for breach of such an elemental thing as the Laws of War! He wriggled his dusty toes and vaguely wondered whether any of his classmates would ever hear of his passing, hear of the miserable end of Cadet Captain Kent. Imagine lying forever in a moldy, dishonored grave beside the pestilential high waters of the Niger. The dregs of his ambition were bitter as gall.

CHAPTER II

"THE POSTE MUST BE HELD!"

AS THE FOOTSTEPS of the orderly died away down the hall outside, Captain Laurier faced the prisoner again and, with a stifled moan, settled heavily back in his roughly fashioned armchair.

"You heard the order I gave?" he quietly demanded as Kent's eyes at last rose to meet his. "You realize, *soldat* Kent, what that means?" He waited in silence for a reply that did not come. "It means I'm going to have you shot. In a way, I will be doing all that was decent in you a kindness, but—"

"But—" Kent's head, with its mass of shaggy blond hair, raised itself slowly. It was almost with dignity that the derelict spoke.

"Why do you torture me like this, *mon capitaine?* Get me shot and have done with it!"

Captain Laurier raised a withered yellow hand that shook like a dead leaf in a winter gale.

"Silence!" he snapped, "I am forced by necessity to give you a chance to redeem yourself. Yes, you!" he said as Kent's eyes widened. "Even you can be redeemed, perhaps. You can't fool me. I've handled too many men during my service in *La Légion.* To my mind you are well born, well educated, and probably were a passable officer once upon a time."

Kent winced at the contempt in that withered aristocrat's face. His every word rang out in that unbearable hot little room like a challenge.

"I find myself soon to die," went on the officer. He spoke heavily and wiped his sweat-covered features. "My Lieutenant Henricot is dead, as you know, from this accursed jungle fever. Gone, too, are the best of my sergeants. The last, Humbert, was sent away trying to find the relief column—I sent him while you snored in drunken stupor in a cell."

Captain Laurier's face contracted spasmodically and a silence fell in which the buzzing of the myriad sticky black flies was clearly audible. Perspiration dark with mud from the river fell from Kent's body with tiny patterings upon the hard earth floor.

With the frenzied gesture of a man who chokes, the captain wrenched open the high, tight collar of his blouse and gasped for breath as he resumed his account.

"Where the relief column is, only *le bon Dieu* knows—they should have been here a month ago. Wiped out probably by Suleiman's slavers. But as I was saying, I sent Sergeant Humbert to search for them; that was ten days ago. From him I have had no word and he was under orders to return on the sixth day."

Puzzled as to why the commanding officer should explain the dire straits of the garrison in such detail to a condemned man, Kent merely stood in his foul rags, staring, and listened.

"This Suleiman has forces overwhelming in number. Half a

thousand men at the least. We have very few. We have no medicines and the garrison dies like cattle of fly sickness; but this *poste* must he held. You have something to say?"

"Yes, sir," replied Kent, and wondered at his own temerity. "Why shouldn't we 'vacuate this rotten fever-ridden hole, retreat to the hills, wait until the relief came up, then reoccupy it?"

Like long-disused machinery Kent's brain functioned slowly and unwillingly. Snatches and phrases other than the obscenities of drunkenness began to return—the language of officers and gentlemen. Under the dirt, Kent's face burned with sudden color. Captain Laurier stifled a groan, poured a glassful of amber-colored water from an earthenware jar and drained the fluid at a single gulp.

"Aha! So we still can think a little, can we?" His fever-bright eyes rested on the tall prisoner. "But no, we cannot evacuate the *poste*," he continued grimly. "First, because in the open Suleiman Tombohko would annihilate us; and second, because to evacuate the *poste* would throw open the whole Volta valley to him. He would murder and enslave thousands of helpless blacks, disarmed and trusting to us for protection. It would be terrible, horrible—no, *mon enfant*, the *poste* must be held! It is that realization which tortures my last hours."

FROM JUST outside the window behind Captain Laurier came the rhythmic tramp of marching men, and a double row of flashing bayonet points passed on a level with the sill.

At that sound Kent felt an icy trickle follow the line of his spine—those marching men were the firing squad. In less than five short minutes he, Roger Kent, would be facing the rifles of those hard-featured legionnaires. All former victims of his drunken might, they would welcome his downfall. As from afar the sound of Captain Laurier's voice broke in on the prisoner's thoughts.

"And now, *soldat* Kent," said he gravely, "I am about to make you a proposal. You have just seen that firing squad go by?"

Like a man in a dream Kent nodded his unkempt head a single time.

"I will give you the choice of being shot by them, or—becoming first in command of this *poste!*"

As though the hand of an invisible giant had struck him, Kent rocked on his naked dirty feet until the chain rattled softly. He blinked stupidly and his bruised, swollen features grinned, revealing yellowed, tobacco-stained teeth.

"You like your rotten little joke, don't you, you goddam Frog?" Resentfully he stared at the stern haggard man behind the desk. "If you were half the man you pretend to be, you'd give me a drink and shoot me. Me in command? Ha-ha-ha!" He burst into low hysterical laughter.

Quite deliberately Captain Laurier repeated his astounding offer, while Kent fell silent and in a maze of conflicting emotions, struggled to collect dimmed, befuddled wits. "You're nutty, then," Kent managed to say. "You're sick—delirious, I guess."

"No, I'm not delirious," gasped the figure in dark blue. "I feel what I do is for the best. Unfortunately you happen to be the one man of officer caliber in this *poste*. Degraded as you are, you are still better than the rabble of common legionnaires." He paused in bitter despair. "Ten thousand black lives are in the keeping of the commandant of this *poste*, and the traditions of the Foreign Legion! *Mon Dieu*—that it must all rest on a drunkard!"

Wildly Kent looked about that bare torrid chamber and his hand sought his throat in dreadful perplexity. Had he forgotten so much? Had he followed the line of least resistance too long? Could he make those savage legionnaires obey him? He knew the task was too great.

Captain Laurier from his chair of ebony and rawhide could guess part of the struggle that was going on inside the chained, half-naked prisoner, towering so tall and dark against the white-washed wall.

"I will disguise nothing," he added with an ironic smile. "The commander of this *poste* will have problems to meet in the next few days that would break the heart of a field marshal. The morale is gone—too much heat, monotony and death. The men are on the point of mutiny, the supplies are low and this terrible fever kills men every day. Sultan Suleiman will surround us before dawn to-morrow—but the *poste* must be held."

There was an appeal in the eyes of the courageous dying officer that stirred something deep in the derelict's being. "You, *soldat* Kent, I believe to be the only man who possesses the quality to drive the men and to hold out to the bitter end. The others, Espada and the rest, would haul down *le Tricouleur* and run to save their precious skins. You will help me, no?"

"I—I—aw, hell, sir," stammered Kent helplessly with outheld hands. "I haven't been an officer in years—I can't—I'm no good—I've forgotten anything I ever knew—I could never do it. Make me *commandante* and I'd be drunk in half an hour—I couldn't live without liquor."

Captain Laurier gave a groan that was half a sob and sank slowly forward on the desk top, lying there with his arms sprawled over the papers and his fingers twitching. Kent started forward with a cry of alarm, but as his fingers brushed the officer's coat, the Frenchman managed to straighten up painfully.

"THE FLAMES of hell itself are burning me—I am going fast," he choked. And his face had assumed a ghastly bronze-green tint. "Here is my offer—accept it and I will appoint you *adjutant** of the *poste*. I will appoint you my second in command—before the whole garrison I will do it—I will make myself live that long, until it is done. Dear God! How my head reels! But you must give me your word of honor," he continued, "the word of the gentleman you once were, that"—Laurier steadied himself on the table by a determined effort—"you will not touch a drop of liquor until the *poste* is relieved."

In abject misery Kent stared stonily at his naked toes to keep his equilibrium. Instinctively he knew he couldn't do it. Fight?

---

* In the French service the *adjutant* is a noncommissioned officer.

Yes. Starve? Yes. Die? Gladly. Keep away from liquor? It had been meat, drink and forgetfulness to him for years. Impossible. With a groan wrenched from his soul, Kent shook his head.

"Think again, *soldat* Kent," pleaded the officer. "If not for your own sake, then for the sake of the helpless blacks that we have disarmed, that France has promised to protect—"

It was without doubt the most terrible moment of Roger Kent's misspent life—saving only that day when he had stood up before a court-martial of his peers to be cashiered. Inside his head was a strange jumble of impulses, some urging him to abandon the struggle, others crying out to him to undertake the burden. Then he spoke.

"May I borrow a coin, *M. le Capitaine?*" he begged. Wonderingly, the gray-haired officer produced an Algerian ten-centime piece and passed it over. Placing the copper on his broken, black-rimmed thumbnail, Kent flipped the coin up to the ceiling where, caught by a wandering sunbeam, it flashed redly in its flight. Then the American caught it between his hands, drew a deep breath and bit by bit revealed the surface.

"You see, sir," he muttered thickly, "I haven't enough moral strength left to make a decision—how dare you trust the *poste* to me?"

"I have no choice," gasped Laurier and drank another glass of the muddy-tasting water.

Suddenly Kent stiffened. He drew his big body erect, threw back his sun-burned shoulders and saluted briskly—a strange, half-naked figure with a face of a tramp saluting in the manner of a soldier born.

"Very well, sir," said Roger Kent in a sharp ringing voice that contrasted oddly with the thick uncertain accents of his previous speech. "I'll try, by God! I'll try, and I'll do my best. God knows if I haven't gone too far down—" The thirst was wrenching at his throat as he spoke and sweat not caused by the heat stood out on his forehead in pellucid beads.

CHAPTER III

SULEIMAN'S ARMY

AN HOUR AFTERWARD the disheartened garrison was, much to its own surprise, paraded in the evening glow.

"Now wot the 'ell?" demanded Jerry of the legionnaire on his left. "Is they abaht to shoot poor old Kent afore the 'ole bloomin' houtfit?"

"Who knows?" replied the other. "But look thou at the gaps in the ranks. Half of the first platoon is gone—Duroche said there were twenty sick of the fever, and there are ten off with Sergeant Humbert. It will be very short and sad when that playful Suleiman arrives," he added as a bugle shrilled "Attention."

A moment later a strange procession appeared from the barracks. In the last red rays of the sun Jerry could see them plainly. First Captain Laurier, his legs wavering under him as two tall orderlies almost carried him forward. Then just behind him strode a tall, broad-shouldered legionnaire whom Jerry at first did not recognize. The cockney started in surprise and smothered an oath of amazement as he saw that the stranger wore the braid of an adjutant on either cuff.

"*Sang' de Dieu!*" breathed the bronzed and bearded legionnaire beside Jerry. "Am I gone mad or is it that devil of a drunken American?"

Then Jerry nearly disgraced himself by dropping his piece on parade, and his small blue eyes were round as twin buttons as he recognized that new N.C.O.

"Gawd strike me pink!" was all he could whisper.

Very briefly Captain Laurier appointed Roger Kent as *adjutant* second in command, while the whole garrison watched in incredulous, bitterly resentful amazement. And nowhere was there a deeper scowl than that on the face of Sergeant Manuel Espada.

"Dios," he murmured. "The captain must be delirious to trust the *poste* to a worthless drunkard." And forthwith, his facile brain commenced to attack the problem of removing that ridiculous puppet. The answer was as easy to him as it was to the majority of those hardened characters in the ranks; to them, force was the only answer to any difficult problem.

Loud and heartfelt were the curses that rang up into the evening sky as the garrison fell out and Kent disappeared in company with the stricken captain. The swarms of homing cranes, crows and ibis circled to avoid the uproar, adding their harsh unearthly croaks to the turmoil below.

"May I, Mihail Chetyre, be damned, twice damned and thrice damned if I stay to have my precious gullet slit," declared a grizzled old Russian who, according to rumor, had once been a bank president in Odessa. "Under real officers I'll fight with the best, but under that sodden wine-skin—*Niet!*"

And that was the tenor of most of their remarks.

"Dat captain-man mus' be crazy wid de heat," said Legionnaire Adipose Brule—and scratched the kinky wool on his cranium in childlike perplexity. "Whaffor he want to set pore ol' Kent up? He's much happier drunk—drinkin'est man Ah ever see!"

Jerry regarded the big South Carolina buck with condescension.

"There ain't nothink my pal Kent can't do ef 'e only wants to," stated the little Englishman solemnly. " 'E'll myke good, you'll see." And Jerry's sharp little face creased in a confident smile with an assurance he in no wise felt.

"What? Dat trash? Him make good?" Legionnaire Brule's enormous mouth opened in a cavernous, contemptuous guffaw. "Yassuh, he'll stay sober when de lil shotes flies 'roun' wid de mockin' birds. Listen to me, white boy. My pappy uster tell me: 'Once a drunk, always a drunk'; an' buhlieve me, pappy, he knew—he died wid a mourner's bench full o' pink baboons an' lavender gy-raffes sitting at de foot of de bed." Legionnaire Adipose swaggered off to mingle with a knot of angry legionnaires clustering about the towering, dominating frame of Sergeant Espada.

"Wait an' see," was Jerry's futile and faint-hearted retort. In the depths of his heart, he, too, doubted that Roger Kent could successfully carry the crushing burden that had fallen on his unprepared shoulders.

JUST AFTER the evening meal, a sullen and disgusted orderly sought out Jerry where he lay motionless on his narrow little cot in the single *chambrée,* where the enlisted personnel of the entire garrison slept.

"Come," growled the messenger. "Our precious *adjutant* is waiting for you." In the rays of the oil lantern he carried, the fellow's gaunt features resembled the face of a famine-struck Rajput Jerry had once seen in India. To-morrow that orderly would be in the fever ward. The little legionnaire shivered.

"Um," thought Jerry as he pulled on a damp white linen shirt, "there's another toff 'eaded fer the 'orspital and the boneyard."

By the dim light of a smoking lamp, the cockney found the newly-created *adjutant* working over a mass of papers, his pen moving rapidly across the paper.

" 'Ullo, cocky," said Jerry when they were alone. "Wotcher goin' to do wiv us?"

"Work hell out of you," was the amazing reply. "You're a corporal, by the by. And speak quietly. I believe Captain Laurier has just died—as he lived, as an example to his men."

Even as he spoke, a hollow-eyed medical orderly girt with a dirtied white apron came out of the captain's room and saluted.*

"It's all over, *mon adjutant,*" he murmured in an awed whisper answering Kent's unspoken inquiry.

Silently the new commanding officer nodded. "Go back to

---

* In the French Army before the War, N.C.O.'s, as well as commissioned officers, were saluted by privates.

the hospital—but wait. How are the sick? Are any of them on the mend?"

"Bad," replied the legionnaire with a discouraged shrug. "They die and die—and there is nothing to do but watch them die. God help us, we have no quinine left—the relief column was to have brought it."

"Stand to attention!" rapped Kent in a tone that made Jerry in the shadows stare in surprise, then automatically stiffen. "No slouching about, even if things are bad. Go back to the hospital and make those poor devils as comfortable as you can."

Then Adjutant Kent got to his feet, went out to the court, and caused the bugler to assemble the garrison. When they stood ranged in silent orderly files, he divided them into reapportioned platoons of equal strength, created temporary N.C.O.'s from the best of them, and addressed them briefly.

"You will obey my orders," he announced crisply, "and obey them cheerfully and implicitly. The first man that questions my orders by deed or voice will be shot."

At that moment there sounded in the distance the report of a single shot. It came from deep in the forest-jungle to the northeast. A thrill like an electric shock ran through Kent as he realized that the slave-raiding Sultan Suleiman Tombohko was investing the *poste* at last—and the relief column had not come.

"Now, then, *mes enfants,* to your posts!"

Sullenly and with deep suspicion written on their lowering brows, the legionnaires climbed slowly to their posts in time to catch a glimpse of a seemingly endless column of men crossing a meadow which separated the *poste* from the vine-matted jungle. Like a whitish river, silently moving horsemen and footmen crossed the open space to be swallowed up once more in the blackness of the forest. Faintly the snuffle of horses and the rumble of human voices carried up to the demoralized men on the walls.

As Suleiman had intended, the number of the slavers brought despair to the stoutest heart in the garrison. There must have been nearly a thousand men in that column, thought Kent, as he lay flat on the floor of the watchtower and peered through the gathering darkness.

"**JUST 'OW** many men we got?" queried Jerry. "We'll need every bloke o' the lot and 'is twin to boot, afore this shindy's over."

"Out of the original garrison of ninety-eight," whispered Kent, "fifteen have already died of the fever and crocs; ten are off with Sergeant Humbert hunting the relief column; and we've got eleven more in the hospital that have to be counted out."

"Leaves us sixty-three," commented Jerry dismally, and dodged nervously as a large inquisitive fruit bat skimmed by his ears.

"Sixty-two," corrected Kent. He sighed, for his stomach tortured him unrelentingly. "Sixty-two men to stand off at least six hundred—Jerry, I can't see how it can be done."

"Steady on, old son," encouraged Jerry. "Yer'll pull orf the job yet. They's a undisciplined lot o' blighters out yonder."

As the words left the little Englishman's lips, from the nearest wall of the *poste* came a spurt of orange-tinted flame that lit the insect-filled night with brief clarity; and the *képi* leaped from Kent's head as though an invisible hand had snatched it away. With remarkable speed the *adjutant* drew an automatic from the holster belted about his waist. He sighted rapidly at a dark blur crouching on a firing platform below, and fired. As the report died away there followed a coughing grunt, a scream of pain and the sound of a heavy fall mingled with the clattering of a dropped rifle.

"Number one," remarked Kent clearly to the darkness below. "Any other skunk who wants the same dose, step right up!" But silence reigned about the besieged fort, silence pregnant with disaster.

"Jerry," whispered the big man, "this will be a lovely mess if the boys can't shoot better than that. Think of it, missed at twenty yards range—perfectly disgusting shooting! Jerry," he added fiercely, and his frame shook with the intensity of his words, "you can't imagine what I'd give for a drink—just a mouthful! I was a damn fool to take the job. I'll have to have a drink soon or I'll go crazy—"

In the darkness Jerry looked up curiously. "Well, why doncher tyke one—pore old Lauriay 'll never know now."

"I won't just yet—gave my word I wouldn't," muttered Kent thickly. "I'm going to try to stick it out a little longer—till morning anyhow. After that I won't promise."

CHAPTER IV

CHALLENGE

THE GRAY, SLOW-DRIFTING mists were still thick over the Goruol River, and hippopotami in the not very distant fens boomed sleepily, as a single Arab on the back of a plunging white horse rode boldly up to the gate of the *poste*. On a short broken branch that still retained a few leaves, the savage-faced emissary carried a square of dirty white cloth. This he waved to and fro. Rising in his stirrups he cried aloud to the curious legionnaires on the wall. He was clad in a blue-and-white-striped *haik*,* with a dirtied red *chéchia*—fez—on his shaved skull.

A blue-jowled Italian drew a bead on the center of the rider's chest just where two cartridge bandoleers crossed each other. and gauged the speed of the horse's gallop. He drew a deep breath and was about to squeeze the trigger when a stinging blow on the side of the head interrupted his little test of marksmanship.

"Fool! Ass-born dog!"

The man glanced up furiously, then wilted. Shaking with rage Sergeant Espada stood over the rash legionnaire, his huge fists balled and his eyes glaring at the Italian, lying prostrate.

---

*   Robelike outer garment.

"Hast thou no wit?" he hissed in an undertone. "Wouldst thou murder Suleiman's messenger? Son of an idiot baboon. By the slaver's good graces we may yet escape with a whole skin the madness of this drunken Americano."

The Italian, glowering, rubbed his cheek, but nodded in comprehension. So that was the way the wind blew! He shrugged and got up again, tortured by an aching head and burning throat.

Kent meanwhile had stalked along the firing platform to the embrasures immediately above the gate.

"No man to shoot," he roared and stood up in plain sight. "Well?"

The emissary, very picturesque in his flowing robes, leaped from his horse with a lithe grace and bowed deeply. Subconsciously Kent noted how the slaver's coal-black skin contrasted with the white stripes of the cloak. Thrice the Arab performed this elaborate salaam.

"To our friends, the Franzwazi,*" he began in sonorous tones, "greetings from the mighty Sultan Suleiman Tombohko, ruler of the Damerdhu, Wandala, Bodhal, Niamey—"

"Granted," murmured Jerry with a snigger at the black's pompous pose. "Git on wiv yer."

"For the Lord's sake, shut up!" snarled Kent from the side of his mouth. "Try to show some dignity—half the battle with these niggers is bluffing 'em!"

From the dusty classrooms at West Point whole pages and chapters began to come back—but still his mind would only work with desperate sluggishness.

"To our valued friend, the Sultan Suleiman Tombohko, we send greetings," returned Kent from above the gate. He stood waiting for the emissary's further speech, carefully studying the intelligent black face below. It was not in the least like those of the good-natured negroes back home. The raider's very modern Mauser rifle was glaringly incongruous with the antique dagger

---

* French.

that dangled from a wide silver-studded belt of finely woven camel's hair.

"Says the Sultan, he goes into his dominions to gather taxes from his vassals beyond the Goruol. He demands free passage to go and come as he pleases. He brings presents to his white brothers," added the ambassador with a meaning laugh.

For a moment Kent stood silent waiting for the man to finish his speech. The two principals of the parley afforded a strange picture in the growing light of morning. The Arab half-breed below in flowing striped robes, their white tinted pink by the sunrise, his Mauser slung carelessly across his back, and the tall soldier above the gate in the trim blue uniform of the legion's N.C.O. For a long minute they silently took stock of each other.

"Sultan Suleiman Tombohko has our permission," replied Kent gravely and with more than a hint of deference, "to come and go as he pleases into the lands beyond the river."

"**MY GAWD,** Kent!" demanded Jerry, in pained surprise, "yer ain't goin' to let that pack o' bleedin' cutthroats through?" The cockney's expression was tragic as Kent ignored the question to watch the dark face with its forked black beard.

The emissary smiled, broadly showing white even teeth. His hand fluttered from brow to heart. On the walls the legionnaires breathed easier. So the new *adjutant* would listen to reason after all. That's luck—perhaps now they would let him live.

"Messieurs les legionnaires will be well paid for the courtesy," the man promised. Among the assembled legionnaires arose a wondering but satisfied murmur. *Peaudzebie!* Perhaps this American had some sense after all! For all his damned superiority and fine airs he was not above taking a bribe. The hard, brown faces broke into broad smiles, and only Jerry was disconsolate and contemptuous of his friend.

"One moment, Sidi," called Kent as the Arab prepared to vault into the saddle once more. "Ere you return to the Sultan your master, there is a detail, an insignificant detail connected with this permission. Sultan Suleiman may freely go across the

Goruol, but first, he and his followers will leave behind all arms save only those used in hunting. His vassals are now disarmed, he will not need weapons." Then Kent added a supreme piece of effrontery. "We will guarantee your safety."

Sixty men guaranteeing the safety of a thousand! The emissary started as though a bullet had struck him. He reined his horse with a cruel jerk that threw it back on its haunches and dropped back to earth again. On his savage countenance was an expression of mingled incredulity and rage.

"Fool, art thou mad?" he snarled and his forked black beard quivered. "Suleiman Tombohko does not lay down his arms at the word of the *Franzwazi* dogs. He needs no protection, insolent one!"

A loud murmur of protest broke out from the men along the firing platforms as they realized the trend the parley was taking. *Nom de Dieu!* The drink-addled fool was putting their collective head into the noose after all—or, to be more exact, their bodies into Suleiman's clutches, which was far worse.

"Nevertheless. Suleiman will certainly drop his arms," reiterated Kent quite unruffled, "if he wishes to pass the *poste*. Otherwise, he is at liberty to turn back."

For a moment the black stood immobile, quite speechless with wrath, while his small horse restlessly tossed its long mane, fretting at the delay, Finally the Arab managed to control his ire sufficiently to speak. In a burst of passionate Arabic he heaped curse after curse upon the legionnaires. At last he quieted somewhat.

"Hearken, O *Franzwazi!*" he concluded in a loud voice that carried to all parts of the *poste*. "The warriors of Sultan Suleiman are as the sands of the desert—do not think to thwart him with thy wretched handful."

"Nevertheless," repeated Kent apparently unimpressed, "we have arms and men in plenty. We fear not Sultan Suleiman. Let him surrender his arms and he may pass—"

"*Kelb ibn kelb!*"* shouted the Arab, and leaping on his horse he drew a yataghan and brandished it at the motionless *adjutant*. "When thou liest naked upon the ant heaps, remember that thou hast refused the clemency of the Sultan!"

He shook the curved blade first at Kent, standing above the gate with the first rays of the sun tinting his bloated cheeks; then at the various embrasures where the legionnaires were muttering hopelessly and angrily among themselves.

"You shall all perish! *Roumi* swine, you shall feed the kites, and the hyenas shall fight the vultures for thy bones."

Realizing that the emissary's threats were shaking the already discouraged garrison's courage, Kent cut short the parley with an abrupt and imperious command to be off. When the Arab lingered to shout more promises of death and torture, Jerry at Kent's command, sent a bullet whistling over the horseman's *chéchia*.

With a shrill valedictory curse, Suleiman's ambassador thrust his naked feet home in bronze shovel stirrups and galloped off toward the silent green forest at top speed. The thud of those fading hoof beats sounded like a knell in the ears of the fearful legionnaires.

THE TRAMP of footsteps hastily mounting the ladder which led to the gate top caused Kent to turn in time to see Sergeant Espada, his dark features ominous and furious, followed by half a dozen thoroughly frightened men.

"Fool!" raved the Spaniard, with eyes that glittered with passion. "Thou are mad! Suleiman will assuredly cut all our throats. Call back the emissary while yet there is time."

"Oui!" bawled a villainous Marseilles Apache, lingering his bayonet. "This drunken scum of the wine shops has cheated us of gold!"

"And ivory—"

They crowded close, hairy, clawlike hands raised, and voices

---

*   "Dog and son of a dog!"

protesting in half a dozen languages, Kent merely folded his arms and stood still.

"Our case is hopeless," added another whom Kent recognized as La-Touche, one of the more decent men among the legionnaires. "To resist is futile—nay, it is suicide." This he said in an undertone as the chorus of protest rose high to the heavens.

Kent knew that his life and the fate of the *poste* trembled in the balance. Jerry quietly cocked his Lebel rifle and carelessly allowed the muzzle to fall in line with the broad, agitated chest of Sergeant Espada, late of the slums of Agadir and the prisons of the Spanish king.

"Messy bloke," thought Jerry; " 'is buttons is dull."

A dreadful doubt seized the American—he couldn't seem to think. In the old days he would have known instinctively how to handle such a situation, but now his brain seemed numb; quite incapable of working smoothly. He realized he must do something—Espada was advancing threateningly and the other legionnaires were gathering menacingly around him like a pack of jackals waiting the signal to spring. Everywhere faces— faces—hostile, filled with hate.

A fiendish voice kept repeating in his ear: "Let them have their way. It's too hard. Take Suleiman's bribe and let the Arabs through. Gold! Money! Ivory!—*drink!* Forget all this in drink— they'll kill you if you don't!"

The temptation was frightful, overwhelming. It was so long since he had made and won a moral decision of any kind. Great God! How his whole being craved the drink!

He opened his mouth to give the assent. Espada must have read the decision, for the Spaniard's small black eyes on either side of his great beak of a nose lit in triumph. Quite unknown to Kent, Jerry's forefinger curled ready about the trigger. Espada would die the instant he touched Kent. Then, from amid the sour river fog that smelled of crushed marigolds, arose the stern face of Captain Laurier, his dead, sunken eyes terrible.

"Your word, *adjutant!* Your word," he seemed to say. "The word of an officer and a—"

Adjutant Kent straightened suddenly and his jaw shut with a click as he stepped forward confronting the sputtering Spaniard with a chilling mask of authority.

"Silence! You cowardly dog—stand to attention!"

Manuel Espada never knew why in spite of himself he stiffened to attention. Perhaps it was something in the quality of that command which made him obey. He opened his mouth to protest, but Kent cut him short with a harsh "Silence! To your posts!"

Though the American had not even motioned toward the automatic at his belt, and stood quite alone save for little vigilant Jerry, the pack shifted uneasily under the *adjutant's* baleful glare. One by one the legionnaires sullenly descended the ladder again. Kent watched them go with a contemptuous smile. But as the last malcontent disappeared, he swayed, and Jerry saw great beads of sweat on his brow.

"Sound the *alerte,*" he snapped as he found the bugler idly smoking a cigarette in the lee of the south wall. "And if you value your worthless life, pay attention to my orders!"

The sound of the high, clear notes of the bugle call ringing out over the tropic dawn seemed to give Roger Kent a little more assurance, but he felt sick and very unequal to the situation. His stomach tortured him and as he strode along the firing platforms he found he was breathing heavily, and though the dawn chill was yet in the air, perspiration stood out on his brow as though he had been undergoing violent physical exercise.

"HO!" GREETED a slovenly Russian, mistaking the *adjutant's* unsteadiness for drunkenness, "see, 'tis our play-acting commandant." He swept his *képi* from his semibald head and bowed in mock deference. "So it pleases your highness to have our throats cut—"

The Russian staggered, reeled sidewise, and fell on his face, senseless and quiet, as Kent, with something of the force that had made him heavyweight champion at the Point smote the mocker on the point of the jaw.

"Throw some water over this insolent dog!" he briefly commanded the men about. "Jump to it! Jacquers, where in hell is the ammunition for this embrasure? Get it!" Without hesitation the man responsible cringed and scuttled off to the magazine.

With an eye that, as long ago, pitilessly detected every piece of negligence, every error of omission or commission, Kent passed along the firing platforms, while the garrison at first responded sullenly, then found itself jumping about as it had not done since Captain Laurier had been taken sick. There was no disobeying that strange N.C.O. who struggled desperately to regain a long-vanished power over men.

Promptly at six in the morning the attack began. From within a distant clump of banyan trees a ragged fusillade was fired.

"Number one," remarked Jerry tersely as a bullet sang through one of the embrasures and struck a legionnaire who had carelessly exposed himself. The fellow uttered a piercing cry and, clapping his hands to a scarlet patch on his throat, rolled from the firing platform and fell to the dusty court below with a heavy thud that sent a chill to the heart of every man present.

"He's not so badly off at that, as we are," grunted the Apache, who was by nature a pessimist.

At each little embrasure crouched a blue-and-white-clad legionnaire, his rifle loaded and ready, a little heap of glistening brass cartridge clips conveniently stacked by his right knee. At regular intervals stood temporary sergeants—appointed by Kent from the steadiest and least worthless of the corporals.

Below the firing platform were the men detailed to carry the ammunition and to act as a reserve. A small heap of brown ammunition boxes were arranged in the center of the court which was approximately sixty by a hundred feet long.

On the top of the watch tower Kent placed the best shots with instructions to occupy themselves solely with the leaders of the enemy—it had come back to him from the dim pages of the past that untrained fighters were under a severe handicap the instant the directing genius became a casualty.

"Gawd," thought Jerry as he watched with undisguised admiration the effective manner in which the new *adjutant* disposed the men. "'E's beginnin' to get the 'ang of it again." He grinned to himself. "Wot did I tell yer?" He challenged Legionnaire Brule as that dusky individual passed by, bent low under a case of ammunition.

The negro sank to the platform and peered cautiously toward the tangle of rubber vines, tamarind and gambier trees.

"Ah sez agin what Ah sez befo'," grunted the black. "'Mos' anybody kin take de pledge an'las' fo'a day or so—Ah sez as Ah sez befo', 'once a drunk, allus a drunk'! Jes' you wait an' see dat white boy to-morrow. Man, he'll be hittin' dat ole bottle wusser'n ever."

Then from afar a shrill horn sounded, and at once a tom-tom commenced to throb, others joined in until the whole forest boomed and frightened monkeys chattered in noisy terror. Above this was raised a human cry menacing and heart-stilling in its volume. A mighty chorus came from the forest and sent hundreds of birds fluttering wildly against the rose-tinted early morning sky.

"*Lah illah il Allah!*" With the eerie rising inflection of a siren, it swelled. "*Ul-ul-ul-Ullah Akbar!*"

Bang-boom-boom, thundered the drums. "Kill! Kill!" their wild rhythm seemed to say.

CHAPTER V

THE ATTACK

AT THEIR SOUND Kent seemed to feel a thrill of excitement and apprehension course down his spine. In that mighty uproar there must be at least many hundreds of voices. What kind of fighters were they? God alone knew. He glanced at the scattered figures in blue and white as they crouched in the crenellated shadows of the white mud walls.

"Oh, God!" he groaned to himself. "We can never drive 'em off!"

"Attention!" he shouted from the tower and saw the brown faces of the N.C.O.'s on the firing platform raised skyward. "Fire in volleys! No one to shoot until the bugle sounds. Rodriguez! Send three of your men to the north wall!"

"Gawd!" cried Jerry in a shaken voice. "Look at the bleedin' beggars! There's millions of 'em!" He thrust out a stubby dirty finger, indicating the edge of the forest where a gleaming of white commenced to appear among the bright green of the jungle. It was like the ripple of foam preluding the advance of a gigantic white-crested wave. Everywhere the undergrowth was stirred into mad activity. High overhead half a dozen black dots were wheeling to and fro—the vultures and kites were gathering.

"Steady!" shouted Kent. "Shoot high rather than low." He would have given much to have had the walls of the *poste* ten instead of eight feet high. If a miracle happened and the garrison escaped annihilation, he'd jolly well see to it that they were raised.

Kent's red-rimmed gray eyes could see the attack taking shape—and his lips, now neatly shaved, were not so loose as they had been; they set themselves tensely.

The wily Suleiman was concentrating his attack from the north with flankers bearing down on the eastern and western walls of the little square-built *poste*. Only the south wall, that which faced the placid Goruol, was unthreatened.

Kent glanced up at the tricolor flapping idly on the bare wood pole. Would it still be there at nightfall? He sincerely doubted it.

Then the first of the slave raiders appeared in full sight. They were stalwart black Haussas, uttering strident war cries and brandishing rifles and spears as they recklessly advanced through grass that was knee-high.

"Um!" remarked Kent tensely, and his mouth was drawn into straight colorless line in the shade of his *képi's* visor. "Lucky they don't seem to care about taking cover. Damn it, but there's a lot of them!"

The bugler who lay beside the *adjutant* merely wet the mouthpiece of his instrument and nodded.

Then hard on the heels of these muscular, half naked foot soldiers appeared the main body of Suleiman's raiders, a great, loose cavalcade riding at a headlong gallop straight at the frail walls of the fort, yelling and firing wildly as they came: enveloped in billowing burnooses, they appeared much larger than they really were.

There were hundreds of them riding little, long-maned horses that reared and plunged with fear and excitement. The level meadow that separated the *poste* from the forest on three sides grew white with those savage black-faced riders and their howling slaves. It was a breath-taking sight, and ever thicker gathered the vultures overhead.

While the legionnaires clutched their Lebels in dogged resignation, the sergeants, too, caught up rifles and moved to empty embrasures, every soul tense for that bugle blast. The galloping men drew dangerously near. Would that strange *adjutant* never give the command? They could see the savage, dark faces of the attackers in detail now. Fula, Haussa, Jekri, Arab—all were there, screaming in barbaric frenzy for the blood of the *Roumi* dogs.

Nearer, ever nearer, surged the attack. Jerry swore feverishly as he saw a sea of black faces, flashing teeth, yellow eyeballs and short black beards—*chéchias* gleaming redly in the light of dawn.

His heart beating like the distant tom-toms, Kent was outwardly cool; he judged the last margin of safety reached, and nudged the bugler who, flat on his back, waited with brazen mouthpiece to his lips.

"NOW!" EXCLAIMED the *adjutant* and snatched up a rifle.

The human wave was about to break over the fort as the bugle blared, raucously, hastily.

Its shrill scream was drowned out in a steady rolling crash of rifle fire, resounding from three of the four walls. A tangle of fallen men and horses appeared as by magic. The others, galloping up from behind, could not stop, and crashed into the dead and dying.

The din became indescribable. Loud rang the shouts of the N.C.O.'s directing the firing, and louder yet the shrill yammerings, the piercing shrieks of wounded horses in dreadful chorus. Ceaselessly the rifles of the legionnaires crackled, mowing down the densely packed, charging men in struggling piles.

"Yah!" screamed Jerry, and fired with cool precision. "Tyke that, yer bloody blighters—" He clawed at his belt for a fresh clip, reloaded and shot down a frenzied Haussa who had gained the top of the north wall.

In spite of the deadly galling fire of the legionnaires the charge rushed on, though at diminished momentum. Arab shots commenced to strike along the walls and the gleam of steel appeared perilously near. It seemed the *poste* must be engulfed.

Kent, from the tower top, had a kaleidoscopic impression of mouthing faces—black, brown, yellow, a few almost white— of billowing robes and shimmering, brandished steel. Now an antiquated flintlock exploded, sending a rain of iron scrap at the defenders, and now a Mauser uttered its staccato bark to hurl a nickel-jacketed bullet *thwack!* against the hard mud walls. The uproar became indescribable. Steadily but completely without intelligent direction—thanks to the marksmen above—the slavers' attack rolled up to the walls themselves, while the veteran legionnaires fired and fired, reloading hastily with metallic snaps of the breech, then cuddling the rifle stocks to their sweating, sunburned cheeks once more. The volley firing became confused and lost as the speed with which the various men reloaded affected the rate of discharge. Unfortunately, a thick smoke cloud from the muzzle-loaded flintlocks, which employed black powder, hung low in the morning chill, masking the ground immediately at the foot of the walls.

"Keep after the leaders," shouted the *adjutant,* and giving the smoke-grimed little Englishman a slap between the shoulder blades he dashed down the ladder and joined the hard-pressed riflemen on the north platform. When he dashed out again into the daylight he almost stumbled across the sprawled body of a legionnaire lying with the shaft of a spear protruding from his breast. Something hummed by Kent's ear with the buzz of an angry wasp as he stooped to retrieve the fallen man's rifle.

"Les baïonettes!" he roared above the crackling shots, and set the example in locking on the long triangular-bladed bayonet of the French infantry, a bayonet which, tapering to a pin-point, makes an excellent lance out of a rifle such as the long-barreled Lebel.

"They come! Help!" roared a deep voice which Kent recognized as that of Espada. "Help us! They gain the wall!" Through the clouds of drifting, acrid-smelling smoke the American could see glimpses of broad steel glimmering along the top of the wall at which the main attack had been aimed.

Courageously enough, the Spanish sergeant and the others had clubbed their rifles and with the reserve legionnaires hurrying to the threatened point they thrust with their bayonets in slow retreat before a mass of howling slavers. The Arabs armed with yataghans, lances and rifles, fought like demons seeking to beat aside those flashing bayonets. It was a decisive moment.

KENT, WITH new-found acumen, realized it, and, raising a shout of defiance he charged along the parapet to fling himself into that deadly struggle with a savage abandon. His nerves snapping under the strain, and rendered savage by deprivation of alcohol, he felt a species of battle madness come over him. A musket flamed not far from his cheek, nearly splitting his eardrum as he thrust and thrust into that choking smoke cloud—then a grinning, evil face loomed up before him, the tribal scars on its slick black skin standing out in sharp relief. It was a colossal Fula tribesman raising a yataghan.

"Back!" snarled Kent, and thrust with all his might. There was a sudden weight on the end of the Lebel and the Fula vanished.

Kent gave the rifle a savage twist to disengage the blade and turned barely in time to face a shrieking Senegalese who towered head and shoulders above his fellows as he grinned in battle-mad ferocity. He raised a sort of tulwar, and aimed a crushing blow at Kent. Employing a parry learned long ago by the banks of the Hudson, the sweat-blinded, desperate *adjutant* caught the center of the descending blade on the hook which finishes the guard of the bayonet's handle. The steel clashed and the tulwar by the velocity of its own descent was dashed from the hands of the Senegalese. Instantly Kent sprang in, driving the steel-shod rifle butt against the black's chin with all his strength. The Senegalese, too, disappeared.

"Stand firm! For God's sake, hold!" he shouted as the deci-mated, outnumbered legionnaires, staggered by the fierce assault, wavered on the verge of a disastrous defeat.

Then raged a struggle such as the placid Goruol had never before witnessed. From the watch tower Jerry could see that the garrison had succeeded in keeping the slavers from all save the north wall, and had wrought fearful havoc with their famed marksmanship. The half dozen sharpshooters under Jerry delib-erately were picking off, one after the other, those tribesmen who seemed by dress or bearing to be leaders.

"Clean th'oo the haid," chuckled Adipose Brule as a tall, gray-bearded rider in a gorgeous green and gold robe toppled side-wise out of the saddle. The negro flipped back his wrist and ejected the shell with a complacent flourish. "Dat makes eight, white boy!"

"Wot's eatin' yer?" demanded Jerry contemptuously as he rolled over to catch up a handful of clips from the pile in the center of the tower top. "Wotcher mean by loafin'? Them niggers ain't 'arf licked yet—look at the beggars!"

He sighted rapidly at the swirl of figures on top of the walls and dropped a sallow *Hajji* from Abyssinia, then a nearly naked Soudanese slave who, with dripping yataghan, had just split the skull of the legionnaire at Kent's right.

"Look at the hadjutant! 'Oo's no good now?" Jerry demanded of Adipose. "Yer carn't expect no more of a man than that!" While reloading he hastily jerked a thumb at Kent, who, side by side with Espada, swung his rifle in a havoc-making arc and by sheer weight of blows was slowly driving back the astonished slavers.

"Dat shore am a fightin' man," mumbled the South Carolina negro. "But jest you wait, white boy—anybody kin fight a man, but booze? Huh-uh!"

ON THE firing platform Kent was fighting a double battle— first against the blood-mad followers of Suleiman, and second, against the havoc which sustained drinking had wrought upon a once powerful physique.

"Lord!" he gasped as he felt the strength leaving his arms. "I can't keep 'em back any longer—" It was as though a broad iron band confined his chest making breathing next to impossible. Red-hot pincers seemed to be tearing at his lungs. His body felt dead—leaden. Enviously he watched from the corner of his eye the untiring efforts of Espada who, bareheaded and with his blouse ripped open and splashed with blood, fought like a demon incarnate.

"Dios!" panted the Spaniard, and whirled up his long Lebel by the barrel. Three glistening Soudanese slaves appeared on the edge of the wall; elsewhere the horde was falling back sickened and demoralized by the fearfully accurate fire from the walls of the *poste.*

"Allons!" Kent panted, and like a battered blue wave the defenders of the north wall rallied and charged along the platform made slippery with the blood and encumbered by the fallen of both sides. In Kent's enfeebled grasp the bayonet barely deflected the foremost slave's powerful thrust, and the edge bit

into the *adjutant's* shoulder, searing the flesh like a hot iron, robbing him of the last vestige of strength.

"Let go," every instinct urged him; "you can't fight any more." The whole scene whirled dizzily before his eyes, but with a strange doggedness he brought his bayonet point in line with the black's muscled chest and lunged with all his weight. As from a distance he heard a cry like that of a wounded horse, and the rifle was wrenched from his nerveless hands as a swirl of fighting legionnaires pushed by with a panted *"En avant!"* and hurled the last of the attackers from the wall. Kent struggled in the grip of an overpowering nausea such as he had never before suffered.

"I can't stand it," he sobbed, and, abandoning the wall, he stumbled off toward the barracks. "I've got to have a drink—I'll go crazy—I gotta get a drink—I'll fight like hell then!"

As he passed a pile of fallen Haussas, one of the seeming corpses came suddenly to life and, with a poniard bright in his fist, lunged at the reeling N.C.O. as he passed. It would undoubtedly have been Roger Kent's death had not Jerry, from his post on the watch tower, adroitly shot the shammer through the heart just as he poised to strike the unwarned *adjutant.*

Kent gave a startled shout and leaped aside as the Haussa collapsed suddenly almost on his own boot heels. Looking up, he recognized the impudent sweat-streaked face of Jerry.

"Thanks, old-timer," called the American. "I'll remember that to you, my boy."

The burning in his throat reminded Kent of his purpose, and with a vague nod toward Jerry he resumed his progress.

Such legionnaires as were still alive and not desperately wounded were jubilantly firing at the hurriedly retreating enemy, and for the most part did not see Kent slink across the court, peering furtively to and fro as he went.

But up on the tower Adipose guessed the *adjutant's* surrender.

"Looky thar, white boy," he grunted, his yellow eyes still lit with the battle flame. "What did Ah say? Thar goes you-all's hero straight fo' de booze. He sho'-nuff kin lick dem low-down, no-'count niggers, but ag'in' dat red-eye he ain't got no chanst!"

And Jerry, as he realized the truth of that remark, rubbed his shoulder which was black and blue from the continual recoil of the steel-shod rifle butt, and sorrowed in the depths of his simple, loyal soul.

"Aw, ye're barmy," he insisted, but without an attempt at carrying conviction. "When Kent 'e gives 'is word—you'll see." He rolled over to study the groaning mound of dead and wounded that in a wide, varicolored swathe surrounded the *poste*.

"Look! Posie," he called. "See that there bloke in the green night-gown? 'E's shamming!" He fired with the word and saw the prone figure's arms jerk convulsively as the bullet struck. That the man had long been dead he knew very well, but it served to change the subject from Kent's moral surrender, a subject on which Jerry preferred not to dwell.

CHAPTER VI

A FRIGHTFUL DILEMMA

"**I'M GOIN' GET** a drink, goddam good I drink!" repeated Kent thickly as he entered the passage leading to the orderly room. The thought seemed to give him new strength, and he licked his lips eagerly at the recollection of a certain bottle of cognac he had espied on a shelf in the quarters of Captain Laurier.

"Liquor—good old liquor—makes a man feel human," he whispered, while on dragging feet he stumbled along the passage to the orderly room, the blood from his shoulder wound drawing long red wales on the white plaster as he brushed against first one wall, then the other. He was surprised not to hear the firing growing fainter with the distance; it even rose in volume.

"Shooting a lot," he thought. "They shouldn't waste ammunition. We haven't got any to spare, and we may be fighting for a week. I'll get a drink, then stop them." At that moment the firing rose to a rattling crescendo, and Kent halted. "Damn fools," he panted, and halted, resting against the cool white plaster. "They have got no sense. Probably whacking off shots at the wounded—as though all the wounded don't die sooner or later in this climate anyhow. They need a nursemaid!"

With that idea uppermost in his mind, and without quite realizing it, Kent halted, turned uncertainly, and with dragging steps returned toward that bright rectangle of light which marked the end of the passage and the opening into the courtyard.

"Lot o' damned children," he repeated angrily. "Waste all their shot—"

Though his throat burned like a lime kiln, he halted when he emerged once more into the sunlight, which was commencing to take on the true intensity of the tropic day, and put a whistle to his lips. He made a wild figure—powder-grimed, hatless, blond hair fallen over his bloodshot eyes, trembling with exhaustion and craving, his white trousers splashed with gore.

"Cease firing!" he croaked, while his eyes ranged along the firing platforms. The farther he looked, the colder grew the chill in his heart. He had not dreamed so many of the blue and white figures lay sprawled and motionless. They lay everywhere, in all manner of fantastic poses, just as the metal spray of scatter-guns and the lonely modern bullets had dropped them.

Here an arm dangled pathetically helpless over the edge of the platform; there was a legionnaire slumped on his knees behind his embrasure as though in prayer. Everywhere were wounded, moaning men in blue. All the enemy within the walls were dead—red bayonets in the hands of Espada and his followers explained the absence of wounded.

"They are gone?" Kent demanded of a yellow-faced Brazilian corporal who was jerking tight the knot of a sling which supported a shattered left arm.

"Sí, they are gone," replied the wounded man, and his teeth gleamed white as he bit to pull the knot tighter. "And so are most of us. One more attack—and then, *pouf!*" He blew out his cheeks with a macabre grimace, jerking the thumb of his uninjured hand at a long row of men lying under the east platform. How big the soles of their shoes appeared! The hobnails on them gleamed dully in the sun.

Then a shrill voice commenced to sing, high up on the top of the tower; it was strictly improvised verse, containing grave errors as to rhythm and tune, but it came as a pæan of triumph which held a note of hysteria:

> *"And pore old Suleiman is a silly Man now—*
> *Sixty little legendaries tort 'im 'ow;*
> *'E thort 'is second nyme was fighter,*
> *But sixty Roumis spelled it blighter,*
> *And pore old Suleiman's Silly Man now."*

"Good boy, Jerry," murmured Kent as the cockney concluded his epic. He took a long pull at the water bottle of a legionnaire who would need it no more, and then called a conference of such N.C.O.'s as had survived that appallingly sanguinary struggle.

SUPPORTING HIMSELF on a rifle, and with the blood from his wound trickling in a diminished stream down his sleeve, Kent picked up a *képi*, pushed it back on his head, and viewed the half dozen grim fighters who answered the summons. Silently he watched them come picking their way over the fallen, while the black shadows of the vultures floated across the sunlit court.

There was, first of all, Sergeant Espada, bloodied and scowling; then there was yellow-faced Corporal Vassos, the Brazilian, his hairless saturnine features grinning triumphantly as he exhibited a bullet hole in the crown of his red and blue *képi*; the veteran Corporal LaTouche, wearing a rag twisted about the base of his grizzled hair, where a lance had grazed him; there were one or two others, trustworthy men.

Very quickly Kent checked the casualties and was appalled

to find that of the sixty sound men who had begun the engage-
ment, only some thirty were still able to stand on their feet.

"And of these," concluded LaTouche, "two have body
wounds—they'll last a day, perhaps two, poor devils."

"None of us will last two days, thanks to good Señor Kent,"
broke in Espada furiously. "And we'd all be alive if he had
accepted the offer of Suleiman."

"Silence!" snapped Kent, and fixed the rebellious one with
bloodshot eye. "Another word from you, Sergeant Espada, and
I'll shoot your worthless head from your body. It's lamentable
that a man who can fight as you have just now fought hasn't the
loyalty of a toad. LaTouche!"

The old Frenchman jumped to attention.

"From this moment you are my second in command. Count
the dead and make a report of the wounded. You, Sergeant Espa-
cla, superintend the distribution of fresh ammunition; warn all
men not to waste a shot. Let the vultures and kites alone; we'll
need all their help."

And again Kent bitterly lamented the non-appearance of
the relief column.

With them was expected a fresh supply of ammunition.
The present garrison had been isolated for some eight months,
during which period a large amount of ammunition had been
expended in the course of patrol duty and target practice.

Under normal conditions what was left in the magazine
would have been an ample supply, but where Suleiman Tombohko went on foray conditions were far from normal.

"Who is this Suleiman?" asked Kent of LaTouche, as they
endlessly studied the edge of the forest from the tower.

"An extraordinary type," replied the veteran, and stooped to
retie his boot lace. "It is said this able gentleman is the son of
an Englishman and a Bedouin mother. His father died when
Suleiman was yet very young; as a result he became an Arab of
the Arabs, bitterly hating his white blood."

"Oh, I see," replied Kent, without turning his head. "But it's a wonder he hasn't learned something about modern fighting. Frontal attacks on fortified posts have been out of date for a good many years."

LaTouche shrugged, and his shadow on the blood-stained boards behind the embrasure mimicked the motion. "It would appear that our good Suleiman doesn't need to learn," observed the veteran, uttering a sigh and giving a significant glance about the dangerously undermanned wall. There was a legionnaire crouching at every fourth embrasure; formerly they had occupied every other one.

"His business for tens of years has been to raid the lands of the Upper Volta for slaves—slaves which he sells in Abyssinia, Arabia and all over Africa. I am told it is a trade that pays well."

A puff of wind from the little meadow before the *poste* brought an odor faint as yet, but incredibly nauseating, and set the weary men behind the walls to wrinkling their noses and swearing.

"Curse the luck!" snarled one. "The dead are but a few hours old—what a bouquet there will be to-morrow!"

Already the ground was black with rending carrion birds, their horrible red bald heads bright in the sun.

SICKENED, KENT divided the survivors of the garrison into two platoons, one of which was always on the walls, ceaselessly ready to give the alarm should Suleiman's cohorts advance again. He then superintended the digging of a huge hole beneath the stones of the floor of the courtyard, wisely placing it as far as possible from the well that supplied the *poste* with water.

In this were laid the dead—German, Pole, Swede, and Portuguese—side by side, all nationality lost in that democracy of death. Then the panting, sullen-eyed laborers sprinkled lime thickly. The diggers then shoveled earth furiously, for the flies circled in hungry, loathsome swarms. It was depressing, back-breaking work.

Toward dusk it appeared that the sagacious Suleiman had adopted a new type of offensive, for from the shelter of the dense haobab thickets and from the lofty mahogany trees of the forest rifles commenced to snap at everything that showed above the walls.

"Snipers' war," commented Jerry, as he got up from a mess-kit of hastily concocted soup and prepared to return to the tower top. "It's a narsty, tire-some gyme—we useter plye it with the bleedin' Pathans back in Hinja. But I hain't yet see the nigger wot could outshoot a real—legendary." And that last word neatly spiked the ire of Legionnaire Adipose Brule, who had risen in sable majesty to obliterate the little cockney.

"Boy, howdy," he sniffed, "but them daiders dot stink," he remarked as he picked up his rifle. "Expect they'll have mo' to say as time go on—unless the buzzards polishes 'em off."

"Yus," agreed Jerry, with a thoughtful frown. "Once hup near the Afghan frontier we had some the like o' these—limburger was violets to 'em." He forebore to mention the pestilence that had resulted from the presence of those same dead Afghans.

"Why myke the boys dahn-'earted?" he asked himself. "Gawd knows we got troubles enough." And what he said was no less than the truth.

FOR TWO interminable days an intermittent struggle went on. Days during which the garrison suffered and swore and watched the fever, aided by the putrefying corpses beyond the wall, make further inroads among the pitifully diminished garrison.

There was nothing to be done, for medicines of all kinds had long since been exhausted.

The air was thick with the poisonous reek in which the vultures flopped and fluttered by day and hyenas chortled and snarled by night. Twice in the long night hours had the garrison flown to arms at the sound of heavy trampling through the underbrush—but it was only a wandering herd of elephants seeking the fresh green grass at the water's edge.

"Where in hell is that column?" demanded Kent savagely, as the twilight of the third day of the siege deepened. "I wonder if Humbert ever found them? Dirty rotters to let us die like this."

"Gawd, matey," murmured a haggard, discouraged Jerry, "they must orl be dead—maybe yer should 'ave tyken old Solomon's offer. We carn't larst much longer, wot I fink. The food's abaht gone."

Kent lifted a face that showed in detail the agony he had endured for the last three days—days that had for him been species of torture more refined than the imaginations of Suleiman's tribesmen could ever have devised.

There were times when his sanity wavered on the brink—times when he half pulled out the automatic at his belt to end a life too miserable to endure. There were times when in the darkness tears of craving had coursed down his cheeks in streams.

"God knows how, but we must hold on," replied the *adjutant,* and passed a hand over his dirty, unshaved chin. "We can't let those devils through to capture and massacre the helpless niggers under our protection." His eyes were clearer now, but there was a tragic light in them. "Jerry, you can't know what this staying off liquor is. It's—it's killing me." Abruptly he turned away.

At that moment came the distant blast of a horn of some kind, and a voice hailed the alert sentries from the outer darkness:

"A truce, O *Franzwazi*," called the invisible messenger. "I bring word from the Sultan!"

Kent raised his head cautiously above the line of the parapet. "I will speak with but one man," he shouted. "Any others will be shot!"

There was the sound of bare feet shuffling over the grass, then a muttered exclamation of disgust as the wind, veering, brought that fearful stench down upon the visitor. Slinking, doglike forms whimpered and vanished among the grasses at his approach, reluctantly abandoning their feast.

"Stand ready," warned Kent, and sent runners to awaken those men who slept the sleep of the exhausted in the malodorous barracks. "This may be a feint."

"I would speak with the chief of *Franzwazi*," announced the Arab messenger boldly. "I have word for his ear."

Then Kent made a serious mistake; Jerry and LaTouche saw the error at once.

" 'E should talk to 'im in private," whispered the cockney, with a dubious shake of his small head. " 'E shouldn't let old Espada and Vassos an' the rest 'ear wot's said."

"You are quite right," agreed LaTouche. *"Monsieur l'Adjutant* is making a mistake of the most grave."

In the damp night stillness every word of the conversation that followed could be heard from one end of the *poste* to the other. With fierce, hopeful ears, the garrison listened with beating hearts for any sort of terms granting them a new lease on lives that seemed to be inevitably forfeited.

Less than twenty men of the small war-worn garrison were now left—five men to a wall fifty feet long.

"The *Franzwazi* are few—"

"Nay, we are many!" retorted Kent brazenly, the darkness hiding the anguish on his sunken features. "Many, strong and well-armed."

"Wot a liar!" Jerry was deeply pained; even he saw the futility of further resistance.

THE MESSENGER shifted his position and white robes glimmered in the light which preluded the rising of the moon. "Nevertheless, the *Franzwazi* lie in the palm of the great Suleiman's hand. He has but to close that hand and ye will be but passing shadows."

"When Suleiman last closed that same hand," reminded Kent, in halting Arabic, "he got naught but very bloody fingers. Do not the voices of your dead tribesmen speak loud enough?"

"Sacré baplême," growled LaTouche from the shadows. "If those voices speak any louder I shall go mad!"

Momentarily nonplused by this rather obvious piece of defiance and logic, the emissary shifted uneasily from one foot to the other. He had not expected anything but an overwhelming eagerness to surrender on any terms Suleiman might choose to offer. Kent stiffened as he heard the sounds of some one silently passing along the platform on the opposite side to that on which he stood—passing around to gain a place at his back.

He glanced at Sergeant Espada, standing huge and silent near by, in pose that suggested anything but quiet resignation, with his hand put in the folds of his overcoat.

"Hearken, O chief of the *Franzwazi*," resumed the man below the wall. "Only yesterday did our great Sultan surprise and destroy a great body of the *Roumis*—dressed as you are dressed. He smote them with the might of his arm and by the hundred they fell. But a few remain as captives and slaves of his slaves."

It seemed as though a hand made of ice had gripped Kent's heart, wringing the blood from it and leaving it hard and dead. Everywhere along the walls did uneasy murmurs break out. Furiously Kent thought for a parry.

"It is as easy for me to lie as for Suleiman," said he coldly. "Go back!"

"Nay!" the Arab's voice rang out triumphantly. "Suleiman lies not; hearken to his words."

Inside the doomed *poste* complete silence reigned, save for the heart-breaking moans of the wretches wasting away from the fever. Every man's consciousness was trained upon that swart emissary's next words.

"To-morrow, with the coming of the sun, you shall see the captives—"

This time Kent's heart sank and his wan face fell into an expression such as might have been seen on that of the Roman Varus when he saw his legions trapped.

"Saith Suleiman, the brave and wise in council: I will give these captive *Franzwazi* their lives, together with their freedom; I will give each man among the *Franzwazi* in the fort of mud two tusks of ivory."

The dimly seen Arab paused to let the full effect of the offer sink into those death-facing legionnaires on the walls. "To each of them I will also give a bag of gold, and to the chief of the *Franzwazi* a kettle filled with red British gold pieces." As Kent, faced with despair, remained silent, the Arab offered yet another inducement. "The *Roumis* are brave warriors; I shall let them keep their arms."

There spoke the crafty Suleiman, thought Kent; he was no mean diplomat. In the darkness behind he could hear the mutterings and whisperings of the legionnaires.

"And if we refuse?"

The messenger paused as though astounded that the idea had ever occurred to the beleaguered white men.

"Then, O fools, ye—die. Die in such a fashion that your children's children will speak of your deaths in whispers."

"What else?" demanded Kent, and felt the oppressive darkness crushing him.

"Two days," called the Arab, "will Suleiman give for the decision, then on the dawn of the third day—Jehannum will gape before the eyes of the unbelievers."

Again Kent was moved to admiration for the astute Sultan's tactics. It was nothing short of genius to allow those two days of grace—two days during which dissension might breed and spread among the hard-pressed garrison.

"In the light of to-morrow's sun will Suleiman show the prisoners—before the fort will he march them. To-morrow noon, if ye have not agreed, they die."

"Go back to your master," said Kent sharply. "Go, and I will give ye my answer when we have seen the prisoners—"

"Rather, *we* will give ours," murmured the Spanish N.C.O. beneath his breath.

"*Inshallah,*" replied the emissary, and quickly withdrew, leaving Kent to face the dark-browed legionnaires and a terrible decision at the same time.

CHAPTER VII

MUTINEERS

AS HE DESCENDED the steps to the level of the courtyard, Kent glanced about and decided that there were not more than five of the remaining twenty he could really trust in an emergency. Terrible odds! Yet somehow the *poste* must be held until the last minute. Perhaps Suleiman was lying and the column might appear.

As his heavy hobnailed boots rang on the stones of the courtyard, the harassed *adjutant* saw Espada advancing closely followed by a dark blur of figures.

"We have decided, *Monsieur l'Adjutant*," Espada announced boldly, "to accept the terms of the Sultan. It is madness to fight longer."

"Indeed?" murmured Kent. "How very interesting!"

"Yes," agreed the rat-faced Brazilian Vassos, "ivory and gold and free departure are better than the ant heap, the torturer's knife and fighting for a cause already lost."

Kent momentarily temporized, fighting for time, while Jerry and LaTouche in the background waited, on the alert for the first overt act of the malcontents.

"Why are you so sure the cause is lost?" demanded Kent. "The relief column may appear any hour."

"Suleiman has captured the relief!" chorused a dozen tense voices. "There can be no hope of rescue—the relief is annihilated!"

"So Suleiman says," objected Kent emphatically. "What has really happened may be quite another matter. The men he speaks of may be from Humbert's little expedition—poor devils. Even if he parades prisoners, there will be not more than a few."

A buzz of conversation revealed that this simple explanation had not occurred, but nevertheless Espada resumed his objections.

"Nay, they are not Humbert's men," he cried. "And even were they his, we will still surrender. We have no medicines. To-day five men fell sick of that cursed fever, and four have died. I, for one, will not stay in this pest-hole. I will fight, but not commit suicide."

The dark mass of men grunted assent and shuffled nearer.

"When the relief comes," said Kent doggedly, "there will be plenty of medicine—there will be decorations and promotions for us all. We will be honored among soldiers, instead of being forever known as the men who deserted their posts in the face of danger. Furthermore, we would be shot as deserters."

A silence fell, and for a moment he felt encouraged; that last sentence had had some effect.

Vassos, however, seized the moment to step forward with a loud: "Never! Suleiman offers us our lives, gold and ivory. What is France to us?"

"Nothing! Nothing!" rose the shouts from all corners. "We will fight no more!" Menacingly they closed in, and Kent saw that to insist would be fatal. He therefore temporized.

"Very well, then," Kent conceded crisply, "to-morrow, when we have seen the prisoners, I will decide—not before."

There was something in that harsh, bold voice that made those men, keyed up to the murder pitch, fall back grumbling among themselves. But their temper was plain to see. Thus far had they fought and suffered, and, short of a miracle, they would go no further.

IT WAS quite futile, Kent realized, to expect the legionnaires, drawn for the most part from the scum and criminal classes of Europe and the Americas, to realize their obligation to helpless Africans under French control. He felt weak and sick inside as he conjectured on what would take place in the morning. Kent was gambling everything on the fact that Suleiman would produce

*The Brazilian slipped inside with the
gleaming blade held ready.*

not more than ten men—the number of Sergeant Humbert's
expedition. If there were no more than ten prisoners, it might
be a trick—and he wondered if the slaver knew of the overdue
column from Lake Tchad.

Should there be ten or less, Kent would very quickly show the
garrison that the Sultan was tricking them. With that as a basis
of objection and conjuring up the probability of treachery and
a massacre if the fort were surrendered, he might possibly stave
off disaster a day or so more. Perhaps—how dared he hope?—
perhaps the long-delayed help might arrive.

"Gawd, matey," murmured Jerry, when the legionnaires had
clambered back to their posts, "yer might as well give hup, w'ile
some o'us is still alive and kicking." He silently uncocked his rifle
and let the butt sink to the ground with a gentle thud. " 'Tain't no
use to myke us orl 'late lamenteds' if the relief's been wiped out."

Kent gazed up into the purple-black sky, where a million
resplendent stars glared hotly down, seeking to follow the example of the pitiless sun. Outside the walls two hyenas broke into

a weird maniacal laughter that echoed eerily on the far bank of the Goruol.

"That's just it, Jerry," murmured Kent, and buried his face between his hands for a moment. "It wouldn't be so hard, if I only knew the truth; but this fellow Suleiman is such a crafty devil, I suspect it's a game on his part to get the men out of the *poste*, then he'll butcher them. Failing, he aims to cause a mutiny that'll accomplish the same result. Jerry"—he sighed, and his lined face was tragic in the starlight—"it's too much. I tell you, it's too much—I can't stick any longer. What if those damned niggers are killed? They've been killed and raided for centuries. Why haven't these poor devils in the fort earned the right to live?"

"Yer will stick, matey," pleaded Jerry. "That damn black feller Brule says yer won't; I—I bet 'im three months' pay—and I—well, I fink yer will stick."

Wearily, Kent shrugged, at the same time clasping his hands spasmodically. "Made a bad bet, Jerry—I'm too far gone—can't stand the strain—I'm really no good—I'll go back to the bottle in another day."

He arose abruptly and tramped off without another word, striding heavily across the court to his quarters, there to catch the first bit of sleep he had had since the siege began.

Once he had disappeared, Sergeant Espada summoned the malcontents into conference in the shadow of the south wall.

"We have had enough of this mad American, then?" The Spaniard's big aquiline face and bristling mustache turned from Vassos to the German, Rhemeier, and so on about the circle of ten.

Each rogue of the number nodded emphatically.

"That last little pleasantry of Captain Laurier's was in poor taste," observed the Brazilian in a sibilant whisper. "Who would have thought this blind bull of an American could be so obstinate? Decidedly, my friends, he must be removed."

"Decidedly," agreed Espada; then, with an air of vast generosity, "and thou, my dear Enrique, shall have the honor and the pleasure of removing our dear *adjutant.*" The Spaniard smiled broadly in the darkness; a cunning stroke, that, for the American had proved indeed a dangerous man to tamper with.

Since Señor Manuel Espada desired one thing above all else—which was to get the aforementioned Manuel Espada safely to the seacoast with as much booty as possible—it was as well friend Vassos should run such risks as might attend the removal of that pig-headed American.

VASSOS GULPED, blinked, but did not dare retreat; nevertheless, he mentally noted that coup against the Spaniard, and who knew but that some time during the long march to the Gulf of Guinea he would find an opportunity of righting that little matter? Meanwhile, the question of removing the *adjutant* must be solved.

"A knife, no?" suggested the sergeant with a wolfish smile. "Bare feet and a quick thrust between the ribs—so!" He made a swift upward motion with his right hand, at the same time uttering a realistic sound in imitation of ripping cloth.

"The removal should be very easy, my dear Vassos," he assured the Brazilian, as that worthy stooped and with a suppressed curse commenced to unlace his *brodequins.* "I happen to know that the big Americano has not slept in three nights. Doubtless, too, he will now be very drunk; it is more than a miracle that he has stayed sober so long."

And, chuckling with macabre pleasure, the worthy sergeant settled back. Señor Espada, in his mind's eye, was already planning the march to the coast. The remaining legionnaires, under his command, would extract every ounce of gold and ivory possible from the fatuous Suleiman; seize and enslave the inhabitants of the first village they encountered, together with what ivory there was to be found; then they would march by easy stages to the head waters of the Black Volta River.

Keeping clear of the territory of the thrice-cursed English Gold Coast colony, the little expedition would seek the coast via Gara, Dabakala, Bonguanu, and through the Ivory Coast to Bandama or Great Bassam. There a dhow could probably be got without too much trouble. It was all very pleasant to contemplate, and as Corporal Vassos, stripped to the waist, bare-footed, and with a needle-pointed Somali dagger in his fist, tiptoed out, Manuel Espada decided that the future was indeed very pleasant to contemplate.

ROGER KENT was awakened by the first tiny twitch of a cord he had adroitly attached to the knob of his door and tied to his hand. Though wearied to the point of exhaustion, he had never lost that soldier's faculty of sleeping with one eye at least partially open.

He was awake in an instant, and in a savage mood—the deprivation of his stimulant had goaded him to a species of frenzy. A dangerous smile played on his unshaved face as he silently arose and, swiftly rolling up his overcoat, thrust it under the coarse gray blankets.

By the cold light of the moon streaming in the window Kent breathlessly watched the door opening inch by inch. Clad only in a pair of trousers, he crouched behind the door, waiting for the murderer to enter.

"Hope to hell it's the Spaniard," he told himself. "He's the brains of the lot."

But the hope died as he caught sight of the dark hair and thin neck of a much smaller man. Vassos! So Espada had sent a puppet—the precious rascal, then, had some respect for him. As the door swung farther open, Kent tensed his muscles and was amazed to feel them rippling freer than they had in many years.

Silently he poised on the balls of his feet, as the Brazilian slipped inside, silent as a shadow, with the gleaming blade held ready and his jet eyes fixed on the shape on the cot.

Very much as a leopard gathers himself, the wiry South American balanced; Kent could see the play of muscles in the naked back quite distinctly as Vassos raised his dagger and sprang, burying the steel deep in the huddled outline.

"You should get glasses, Señor Vassos; your eyesight is deplorable," remarked Kent, and, as the other whirled with a squeal of fear, the blond *adjutant* caught him a terrific blow on the point of the jaw.

The Brazilian's long, narrow head snapped back. He fell heavily alongside the cot, caving in the back of his skull upon the corner of an iron-bound chest that lay against the wall. Revealed in the moonlight, the dark limbs writhed aimlessly a moment; then a purl of blood bubbled from between Vassos's lips and trickled down his chin onto the floor. Finally he lay still with only a minor muscle or two shuddering dreadfully.

"Not even a good fight," grunted Kent savagely, and stooping, he easily heaved the limp body over his shoulder. With the warm slack limbs horridly caressing his back, and with the smell of the dead man's unwashed body strong in his nostrils, Kent strode along the corridor, past that dreadful hospital room where the sick and wounded whimpered ceaselessly for the medicines that did not exist, out into the broad moonlit courtyard.

Under the shadow of the south wall crouched a group of men. Kent sensed who they were and chuckled under his breath. Quite easily the big *adjutant* strode to the center of the court and there flung down the body, surprised to find that he was not even breathing hard from the exertion.

"Hey, Espada!" he called to those dimly outlined figures. "Next time, come yourself!"

Then, as he stood there, massive and fully revealed in the moonlight, Roger Kent suddenly threw back his head and laughed and laughed until the jackals beyond the walls joined in. The effect was wholly horrible. The eerie chorus swelled louder and louder, rending the night with a ghastly nerve-shaking merriment.

"He is mad!" breathed Espada fearfully, and involuntarily crossed himself. "The *adjutant* has gone mad!"

CHAPTER VIII

SULEIMAN'S CAPTIVES

DURING THE REMAINDER of the night Kent, sitting on the top of the watch tower, viewed the moon rising in full splendor and pondered upon the wisdom of imprisoning the insubordinate Espada and the other known malcontents in the cells; but, as Jerry reluctantly pointed out, it would diminish the pitiful handful of the garrison by at least five rifles, and these could not be spared.

On the other hand, the certainty that the Spaniard would further attempt to force a surrender made the decision to leave him at large an exceedingly difficult one to make. From the forest came the sound of drums, and the lofty tree tops reflected the red glare of many camp fires whose smoke climbed in tall white columns up to windless sky.

"I am staking everything," said Kent in a low voice, "on Suleiman's not being able to produce more than ten prisoners. Somehow I can't accept the idea that the relief has been wiped out."

"If they hain't been scuppered," commented the small legionnaire bitterly, fanning away the mosquitoes, "they 'ad better come in a 'urry."

During the night two more of the garrison, Adipose Brule for one, came down with the pitilessly ravaging Coast fever, thus reducing the garrison to some eighteen sound but hopeless men. To the dew-soaked *adjutant* it seemed ages before the sun at last appeared above the horizon and revealed the bullet-pierced tricolor still flying.

"And now we'll know," muttered Kent as, warned by the distant blast of a horn, he mounted the parapet to see whether Suleiman Tombohko could make good his boast or not. At some distance along the wall Kent was not surprised to observe Espada, glowering watchfully out over the mist-veiled mead-

ows where the dew yet sparkled on a host of bright plants and
flowers. Then Roger Kent realized that the moral as well as the
physical struggle between him and Espada must shortly come
to a climax.

Every soul in the *poste*, realizing that the show-down had
come, dragged himself to the walls, even the yellow-faced sick
and the wounded were there. As a single Arab horseman, clad
in flowing white burnoose, galloped up to the walls Kent felt a
thrill of fierce excitement course down his spine.

A complete silence fell over the bullet-pitted walls, in which
the drumming of the horses' hooves carried clearly to the men
on the wall. The *adjutant* was seized with an inspiration as the
Arab drew near. Cupping his hands, he bawled out to an imaginary company of men: "Sergeant Lenoir, send your platoon to
the south wall. Leave ten men behind to bring Sergeant Vasskyj's platoon up to thirty. Send forty to the north wall." And
so on, while Jerry profanely marveled at the fluency of Kent's
prevarications.

"Thirty men, if yer please! 'E's made a 'undred and fifty men
out of the air. Oh, 'e's a deep cove, is our *adjutant*."

Disconcerted by the bawling of orders, the Arab pulled in
his stallion with an air of surprise. It had never occurred to that
swarthy individual that the little *poste* could hold so many men.

Kent at once recognized the voice of the rider as that of the
emissary who had spoken the night before.

"Hearken, O *Roumis!*" he shouted. "As the great Suleiman
has promised, he will now parade the *Franzwazi* prisoners.
You have but to gaze at yonder vale. Look well, O *Roumis*, for
there will you see them pass." He laughed in shrill mocking
triumph, pointing out with a thin brown hand at a little break
in the forest's outline.

THE ADJUTANT'S heart sank, yet he hoped against hope
that the prisoners would be the few from Sergeant Humbert's
missing reconnaissance party, so he merely nodded carelessly.

The Arab, his burnoose hood thrown back, sat on his horse

like a centaur, though the animal curvetted and plunged, mad with the pain of the cruel Moorish bit on his bangle-hung bridle.

"And remember, O *Franzwazi*," reminded the emissary with grim pleasure, "if yonder rag still flies in the evening mists, each of these prisoners shall die."

So saying, the Arab, with a last derisive guffaw, wheeled and dashed back at a mad gallop toward the edge of the forest, leaving a shaken and thoroughly unhappy adjutant to face an incipient mutiny.

Hardly had the messenger disappeared than the booming, menacing notes of the tom-toms commenced to throb in the forest, and the carrion birds which had already congregated fluttered off on vast pinions, fanning a foul breeze on the watchers and uttering hoarse savage cries of alarm.

Boom! Boom! Ta-thunk—thunk! rattled the war drums until myriad monkeys fell to shrilling in defiance.

" 'E's going to attack," cried Jerry excitedly. "Yer was right, matey. 'E ain't got no prisoners arter orl."

It was almost with a sense of relief that Kent in a vain gesture ordered the legionnaires to their posts. Far better to die in defense of his word than at the hands of the amiable Sergeant Espada and his rabble. To allow mutiny was bad soldiering.

Soon the clumps of baobab, mahogany and mangrove sheltered thick masses of white-robed slavers to a number well over a thousand. Their white robes reminded Kent of snow under fir trees.

"Millions of 'em. Orl hup wiv Kent & Co., what I fink," opined Jerry in awed tones. "Wot for does that bally blighter waste time wiv parleys?"

"Nothing but a fear of the white man's superior arms and intelligence," replied Kent grimly, but none the less the cockney's chance question gave him the germ of an idea. "I wonder from which side the attack will come? Not that it matters a continental. We'll go under at the first rush."

He sighed long and bitterly. He had fought not only with

Suleiman, but with himself. And now all that suffering and
privation had gone for naught. It was the irony of fate. Soon
those damnable tom-toms would change their beat to the battle
rhythm and there would be a swift end to all his problems.

To the intense surprise of the surviving legionnaires, the
masses of enemy remained at the edge of the forest, falling back
to either side of the little glade the Arab had indicated. Kent
leaned far out over the walls and stared at the spot.

"Keep a careful count," he said to LaTouche and Jerry, who
knelt beside him. It was as if he saw his hope of salvation being
written against the emerald green background of the forest. A
long blood-hungry yell arose from the slavers.

Kent watched with bated breath the distant appearance
of a tall figure in the blue and white of the Legion's tropical
uniform. It was too far to recognize the man's features, and
Captain Laurier's glasses had been smashed in Kent's struggle
with the Brazilian murderer.

Again a fierce shout arose from the assembled followers
of Suleiman, and the *adjutant's* heart turned to ice as he saw
that the unfortunate European was imprisoned in a species of
wooden collar. The distant prisoner's hands, furthermore, were
tied behind his back.

"WHAT'S THAT fing abaht his neck?" whispered the little
cockney in a strained voice. "Hit looks like wot they put around
the cows at 'ome."

"It's the branch of a tree, the slaver's yoke," explained Kent
briefly, and his blue eyes were tragic in the brown of his face.
"They cut a very heavy branch that forks, put the prisoner's neck
into the fork, and pass a bolt through behind. The stem hangs
to the ground. The idea is to interfere with the poor devil's legs
if he tries to run."

Presently another loud cry heralded the appearance of a
second figure in blue and white. He, too, was hustled across the
gap under a shower of blows and was swallowed up in the Arabs'
ranks on the opposite side of the interval.

"Three," counted Kent, and felt his pulses hammering furiously.

"*Quatre,*" said LaTouche, his wrinkled old face impassive.

"*Cinco,*" murmured Espada down the wall. "Our precious saint of an *adjutant* can find no more excuses. Here is proof enough."

Though enough proof had already been furnished to the majority of the garrison, Kent, for some unfathomable reason, could not rid himself of the idea that the whole brutal spectacle was a subterfuge. He firmly believed that ten prisoners at the most would be seen.

But as the eighth bent figure came into view, dragging its yoke of shame, he felt a constriction in his throat, and, like a man reading his death warrant, watched the appearance of the ninth and the tenth man. Would there be any more?

He leaned far out over the parapet, the sun's first rays lighting a profile that had become strangely strong and clean-cut of late. They tinted the blond bristles on his square jaw. Over the *poste* reigned a silence complete and ominous.

Espada was straightening his big body, and his narrow eyes were riveted on the distant mass of enemy.

"Oh, God," breathed Kent as yet another figure in blue and white appeared, and he felt the roots of his hair tingle. "Suleiman has wiped out the relief after all!"

One by one in a sad procession, urged along under a shadow of blows, the prisoners passed, to the number of forty-five. Then with a final triumphant thunder of tom-toms, the whole Arab mass retreated into the forest again, leaving the hollow-eyed handful in the *poste* robbed of their last hope.

CHAPTER IX

A GHASTLY THREAT

DAZEDLY KENT TURNED away from that horrible forest
with its hidden threat of death. He heard a heavy tread advancing rapidly along the firing platform, and for the first time found
himself able to think quickly and clearly. He knew what he was
going to do, and, in spite of his bone weariness, his movements
were quick and decided.

"Cover Rhemeier, when they come near. Follow my lead for
the signal," snapped the *adjutant*. "LaTouche, you cover Lenoir
and keep him covered. You'll die if you don't." There was no
mistaking the purpose of the three men advancing along the
platform.

"Gawd, Kent," protested Jerry, nevertheless obediently cock-
ing his rifle, "you ain't goin' to fight no longer, are yer?"

"Do what I tell you," growled Kent; and with his automatic
held hidden in the skirts of his wide, dark blue overcoat, he
waited for Espada's advance.

"Doubtless," began the Spaniard, with malevolent sarcasm,
"our good *adjutant* intends to fight further, no?"

"That's a good guess, sergeant," the big American replied
briskly. "I wish you could join us, but I can't have the defense
further hindered by you. Consider yourself under arrest! You
and Rhemeier and Blanco will at once lay down those rifles and
whatever equipment you now wear."

Speechless with wrath, the huge Spaniard raised his Lebel
and sprang forward, but stopped with a startled shout as Kent's
automatic swung in line with his eyes. Promptly LaTouche and
Jerry covered the other two.

It was very neatly accomplished. The three principal malcontents were quickly stripped of all weapons and equipment, then,

helplessly fuming, they were marched off to the cells beneath the water tower. Although the rest of the garrison hurled curses and threats as Kent and his prisoners passed, they offered no resistance.

"Fool!" venomously gritted the Spaniard. "Blind American boy!" He thrust his big hands through the bars as Jerry turned the key on the mutineers. "Think not that you have won—*Dios,* no! You will join the carrion outside when Suleiman's truce is done. Rest assured, *mi amigo,*" he added malevolently, "that the brave men you condemn to death in this *poste* will not allow your madness to last much longer!"

As the doors of the cells clanged on the two other prisoners, they broke into a storm of heartfelt blasphemy, and heaped all manner of threats and abuse on the granite-faced *adjutant's* head. As LaTouche and Jerry accompanied the iron-willed N.C.O. out of the musty cellar, Jerry laid an imploring hand on Kent's arm and fiercely demanded to know the reason for his refusal to negotiate.

"I fink ye're barmy," he protested. "Wot good does it do to get us all killed? Yer saw Suleiman has caught the relief good and proper. There was no less nor forty-five legionnaires in chokey."

"Yes," admitted Kent wearily. "I know it looks bad, but the psychology of Suleiman's offer is wrong. I don't just see why— but it's wrong."

"'Is si-cholera—'ell!" spat Jerry in real indignation.

"His psychology, as *Monsieur l'Adjutant* says, may be wrong," broke in LaTouche, "but there will be nothing wrong with Suleiman's bullets to-morrow morning. Come on, now, haven't we fought enough?"

"NO," SAID Kent heavily, and passed a hand over his furrowed brown forehead. "We haven't fought enough until the last man is dead. It's our painful duty to fight this little row out to the bitter end, no matter how black things look. Besides, I have been thinking. Why should old Suleiman offer us such liberal terms when he must know that we're at the end of our rope? If he'd really wiped out the relief, he'd go right through this *poste* as though it were an ant hill."

"Yes," objected LaTouche bitterly, "but please tell me where he captured the forty-five legionnaires we saw with our own eyes? It is most unlikely that there should be two expeditions of legionnaires in this vicinity. Heaven knows that the Legion is stingy enough with troops. Of a certainty these miserable ones must be from the relief column. Can you not see it will avail us nothing to die of fever? The blacks will be captured and enslaved none the less."

Kent was almost shaken from his determination. It seemed that no possible hope remained to them. Did not these poor old devils of legionnaires, who had suffered so much, deserve the right to live? Undoubtedly the next attack would be the last, and Suleiman would break through nevertheless and carry out his raid in triumph. Why not, therefore, spare the lives of these eighteen starving, fever-shaken men?

As they reached the doorway leading into the sunlit court-yard, Kent paused.

"My friends," said he, "it is a terrible thing to ask of you—to continue to fight. I don't know why, but I feel certain that this parade of prisoners is in some way a trick."

LaTouche silently shook his head. "There was no trick—I counted forty-five myself."

Kent continued: "Suleiman Tombohko logically has no reason why he should offer us terms—but he has. The answer is, he must fear something."

Then LaTouche made a suggestion. "Perhaps it's because the river is rising and the black devil fears that he'll be unable to cross after a few days. The ford would then be too deep."

"That may have something to do with it," admitted Kent dubiously, "but I feel sure there is something else back of his willingness to retreat. No, my friends, I'm sorry—but I don't think we shall surrender just yet."

"But, *mon adjutant*," concluded LaTouche gravely, "have you the right, on such vague hopes as are left to us, to condemn to death those unhappy devils in Suleimai's clutches? Remember," he warned, "Tombohko has promised to execute them to-night unless the flag is lowered."

Jerry, too, made Kent's decision harder. "Even if yer lets 'im do fer the chappies 'e 'as," he pleaded, "wot for do yer 'ang on? The froggies could never blyme yer. Gawd, wot a fight ye've made! Woncher 'aul down the old rag? Ye'll save the lives of eighteen true men." His pleading eyes all but shook Kent's resolution.

He groaned. "I'd die ten times over rather than make this choice—but—I have no choice. We must fight to the end."

In vain did LaTouche and the little Englishman argue. The many points they brought were undoubtedly true, and to the most of their objections Kent could find no answer; yet he shook his sunburned head and doggedly refused permission to accept the extraordinary offer of the Sultan.

EVEN MORE were his suspicions of Suleiman's peculiar behavior aroused that evening. Just as the sun was about to sink over the feathery tops of the palms, with great ado the slavers marched forth a group of only five heavily chained legionnaires at a distance of some two hundred yards from the *poste,* and there lined them up, a motley crowd of Arabs standing ready with guns about them.

Again came that galloping emissary and shouted up to the walls. "Have you accepted the terms? Remember that these *Franzwazi* die when I return."

Kent stood like a figure of granite while even the most loyal members of the garrison implored and berated him to surrender to save the unfortunates who sat hopelessly waiting the firing squad on the far side of the meadow. Anguish such as he had never before experienced filled Kent's heart, and his hands at his sides clenched and unclenched themselves in an excruciating agony of mind that none of the men about could possibly understand. It would be so easy to say "Yes." Then as he glanced across at the five solitary figures on the far side of the meadow he seemed to see the helpless, disarmed negroes who had been slain and harried by the hundreds—now living under the protection of France.

"No," he announced briskly, "we are not going to surrender. Not unless Sultan Suleiman produces all forty-five of the prisoners and shoots them under the walls of this *poste!*"

The bronze-faced legionnaires stared in astonishment at one another. *"Nom de Dieu!* Indeed he is mad!" They fell back from Kent as though he might at any moment fly at the nearest of them.

The emissary below was clearly taken aback. Here was something he had not in the least expected, and he seemed unable to cope with the situation.

Then, haltingly and with palpable embarrassment, he looked up at Kent again and stroked his black beard as though in a quandary. "Suleiman," he cried at length, "is merciful. He will shoot but five of the legionnaires."

Now it was the turn of the legionnaires to wonder at the Arab's reply. Why should Suleiman thus illogically be disposed to mercy? Why should he balk at executing forty-five instead of five of the *Franzwazi* he had hated since boyhood?

Kent felt his advantage at once, and his drawn features lighted up with hope. "No," he insisted, "we shall not surrender until the other forty are led out beside the five and here executed."

Jerry came to the decision that Kent's mind had broken under the terrible strain he had endured. " 'E's batty," he solemnly confided to LaTouche. "Pore Kent's clean batty!"

The Arab, after hesitating a moment, galloped off with the statement that only the five legionnaires should be executed, even though Kent had agreed to surrender the moment all the forty-five legionnaires lay dead.

Presently, far across the meadows, a ragged volley was fired, and when the tribesmen moved aside five blue and white figures lay motionless on the sunset-tinted grass.

As the echoes of that fusillade died away, Nytteus, a nervous, blue-jowled Belgian, went quite mad and rushed at Kent, shrieking "Assassin!" at the top of his voice. "Murderer!" he cried as his bayonet gleamed bright. "Monster! You could have saved our comrades. Will you not be content until we, too, are dead?"

Kent side-stepped the madman's aimless rush and dropped him with a hard blow to the jaw. Shaken and white-faced, the harassed *adjutant* ordered the weeping, groveling maniac to be carried down to the cells.

"Too bad," sighed Kent, "but it can't be helped. This *poste* must be held! Don't you see?" he demanded, turning to the thirteen scarecrows who were too cowed by the horrible events of the last few days to offer resistance. Without the leadership of Espada they seemed resigned to their fate. "Don't you see that Suleiman hasn't destroyed the relief? How he managed to get these forty-five men in uniform I can't imagine, but if they were all prisoners he would have taken me at my word and shot them outright to get the fort. I tell you"—his voice grew strong with conviction—"the relief has not been destroyed, and we must hold out."

CHAPTER X

STRATAGEMS AND TREACHERY

IT WAS THE acrid smell of burning wood that warned the garrison that somewhere an unknown mutineer had set the *poste* afire. Before they discovered the yellow flames licking eagerly at the subterranean storehouse all but a small fraction of the food had been destroyed.

At Kent's command the hard-driven defenders dashed pails of water over the blaze and, choking and coughing, stared with hopeless eyes on the charred remains of the food supply.

"It was lucky, perhaps," observed Legionnaire Vasskyj with a grimace, "that the flames did not reach the dynamite, else our merry little company would have been in even smaller bits than Monsieur Suleiman will carve us to-morrow night."

Kent nodded dumbly. This seemed the crowning blow of his misfortunes. Without medicine, reduced to a few rounds of ammunition, and now without food. Further defense could last but a few miserable hours. In the morning Suleiman's howling masses would put an end to the struggle. For that prospect Kent was thankful. How tired he was, even too tired to feel that incessant gnawing desire for alcohol in his stomach. Then, in the midst of his despair, came a sudden ray of hope like the steady beam of a beacon on a tempestuous night.

"It just might work," he told himself. "If I only could bring it off!" And for the first time in days a real smile lighted his bearded features.

At the same time, unfortunately for the *adjutant*, Legionnaire Jerry Hawkins had come to a reluctant decision. "If pore ol' Kent is so barmy he can't tell when 'e's licked, Gawd 'elp me, I'll just naturally 'ave to save 'im." Half an hour later, when the moon silvered the rank-smelling river mist, he found an opportunity to drop silently over the wall, and, with a grim smile on his pinched features, marched straight across the meadows toward the camp fires of Suleiman Tombohko.

Hardly had the little cockney disappeared from the *poste* than Kent, with the germ of an idea growing in his mind, sought everywhere for him. From the top of the watch tower to the moldy cellars of the *poste*, past the cells where Espada and the others cursed and railed, high and low he searched; but nowhere was even so much as a button to be found of the Englishman.

"He must have gone 'on pump,'"* said the *adjutant* bleakly, and felt a cold, deadened sensation in his brain as he realized that the man he had most trusted had deserted him in his hour of need. "And I wanted to show him," murmured Kent—"show him I'm not wholly a rotter; I wanted to repay him for saving my life."

---

* Deserted.

Hopelessly he stared out over the billowing fog. It was too late now, and Jerry's faith in him had died. Kent knew at that moment how Anthony must have felt when he saw the Egyptian fleet deserting him at Actium. Here and there a despondent legionnaire slouched on the walls, looking at him with hostile, fearful eyes. Only the *adjutant's* new-found domineering personality kept any semblance of discipline.

"It's a damned shame," he reflected bitterly, "that Jerry couldn't have waited an hour longer. How he'd jump at this new idea!"

For a long time Kent had sat in his quarters pondering over the peculiarly inconsistent policy of Suleiman Tombohko.

"I'm right; he can't have touched the relief; it was Humbert's lot he captured." In the recesses of his mind something clicked, and he seemed to see again that narrow defile, crowded on both sides by the yelling Arabs; saw again the prisoners passing, one by one—swallowed up in the ranks on the far side of the defile.

"Oh, of course!" he groaned. "It was a trick. If my brain wasn't pickled, I'd have seen it at once. The old devil never showed more than one man at a time. He kept 'em at a distance and passed the same five men across that gap—ran 'em round behind the tribesmen. The goddam old fox!"

He chuckled as he saw the whole trick unfold itself. "The relief column must be pretty close or else he'd wait a little longer and starve us out." But at the same time Kent knew that to explain this to the twelve remaining legionnaires, and ask them to believe it, would be impossible.

AS HE sat there a damp breeze smelling of rotten vegetation came up from the river, and the mist rose thick and white from the fen. Never had Kent felt so utterly alone, so thoroughly discouraged; yet, with a strange new determination he numbly sought to prepare for the last phase of the defense.

In dead silence he made his way to the storehouse of the *poste*, and there filled a species of wicker knapsack with long sticks of dynamite from the little blue boxes. He eyed the yellow-wrapped cylinders with a savage gleam in his eye, and his mind began to work out the details of his last attempt to stave off disaster.

Into his pocket he crammed a notebook and then buckled on his automatic and caught up a bugle which had lain neglected in a corner of the orderly room since the bugler had been laid along with so many others in that vast grave under the south wall.

"There'll be hell to pay if the poor devils find out I'm gone," he thought as he silently made his way across the south wall; then, waiting until an especially thick stratum of fog came rolling up, he dropped as gently as possible over the wall, hoping fervently that the shock of his fall would not set off those deadly yellow cylinders strapped on his back.

He landed on hands and knees in the dew-wetted grass at the base of the wall, and remained silent a moment, looking to the right and left; then he cautiously commenced to advance, the heavy dew wet on his hands, but started back with a suppressed cry of alarm as a large evil-smelling shape rose from the thickets immediately in front of him. Kent breathed a sigh of relief as he realized it was nothing but a pair of hyenas that had dragged part of their ghastly meal to the shelter of the bushes.

With renewed courage he moved off, circling to the right around the *poste* and gaining a position some hundred feet beyond the north wall. With a grunt of satisfaction he halted and eased the wicker knapsack to the ground.

With deliberate haste Kent selected three of the deadly sticks and, taking a bearing on the walls, concealed them in a tuft of *esparto* grass, then ripping a sheet of paper from his notebook, wrapped it around the little bundle of explosives.

This improvised mine having been satisfactorily arranged, he crept on hands and knees through the billowing mists to a hollow rotting log which lay some fifty feet beyond the tuft of grass. There he repeated the maneuver and, glancing back, had glimpses through a rift in the fog veil of the walls rising stark and forbidding in the moonlight.

He experienced a warm little thrill of exultation as he saw the tricolor fluttering strong in the night breeze and realized that he, with the help of but two loyal men, had kept that flag where Captain Laurier had raised it.

It took him half an hour to distribute the dynamite sticks in a wide double semicircle, one series arranged much closer to the *poste* than the other. Drawing from the recesses of his returning memory, Kent skillfully arranged the mines so that they could be detonated with a maximum of damage to forces advancing along the general course they must follow to attack. Some of the yellow sticks he concealed among the robes of the bloated and decaying dead, some he hid in clumps of dewy nodding flowers, always placing a white sheet from his notebook to mark the spot.

SWEAT WAS streaming down the *adjutant's* forehead, and his body, beneath the coarse dark-blue uniform, was wet, by the time the last sticks were placed to his satisfaction. Then, carefully hiding the hamper for future reference, Kent boldly marched down to the river's edge.

He noted with grim amusement the unfinished pier at which he had labored, and wondered if the guard who had sat above him that fateful afternoon would have recognized his ex-prisoner. He tentatively fingered his chin and cheeks, then smiled in the darkness. Gone was the flabby, bruised softness of his cheeks. They were hollow now, but bronzed and healthy. Gone was his shambling gait, his heavy, hang-dog look.

As the *adjutant* strode along it was with the vigorous stride of a man who respects himself and demands respect from others. The blue eyes, had they been visible in the darkness, were clear and steady. He progressed along the muddy, reed-grown shore with a distance-eating tread that carried him quickly away from the doomed *poste*.

Myriad night animals squalled and called in the darkness, and once a large leopard, surprised as he lapped at the water, fled with a heart-stilling screech that lifted the hair on Kent's head. Curious bats of varying sizes circled persistently about his head as they gorged themselves on the clouds of mosquitoes and other night insects that in humming swarms infested the broad Goruol.

At last the American halted, and, in the shelter of the reeds, squatted on a stump that was damp with mold. Brushing aside the buzzing insects with one hand, he warmed the mouthpiece of the bugle in the hollow of the other and grinned to himself.

"I'll have to sound 'assembly' as the American Army does it," he murmured, "but there shouldn't be a chance in a thousand of those poor devils at the *poste* ever being able to tell the difference. If I can only get them to stick it until morning!"

He pulled a bloodstained dirty rag from his pocket and carefully stuffed it in the throat of the instrument with the intention of making the call seem to come from even a greater distance than it actually did. "Hope this gives Suleiman bad dreams," he thought, and, filling his lungs, put the cold mouthpiece to his lips. Fortunately he had learned in idle moments at the Point to sound various bugle calls of the American Army.

Deciding on "Taps," he began. There were frequent breaks and many false notes in the call he blew, but in that heavy, damp stillness the strains carried faintly to both the camp of the slavers and to the beleaguered *poste*. "Pretty sour," he remarked disgustedly; "any Boy Scout could do better, but it just might work."

Tucking the bugle under his spacious overcoat, he made his way hastily toward the half built pier. He could hear as he skirted the camp of the slavers the excited murmurs of Suleiman's followers, and he wondered what that crafty veteran was thinking at the moment. Doubtless Tombohko was in a state of horrid doubt, and it was almost with a feeling of exultation that he made his way from thicket to thicket, ever nearing the walls. He prayed that no vigilant legionnaire would fire at him as he placed the wicker hamper he had employed for the dynamite against the walls. With its help, his fingers could just reach the coping of an embrasure, and he silently hauled himself, increasingly alarmed that no one challenged him.

A moment later he was lying flat on the firing platform

looking about with anxious eyes, as he found the walls to be completely and utterly deserted. There was not a soul to be seen anywhere, and he wondered if the garrison had not surrendered *en masse.* Defeat's cold finger clutched at his heart.

Were all his fine plots and plans to go for naught? Hopelessly he stared about the tenantless walls. "Well," said he aloud, "how can you buck the game if the cards are stacked?"

AT THAT moment, however, he caught the distant murmur of voices, and on tiptoe made his way across the courtyard toward the barracks. There, by the light of a single smoking lantern, he found not only the twelve loyal legionnaires, squatting in a large semicircle, but Espada and his two ringleaders freed and holding forth at length.

"See how our brave *adjutant* deserts us!" stormed Espada, with a wide sweep of his hands. "For all this braggart's fine pose and all that, the *coquin* runs off with his tail between his legs, leaving us to the knife of Suleiman."

"Yes, yes," cried the assembled legionnaires, "but what of the bugle call? Would it not appear that the *adjutant* was right after all?"

"Bugle call, bah!" the worthy sergeant spat in disgust. "It is a trick."

"But we heard it with our own ears," broke in two of the others. "Louis was on the east wall and I on the north. We both heard it. *Nom de Dieu!* It must be the relief at last."

Kent, unobserved, stood in the doorway watching the conclave. By the feeble light of that single lantern set on the floor, the legionnaires argued stormily, and their fleshless, deep-lined faces revealed in every detail the privations they had endured. Like an anarchist orator, Espada towered over them, his sweeping black mustaches quivering with the intensity of his arguments.

"Yes," he said scornfully, "there was a bugle call, but this Kent animal is crafty. He will do—"

Kent, as he watched the big man's face, realized that the Spaniard, more intelligent and guileful than the rest, had undoubtedly seen through the little stratagem Kent had employed. He knew he must stop that little speech before it was completed and the fat landed in the fire.

So with a loud "Hands up!" he advanced into the circle of light, amid a chorus of startled cries and oaths. LaTouche alone seemed pleased to see the *adjutant* alive and unharmed. The others fell back sullenly, leaving Kent and the Spaniard face to face. At the same time Espada realized that he must stake all on disposing of Kent; for, should the relief column arrive now, his shrift would indeed be short and there would be no lucrative march to the coast.

Courageously enough the Spaniard lunged straight at Kent, who had unwisely neglected to throw off the safety catch on the automatic he leveled. Kent pressed the trigger, but no explosion followed, and in the last fraction of the moment left to him he had barely time to sidestep. Espada's fist knocked the gun from his hand.

Kent was fighting at a grave disadvantage, he instantly realized, for Espada was clad only in boots, trousers and the thin cotton shirt of the legionnaires' uniform, whereas he himself wore the heavy cumbersome overcoat, together with a pistol and other equipment. For a moment the two antagonists squared off, gauging each other, and gray-bearded LaTouche, in summing them up, felt little confidence in the outcome for the *adjutant*. The olive-faced Spaniard was at least a head taller, immensely broader, and more powerful.

On the other hand, Kent was by far the quicker of the two. The vital question lay in how far the American had recovered from the effects of his long years of intemperance.

Kent, his eyes fixed on the oncoming Spaniard, flung off his *képi* and edged around to give himself more room, while Espada laughed scornfully.

"Come hither, little Americano," he jeered, "and Manuel

Espada will break thy neck for thee. The others you may deceive with your vile plots, but not me. Come, *perrito,* ere I—"

HE ADVANCED no farther, for Kent, fearful lest the mutineer betray his artifice, sprang forward, aiming a lightning blow at the Spaniard's face. It landed, but only as a glancing blow, for the sergeant, too, was quick. As Espada leaped aside, he aimed a shattering kick at Kent's kneecap, and had it landed it surely would have ended the struggles of that courageous individual against a fate which piled ill fortune mountain-heavy upon him.

The American, however, succeeded in turning aside and avoided the flashing boot with a quick sidewise motion, but a sledge-hammer blow of the giant Spaniards fist he could not escape. Like a pile driver it impacted on his cheek—caught him ere he could recover his balance. A thousand fiery stars winked before the *adjutant's* eyes and he rocked on his heels. It seemed as though that smashing blow had robbed him of all his strength, leaving him sick and dizzy.

"You must not lose!" shouted a small voice in his brain. "You must hold out a little longer." He shook his head to clear his senses and actually was able to drive his left hand full between the Spaniard's eyes, as the other charged in.

Espada flinched as does a bull when the picador's lance stings his flanks, and had Kent been able to put his full weight behind the blow that deadly struggle might conceivably have ended then and there; but the berserk Spaniard merely flung his big head sidewise to rid his nose and mouth of blood that poured into it from a bruised and inflamed nose.

Espada again rushed in, and Kent, fighting desperately, warded him off with a series of short left-handed jabs that stung his antagonist, but otherwise wrought no damage. The Spaniard, completely unskilled in the science of boxing, kept rushing in, aiming flaillike blows at Kent.

Sooner or later, Kent realized, one of these sledge-hammer blows would land and so put an end to the battle. Gasping for breath and terrible in the intensity of their struggle, they went around and around the dimly lit room, while the hoarse cries of the legionnaires, encouraging the massive Spaniard, rang loud in Kent's ears. If there had been but one encouraging voice bidding him, Roger Kent, to fight on, he would have felt better, but that complete silence stung him to the quick. Even old LaTouche was silent.

At last Espada, goaded beyond endurance by his inability to reach his antagonist, abandoned his bull-like rushes; then his teeth gleamed in an evil smile as his hand flashed to the back of the waistband of the baggy white trousers he wore, and in an instant a long-bladed knife gleamed in his hand.

"Mucker!" panted Kent. "Why in hell can't you fight fair?"

But Espada, with a guttural *"Carajo!"* was upon him. The American desperately sought to knock aside the glimmering knife blade, felt the steel enter his left forearm. Then Death looked him squarely in the face. That a number of muscles were cut the cornered *adjutant* knew instantly, for with a twinge of terror he found that several fingers of that hand refused to stay closed.

"This will be all," he thought, but he nevertheless fought doggedly on, vainly seeking to drive off the big man. Espada sprang forward, a grin of savage triumph on his face, as he sought to follow up his advantage. Desperately, Kent looked about for a means of escape. In a vague sort of haze he caught sight of excited, scowling faces waiting at the far end of the room. They were hugely enjoying the prospect of his fall.

What he would have given to have seen Jerry's plain, friendly face among them! But Jerry was not there; Jerry had deserted. Then his despairing eyes circled the floor for the last time and fell upon a dully gleaming object. It was the automatic he had neglected to disengage on entering. There lay his sole hope.

HE RETREATED toward it, raining blow after blow at the Spaniard, who, supremely confident of his advantage, did nothing more for the moment than to plunge his knife again and again in the warding left arm that Kent had deliberately sacrificed as a buffer.

It was slashed and bleeding in a dozen places by the time that Kent stood over his weapon. Then, with a loud, disconcerting shout, he rushed headlong at Espada, fastening his right hand on that of the Spaniard and throwing all his weight forward at the same instant.

"Sangre de Cristo!" shouted the sergeant in triumph. The fool had played right into his hands. Manuel Espada knew he was stronger than the American, and that once he had his arms around him it would be over with that accursed Americano.

Dexterously he thrust his leg back of Kent's twisting him over. For a moment the two struggled in a straining deadly embrace, then fell with a dull thud to the cold, damp floor, Kent holding on for dear life to the knife hand and watching for an opportunity to reach the fallen automatic with his mangled, dripping left.

A terrible doubt seized the *adjutant* as to whether he could yet manage that crippled hand sufficiently to pull the trigger. It felt quite dead and useless. God! If it were! His breath was short, and the increasing pressure of Manuel Espada's massive left arm seemed to be crushing the life out of him.

Slowly the Spaniard was forcing the gleaming blade toward the American's chest. Try as Kent would, he could not halt that steady, menacing downward motion. Shortly, in spite of his frantic struggles, the knife would enter his chest. He groped madly for the automatic, and at last encountered it.

To his dismay, only two of his fingers would obey his commands, the thumb and first finger. The world was spinning darkly before his eyes as he fumbled to get the weapon into such a position that it could be fired. Unfortunately his fingers had grasped the barrel on first contact. The knife point was actually slitting the rough blue cloth above his heart, and Espada was preparing for a final effort that once and for all would remove the headstrong American.

The Spaniard gathered himself and set his weight. Kent, knowing instinctively that this was the last phase of the struggle, groped madly to bring the automatic in position. At last it was accomplished, and awkwardly with the left forefinger Kent felt for the safety catch. Its hard, rough surface moved, and, pressing the blunt muzzle deep to the Spaniard's side, he pulled the trigger just as the point of the knife entered his own body.

There was a muffled, thunderous roar in the confined space of that small room; then Espada's body went limp and heavy as lead, pressing the half-conscious American to earth. The knife fell from the sergeant's nerveless fingers and remained half supported in position by the thickness of the *adjutant's* overcoat.

Espada uttered a long, sobbing sigh, then relaxed, and in spite of their hate the onlookers uttered an unwilling cry of tribute. In an instant old LaTouche was kneeling beside Kent.

"*Tu es blessé!*" he cried. "You're wounded! *Dieu*, but that was a splendid struggle! Have no fear, *mon ami*, the men will now follow you to the end."

CHAPTER XI

CHOOSE!

AFTER THE GRIZZLED corporal had roughly bandaged the deep and painful slashes in Kent's left arm the American gathered the last little remnant of garrison together while he fed their hope on the sound of the bugle.

"They can't be far away," he panted; "perhaps less than ten kilometers; and in the morning we must surely see them coming to our aid. But a few hours more of resistance, and we'll have won such a struggle as few can equal in all the history of *la Légion*."

But even while he spoke his conscience tortured him as he saw the confidence reinstilled in those sweat-streaked faces. If they only knew that the whole affair was a sham, every cheering word a black lie! It was a terrible load his conscience was carrying.

"And now, men," he continued, "I will tell you how we may yet hope to drive the followers of Suleiman in defeat back into the jungles." Forthwith he spoke of the dynamite which he had placed, and roughly assigned the mines to the few men who were left. "You will wait until I give the signal; then shoot at the white markers I have tied around the sticks. They should make a nasty piece of fireworks."

"Nom de Dieu!" was all they could cry as they saw the trap gradually revealed. "The old black devil will be annihilated!"

Gone was the hangdog hopelessness. On the faces of the men beamed confidence as they believed they saw honors and glory within arm's reach. Kent, alone in his agony, knew that the hope of relief was vain. Somewhere that column must be, but how near or how far he could not possibly guess—all he could do was to struggle doggedly, blindly to the end of that living nightmare.

Fervently he hoped that the attack of the following morning would once and for all settle his problem. He felt much like a man who, swimming under water, seeks to gain the far side of a raft. His lungs are bursting and his head roars, and he wonders whether he will ever be able to gain that shimmering patch of light water ahead.

Long before sunup every available rifle had been collected, loaded and stacked about the top of the watch tower. As there were but twelve men left, Kent reluctantly decided to abandon the long, indefensible walls and to stake his all on a successful defense of the watch tower. Searching the belts of the fallen, the weary legionnaires collected a pitiful ten rounds of ammunition per man.

During those long, black hours Kent more than ever missed the cheerful optimism of Jerry, and wondered what peculiar flaw in the cockney's nature had tempted him to desert in the last minute.

"Poor devil, he's probably been cut to bits by now," he told himself. "Why did he do it?"

With a load of rifles held in his undamaged right arm, he strode along the firing platform to the entrance of the tower. As he paused to open the door something flashed through the air and lighted at the *adjutant's* feet.

He started back hastily as he recognized the missile to be an Arab lance tufted with a waving frill of horse hair. But what aroused his curiosity was that wrapped about the middle of the handle was a ragged square of paper.

He peered cautiously into the grayness below the walls, and listened intently, but there was no sound. Greatly mystified, he silently leaned the rifles against the tower in an orderly row, then plucked the message from the shaft.

His heart pounding with a vague alarm, he stepped into the tower and, by the light of a match, read a message which turned his body to ice. It was from Jerry.

It read:

> DEAR KENT: i thinks you are barmy enuff to keep on fiting, so have taken a way to make you stopp. i have went to the nigger and surrendered. i have told him he can kill me in the morning if you don't haul down the flag before sun up. i know you will not let you old pal Jerry be killed—i am doing this for yure sake. P.S. For God's sake. Haul down that dam flag, these blokes are narsty.

HAD NOT Kent suffered so many trials and sorrows during the ghastly days just past, he would have been transfixed with horror. As it was, he sank to the lowest step of the stair in a species of numb agony. He must either condemn a loyal and unselfish friend to an indescribably terrible death, or lose the *poste*.

Of all the many frightful decisions he had had to make, this was by far the worst. In his mind's eye the *adjutant* could see Jerry standing on the edge of the forest, his little blue eyes confidently fixed on the tricolor, watching and believing that the friend whose life he had saved would not condemn him to a dreadful death.

Wise Jerry, to have thought it out so perfectly—to have found so unerringly the weak joint in his armor! To have appealed to that sense of loyalty which above all distinguishes the man from the mucker! Try as he would, poor Kent could not bring himself to make an immediate decision. It was too much for his over-wrought brain, and then it was at least some half hour before sunup. During that time he would plumb his soul on the course he must follow, but he knew he could not bring himself to think of condemning Jerry to death.

No more could he bring himself to contemplate surrender, after having lost so many lives and caused so much suffering. Silently he gathered up the rifles and, with his wounded arm giving him acute agony, climbed the stairs one at a time to the platform above.

At last a tinge of pink tinted the sky to the westward and bit by bit the details of the surrounding country, now as familiar as the back of Kent's own hand, commenced to show up in greater distinctness.

The *adjutant*, weak from the loss of blood and with his left arm secured in a rough sling, was making the last preparations for defense. As the increasing light permitted the white markers on the dynamite sticks to be seen, he assigned specified riflemen to each group.

The eager legionnaires peered anxiously about, as though they expected each moment to hear a fresh blast on that hope-instilling bugle. They kept looking up the river with hope written large on their haggard faces.

Deeper and deeper grew the rose color on the horizon, until the stars paled and vanished by hundreds. Kent, as in a dream, glanced alternately from the horizon to that flag which flapped overhead. Within him raged such a conflict of mind as drives men mad. A thousand kindly things little Jerry had done rose before his eyes. It was but three days since the Englishman had saved his life when he fought on the wall. At the time he had vowed not to forget, and now—

"The sun will soon be above the horizon," remarked LaTouche eagerly. "I hope the commandant of the column does not delay. *Nom de Dieu!* with but ten rounds apiece we cannot fight long."

A single wandering cloud was directly above the path of the sun, and with hollow, agonized eyes Kent watched the color of that cloudlet grow brighter and brighter.

Uttering a stiffled groan, Kent got unsteadily to his feet and stumbled across to the halyards of the flagpole. With his good hand he reached for the knot.

"What are you doing?" demanded one of the legionnaires as Kent awkwardly commenced to lower the flag. "You aren't going to surrender now?" An echo of startled voices rang in protest, but Kent, heedless of their frantic protests, hauled downward with sharp, decided motions, until the flag floated at halfmast. Then, with something like a sob, he retied the knot, leaving the tricolor fluttering some ten feet from the wondering men on the platform.

"To your posts," snapped the *adjutant* harshly. He turned away and caught up his automatic pistol; then sank at one of the embrasures and knelt with eyes closed.

The sun had become a glowing, copper-colored lozenge above the tree tops when Kent once more opened his eyes. The legionnaires were squatting about, looking down on the deserted *poste* with curious gaze. Then in the depths of the forest recommenced the clamor of tom-toms. Sultan Suleiman Tombohko was coming for a last decisive attack, an attack which would forever blot that troublesome little fort from his dominions.

CHAPTER XII

THE LAST ATTACK

"AS YOU VALUE your lives, no man is to fire until I blow the whistle," warned Kent when the first of the slavers appeared at the edge of the forest.

Boom-boom! Boom-boom! roared the drums in a rising frenzy.

As before, the slavers came on in a wide, formless charge. The footmen hurried ahead, soon to be overtaken by the massed, wildly shouting horsemen. There were hundreds of them, fiercely determined to terminate this tiresome struggle once and for all.

They came on in a resistless, colorful torrent, and the handful of men on the tower were shaken with a terrible fear that their plan of defense might fail after all.

The twelve lay flat on their bellies on top of the tower, each man sighting steadily on his square of paper, waiting for that fateful whistle blast.

The noisy charge came nearer and the thunder of the horses' hooves filled the air. Bullets, fired by the infantry, commenced to strike the watch tower, then for a little space the attackers hesitated when no rifle shots came from the walls.

They gathered courage, however, and nearer and nearer they came. At their head was a big man in a green *haik*, waving a scimitar that flashed redly in the sunrise behind him; at intervals came solid masses of cavalrymen, dashing at headlong speed toward the walls.

Now they were passing by the first of the paper markers. Kent prayed that no horse would accidentally tread on the hidden explosives—but consoled himself with the knowledge that a horse will invariably step or jump over an obstacle, no matter how small, rather than tread upon it.

On came the slavers, their weapons flashing in the sunlight

and their voices making the morning hideous with their blood-thirsty *"Lah! lah! illah! Allah!"*

"Steady," called Kent in a voice of ice. He could not rid himself of the vision of Jerry lying dead. It required the iron discipline of the Legion, a vast amount of self-control, to make the rifle-men withhold their volley until the horsemen were almost at the walls and the footmen well within the outer line of white markers. Then with a great lifting sensation in his being, Kent put the whistle to his lips and blew a short single screaming blast.

WHAT FOLLOWED Kent only remembered in a disjointed succession of scenes, as vague and indistinct as a nightmare.

The effect of the crudely improvised mines was frightful, utterly appalling. The legionnaires' bullets, striking squarely among the dynamite sticks, detonated them instantaneously with thundering vivid yellow sheets of flame that hurled tall plumes of smoke, fire, and soil far into the air, blasting every living thing for yards about with a rending white-hot hand. The tower, solidly built as it was, swayed beneath the shock of that first series of stunning explosions. For a breathless moment all was still.

The Arabs, such of them as were yet alive, halted, petrified with a nameless terror; the legionnaires ceased fire, appalled at the power of their own weapons. Great streaming craters of earth had opened about the spots where the dynamite had been hidden, and a ghastly shambles of torn, red-stained white bodies stretched away on either side of the *poste*.

Suddenly the terror-stricken slavers screamed in complete abandonment. They retreated madly in all directions. Then the legionnaires turned their rifles upon the second and outer line of mines between the broken slavers and the forest, and the frightful tragedy was repeated.

The exploding dynamite shattered the masses of retreating slavers, killing many of them by the sheer concussion, and raining a mass of horrible débris upon the *poste* and forest. Some gruesome bits even fell into the oily Goruol, where ripples

spread in wide concentric rings. Birds in chattering terror fluttered madly to and fro.

As the tower again swayed under the repeated concussions,
Kent was knocked to his knees. All he knew was that of Suleiman's forces but a broken handful remained, fleeing with the
blind sightlessness of the utterly terrified, flinging away their
weapons and anything else that hindered their headlong flight.
In an incredibly short time all that remained in the stricken
field were its mounds of dismembered dead and the shrieking
wounded.

"There," breathed Kent. "I guess Jerry will sleep better now."
So saying, he slipped gradually to the shell-littered platform to
slump senseless against the embrasures.

Step by step the legionnaires clambered down the tower to
the walls, and for the first time in ten days flung open the gates.
In their midst they carried the senseless form of their *adjutant*.
Very tenderly they laid him in the shade of the south wall and
poured water upon his white and tortured face, but still he would
not wake.

"Il est bien fini," murmured LaTouche brokenly, and the tears
coursed down his weather-beaten cheeks as he felt how slowly
beat the American's pulse.

THE GARRISON was not in the least surprised when, late
that evening, a little group of strange legionnaires came marching up cautiously to the *poste*, their eyes wide with horror and
amazement.

In their midst strode a short, red-faced individual who turned
to the leader and said:

"Hi 'opes as 'ow Kent ain't took the big jump. 'E were an A-1
scrapper, 'e were."

The garrison, if such a pitiful handful could be called a garrison, stared with amazement as they recognized the form of
their lost companion Jerry among the perspiring advance guard.

"Allo!" called LaTouche in amazement. "We thought you

were cat-meat long before. How does it happen you are still here?"

"Oh," explained Jerry, with an air of vast condescension, "the bally niggers forgot orl abaht poor little me when Kent's fireworks went orf. They thort to keep me until the rest of yer was prisoners too. And wot the narsty blighters intended to do to us! Where is Kent?"

"*Monsieur l'Adjutant* is dying," murmured LaTouche, crossing himself. "Since the assault was defeated he has lain as one dead."

In wide-eyed alarm and with the gaping *sous-lieutenant* of the relief column at his elbow, Jerry brokenly demanded to be led to Kent's bedside, and as he saw the long form of his friend lying white and motionless on the cot he broke into a broken sobbing.

"Kent," he cried, "Kent, ol' mate, if I 'ad only known of your little gyme. I didn't know." A faint motion of Kent's eyelids raised a hope in the cockney's heart. "Kent," he cried, "it's me— Jerry! Kent! Yer carn't die arter all this! Didn't yer understand? The relief 'as come!"

Slowly the American's eyes opened and he gazed at the anxious Englishman with a little weak nod of recognition.

"I don't know how it is," he said faintly, "that you are alive. Perhaps it's I that is dead and I am dreaming all this."

"But no, *adjutant*," broke in the *sous-lieutenant*, eager to have his share in the conversation on such a glorious occasion, "you're not dead. You'll live to be the *beau ideal* of the Legion, and we have come to save you from Suleiman."

"Thanks," whispered Kent with a wry smile, "but I expect Suleiman's present somewhere—but not voting."

The *sous-lieutenant* pulled a flask from his pocket and put it to Kent's lips.

"No, thank you," said the wounded man. "I've already had more than my share—"

"His share?" cried the *sous-lieutenant*. "Poor devil, he's delirious!"

He turned to Jerry, but that hard-bitten individual was looking at the vast common grave in the courtyard. "Gawd!" he murmured. "I wish that Adipose nigger was 'ere—'im wiv 'is everlastin', 'Once a drunk, always a drunk.' Wot a liar Hi`d call 'im!"

THE RENEGADE CAID

Hopeless, untiring, Lemuel Frost of the Foreign Legion and his companions stake their lives to stem the relentless advance of a terrible enemy of France

CHAPTER I

RAIDING TRIBESMEN

THE SERGEANT'S LONG legs swayed gently to the stride of his camel as he rode slightly in advance of three hard-featured, unshaved men in the blue and white uniform of La Légion Étrangère—last of the world's mercenary regiments. He seemed to be drowsing, for the sun, glaring on his sweat-sodden white neckcloth, no longer beat down with the pitiless, furnace heat of midday.

But Sergeant Lemuel Z. Frost was very far from drowsing. His brown eyes, so deep in hue as to seem black, and narrowed by the glare to mere slits, flickered endlessly back and forth like those of a Comanche, Sioux or some other plains Indian, noting every tiny depression and shadow in the vast, red-hued desert stretching away toward the heat-distorted horizon.

"This heat makes little old Death Valley seem like a perfoomed garden! Hope everythin's O.K. at Samah."

With the thought his eyes flickered over the red ridges to the left. Somewhere out yonder lay the tiny white-walled *poste* of Samah, one of many such barriers to the spoil-hungry raiders of the Arabian Desert.

Suddenly he stiffened; far away in the direction of Samah rose a tiny plume of whitish smoke, rising almost vertically in the windless atmosphere into the aching blueness of the sky. Sergeant Lemuel turned toward the rear a lean, hard-bitten face that was remarkably like an Indian's and marred on the right side by a long whitish scar running from the corner of a straight, thin-lipped mouth to just below the high cheek bone.

"Hey, Harold! Mosey up alongside!" he called.

The smallest of the three Legionnaires grunted, spat and kicked his mount into an awkward trot to ride up, sparrow-like,

red features alert. From the deep shade of his *képi's* leather brim, two small and very bright blue eyes fixed themselves upon the American's intent brown face.

"Wot's bitin' yer, Lem?" he demanded, as his buff-colored *mehari*—riding camel—slowed to a fast shuffling stride that stirred lazy puffs of reddish dust.

"See that there smoke?" The sergeant's wide brown hand, decorated with an eagle bluely tatooed on its back, indicated the smoke column. "Don't look too healthy, do it? It's a damn sight too near to the *poste* to suit this ornery *soldado*."

"Carn't see it," replied the other, after searching the desolate stretch ahead. "But I do see somethin' else. Look down by that *wadi* yonder!"

The American's narrowed eyes flickered to a deep gully that lay, a blue-shadowed slash in the desert's face, some two miles

They found the poste
a place of horror.

to their right. Lemuel's flat, blue-clad back stiffened in alarm; into that gully was galloping a long line of camel riders.

"Well, I'll be damned!"

Lemuel's horny hand shot to a battered pair of field glasses swaying on his chest, but before he could get them out, the last of that quick-riding column had vanished as though swallowed by the hot clay and sand of the desert.

"Now strike me peculiar pink!" grunted Corporal Harold Hackbutt of the Sixième Compagnie, as he further shaded his eyes with a stubby hand bearing a generous crop of reddish bristles on its back. "It's a raidin' *'arka*,* all right, but that's the first time *I* ever seen Arabs sportin' dark robes."

---

* *Harka*—raiding expedition of no special size.

"Same here," grunted Lemuel, jerking his bridle rein. "Shake a leg, son; I reckon we'd better slip down into this arroyo and make ourselves harder to see."

"Wot do you think them beggars is, Lem?"

"Hard to say. 'Tain't none o' the Druses, 'cause they always wear white or stripes—leastwise, their desert tribes do. The mountaineers is different—they wears blacks and browns, as you'll recollect, eh, son?"

The sweat-bright faces of both Legionnaires creased in reminiscent grins, the vicious fighting of the recent Jebel Druse campaign still fresh in their minds. No Legionnaire who had fought that ghastly campaign would quickly forget the fierce charges of the shaggy Hauran mountaineers, whose habitat now lay not far behind, a black basalt mass rising sheer from the red plains.

"THEY SEEMED to be ridin' in formation o' some kind, Harry. Might be British. We ain't so far from the Trans-Jordan border, you now."

"Them blighters British?" The cockney shook his head until the white *képi* cover fluttered. " 'Ell, no! If they 'ad been wearin' khaki we couldn't 'ave seen them 'arf so good."

Amid an avalanche of hot pebbles the sergeant guided his *mehari* down a steep slope of crumbling rock; while a sharp uneasiness rose within him. There was something queer about these strange, hard-riding raiders. To what tribe did they belong? What was their objective? Where were....

Suddenly the sergeant's blue-clad arm shot skyward in an unmistakable gesture of alarm; whereupon Harold and the two other Legionnaires, big, brown-faced men with brutal, clean-shaved faces, set their weight back, jerking their camels to an abrupt halt. It was significant of the deadly peril in which they existed that the rifles were unslung and cocked without command.

"Down!" snapped Lemuel, black eyes a-glitter. Placing his dusty hobnailed shoe on the base of his snuffling camel's neck, he pressed vigorously; whereupon the ungainly brute uttered a low, bubbling groan and with jerky motions like those of an awkwardly folded camp chair, sank to earth and snapped half-heartedly at his rider's knee.

"These damned A-rab canaries will be the death o' us yet," snarled Lemuel, as he stooped to adjust the knee halter. "Why in hell can't they be quiet? I ain't aimin' to get impaled on no young palm stump just yet. Shut up, you cross-grained devil!"

"Your orders, *mon sergeant?*" inquired Legionnaire Maillot, a villainous ex-Apache from Marseilles. His gap teeth shone yellow in the strong sunlight as he advanced, his long Lebel held ready—even when mounted the splendid marksmen of the Legion spurn the shorter Gras carbine. He was jerking open the flap of his black leather cartridge clip containers, his deep-set black eyes lighting with the joy of coming battle.

"Sounds like camel riders a comin' up this arroyo," was the sergeant's reply. "We're out o' sight, so if we stay quiet and them damned camels will stop their blasted yelpin' mebbe we can avoid a set-to."

Realizing that a "set-to" would probably end unpleasantly— the Druses are not fond of men in French blue—the reconnaissance party took up the best positions that could be found behind convenient bowlders at the head of the gully, as far as possible from that mysterious column of camel men. Who were they? More of those dark-robed raiders?

The rocks were still scorching hot from the midday heat they had absorbed. Though the sun was reddening and plunging toward the western horizon with satisfactory speed, the four Legionnaires bitterly resented their enforced proximity to the hot earth, which exuded scorching air currents that sent rivulets of perspiration trickling beneath the heavy dark blue overcoats they wore.

NOW, IF it comes to fighting," whispered Lemuel, his hard black eyes embracing all three of the tensed riflemen, "wait for my order. *Feux de salves!* Volley fire and yell like hell!"

Bulgakan, a blond Russian Legionnaire whose huge bulk lay sprawled on the far end of the line, nodded several times, a blue-black shadow mimicking his motion on the dry, lifeless clay. Next to him Legionnaire Maillot licked thick lips that were brown and cracked from the heat. Corporal Hackbutt with characteristic *sang-froid* disposed bright brass cartridge clips in a neat, convenient row before him and scowled.

"Just our bloody luck, Lem," Harold growled, blowing a sweat drop from the end of his pointed nose. " 'Ere I'd thought we'd finished this 'ere reconnaissance wiv nerves 'ale and 'earty, and now look wot's 'appenin'."

"What'll happen next is you'll get a thick ear if you don't shut that noisy trap o' yours," promised Lemuel; then he flattened like a frightened quail, big, bronze-hued hands tightly gripping his Lebel.

Even his war-tried heart began to pound when, with the complete silence of a drifting shadow, there trotted into the gully below a strange vision. He was a dark-faced Druse in white robes which at that distance seemed oddly marked. Three, four, five, six others rode into sight; then after an interval three or four more appeared, swaying oddly in their brass-mounted saddles.

Gradually Lemuel's jet eyes widened and into his Indian-like visage crept a look of puzzled surprise. He glanced sidewise. The other three riflemen, too, were gaping in astonishment; for the snowy *djellab* of the leading Druse was spotted with blood flowing from a hideous face wound. The white *mehari* he bestrode shuffled wearily along, head swaying dispiritedly at the end of its ungainly long neck.

To the American's intense surprise, the other riders also bore the marks of conflict. Of the ten that appeared, only three or four were without wounds of some kind.

Nearer and nearer rode the fugitives, obviously survivors of a disastrous skirmish. The details of their equipment now showed more clearly. Scarlet and green saddle cloths; archaic, gold-hilted tribal daggers, hooked like the bill of a bird of prey; goatskin water bags, modern pistols and rifles.

When the Druses were yet some fifty yards away, the man with the face wound swayed weakly, lost his grip on the saddle horn and suddenly plunged from his camel's back, to lie a tumbled heap of blood-splashed robes among the small round stones in the bottom of the gully. His camel halted and lowered its sweat-darkened head to sniff at its late rider.

Clearly the muttered words of the next Druse carried up to the curious watchers crouching behind their stones. "*Bismillah.* God wills it. May the soul of Ibn Cheil pass to the Seventh Circle of Paradise!"

But the speaker, a big hawk-faced tribesman with a black forked beard, made no gesture to halt, nor did any of his followers. Reluctantly the fallen man's *mehari* abandoned the corpse, and halter rope dragging, fell in with the last of the beaten force now passing directly below the bewildered Legionnaires.

IT WAS very tempting to see those dark-featured, unmissable targets not twenty yards distant, riding by utterly unaware of their peril. They were enemies, too—fierce Druse nomads of the sort who made life a continual nerve-racking hell for the small Legion garrisons scattered among the heat blasted foothills of the Hauran mountain range.

Bulgakan scowled, rolled pale blue eyes imploringly to Lemuel, and licked his lips for all the world like a hungry dog. Maillot's calloused forefinger had crept around the trigger of his Lebel and he cuddled the stock to his swart, unshaved cheek. Over the rifle's sight he had already picked out a minor chieftain for the first bullet—a rich young Tchek with two gold-hilted daggers tucked in his girdle.

It was not that Lemuel had any moral scruples against shooting from ambush. He would have been very glad to wipe out that sorely stricken party: had he not seen handsome young Lieutenant Dinard, neatly disembowelled and minus ears, nose and eyelids, sent into camp lashed to a foundered baggage camel? A gift from these same Druses.

But, crafty veteran that he was, he restrained himself. Who knew what might be out of sight down the gully? It must be a terribly efficient force that could inflict such a crushing defeat upon the hardy warlike Druses. Had it anything to do with that long column of dark-robed riders?

Now the retreating Druses had all limped by: the badly wounded clinging desperately, doggedly, to the high peaks of their camel saddles; the unwounded ones somber-eyed as they dejectedly goaded their long-legged mounts to an even swifter walk.

It was only when the low gurgle and whining of the camels had faded in the distance and the last rider had been lost to sight around a bend in the gully that Lemuel made any motions. Even then, though tortured by heat, he delayed a full ten minutes lest some straggler, mounted on a wounded camel, might come up and give the alarm.

"Allons, mes enfants," he said at last, and wiped great drops of sweat from his straight black brows. "Reckon we can amble down and throw a eye over that late-lamented cutthroat."

In silence the four men in blue and white scrambled down to bend presently over the gray-faced Druse.

" 'Ello! The bloody devil's still breathin'," observed Harold, "Watch 'is blinking chest...."

He dropped to one knee and rough-jerked the *djellab's* hood away from a dark, predatory face that lacked one cheek, an ear and part of the skull. Eyes, dim but yet retaining intelligence, opened, and on beholding the dreaded uniform of the Legion the tribesman made a feeble effort to spit; but as his left cheek had been entirely torn away leaving the teeth and bone exposed, this amiable effort was quite without success.

"Sacré mecque!" Legionnaire Maillot's snaggle teeth shone in a wolfish grin as he set down his rifle. "No use wasting a good shot on such. Here!" Stooping he caught up a great round, reddish

stone, heaved it to his shoulder, and grinning wickedly came striding toward the wounded Druse who watched him from venomous black eyes.

"Ah!" grinned Legionnaire Bulgakan in simple pleasure. "How nice! Our friend is thinking of his partner who was skinned aliv'e last month."

NEARER STALKED the brutal-featured Apache, the stone ready balanced, the Druse watching him from dim, malignant eyes.

"Lay off!" suddenly rasped Lemuel. "This hombre's goin' to peg out pronto, anyhow."

Maillot halted, scowling. "But, *mon sergeant,* 'tis too easy a death for this black dog."

Lemuel's jaw shot out. "You heard me! Drop that dornick," After the stone had thudded to earth the American thrust the *képi* to the back of his head and speculatively eyed the stricken native, just then writhing with a spasm of pain.

"Harold" he announced. "There's a few things I'd like to know about these here goin's on. To pull through with a whole hide we gotta do some fast thinkin'. Just you hike up to them left-handed gyraffes o' ourn and fetch little Lemuel a water bottle."

"A wot?" The cockney seemed intensely surprised, almost pained; for this war between the Legion and the Druses was without romance, without glamour or mercy; it was a dreadful, savage struggle in which the weak and helpless perished as slowly and uncomfortably as possible.

"A water bottle—canteen—get it pronto!" snapped the American. "And now you two, haul this nigger into the shade."

Muttering resentfully, Bulgakan and Maillot picked up the dying Druse and with no special tenderness deposited him in the shade of a great red rock.

"*Maiah! Maiah!* Water!" choked the Druse convulsively, lifting a small dark hand to his blood-streaked throat.

"Now you, Maillot, forget your buddie and listen to orders."

Lemuel was very brisk and businesslike. "You speak the A-rab lingo, so as soon as we've watered this here faded rose a bit I want you to ask him some questions."

" *'Cré nom de Dieu!*" The Frenchman spat in disgust; but knowing the hard fists of Sergeant Lemuel Frost he obediently squatted on his heels and prepared to translate, after Corporal Harold had tilted a tin cup full of water into what remained of the Druse's mouth. Lemuel nodded in satisfaction when bewilderment and gratitude indescribable lit the stricken native's features.

"Ask him what happened."

In swift, guttural Arabic, Legionnaire Maillot obeyed. Then in a feeble, blood-choked voice the Druse commenced to speak.

Maillot's red, battered features were lifted to Lemuel "This *vaurien* says his raiding party fell in and fought with warriors from a strange tribe—probably gun-runners from Tiflis. This sacred grandson of murderers also says the strangers are fierce warriors, terrible white men, leading Arabs from a far country. What next, *mon sergeant?*"

"Find out where the skirmish was. See if you can't get a better idee o' the nationality o' these hostiles."

Bending low, for the Druse's voice was growing constantly weaker, Legionnaire Maillot listened, then uttered a low cry of astonishment: "He says the razzia, the foray, was made by the followers of a white man called Caid Rouazi Dial Allah." Maillot scratched his dirty blue-black head. "Rouazi Dial Allah— that means 'Fist Blows of God.' Our dear little cutthroat also would have us believe that this white man has become one of the True Faith—that this Caid fights as do the Roumis. The Druse *harka* was massacred—almost wiped out. *Dieu de Dieu!*"

AT THIS, Lemuel's craggy features fell into a tense, thoughtful expression; and while Bulgakan and Harold maintained a vigilant lookout up and down the gully he put question after question.

"What's this gay Caid's objective?"

The dying tribesman groaned a little before replying, and the bright arterial blood pumping from that ghastly wound seemed to flow slower, as though the supply were nearly exhausted. How red it shone on the white robes and on the hard, sun-dried earth!

"This renegade Caid has sworn to make a kingdom for himself. He plots to inflame the desert tribes against the French in Syria, and the English in Palestine and Transjordania."

"Going to lick France and England, eh?" commented the American with grim humor. " 'Pears like this bad hombre ain't afraid of a fight."

It appeared on further inquiry that the Caid Rouazi had three main objects in mind. One was to capture a Legion supply depot at El Kufr lying at the end of a narrow defile on the far side of the Hauran mountains; the second was to intercept and capture certain supply trains due at Nasib on the Damascus-Bagdad railway. The gentle Caid had heard that machine guns, which he could use very handily in his business, were being shipped in quantity to the none-too-well equipped desert garrisons.

The third and not the least of El Rouazi's ambitions was to indulge in a wholesale slaughter of Christian natives then assembled for a fair at Melal-es-Sarrar, not far to the southward. A thoroughgoing massacre, the Caid firmly hoped, would cause the fanatic tribesmen of the Jebel Druse, El Jah, and Jebel Zumleh to rise and join him in casting out the hated Europeans, once and for all.

"Nice little program," commented Harold. "I *don't* fink!"

"Ask the nigger how many men this Caid's got," directed Lemuel, eyes narrowed with concentration.

But when the Legionnaire Maillot put the next question the wounded man's eyes had nearly closed and the blood flow had ceased.

"Come on, *sacré cochon noir!*" Maillot rasped, shaking the gore-splashed Druse; but the only result was to evoke a sudden last rush of blood. Then the glazing eyes, strange-white in that dark face, gradually open and the robes lay still over the tribes-man's narrow chest.

LEMUEL WASTED no time in regrets. A razzia of major importance was afoot; and the more he thought of that pillar of smoke in the direction of his *poste* the less he liked it.

"Wish to hell we knew how many there is in this funny *harka*. Well, snap out of it, you *soldados*. We got a heap of a way to go yet, and I ain't figgerin' to tangle with these strangers outside the *poste*. Anybody that can lick them ornery Druses to such a frazzle is tough meat!"

With more than their usual swiftness the Legionnaires cast off knee halters and with whistling cuts of camel whips urged the foul-smelling *meharis* to their feet. Then with Lemuel riding in the lead, his long legs in dirtied white canvas crossed and locked before the pommel, the reconnaissance party cautiously made their way down into the gully and passed the dead Druse who lay staring up into the afternoon sky with a fixed and grave interest.

Swaying and jolting in the saddle, they trotted down the gully toward the vast undulating expanse of desert. Suddenly they rounded a corner to behold the whole, wide-flung horizon.

"*Yei Bogu!*"

"Gorblime!"

"*Bigre!*"

Each in his own way expressed dismay; for in the direction of the *poste* at Samah there rose an ominous pale gray cloud that hung in grim significance over a tiny white speck barely visible through Lemuel's glasses.

"Now may I be a long, tall son of a buzzard," swore Lemuel. "They've tackled the *poste,* and the boys is in trouble there."

Instinctively his mind flew to the one man in the garrison who mattered: Reb Carver, that rangy, black-haired Louisianan who for ten years had shared his travels, dangers and pleasures. The sergeant's jaw shut with a click.

"Guess Reb'll take care of himself. He always has," he muttered. "But it sure looks bad! Come on, you unplucked gallows birds."

And with faces that betrayed alarm in varying degrees, those stalwart men in blue and white lashed their long-legged *meharis* to a swift but lumbering gallop.

CHAPTER II

FIRE AND TORTURE

DUSK WAS DEEPENING into twilight when the reconnaissance party galloped around the last barren hog-back hiding Samah from view.

"It's bad, orful bad," grunted Harold excitedly. "Look, Bulky! See the red glow on that 'illside?"

A moment more and the panting, lathered *meharis* were ridden into full sight of the flame-spouting *poste* at Samah. Long banderoles of fire were licking up the flagstaff, were billowing from the watchtower to dye the whitewashed mud walls crimson.

"Steady, now!" cautioned Lemuel, slowing his camel. "There's like to be some o' them raiders still 'round."

The gaunt American sergeant's voice was strangely low and thick; and all three of his followers knew that he was thinking of the gay and fearless Reb Carver.

An icy hand clutched Lemuel's heart when he thought of Reb. Did the big Southerner lie among those blackly sprawled figures scattered on the slope just outside the crumbling white walls? Or had he escaped? Lemuel's mouth set itself in a straight colorless line—common sense told him there could be no escape from Samah, standing as it did on the crest of a little hill with hard clay sloping bleakly away on all sides. Still, Reb was wise as an old he-coon.

Silent as drifting shadows, and with Lebels tightly gripped, the four Legionnaires dismounted, knee-haltered their panting camels and deployed to reconnoiter. The nearer they came to the burning *poste,* the longer grew Lemuel's leathery features and the narrower his keen black eyes.

A billow of spark-laden smoke swept down from the *poste,* bringing a dreadful smell like that of a steak scorched by a careless cook. Burning flesh! Nauseous and speaking eloquently of the dreadful fate of those Legionnaires who had perished within, the wind and smoke drew tears from the eyes of the anxious reconnaissance party.

"Reb!" called Lemuel. "Reb! My Gawd, boy, where are you?"

Into the veteran's mind flashed a series of pictures: of himself helpless on the ground, of Reb Carver swinging a clubbed Enfield, fighting off a murderous circle of dark-faced Revolutionistas. But for Reb's help that day, Lem Frost's bones would now be moldering in the Guatemalan jungle.

Another picture was of himself and Reb as two khaki thunderbolts launched at a machine gun nest. Side by side they raged, bayoneting the screaming, gray-clad gunners who outnumbered them three to one. And after the push was over, hadn't they got drunk?

And now, what had happened to Reb? He simply must be around somewhere! No one could kill Reb. He was tougher than rawhide.

TO THE American sergeant's experienced eye, the trampled ground gave much information. Here was a heap of empty cartridge cases. There were boot marks, mingled with the footprints and slipper marks of native feet.

That Druse had not lied! It was a force of combined Arabs and Europeans which was invading southeastern Syria.

They must have been disciplined, too. A long line of footprints showed where the raiders had fallen into ranks; a little farther on, part of a machine gun belt bespoke the completeness of Caid Rouazi's equipment, and on the white walls up above one could see the bursts blackly marked. Though not a single dead enemy remained before the *poste*, dark pools scattered over the hillside revealed that the defense of the garrison had not been entirely in vain.

Steadily Lemuel's fears grew as he commenced the final climb. Just ahead of him lay a body, dark and strangely flat, the first of the massacred garrison. When the flames shot suddenly higher, Lemuel bent to recognize Carrora, the Italian senior sergeant. He had died terribly, for his hairy, naked body lacked several major parts, and in the dead man's eyes was an expression of surpassing agony.

"Bad as the Druses, these here renegades!" muttered Lemuel. Had they done that to Reb? He felt sick, despairing. No, he told himself savagely, Reb was resourceful; had escaped.

Up and up he climbed, circling about or stepping over one ghastly corpse after another. How eloquently they told of the merciless onslaught which had made another large gap in the ever melting ranks of the Legion! Yes, the recruiting offices in Marseilles and Sidi Bel Abbes would be busy for weeks to come.

Glancing sidewise, Lemuel could see Harold advancing, sharp little features twitching with disgust when a plume of black, oily smoke swung down the hillside to envelop him. Up to the smoldering, shattered gate, through it and into the court-yard, Lemuel's long legs carried him. Just then a strong puff of the desert night wind fanned the ruins of the barracks into a great sheet of flame; and Bulgakan uttered a hoarse cry.

At the sound of his voice Lemuel whirled, finger on trigger, fully expecting to see a dark swarm of enemies come galloping up the hill. But the flat-featured Russian was staring fixedly at a section of wall to the right. Suspended against the flame-lit white surface was an object that glimmered palely. The structure of that distant outline was somehow familiar. Lemuel was suddenly reminded of church. Then his breath went out with a long, shuddering hiss.

"Blime!" choked Harold. "It's a man, and—and—"

There was no need for him to explain further. They all saw what had happened. Lemuel, tallest of the four, now stood in a frozen gesture, lean head outthrust, staring in fixed, incomprehending horror. Coarse and brutal though they were, Maillot and Bulgakan also gazed in shaken awe, while Harold cursed endlessly beneath his breath.

THEN SOMETHING like a low groan sounded from the fire-lit section of wall. Lemuel galvanized into action, and with the help of the others wrenched out the four long bayonets by which Reb Carver's hands and feet had been spiked to the wall.

"Reb! Reb, old pard—you ain't dead! Pull yourself together, Reb—I—oh, God!"

Terrible was Lemuel's anguish. For perhaps the first time in thirty years, tears coursed down his scarred and powder-stained cheeks, as he saw how near death was his comrade.

"Quick—you, Maillot! Get a canteen off'n our camels. Harold, put your coat beneath his head."

In silent grief the cockney obeyed, while Lemuel stripped off his heavy blue overcoat to tuck it over that gaunt, pain-racked figure. How very white, damp, and sunken the features looked! Only the false color of the flames gave them life. It was strange how those rough men, even then in danger of their lives, took time to think of every possible means for easing the tortured Legionnaire's last moments.

When the water trickled past his dry, contorted lips Carver showed the first signs of life.

"Reb—*Reb!* Don't leave me!" implored Lemuel, fiercely. "I just can't soldier without you!"

But the other's black-haired head moved ever so faintly on Harold's coat.

"Cain't, Lem. That Roossian devil's fixed me… fer keeps."

"Tell me who he is!" pleaded the gaunt sergeant with terrible intensity. "Tell me! I'll kill that swine by inches!"

"A Russky man in garrison recognized him… He's famous—name's Michailov."

From Lemuel's elbow came a loud grunt of surprise from Bulgakan.

"Michailov!" he snarled. "No wonder! In all the Little Father's army never was a better soldier nor a crueler—"

"Keep that for later!" snapped Lemuel, tilting more water into the bloodied lips. "You all beat it—git! Go look around, make yourselves useful."

Only Harold realized how great was the agony in the American's soul. He laid a sympathetic hand on Lemuel's arm, and said quietly: "All right. We understands, matey—and we're terrible sorry."

Heads bent, the three moved off; black, martial silhouettes clearly seen against the leaping, crackling flames which soared ever higher into the night air.

For a while the friends talked; spoke of joyous adventures together, of loves, of perils; and it was only when the Dark Angel hovered very low that Lemuel forced himself to think of duty once more.

"Tell me, Reb," he whispered, trying to forget how horribly cold that torn and mangled hand had become, "tell me. Where's this son of a buzzard headin' for next?"

"An escaped prisoner o' his'n came in," the dying Southerner answered in a voice now almost inaudible, "and 'lowed as how Michailov—natives call him Caid Rouazi Dial Allah—aims to take our *poste* at El Juweilil."

"So that's his game! Um Wulad after that, I s'pose."

"He'll take it, too. He's smart soldier with a real army. Three or fo' thousand camel men, auto rifles and m.g.'s—all unifo'med—green cloaks, white pants and blouses and red fezzes—recognize 'em easy. You-all gotta stop his gettin' them guns off'n them trains, and his massacre o' the people at the fair at Melal-es-Sarrar. God help you all if he pulls that off; whole damned Druse country will be a rarin' again—hell to pay… Lem?"

"Yes," choked the sergeant. "Anythin' I can do?"

Reb Carver's lips twisted into a tired smile. "Chuck another overcoat over me, I—I'm gettin' kinda cold; then talk to me about home."

SILENTLY LEMUEL obeyed, tenderly tucking in Bulgakan's overcoat on top of his own; then, taking the Southerner's chill hand in his, he commenced to speak of the great emerald-green forests and bayous of Louisiana, of hounds belling hot on the trail of a lordly buck, of the bright-winged ducks that skim the cool green waters.

At the far end of the courtyard the three Legionnaires stood silently watching, listening to the steady rise and fall of Lemuel's voice. Suddenly it fell silent, and the black outline of the speaker's head sank forward between shadowy hands. So he remained a long five minutes, shoulders a-quiver. Then he got up.

"I allow we'd better be gettin' along," Lemuel muttered. "We got a lot to do."

"Wot are we goin' to do?" demanded Harold, his eyes determinedly fixed on the throbbing embers at the far end of that ghastly courtyard.

Lemuel's wide shoulders lifted in a deep sigh. "I'm goin' to kill that Roossian swine with me own hands."

Suddenly the bronze-featured sergeant remembered, and whirled on Bulgakan: "Say, you act like you knows somethin' about this Michailov guy. Do you?"

Without a word the Russian slipped off his dirty suspenders and slid up his shirt to reveal long, rough scars in a purplish crisscross design that climbed up his back. The flesh was strangely twisted and puckered—altogether ghastly by the firelight.

"Has Leon Bulgakan known Prince Michailov?" The Russian's deep laugh sounded like the growl of an animal. "He ordered that done!"

"So you want him, too," remarked Lemuel, with forced calm. "Appears to me there's going to be a row as to who gits first crack at this Roossian devil. But who is he, aside from all this personal stuff?"

"He was colonel in the Little Father's cavalry," replied the Russian Legionnaire. "Good officer, too. During the great war he was on staff of Grand Duke Nicholas in Armenian campaign. Prince Michailov was clever, very clever; he beat Turks right and left. Yes, his highness was a brilliant strategist."

"And then what happened?" the American cut in. "Snap out o' it! We ain't got all night."

"When *sacré* Bolsheviki come, he sell his whole brigade to Trotzky; then when Wrangel fight, he sell out the Red forces. Oh, yes; Prince Michailov's coat is turned very easily. But Bolsheviki chase him out of Ukraine."

"Wot's all them 'orrid scars on yer back?" inquired Harold.

"A knout," was Bulgakan's grim reply. "A favorite amusement of Alexander Michailov. He order that done when we are fighting the Hungarians up in the Carpathian Mountains."

"Why?"

"I didn't see him in time to salute," was the Russian's reply.

"Nom de Dieu! And for that he made cat's meat of your back?" growled Maillot uneasily. "So this is the monster we are fighting?"

Lemuel, who had not spoken for several minutes, stood gazing fixedly at the spot where rested his friend. He looked up suddenly:

"Come on! We'd better get back to them camels and mount up."

"GOING AFTER Michailov?" demanded Harold.

"No, that'll have to wait. Our first job's to try and reach Um Wulad before his raiders does. The *poste* at El Juweilil may hold him up a bit. Then mebbe we could sprint through that pass with the funny name. What's it called?"

" 'Saladin's Throat' is wot the bloomin' natives calls it."

"Well, it's the only pass through the Hauran mountain range

for a good two hundred miles each way. Now, if the Um Wulad garrison and the supply depot garrison at the other side of the pass could concentrate and take up positions in the pass, they might hold up old Michailov's advance long enough for armored cars and cavalry from Suweideh and Mejmar to reach El Kufr."

"Then yer idea is to ride 'ell fer leather to warn Um Wulad?" Harold frowned, while shouldering his Lebel. "Say, Lem; I just 'appened to think—unless they 'ave changed the C.O. there, we're goin' to 'ave a 'ell of a time. Lieutenant Von Maxenzee—'e's the bleeding Austrian wiv manners none and 'abits narsty, whose platoon bolted at Tibneh. Remember?"

"He'd better listen," growled Lemuel, starting off toward the ruined gate. "God help the poor nigger people on the far side o' the mountains, if this here Michailov buzzard gets loose!"

The four had just quitted the *poste* when from behind a not distant rise came the sound of a guttural song. Bulgakan's flat red face quivered, and he started as though a scorpion had stung him.

"Vite!" he rasped, throwing off his rifle's safety catch and breaking into a trot. "Quick! To the camels! 'Tis one of Michailov's patrols—that is the Cossack crow song!"

Like jackals skulking from a ruin the four Legionnaires silently left the scene of tragedy, and shielded by the noxious smoke, made their way hurriedly downhill to where their camels were twisting long, snake-like necks in angry impatience to be at water troughs.

All went well for a time. The deep, hoarse voices roared out verse after verse of the song. The Legionnaires could see the men now, a dozen or so still astride their camels, watching the play of the flames. Paces, uniforms and camels all were dyed red. Behind them was the velvet blackness of the night.

Then Lemuel's camel emitted a long, gurgling groan of disappointment while it was being cinched. The dark-browed sergeant's heart nearly stopped. Abruptly, the distant song ceased; and from the pitchy darkness—the moon was yet but a golden promise on the horizon—came the subtle clanking of stirrup irons and the cautious click of rifle bolts being drawn back.

As if by magic the Russians faded from sight into the gloom; and now the Legionnaires needed no word to speed them. In frantic haste they cast off the knee halters and lashed their sullenly whining brutes to their feet just as there broke forth a deep, ringing war cry which was quite unlike the familiar *"Ul-Ul-Ullah Akbar!"* of the fierce Moslem desert dwellers. This war challenge rang far more eerily through the darkness:

"Hourra! Hourra! Hourra-a-h!"

Hoarse, bloodthirsty and savage, it sent an icy rivulet trickling down Lemuel's spine. Battle yells and charging shouts he had heard and used a-plenty during the long years of his campaigning, but this was the first time the veteran had ever listened to that wholly barbaric Cossack yell which, since the Middle Ages, has terrorized eastern Europe:

"Hourra! Hourra! Hourra-a-h!"

The raiders seemed to be on all sides.

CHAPTER III

THE DOOMED POST

OF THE WILD headlong ride that ensued, Sergeant Lemuel Zebulon Frost retained only disjointed impressions. One thought, one realization crushed out all others: Reb Carver was dead. Somehow he could not bring himself to believe it. Gay, hot-tempered Reb lying back there in the *poste?* Impossible!

Even when the pursuing patrol became visible in the first rays of the honey-colored moonlight Lemuel remained incapable of thought, so stunned, so overwhelmed with grief was he. Only when the foremost riders, two darkly seen camelmen in somber flowing robes and Mussulman fezzes, outdistanced their companions and, with lances leveled, bore swiftly down on the fleeing Legionnaires, did the American arouse himself and the battle fire commence to burn in his narrowed eyes.

It was characteristic of Harold that he was the one who reined in to reenforce Lemuel, whose camel, wearied by the greater weight he bore, was lagging a little.

"One apiece, old egg," he grunted.

"Thanks, son," muttered the sergeant; "but I'm goin' slow a-purpose. I aims to intervoo that foremost Roossian with the fancy pig sticker."

Glancing backward, Frost discovered that the main body was a good hundred and fifty or two hundred yards behind their overanxious leaders, both of whom brandished long, slender lances while flogging their splendid racing camels to even greater speed. On beholding the big Legionnaire's *mehari* slacking its pace, they stood in their stirrups and settled their lances significantly.

"*Hourra! Hourra! Hourra-a-h!*" they bawled and, swaying to the weird gallop of their mounts, came charging up.

"Bloody fools! Clean balmy to get dotted one," chuckled Harold, when Lemuel jerked out his automatic. "Silly idiots, they orter know better!"

This was hardly fair, as neither Cossack could be expected to know that the hawk-faced Legionnaire now riding but a few yards before their twinkling lance points was an ex-Texas Ranger, whose bullets seldom went astray.

" 'E'll pot 'em in a minute." But just in case of accident, Harold unslung his Lebel and rode prepared to repair any possible error.

"*Hi-yah!*"

The American cavalry yell rang out as Lemuel suddenly whirled in the saddle, raised his N.C.O.'s automatic, and swiftly sent a bullet into the leading raider at precisely that point where two cartridge belts crossed on the Cossack's white uniformed breast.

Spasmodically, the rider stiffened, swayed; then the lance

glimmered like a wand of silver crazily brandished, as the rider's hands shot skyward. Without a sound the dead man slipped from the saddle and rolled over and over on the ground like a child at play.

Lips writhed back in a smile of savage satisfaction, Lemuel shifted his aim to the other, who, nothing daunted, bent lower in the saddle and dashed forward. He pressed the trigger, but to his utter dismay no report ensued. The Russian's broad-headed lance flashed in the moonlight. His body gave a powerful surge to drive the point through the Legionnaire's torso; but by a dexterous twist the American avoided the Cossack's murderous thrust by a scant fraction of an inch. *R-r-rip!* His overcoat was shorn apart. A yelling, bearded face loomed close; instantly the veteran shot out his long arm and swept the green-cloaked camelman from the saddle to the back of his own *mehari*. Fists beat in Lemuel's face, tore at his eyes; but the sergeant's long fingers, strong as steel springs, closed upon the prisoner's hairy throat.

FEARFULLY HAROLD poised his rifle, watching the deadly, frantic struggle taking place on the back of Lemuel's blindly galloping camel. He saw the Russian wrench a Cossack dagger from his belt, saw its blade glitter evilly in the moonlight; but failed to note that, as the razor-sharp dagger descended, Lemuel's head had flickered sidewise to catch the descending wrist between strong white teeth: so Harold with remarkable accuracy drilled Lemuel's prisoner through the chest. In pained surprise he heard the gaunt American curse when the captive Russian sagged and went limp.

"No use to me now, damn the luck!" was Lemuel's bitter reflection, as he let the sweaty, foul-smelling body flop to earth. Then in fury he turned on the grinning cockney.

"Blast your interferin' hide!" he snarled. "What for d'you think I take a prisoner? To have you drill him for your own amusement? You damn little cockney rat!"

Then, on seeing the pained amazement in the Englishman's

face, Lemuel hastened an apology: "Sorry, son; I orter be thankin' you. I—I guess Reb's got me kind o' upset. But I wanted to get some acc'rate dope on this renegade Roossian's plans. Well, we ain't far from Um Wulad, judgin' by that ridge yonder."

Setting straight the *képi* which dangled about his neck by its chin strap, Lemuel next cleared his jammed automatic, returned it to its holster, and then intently scanned a long moonlit hill ahead. Reminded him of a Texas hog-back, it did; but he knew that on the other side lay the oasis and *poste* of Um Wulad.

In that *poste* there should be quartered some forty or fifty hard-bitten Legionnaires of the Seventh Company. But as his camel slowed to climb the slope, Frost found himself wondering if he would be in time. Had Michailov headed straight for this *poste* after obliterating the one at Samah, or had he paused to blot out El Juweilil in passing? Lemuel and the others would know within a few minutes.

He glanced back to see the last of the pursuing patrol, numbering perhaps eight or nine, halted by the bodies of their slain companions, evidently quitting the chase.

"Bloody butchers—I wonder if we will shake 'em off? Oh, Reb—Reb, old pal—I'll kill that devil or die tryin'!"

On through the cold night air of the desert galloped the four survivors of the massacred Samah garrison. Lucky they'd been out on reconnaissance, reflected Lemuel, or he, Harold, Bulgakan and Maillot would be nothing more than mangled lumps of flesh—jackal food.

As the crest of the hill drew near, his heart commenced to thud more quickly. Would they find flame and desolation ahead? The plain dark with enemy raiders? He listened, but to his ears came nothing but the soft hiss off sand and clay under the broad pads of the *meharis'* feet.

"Close in!" he called in an undertone. When the shadowy riders drew abreast he added: "If Um Wulad's been took, we'll circle to the right and try for the pass. Every man for himself; somebody's got to git through with the news."

Up, up they rode. The crest was just a few yards ahead; eight eyes were wide with expectancy. Three strides more—up and over! A great warm tide of gratefulness swept into Lemuel's being. Dominating the scattered native dwellings and towering over the idly stirring date palms lay the *poste*, neatly white and apparently lifeless; but the faint twinkle of moonlight along a rifle barrel told the breathless sergeant that here and there a sentry walked the walls.

FIVE MINUTES later he was riding toward the gates bawling *"Aux armes!"* at the top of his lungs. "To arms!" They must hurry! At any minute the onslaught of Caid Rouazi's swift cohorts might invest the *poste*.

When they galloped closer a figure stirred above the main gate, and a silhouetted head stood black against the stars.

"Qui vive?" challenged the sentry, an evil-faced Greek.

"Ouvrez vite! Open up, you idiot!" roared Lemuel. "We're of the Sixth Company, at Samah." That slow fool—couldn't he realize that every second meant life or death?

Harold growled an anxious aside to Maillot: "The man's blarsted slow. I see the Seventh ain't forgot 'ow we showed 'em up at Tibneh. I'll bet yer a month's pay, cockney, that damn Austrian lieutenant won't believe Lem. He 'ates the sight o' Lem because Lem's platoon saved 'is blinkin' little shirttail, that day."

A few moments later in the *poste's* orderly room Lieutenant Karl von Maxenzee stared with insulting disbelief on the hollow-eyed, panting sergeant.

"Quelle sottise!" he snarled. "What foolishness! Do you mean to tell me, stupid, that there are Cossacks roaming the Red Desert?"

Lemuel, standing at rigid attention, felt his heart sink. It had never occurred to him that even the stupid and arrogant von Maxenzee would refuse to be warned.

"Before God, *mon lieutenant!*" he cried hoarsely. "It is the truth! Quick, sir! Your only chance is to order the garrison into the pass—'Saladin's Throat'—where you could hold the Caid back while we ride ahead and raise the garrison at El Kufr."

The pale blue eyes of the Austrian lieutenant were hard as bayonet points beneath their puffy, red-rimmed lids.

"*Garde à vous!* Care! Since when does a slovenly dog of a sergeant presume to give advice to an officer?" he snarled. "Bah! For your childish fears and imaginings I care not that!" He snapped strong brown fingers and turned away, a stiff erect figure in dark blue.

Sickened, desperate because of the time that was being lost, the American stepped forward, his hands imploringly outstretched:

"But the lieutenant's *got* to believe! Your garrison will be wiped out within twenty minutes, and they'll die a death a nigger's yellow dog doesn't deserve. No—no! Listen to me! I tell you this Russian butcher's got two or three thousand men, with machine guns."

"Silence, insubordinate swine!" broke in Lieutenant Maxenzee with a chill, menacing voice. "I think that you must be drunk, sergeant, or else gone crazy with the heat. Understand, fool: I'll not believe a word of this nonsense and I'll not order a man out of this *poste!*"

His thin red features, lit by an oil lamp, showed that like most weak characters, von Maxenzee mistook obstinacy for determination.

PRECIOUS, RELENTLESS seconds were flying, Lemuel knew. Seconds which meant success or failure for Caid Rouazi Dial Allah's bold raid into the rich plains of Syria. His blood ran cold at the thought.

What would the subject tribesmen think if the renegade Caid successfully defied the might of France, captured supply trains, and seized an important supply depot far within the territory defended by the supposedly invincible Foreign Legion? And what about those poor devils now singing and dancing at the fair in Melal-es-Sarrar, sublimely unconscious of the impending avalanche of death and destruction?

All this flickered through Lemuel's mind as he stood, a tall bronzed figure, at attention before the commandant's desk, with the reddish rays of the oil lamp deepening the ridges of his cheek bones and tinting the long scar purple.

"You always were a pack of timid braggarts in the Sixth Company," continued the worthy lieutenant provocatively. "Now, we of the Seventh—"

As von Maxenzee had hoped, this was too much. Lemuel's anger flared.

"So you think so? You damned yellow Dutchman! Who ran like hell when the Druses charged at Tibneh? The Seventh! Who cost us a whole platoon to win back what your cowards lost?"

Livid with wrath and evil satisfaction, Lieutenant von Maxenzee sprang to his feet, pale eyes aflame.

"Du lieber Gott! Here's insolence!" he barked, while his hand flew to draw his pistol. "Cowards, eh?" He wrenched open the holster, then checked himself. "No, we'll keep you for court-martial… Sergeant Louvadis! Put this insolent trickster under arrest!"

The door of the orderly room swung open to admit a lowering, thickset Greek sergeant.

"Arrest him!"

Lemuel was a soldier to the core, with a soldier's mighty respect for military law and the dire penalties it can inflict. He realized that if he did not do something very rash, he and the three other men of the Sixth Company would be immediately imprisoned. Later they would be slaughtered and tortured with the rest, when Michailov's trained troopers assaulted this *poste* as they had annihilated those at Samah, and by this time, El Juweilil.

"Arrest that man!" Shaking with passion the Austrian stood,

accusing finger leveled, his face scarlet to the roots of his stiff, blond hair.

Casting discretion to the winds Lemuel got into action; and by so doing established claim to a firing squad. With a movement so swift that the weapon seemed to flow into his hands, he wrenched his automatic from its holster; and before either the officer or the startled Greek could move a finger they were both covered by that deadly black tube.

"So!" snarled von Maxenzee, backing away. "You want to rot in the penal battalion!"

"No—and I ain't going to, either! Put 'em up, or I'll drill your worthless hides!"

Harsh, like the clash of a bayonet dropped on a stone pavement, was the American's voice as with weight balanced on the balls of both feet he surveyed the sullen pair whose hands had crept to the level of their shoulders.

"IF YOU'RE so damn' blind and dumb, that you won't believe me, I ain't going to stay and die with you! No—keep 'em up and don't move! If you say another word, Mister Dutch Lieutenant, I'll enjoy killing you. I've earned a death sentence already, so I wouldn't stick at bumping you off. No—stand still, sergeant; 'less you want a bullet through your greasy craw! Now, both of you, about-turn!"

Reading death in those blazing black eyes, officer and noncom obeyed. Then Lemuel darted forward, plucked the pistols from their holsters and jammed them into his belt.

"*Verdammt Amerikaner Schwein!* You'll die for this!" rasped von Maxenzee.

It was quite clear to Lemuel that the Austrian would never rest until a firing squad of the Zephyrs—the terrible Bataillon d'Afrique, penal division of the French army—had disposed of the audacious American. But what the hell? The poor fool would be hacked into filets inside the next hour.

In a moment Lemuel had gained the door, had leaped through, slammed and locked the door from the outside, and shoving aside a frightened corporal, bounded below, bawling for Harold and the other two men at the top of his lungs.

He found them in the courtyard, wet of head, face and chest, reveling in the coolness of water drawn from a well freshly blasted through the hard basalt underlying the desert. Striding forward, Lemuel realized that the well was not more than half completed, for various tools lay neatly stacked to one side and several square blue boxes under guard of a special sentry bespoke the presence of dynamite. At Lemuel's word, the three donned their *képis* and fell in beside the camels.

"Wot's up, Lem?" muttered Harold, when he saw the grim expression on the sergeant's bronzed, sweaty features. "Had a run-in wiv the dear little Austrian?"

"Yep, he's out for my scalp. You can hear him yelping from here. Shake a leg, you worm-casts!"

Scowling at the metal number sixes stitched to the visitors' collars, various members of the garrison stood undecided, then looked uneasily about as from the depths of the *poste* roared a furious voice, its words indistinguishable with passion.

"You!" snapped the American sergeant to the Legionnaire on guard at the gate. "Open up, pronto; we're goin' on!"

When the man hesitated, Bulgakan, who was not as slow as he looked, lashed bis camel forward, shoved the startled sentry to one side, and flipped up the stout top bar, while Lemuel expertly leaned low in his saddle and shot back the other, and pushed open the gate, screaming on unoiled hinges. Like four pale shadows the reconnaissance party quitted the doomed *poste* at Um Wulad, galloping off amid volleys of curses from the garrison and a chorus of wild barking from all the ribby curs in the oasis.

"Damn' blind fool—wouldn't listen!" raved Lemuel when the single-storied, whitewashed houses of the native village lay a few yards behinds. "That's torn it for fair! There's no one to hold the pass now."

A sense of angry desperation settled upon the sergeant when

he reflected upon the gravity of the charges to which he had laid himself open: insolence, insubordination, and threatening an officer! It was just another burden to the load of sorrow and anxiety already riding his weary shoulders. First Reb, then Michailov, and now… Surely the odds were too great.

"Guess there's nothing to do," he muttered audibly, "but to 'go on pump'—desert as soon as the dust settles. I've sure got myself in a three-ply, man-size mess."

BEFORE HE could speak further came the vicious *crack* of a rifle from the top of the hog-back they had crossed in coming from Samah, telling the four that Michailov was already upon the doomed *poste!* Lemuel's heart stopped while the report echoed and reëchoed menacingly among the low foothills surrounding the oasis of Um Wulad, for near at hand had sounded a queer little grunt. Many times before had the veteran heard such a grunt.

He whirled in the saddle just in time to see Legionnaire Maillots dirty hands fly spasmodically to an invisible wound in his side. Then with an expression of intense surprise on his hard, moonlit features, the Apache toppled sidewise and, taming a half somersault, fell to lie very still on the thick dust of the reddish caravan track.

Bullets hissed and moaned all about the three as the first shots sounded from the *poste*. A bugle shrilled brazenly, despairingly, several notes of the *alerte* sadly flat.

"Gawd help us!" Harold uttered a low cry of alarm. "Will yer look at 'em come! There's thousands of 'em!"

While the *meharis,* refreshed by the rest, bounded past the last silver-trunked palms, Lemuel looked back to see the dunes black with ranks of camelmen who rushed down over the bare, clay foothills like an engulfing, sable wave. Maillot was undoubtedly dead; so the three lashed their camels to top speed, chilled by the dreadful, barbaric shout that arose once more to fill the beautiful night with terror.

"Hourra! Hourra! Hourra-a-h!"

From the *poste* came an answering shout, feeble in comparison, but dauntless in its lack of fear.

The night wind was now rushing evenly past Lemuel's set features. Could they reach El Kufr in time? He was beginning to doubt it. Who would have thought that the renegade Caid could travel so fast! His forces must be wonderfully organized and mounted.

Frost cast a brief glance at his companions, hunched like jockeys on their camels' backs, busily plying their whips. Bulgakan's flat, savage face was turned to the rear, watching in manifest fear the terrific onslaught on the little white *poste*.

Jewel-like flecks of fire flickered even then from the crest of those long, low walls. Somewhere a machine gun got into action, its staccato bark splitting the night's stillness. Then another spoke and another, lashing the *poste* with a deadly, leaden blast that crippled the defense ere the struggle was well begun.

Most terrible of all were the agonized shrieks and howls arising from the native village. These grew ever louder, more poignant and frightful; from which the fugitives guessed that a company of camelmen was sweeping through the hamlet's two or three streets, hacking, hewing down the terrified natives as the Huns of old rode roughshod over the rich provinces of Rome. Arose the shrill, tortured screams of women in anguish; the weak, pitiful bleat of some child who realized that its scarce-begun life was already ended.

In less than three minutes the white-walled *poste* was closely invested with a ring of fire. Dearly was von Maxenzee paying for his arrogant incredulity!

"It all depends," Lemuel was panting to Harold, "how long the garrison can hold 'em up. Course they'll fight to the last man; but they ain't got a chance. Damn, I hope they's some machine guns at El Kufr! Chuck away your ammunition, boys, all except two or three clips; then shed anythin' you can spare—ride light's the word; we're in for the race o' our misspent lives… Hell! We've been seen!"

Galloping at headlong rate down a moonlit hillside was a dark column of camel riders. Their unmistakable intention was to cut off the retreat of the three Legionnaires before they could gain the wide plain sweeping to the not very distant Hauran mountains.

CHAPTER IV

ONE JUMP AHEAD

"IT AIN'T NO use. They'll ketch us!" Lemuel's breath was whistling into laboring, aching lungs; tough though he was, the half hour's hard galloping was telling on him. He made a strange, unsoldierly sight—black hair whipping in the wind, without overcoat, without cap, without blanket roll or rifle, retaining only four pistol ammunition clips tucked in bis wide blue waistband. He turned to watch the dark outline of pursuers grow ever more distinct.

"We'd be all right if only our mounts was fresh," was the cockney's panted observation. "That blarsted pass ain't but 'arf a kilometer away... Blime, look at Bulky leg it! One taste o' dear Michailov is enough for 'im, I guess."

Too spent to reply, the American sergeant's bloodshot eyes searched the surrounding moon-frosted hillsides, seeking some rugged area which might afford opportunity of casting off those relentless pursuers whose lance points twinkled less than half a kilometer behind.

"We gotta get to El Kufr!" he kept repeating. "We *gotta!*"

While his lean body pitched and swayed to the *mehari's* gallop, Lemuel's warwise brain tackled the problem with the experience of twenty turbulent years. But he found no answer. How was he, with only two men now, to prevent the slaughter of the garrison at El Kufr? Save the supply trains, and halt the wholesale massacre of the Christian natives at Melal-es-Sarrar?

The prestige of France herself lay in his hard brown hands; and were he not able to devise some means of thwarting Michailov's raid, uncounted thousands of lives would pay for it!

His black eyes ranged ahead, studied the rugged, somber outline of the Haurans reaching up like sharp, sable fingers to grasp the blazing stars. Somewhere ahead lay that narrow slash through the mountains, called Saladin's Throat. How far away was it?

To the harassed sergeant's further alarm his camel and the others began to show distinct signs of tiring; their spongy feet landed with stiff, unexpected jolts that made them lumber off on tangents. How terribly loud was their labored breathing!

Dashing the bitter sweat from his eyes, Frost examined the hills to the right, and stiffened convulsively. What was that glimmer of white up there? While the wind rushed past he watched, hoping against hope that he had been mistaken. But no, the white blur materialized into a long line of camelmen advancing at top speed, who eliminated any chance of winning a passage into Saladin's Throat.

It must be, Lem decided, a raiding party of the fierce Jebel Lejehis; there was no mistaking their distinctive black turbans.

"Cooked and cooked for fair!" Like a delirious man Lemuel blasphemed in his despair, "Cain't keep on, and 'tain't no use to turn back!"

Harold and Bulgakan had not yet seen the new menace. He called to them, and quite without knowing why, shouted:

"Keep right on ahead!"

At the command, they looked up and automatically reined in, but started on again. Oddly enough the desire burned in Lemuel's brain to die as near as possible to the goal. Yes, it seemed better to perish beneath the razor-edged *flissas* of the Jebel Lejehis than the lances of Caid Rouazi's hard-riding barbarians.

ON AND on galloped the meharis, carrying their riders toward the death waiting ahead. It struck Lemuel as a cruel irony that they should be actually urging their beasts toward certain death.

"Think fast, boy!" he told himself. "Think fast, or you'll be cold monkey meat inside o' two minutes!"

A dense swarm of black-turbaned, white-robed riders had gained the same track along which Lemuel and the other fugitives were racing; and after a momentary hesitation, the tribesmen closed in, obviously surprised that the trio neither halted nor turned aside.

The fatal seconds ticked relentlessly by. Nearer and nearer! Lemuel could clearly see the jolting trot of the enemy camels, now sharply silhouetted against the golden glory in the sky, for the moon was rising squarely behind the tribesmen, tinting their thin lances.

A fugitive hope entered the American's brain. Why had the Lejehis not yet opened fire? He would have given much to know; he guessed it was because of the absence of the distinctive dark overcoat, which made each Legionnaire appear to be white clad, for in the desert garrisons the trousers and undershirts are white.

"They won't wait any longer." He could see the carbines coming to shoulder and felt his throat suddenly become dry and burning. Too bad; he very much wanted to live in order to avenge Reb. Well, maybe this wasn't so bad….

But how about the helpless souls merrymaking at the fair? "Think, boy—think! There must be a way," he told himself savagely. "But it ain't by fightin' a way through—they's nigh thirty or forty o' 'em ahead." He glanced back. Out of sight for the moment were the followers of Caid Rouazi.

"So long, Lem! Don't let 'em take yer alive." Harold reined over, his small pinched face ghastly in the moonlight. "It's all very queer, though; why are these bloomin' natives raidin' in the dark?"

In a flash the answer occurred: "Reckon they're on their way to join up with old man Michailov!"

Only a hundred yards separated the white-robed men from the three sweat-bathed fugitives. The crisis was inescapably at hand!

In the American's brain seethed a mad maelstrom of confused thoughts, of desperate plans and cunning subterfuges. Nearer and nearer! A preposterous idea presented itself—a Yankee bluff.

"Bulgakan!" he yelled. "And you, Harold! We're scouts belongin' to Michailov's gang. See? We're bein' chased by Druses. Get me? Mebbe they got a Roossian with 'em, so you hail 'em, Bulky—bluff 'em; it's our only chance!"

"Cunnin' old fox," thought Harold and prayed that no Lejehi would fire.

Not far ahead the moonlight glistened ominously on many a rifle barrel and drawn scimitar when the tribesmen, deeply puzzled, pulled their camels to a halt, to watch in mingled suspicion and amazement the headlong approach of three weirdly dressed Europeans. No Legionnaires these, they thought—the gallopers wore no *képis*, no overcoats, and made no effort to unsling their rifles; Lemuel had insisted on this.

The Tchek in command grinned thinly to himself. "If they prove French, they seem good strong men who should last well under the torture."

"Allahu Akbar," piously added the worthy Tchek, then he drew his Luger automatic. "We shall bring gifts to the Caid Rouazi."

JUST THEN Bulgakan, racing along a few strides in advance, raised his right hand above his close-cropped blond head in the universal signal of peace, and with stentorian tones inquired in Russian if there were a follower of the great Caid Rouazi among the ranks of the Jebel Lejehi.

Then did the Lejehi leaders questioningly eye one another. French they were familiar with, but not this hoarse, guttural tongue.

The three Legionnaires were almost among the suspicious, dark-featured Lejehis when for the first time the tribesmen detected the sound of pursuit. As an excited, high-pitched babble of Arabic broke out, Lemuel sensed the psychological moment, turned in his saddle, and pointing to the rear, gasped: "Jebel Druse! Jebel Druse!" at the top of his lungs.

Even as the words left his lips, the veteran's bloodshot eyes flickered searchingly from one to the other of those fierce, predatory features crowding aggressively toward him.

Would they believe? Everything swung trembling in the balance. Lances and swords swung up, poised for action.

But not for nothing had the Druse and the Lejehi tribes been sworn enemies for uncounted centuries.

"El Druse! El Druse!" The words leaped like wildfire down the white-robed column.

The hawk-faced Tchek eyed Bulgakan narrowly; and then the conclusion Lemuel had hoped he would make leaped into his mind: Ah! So the pariah-sired Druses had cut off a detachment belonging to Caid Rouazi?

Panting and trembling in every limb, Lemuel watched a fierce joy light the Tchek's features as, standing in his stirrups, he brandished a carbine, faced to the rear and shouted the command to charge:

"Elkoddam! Ul-Ul-Ullah-Akbar!"

In an instant the Lejehi raiding *harka* had deployed into a long double rank. Gun breeches clicked and scimitars were drawn with sibilant *zweeps* that played sweet music in the ears of the Legionnaires.

Nervous moments followed for the bareheaded, wild-eyed sergeant and his two surviving followers. Lost in the depths of the Lejehi array, they unobtrusively urged their camels toward the rear ranks, past tribesmen intent only on slaying the hated Druses. For safety's sake they repeatedly shouted "Caid Rouazi!" and found that the name worked like a charm.

Once deployed, the white-robed band took up a trot, raising the fierce cry of *"Ul-Ullah-Akbar!"* until it swelled like the tones of a mighty organ.

"And now, gents," muttered Harold joyously, "there's goin' to be the best little Donnybrook yer ever 'eard tell of!"

With breathless, terrific speed the battle was joined. Those hard-riding followers of the Russian renegade swept around a low hillock to find themselves suddenly confronted by a long line of howling, murderously inclined tribesmen, with not a second's time for parleying.

LEMUEL, RIDING anxiously in the rearmost rank, watched with professional interest and no little alarm the expert way in which the dark-robed Cossacks closed up, lowered their lances, and uttering a terrific *"Hourra! Hourrah!"* hurled themselves in resistless momentum upon the eager Lejehis.

"Shall we flee?" panted Legionnaire Bulgakan, eyes wide and sweat-soaked chest heaving.

"Not yet, son, not yet," was Lemuel's muttered reply. "We'll wait till these hombres lock horns good and proper and forget all about as."

And lock horns those combatants did. Lances snapped, pistols cracked viciously, camels went sprawling to the ground to be trampled upon by their fellows until they howled in agony. Steel rang on steel, bodies met with dull, sickening impacts and shouts, yells, screams arose from the wild mêlée.

Once the battle was fairly joined Lemuel had no trouble in foreseeing its outcome. One last look he cast at that mad tangle of fighters, to see the long lances dipping and thrusting, to see gleaming blades circle and whistle down.

On and on the three must go. On to El Kufr, to bring the news of disaster. Lashing their *meharis* to fresh efforts, the trio sped off. All went well until a straggling Lejehi mounted on a lame camel, unaware of the trio's identity, spied the fugitives. Prompted by some imp of misfortune, the tribesman whipped up his Mauser rifle to take a long range shot at the three bobbing targets.

Neither Harold, riding as he had never ridden before, nor Lemuel, his mind frantically seeking for inspiration, noted how

Legionnaire Bulgakan hunched up, coughed two or three times, then wound both his great hands around the saddle horn, spitting out a dark trickle which commenced to ooze from the corners of his mouth.

"We've got to get to El Kufr; if we don't warn 'em no one else will!" Lemuel kept telling himself, and found comfort that the din of battle was fading. He glanced backward. "What fighters them Roossians are!"

Though the Caid's men were outnumbered, he saw that the Cossacks had overwhelmed the larger Lejehi force and were now engaged in mercilessly hunting down fugitives.

The American's face grew ever longer. Evidently the Caid's men would take a lot of licking; no undisciplined mob were his three or four thousand camel troopers. What a superb soldier this Michailov must be! He who had murdered poor Reb.

Lemuel's gloomy train of thought was interrupted by the sight of a narrow black ribbon that seemed to split apart a mountain peak not far ahead. He knew it must be the pass called Saladin's Throat, beyond which lay the important supply depot of El Kufr.

Grinning in fierce delight and anxiety Harold drew alongside, ignorant that Bulgakan was now swaying like a drunken man in his saddle.

"There's the pass! Blime, Lem, if they ain't no more Lejehis we'll win through yet!"

But Lemuel, thinking of that deadly force behind, was weighing their chances and finding them pitifully small. "How could he save both the supply trains and the pilgrims?"

HE HAD found no answer to the question when the blackness of the defile swallowed them up.

How utterly lightless it was in the gorge! How narrow! The three camels, stumbling continually, could barely ride abreast. High overhead shone a few stars, toward which the mountain sloped sharply on either side. In many places Lemuel noted that the rock formed sheer walls.

As no shot greeted them and no ambushed force surprised the Legionnaires, Lemuel's heart commenced to beat a little slower. Not a quarter of a mile ahead lay El Kufr, the supply depot, with a garrison of a hundred well-armed men. Yes, he had won the first step; though perhaps it was nothing more than a temporary stay.

In another twenty minutes a force equipped with automatic rifles and machine guns would advance in an attempt to block the pass until strong columns from the Suweideh and Mejmar garrisons could arrive to defeat Michailov's barbarians in pitched battle.

Then came an agonizing thought: If the renegade Caid were kept on the east side of the mountains, he could yet massacre the pilgrims at Melal-es-Sarrar and deal a death blow to French prestige. On the other hand, if he won through Saladin's Throat he could seize and loot the supply trains of their invaluable material. What should Lem do?

He was still pondering when the gloom thinned and through a narrow gap the rich, rolling plains of Syria came into view. And there was the depot, its embrasured walls pristinely white in the moonlight.

Out of the pass lumbered the American sergeant's camel at a heavy faltering gallop that jolted every bone in his body; just behind rode Harold; but there was no trace of Bulgakan. What had happened to him? "I suppose he's fallen!" Lemuel muttered. "We ought to go back, but...."

CHAPTER V

DOOMED MEN

WHILE FROST WAS still debating his course the Russian Legionnaire rode into the moonlight, arms locked weakly about the saddle horn and his shirt front dark with splashes of blood. Poor devil! Shot through the lungs.

At a glance Lemuel realized that he had lost another sturdy Legionnaire. The veteran sergeant had seen too many men thus wounded to be mistaken. Well, Bulgakan would probably be able to reach the depot, now only four hundred yards distant.

By tacit consent he and Harold, with that loyalty of the Anglo-Saxon, turned back and one on either side tenderly supported the weakly swaying figure. Thus they rode straight toward the square little fort, which, dominated by a high watch-tower and lying at the foot of a great black mountain, looked remarkably like a toy building.

"Aux armes!" yelled Lemuel. "Turn out the garrison!"

" 'Urry! Open the blinkin' gate—*aux armes! Aux armes!"* To make his thin voice more carrying Harold dropped the bridle and cupped his hands.

Ten minutes later Lemuel, haggard, wild-eyed and trembling from his exertions, was addressing a thoroughly dismayed sergeant.

"Dios de Dios! We are lost!" cried the fellow wildly. "There are only four men left in the depot—"

"What!" A roar like that of Niagara sounded in Lemuel's ears. Four men! He felt sick and shaken, four men! "Where are the rest?" he snapped.

"Left at sundown for Nasib to escort supplies due on that *sacré* supply train to-night. But this invasion?" The speaker, a big blue-jowled Spaniard, glared at Lemuel from frightened black eyes.

On the American's face he read only a part of the hopeless-ness, of the agony tearing that big man's soul. This was the last blow, the ultimate stacked card. Only four men! His wild ride had been then in vain.

"Invasion? Oh, yes; thousands of 'em. Listen here, sergeant—what's your name?"

"Martinez."

"You got wires from here to Suweideh and Mejmar?"

The other, yet damp and bleary with sleep, nodded his disheveled head vigorously.

"O.K.—show 'em to me!" Lemuel rasped. "Hurry, you damned garlic destroyer!"

Three steps at a time Lemuel's dirty white form bounded up the stairs leading to the commandant's office; while Harold tongue-lashed into frantic haste the other three men of the depot's garrison, and dashed below to secure metal strips of Hotchkiss ammunition for a brace of canvas-shrouded machine guns standing along the walls.

HOPELESSNESS SUCH as he had never known before gripped Lemuel's soul. Hell! He'd fought, planned and schemed; but everything had gone wrong! Samah lay in ruins, Reb Carver was dead, von Maxenzee had refused to listen; and now to find the supply depot guarded by only four men! Sickened, he realized that nothing in the world could prevent the success of Michailov's raid, and its even more terrible consequences. There was absolutely no-way to stop him in the pass. What could seven men, one of them badly wounded, accomplish?

A stride behind the thoroughly frightened Spaniard, he burst into an office lit only by a shaft of moonlight. All his eyes saw was a telephone standing on a rough wood table. Shaken with futile rebellion at Fate he snatched up the instrument and gave the crank a vicious twirl.

"Hello?" he panted. "Hello!" Silence. He could feel the Spaniard's dark eyes fixed upon him, questioning, fearful. Still silence. He spun the crank again. Were they all asleep at Suweideh? Beside himself at the delay, his eyes roved about the shadowy office and fell upon the Spaniard.

"Well!" he snarled. "D'ye think this is the time for a rest cure? Get to hell downstairs and lug up some ammunition, or you'll be playin' a banjo before the pearly gates in half an hour!"

But the big sergeant shook his head in a gesture of despair.

"Yesterday we issued all but a very little ammunition to Um

Wulad. In all the depot there are only two machine guns fit to fire. New ones are coming on the supply trains."

"Yeah, and won't dear old Michailov love to have 'em!... Hello!" Lemuel savagely spun the crank until the whole instrument quivered and the buzzer hummed like a rattlesnake.

"'Allo!" At last a voice sounded sleepily over the wire.

"Supply depot speakin'!" snapped Lemuel, seeking to use the shortest means of expressing the situation.

"They's a big raid on. Enemy *harka* drilled by Europeans— three thousand o' 'em, at least."

"What—what?" sputtered the voice at the other end of the wire.

"Listen, you idiot! Get every word I say, the first time. Them raiders is due here at El Kufr any minute now, aimin' to seize the supply trains Nasib."

"'Allo!'Allo! Who is this speaking?" A new voice had cut in.

Lemuel groaned, exasperated beyond words. Evidently some one in authority had interrupted, so he must waste vital seconds in repeating his message.

"Send every man you can!" snapped Lemuel, his gaze fixed on the dark gap marking the pass, which was visible through the orderly room window. "Yes, urgent is right!... What? How long will it take them mounted Legionnaires to get here? Two hours? It'll be too late... The armored cars, they have to detour? Can't they do better than an hour and a half? This Michailov will have made his raid and got out by then. Every second counts. To play safe I suggest you call Mejmar in five minutes, coöperate with 'em. I'm calling now, but the wire may be cut any second."

CLICK! HE slammed down the receiver; then his trembling sweaty fingers flipped over a nickeled lever, tipped with a red rubber handle, and spun the battery crank again. After a struggle of five minutes the frantic American succeeded in arousing a drowsy orderly. Having learned by experience by this time, he demanded to speak to the commanding officer directly. He told the story with his eyes riveted on the pass—how near was the Caid Rouazi now?

It appeared that at Mejmar only three armored cars and a half squadron of Chasseurs d'Afrique were available. Yes! They would start immediately. Sergeant Frost was to hold the depot as long as possible.

Meanwhile, in an undercurrent of thought, Lemuel pondered. With wholly inadequate forces at his command, how could the pass be held? After deserting the telephone he dashed below and passed through a long supply room where a number of solidly built, blue-painted boxes lay stacked almost to the ceiling.

"What's that?" he demanded of Martinez.

"Dynamite, for use on the new well at Um Wulad."

Dynamite! Hope soared into Lemuel's weary brain, and in fierce excitement he spun upon the Spaniard.

"That's the ticket! Quick!" he demanded. "Where d'ye keep the fuses and detonators?"

In that inimitable shrug of the Latin, Martinez's naked shoulders shot up. *"No hay!* None left—all shipped to Um Wulad!" he cried dramatically. "There is a fresh supply coming on the train."

"On that train! Oh, yes; every damned thing we need's on that train!"

Train! Train! The word hammered crazily in Lemuel's harassed brain. Why did everything depend on that train? He stared blankly at the neatly stacked cases. Dynamite! Case after case of it. Dynamite! Useless as chalk. There was no means of exploding it.

True, they might, if there were time, clamber up above the pass and hurl some sticks below, but they would be performing a fruitless self-sacrifice. They would never live to hurl a second stick; and though the first explosion might blow a few dozen men to atoms, it would in nowise effect a halt of Michailov's determined advance.

ARRIVING ONCE more in the moonlit courtyard, Lemuel

found Harold and the three other Legionnaires smeared with oil and cosmoline, squatting grimly behind a pair of rakish, thin-barreled Hotchkiss machine guns, both of which, in their present position, were incapable of completely enfilading the pass. Almost hungrily the slender black snouts peered over the white battlements.

Lemuel would have found some measure of comfort in them had there been more than a few dozen metal ammunition strips, each of which holds but thirty rounds. For the impending action it was a pitiful, perilously inadequate supply.

"Dynamite!"

The word throbbed and darted about his brain. Somehow it could be used! Granted enough time, its mighty power might be utilized. Bitterly the gaunt sergeant cursed the absence of fuses and detonating apparatus. What was the solution?

In his mind's eye he could see hordes of shaggy Cossacks scaling the depot's walls, killing the defenders, capturing the post, then galloping on to surround the trains and finally riding back, herding baggage camels that groaned beneath burdens of spoil.

Seven men to check the advance of at least three thousand? It could not be done. Dynamite! Dynamite! Then suddenly, like a star shell bursting on a cloudy night, came an idea, and Lemuel's rat-trap mouth twisted with grim humor.

"That's the ticket!"

While the wide-eyed Legionnaires listened he hurriedly explained his plan, and saw the drawn, hopeless faces about him gradually relax, to become at last wreathed in murderous smiles.

Under Harold's leadership Poullot and Andrada, two of the depot's tiny garrison, darted off along the firing platform to the supply room where those deadly blue cases were stacked.

"Shake a leg, you devils!" shouted Lemuel as he, with Martinez and the fourth man of the depot's garrison, sprinted to the sleeping quarters to gather up every spare sun helmet or *képi* they could find. A few instants later Lemuel staggered out, long arms filled with assorted headpieces. Following him was Martinez, a man of extraordinary strength, bearing a huge bundle of spare rifles; lastly appeared the third Legionnaire, similarly laden.

Slumped on a firing step, Legionnaire Bulgakan stared for the last time upon the peaceful lustrous moon, then with eyes that had grown enormous, watched his fellows and continually wiped away the dark froth which welled to his quivering lips.

It was a weird, almost grotesque procession which presently stepped off toward the pass. Each of the six sound men was bent under a heavy burden, and behind the little column rode the slowly dying Bulgakan, who clung doggedly to the saddle of a *mehari* on his way to meet the certain death for which he had volunteered. The blackness of the pass swallowed them up.

"Oh, God, just hold them butchers up twenty minutes more!" was Lemuel's silent prayer; but deep within him he doubted that the plea would be granted, since both hard and fast rode the followers of the renegade Caid.

CHAPTER VI

THE TRAP IN THE PASS

LEGIONNAIRE BULGAKAN'S WHITE face looked strained and almost ghostly in the moonlight when Lemuel hastily tucked an overcoat behind the Russian's back to keep him in a sitting position. Deliberately he laid a cocked and loaded rifle across the dying Legionnaire's gruesomely spotted white trousers; then he held out his hand to clutch the doomed man's cold fingers an instant.

"So long, Bulky; you're a game devil to do this. I'd do it myself if you weren't peggin' out. Remember, now: all you gotta do is to wait till the pass is full o' the Caid's men, then fire into the thick of 'em as long as you can." He peered anxiously into Bulgakan's flat, sweat-dewed features. "Sure you can stick it out all right?"

"Leon Bulgakan would live till hell is ice-coated," the Russian murmured savagely, "if he thought he could kill the butcher, Michailov." So saying, the Russian Legionnaire wiped the froth from his lips once more and raised his hand in salute. "*Au revoir, mon sergeant;* I'm glad to die like this. The dynamite will be quick."

Lemuel again gripped his hand, and turned away suddenly. First, Maillot, then Bulgakan—who would disappear next from the roster of the living?

" 'Urry up there, Lem!" The cockney's anxious voice floated up from the blackness to that narrow, rocky shelf on which rested the wounded Russian. "I fink I 'ears 'em comin'."

BEFORE COMMENCING the downward climb, Lemuel cast one brief glance about the dark walls and slopes hemming in the pass. Here and there a rifle barrel pointed down into the chasm, and realistically fixed beside the stock of each weapon was either a *képi* or a sun helmet.

Yes, they were as cunningly hidden as the brief time had permitted. Not plainly visible were the pseudo-riflemen, but they could be distinguished from below if cause were given sharp eyes to study the slopes above. Well, Bulgakan's shooting would certainly draw that attention.

The six able men had worked like mad, and as a result of their frantic endeavors, quite a number of clefts and pinnacles for a quarter of a mile each held a rifle pointing into the pass, and a helmet beneath which was arranged three or four long yellow cylinders.

As Lemuel scrambled downward, there came to his ears the distinct clank and clatter of accouterment from the Um Wulad end of the pass; whereat a savage grin drew his thin lips back from white and even teeth. Michailov, otherwise the Caid Rouazi Dial Allah, was advancing in force!

Immediately the six took up the *pas gymnastique*—that swift trot of the hurrying Legionnaire—and dashed back toward the depot.

Back to El Kufr they raced, while the American sergeant plotted to make his victory overwhelming and complete. Yes, there might be time to drag forward and mount one of the Hotchkisses at the mouth of the gorge, where it would be in position to mow down any raiders who chanced to escape the general annihilation.

Leaving Harold and two other Legionnaires confidently crouched by the Hotchkiss remaining above the depot's main gate, Lemuel, still coatless and *képi*-less, hurried forward, with Martinez and Poullot a stride or two behind, sweating and grunting beneath the weight of the Hotchkiss and its ammunition.

"Lucky this damn' thing's air-cooled," panted the American, "A water can would be the last straw."

When the three regained the black entrance to the pass, they selected a position in the shadow of the cliffs among a clump of bowlders, and there mounted their lean-muzzled weapon.

The sounds of the approaching camelmen grew louder. Gurglings, clankings, voices, all confused by the straight black walls, came winging forward. The point and advance guard could not be far away, thought Lemuel as he carefully set the tripod's jamming handles.

WITH MARTINEZ lying alongside ready to feed the stiff strips of ammunition into the mechanism, and with Poullot crouched, tools in hand, prepared to clear minor jams, the American sergeant sighed in satisfaction on hunching himself over the breech.

"Point-blank range—to hell with sights! Now, Reb Carver, watch little Lem and Company learn these Roossians a lesson in machine gunnin'."

He squinted along the barrel. Yes; the alignment, squarely on that black opening, was correct; set just where the cone of fire would be most crippling.

Still gasping and sweat-sodden from their exertions, the three Legionnaires lay flat behind their sheltering clump of bowlders, staring into the velvet blackness of Saladin's Throat, conscious that a host of subtle sounds was growing distinctly louder.

"*Bueno!*" muttered Martinez nervously, and laid his automatic on a stone beside him to be readily snatched up should need arise. "Now they come! *Sangre de Dios!* I hope your dying Russian won't fire too soon."

"He won't," Lemuel grimly assured his mahogany-featured companion. "He's a wise boy, is Br'er Bulgakan, and he aims to polish off as many as he can."

The three stiffened and crouched lower, for somewhere in the gorge a pebble had clicked against another and a camel snuffled noisily. Eyes wide, the machine gun's crew stared into that pitchy blackness before them. Nothing visible yet. Then came the sound of low voices.

Lemuel's pulses throbbed. Ah! A shadow blacker than the rest loomed indistinctly amid the gloom. Another, and another. The roots of Lemuel's hair tingled under the suspense.

Yes, the column must be squarely in the pass; now was time for Bulgakan to fire! Involuntarily his lean body contracted, his head bent lower, prepared to endure the deafening roar which would ensue. Eternal seconds dragged by. Still silence.

STEADILY THE number of those darker shadows increased, assumed definite shapes. A whole rank of them. Hell! Bulgakan was misjudging, but he'd fire now. Many of the raiders must now be clear of the dynamite-planted area. Oh, well, the Hotchkisses would settle their hash in a hurry.

Out into the moonlight rode the first raider, his lance swaying gently and his shaggy head, surmounted by a fez, turning ceaselessly this way and that. Then another. What was the matter with Bulgakan?

Whispering fearful imprecations, Sergeant Martinez crouched lower behind his stone, an ammunition clip held ready. Reluctantly Lemuel's gnarled forefinger came in contact with the oily coolness of the Hotchkiss's trigger.

What was the matter with Bulgakan? The fool had been given his instructions! Three full ranks were now out in the moonlight, and Lemuel knew he could not allow those camelmen to advance much farther.

Conscious that his heart hammered like a riveting machine, he bent forward, found the center of that dark-robed column, and settled his shoulder firmly into the Y-shaped rest. He'd wait until the first rank reached that big flat bowlder over there.

"*Diablo!*" Martinez was breathing as though he had run a half-mile race. "That Russian idiot has ruined everything!"

Lemuel's somber eyes fixed themselves on that flat stone, glimmering palely in the moonlight. A shadow wavered black across its surface; venting a despairing curse, he squeezed the trigger.

Rat-tat-tat-tat-tat-tat-tat-tat!

Towering cliffs magnified the machine gun's roar, as with curious, crazy motions the foremost raiders and their *meharis* collapsed into an inextricable, kicking heap. Shrieks and yells arose. The advance guard halted, milling undecidedly. Behind them the main body jammed up, yelling to know who was wrong.

"Bulgakan!" choked Lemuel. "Why doesn't Bulgakan shoot?"

The bitterness of a general who sees his carefully planned victory thrown away by the stupidity of an underling invaded Lemuel's soul. True, the advance had been halted; but only momentarily. He was soldier enough not to deceive himself.

Rat-tat-tat-tat! Just to finish off the stragglers.

A DARK mass of camelmen had formed and was trotting determinedly forward. He let them reach that white stone again, then the Hotchkiss again sent its hail of whistling lead into the mass of closely packed riders.

Many of them fell, choking out their lives; but others, galloping out on either flank, almost won clear; and the sergeant was hard put to traverse his weapon in time to cut them down. Some time soon they would break away, and then—taps for Lemuel Zebulon Frost and Company.

"Bulgakan!" What was wrong with him? Then suddenly the American realized what had happened, and bitterly cursed his folly in placing the dying man above the defile. Bulgakan had lost consciousness, probably had died shortly after the American sergeant's departure. Of course, Lemuel reminded himself, he hadn't wanted to condemn a sound man to sure deaths and Bulgakan, though dying, had looked strong.

So the game of life and death was lost, after all. All would be over soon; only three strips of ammunition remained beside the Spanish sergeant.

"*Ah, Dieu!* We are lost!" Poullot commenced to whimper in fright and beat grimy fists together in pathetic despair.

Rat-tat-tat-tat!

Now the machine gun's fire seemed to have no effect whatsoever in checking that steady onrush of Caid Rouazi's raiders. Dozens fell, but dozens more escaped on the flanks, and now yelling their fiendish "*Hourra! Hourr-a-a-h!*" came riding squarely down upon the machine gun crew, lances leveled.

Bellowing like a bull from his native land, Martinez stood up and gamely emptied his automatic into the onrushing horde, then, conserving the last shot and knowing too much about the fate of Michailov's prisoners, pressed the pistol to his own temple and fired.

Sick with disappointment, Lemuel steadied the Hotchkiss until a dry click told him its last shot had been sped. Only then he gripped his automatic and looked up. Almost above him was a yelling, bearded Cossack, lance point, leveled and mouth wide open. Like a fearsome, hairy gargoyle he bore down on the doomed American, who had just time to whip up his pistol and fire.

Lemuel's shot, sped in too great haste, pierced the camel's head, killing it instantaneously so that the ungainly animal stumbled, slid forward and of its own momentum crashed heavily upon the machine gun and gunner, burying them both beneath its quivering, hairy and malodorous form.

As he sought to leap clear something struck Lemuel's head a vicious blow, and, knocked flat by the falling animal, he collapsed, to be bathed with its blood.

CHAPTER VII

ONE MAN'S WORK

WHEN THE BLACK shades of complete unconsciousness lifted from Lemuel's brain, his first thought was that his right leg ached abominably; his second was that a powerful, sour reek was stinging his nostrils; and the third was that somewhere many rifles and a machine gun were firing intermittently. Subconsciously, he knew enough to lie still. About him moved shadowy figures. He couldn't seem to see well; gorge, moonlight, rocks, and corpses all whirled giddily about. What was going on?

By a supreme effort he rallied his wandering wits and forced them to fall into position, like an expert drill master. Answers to the three questions he discovered almost immediately: the pain in his right leg was caused by the fact that a dead camel lay across it, forcing said limb among stones which were both hard and sharp; the sour stench was also due to the camel; but the third question?

He warily opened his eyes a narrow crack to see the jewel-like flash of rifle fire raking the darkness around the depot. From above that structure's main gate spat the fire and chatter of a single machine gun fighting overwhelming odds.

"Harold, good old Harold!" he mused, while fighting for strength. "You can always trust the limeys to stick in a pinch."

At first marveling to find himself alive, he decided that his present safety lay in the fact he was liberally smeared with the dead camel's blood. Also being clad in white he had escaped the attention of all save the first rank of Caid Rouazi's forces.

As the scene whirled less madly about, the agony in Lemuel's

heart grew sharper. He had failed! For all his efforts and schem-
ing, the renegade Caid had broken through; and now Harold
and the others in the depot must die.

Some little distance away he could see a straight-backed,
motionless figure surrounded by many officers and sitting on
a splendid thoroughbred white *mehari;* it must be Michailov.
The rider wore beneath a long dark cloak a white uniform that
glittered with decorations, and set on his thin head at a rakish
angle was a Mohammedan fez. On the Caid's chest hung a pair
of powerful field glasses and a snap case, while at his belt an
automatic kept company with a Cossack dagger.

Quite calmly the silver-bearded veteran directed the invest-
ment of the depot, dispatching now a messenger here, now a
galloper there. This time there would be no burning; the worthy
Prince Michailov could very handily employ the immense quantities of wheat, blankets, cartridge belts and other supplies the
depot contained.

LEMUEL, AS he lay motionless and half buried beneath the
camel, could watch with dreadful clearness the taking of the
depot.

Far out to either flank of the white moonlit structure the
renegade Caid sent strong detachments of dismounted riflemen, who took cover with drilled precision and who kept wary
eyes upon the death-spitting machine gun above the main gate.
Then, like the closing jaws of a pincer, the flanking detachments changed direction, and uttering a heart-shaking *"Hourra!
Hourr-a-a-h!"* some two hundred men simultaneously charged
the walls.

"Hourra! Hour-r-a-a-h!" How awfully the cry reëchoed in
the gorge behind the helpless sergeant! Sick at heart, he beheld
Harold and the other machine gunners pick up their weapon in
a desperate attempt to train it upon the attackers charging from
the left, even though a dark swarm of raiders was also swoop-
ing in from the right. No use. The Hotchkiss had time to emit
only a few staccato reports; then its gunners were engulfed in

a swarm of attackers who leaped cat-like to the walls. Swords gleamed, rifles flashed for a little while; then a silence fell, pregnant with tragedy.

"Poor Harold!" murmured Lemuel, bitterly. "Another man gone... He was a damned good soldier, too."

Prince Alexander Michailov was not one to ignore the value of time, and he was already three-quarters of an hour behind his schedule; so hardly had the last rifle cracked than a bugle shrilled some unfamiliar call which sent all but a single platoon scrambling up into the saddle. While the sergeant looked on, the Russian's perfectly disciplined little army swiftly formed into ranks and, moving off in column, trotted out over the broad plains of Syria like a dark stream.

Now safer from detection, and obeying the instinct of self-preservation, Lemuel tentatively placed his free foot on the dead *mehari* and shoved. Ha! The imprisoned leg had moved an inch or so. Suddenly he relaxed; not far away a badly wounded Cossack was lifting his head.

"Dunno what for I want to live," Lemuel reflected dully. "Reb's dead; Harold, Bulgakan and all the rest are dead; and Michailov's loose."

He tugged again, while sharp stabs of pain traveled through the imprisoned right leg. Momentarily exhausted, he lay still to view in grim satisfaction the havoc his Hotchkiss had wrought during its brief career. By tens and twenties lay the dark-robed raiders, mingled indiscriminately with dead and dying camels. Not a bad five minutes' work.

By the time Lemuel got his leg free, Michailov's column was far on its way to Nasib, moving like a long dark snake over the moon-silvered plain.

"I allow they'll get them trains inside of half an hour, and clear out before—"

BUT SUDDENLY there came to the battered American's ears a tiny sound which stirred his flagging pulses. It was the ever-so-faint cough of a locomotive getting under way!

In overwhelming relief he lay back, while the blood quick-
ened and leaped through his veins. Of course; he'd forgotten
that the commanders at Suweideh and Mejmar could and would
communicate with the railroad authorities at Nasib. Even now
the precious trains were being hauled away, roaring off through
the night beyond reach of Caid Rouazi Dial Allah.

The sergeant's feeling of triumph was instantly dampened by
two realizations: first, Prince Michailov was still quite at liberty
to loot the depot of its military stores; and second, after returning through the pass he would be free to carry out his massacre
of the pilgrims at Melal-es-Sarrar!

An idea sprang to Lemuel's mind. He sought frantically to
free himself. At last his leg slid from under the camel's warm,
hairy body. Though badly bruised and cut in several places, the
limb was not seriously injured. He listened, and heard again the
puffing of busy locomotives. Watching the distant black streak
marking Michailov's advance, he could not tell whether the
column was yet in motion or not.

Then, from far to the north, a delicate arc of fire soared into
the purple heavens, and an instant later three tiny pin points
of green flame flared with brief intensity, then went out. Automatically Lemuel's sunken eyes flickered southward, watching
tensely, breathlessly. Then, in answer to the first, another jeweled
parabola soared up to spew forth two red balls of fire.

"Thar she blows!" grinned Lemuel. "Them rockets is the glad-
dest sight I see since the Armistice."

Wheezing in an effort to suppress groans, the sergeant painfully hauled himself into a sitting position, his gaze yet fixed on
Michailov's distant column. What was the raider going to do?

He was not long in finding out. Almost at once the distant
black streak widened, then contracted into a huge, sable dot.
Little shivers, cold as glacier water, flickered down the American's back. So Michailov had decided to retreat!

Skulking on hands and knees lest the guard remaining in
possession of the depot catch sight of him, he commenced to

crawl off into the blackness. Lemuel's progress was painfully slow. Once, to prevent a warning outcry, he was forced to strangle an Arab wearing Michailov's uniform. For some moments the fellow, suffering from a ghastly abdominal wound, had silently observed the sergeant's approach until the two found themselves face to face over a dead camel.

It was a terrible sight the American sergeant presented: white shirt and trousers splashed with the gore of the *mehari* he had shot, hair falling over his forehead, and from behind the straight locks his gleaming dark eyes shone as, pistol yet in hand, he crept forward over the sprawled body of the camel.

When the Arab hailed him in what Lemuel thought must be Russian, he made no answer; and reading sharp suspicion in the fellow's eyes, he hurled himself forward and gripped the native's windpipe barely in time to suppress a betraying cry.

A LAST look cast back to the plains showed Lemuel that the situation was becoming clearly defined. In the center, the renegade Caid's column was in full retreat; to the right, and still very distant, armored cars from Suweideh were rushing forward with their headlights glimmering faintly. Presently, when the cars came closer, those lights would go out. To the southward, but farther away, had appeared a long irregular column, which to the veteran's trained eye meant just one thing: it was the half squadron of Chasseurs d'Afrique hastening toward El Kufr at an extended gallop.

Unless something were done promptly, Caid Michailov would be back at the depot again, and, picking up his spoil, could gallop on through the pass and out into the endless wastes of the Red Desert, where he and his camelmen could with impunity mock the efforts of armored cars and cavalry.

Fifteen minutes later Lemuel was panting at the foot of that cliff upon which he had left Bulgakan. With his wounded leg causing him untold suffering, he commenced to hoist himself upward, the automatic's trigger guard gripped between his teeth. Endless, pain-dimmed æons seemed to pass before he caught sight of Legionnaire Bulgakan seated just as he had been left, but with his great blond head tilted back and his mouth sagging open so that the moonlight just touched the points of his teeth.

It was astounding how quickly the Renegade Caid's men had retreated. Already from far down the pass came the grunt and whine of camels, whereat Lemuel's heart commenced to thud more wildly. Would the Russian's men, less cautious than before and hurrying from pursuit, see all of the nearly hidden sun helmets and *képis?*

"I reckon mebbe I could see some more myself if I was to shinny a little higher."

Then he had an idea. He picked up the stiffening corpse of his late comrade and arranged it in a crouching position in plain sight and with its rifle apparently poised for action. One of the riflemen, at least, would be convincing!

"There y' are, Bulky," he muttered, steadying the Lebel with a pair of stones. "Give 'em hell, boy!"

Subconsciously he slapped the cold shoulder and shivered, then resumed his climb until he reached a point from which he could see more than a dozen of the hidden pseudo-riflemen.

Like a stalking Apache he flattened out and merged with the summit of a particularly solid shoulder of rock that lay well above the line of dynamite charges. Behind him he found a shallow crevice in which he might find a measure of protection from the blasts to come. That was lucky.

Would his scheme work out as planned? Everything depended on whether the Russians would fire singly or in a volley. A volley would blast away a good part of the mountain and bury Michailov's cohorts beneath tons of basalt; but a single shot, while doing some damage, would only serve to give the snare away. Well, time alone would reveal the answer.

WHILE WAITING, Lemuel shifted his weight and felt something dig into his thigh. Reaching down, he tested the offending outline, then a grin spread over his unshaved features—it was his sergeant's whistle.

"A break at last!"

Setting the metal tube between his lips, he crouched low and peered downward. From the darkness below had come the indistinct murmur of voices. Into the gulf dark-robed camel-men were commencing to ride, just as a throbbing glare of fire redly lit the black crags above. So Michailov had fired the depot! Well, it would give the avenging Chasseurs, Legionnaires and armored cars light to shoot by.

"Boy, baby! Look at 'em come! Tough-looking hombres, and I don't mean mebbe!"

Now the retreat was in full sway. Rank after rank of camel-men trotted silently by, their lances, slim and straight, pointing to the stars above. Where was Michailov riding?

"When them scouts gets abreast o' that last helmet, it'll be time to sound off," he told himself, and gripped his automatic tighter.

Never, during the thirty-odd years of Lemuel Frosts soldier-ing, had his nerves been keyed quite so tight as when he watched the Russian vanguard advance foot by foot toward that fatal last white blur. Did any of those tight-riding raiders guess that for them the sands of life were running low, lower and lower?

Now? No, a moment more....

"Take a look at this, Reb!"

After drawing a deep breath that sent air hissing into his lungs, Lemuel set the whistle to his lips and blew. Hardly had its shrill blast faded when he shouted in hoarse parade-ground accent:

"Preparez les feux de salve! Volley fire. Ready—aim—"

Purposely he delayed before roaring the last command to his imaginary force. Dozens, hundreds of faces were tilted upward, searching the mountain-sides. Ah! The raiders were now unslinging their carbines, with hasty but precise motions. Their N.C.O.'s were bellowing incomprehensible commands.

"Fire!" roared Lemuel, and emptied his automatic pistol into the thick of those cool, collected camelmen. The echoes

helped—they magnified and multiplied his shots into a crashing volley.

Exultation gripped Lemuel when a deep, guttural command rang out. He hurled himself back into the crevice, pressed hands to ears, and waited.

Fire flashed from a hundred carbines scattered along a distance of perhaps quarter of a mile; then it seemed that a fierce, white-hot volcano had erupted in that dark defile known as Saladin's Throat, and all went black before Lemuel's eyes.

THE RELIEF columns, rapidly, converging upon El Kufr, halted in bewildered alarm on beholding vast sheets of green and orange flame soar high into the night, apparently from the depths of the mountains, reaching, licking toward the pale moon. Cascades of blinding fire billowed up, lighting the rugged crags, the towering peaks, the vast plains, and the faces of the soldiers with a glare brilliant and brief as a titanic flash light.

Comparative darkness descended, while a thunderous report roared out. On its heels came successive detonations as those few dynamite charges not exploded by the Russians' volley went off of their own accord.

"*En avant!* Slay these renegade dogs! Slay, *mes enfants,* and spare not!" roared Commandant Le Nollet. Whereat his Chasseurs grinned like winter wolves and spurred their weary mounts to the charge. On the right of the cavalry four swift gray armored cars, each mounting two machine guns shot past with cut-outs open, to skim forward over the level plain like uncouth monsters.

From the north came more armored cars and two troops of mounted Legionnaires, all fresh and eager for the fray.

Back out of the earthly inferno of the pass streamed hundreds of black, fleeing figures; who, escaping death behind, now found themselves completely hemmed in by less numerous but fresh and eager French troops.

With courage worthy of a better cause the green-robed soldiers of Prince Michailov rallied, formed some sort of line, then advanced upon the Legionnaires.

The ensuing struggle was as bitter as it was brief. Caid Rouazi's forces, though in the majority and not demoralized by the cataclysm which had blotted out a good half their number, were no match for the swift armored cars that raged back and forth through their ranks, machine-gunning them furiously.

Weirdly, the crimson glare of the burning depot lit the scene of battle, revealed mounted Chasseurs and Russian lancers thrusting, hacking and hewing to the end; revealed blue-clad, brutal-featured legionnaires, their dripping bayonets redder than the fire, thrusting, shooting, then thrusting again.

OF ALL this Lemuel was unconscious, for he lay completely insensible in that crevice into which he had hurled himself. He witnessed nothing of the fearful avalanche in the pass, when towering pinacles of basalt tottered, crumbled, and crashed down, annihilating hundreds upon hundreds of men who screamed in vain terror.

Nothing of that appalling success of the trap could he appreciate, nor the grim irony of the fact that Caid Rouazi's men had been their own executioners.

At last, a cool wind blowing up the pass carried off before it clouds of rock dust and the fumes of burned dynamite, and fanned Lemuel's throbbing forehead until he regained a measure of consciousness. This was difficult, for the terrific concussion had started minor hemorrhages from the nose, mouth and ears.

He became aware of rifles and machine guns going off somewhere in the distance. Quite without knowing why, he blindly struggled to his hands and knees. Dimly the idea penetrated that there was fighting going on. He was a soldier; his place was in that fight.

Weak, dizzy and almost delirious, Lemuel climbed down, then staggered on toward the mouth of the pass. It was slow, terribly slow going, for jagged heaps of rock must be climbed over, rock that completely covered the floor of the defile.

Just a little ahead he seemed to see Reb Carver, gaunt, long-legged and grim.

"Come on, Lem," the ghostly figure seemed to say, and beckoned with an imperative forefinger. "The guy that murdered me is out yonder. Till you git him, I cain't rest easy."

Much like a wounded animal, Lemuel crawled from block to block of cold dusty stone, slowly but surely winning his way back toward the fire-gutted depot.

At last the plains were visible again, and Lemuel could see that a remnant of Caid Rouazi's forces crouched behind bowlders, reorganized now and firing with telling effect into the ranks of the Legionnaires, who were finding a vast difference between this well-controlled and accurate fire and the ragged, poorly sped volleys of half-civilized natives.

Fight as they would, the end of Michailov's command was nevertheless in sight. Hemmed in on three sides by the mountains, with their retreat cut off by the choked pass, the raiders fought with the dogged energy of the doomed.

Suddenly, to their right, the dynamite remaining in the depot exploded with a terrific detonation that made the earth tremble like jelly beneath Lemuel's feet. A vast geyser of flame spewed skyward; and as in a dream the American had an impression of the depot's walls falling outward, of curious dark objects flung into the reeling heavens, of the whole plain suddenly lit with the light of noonday.

Crash! Darkness—terrible, stunned darkness. Debris commenced to rain down, and this time the Caid's forces broke up for the last time. Like frightened rabbits they darted hither and thither—some were struck down by the falling stones and timber, others vainly attempted to scale the mountain-sides. The hardiest souls hurled themselves forward to perish on the bayonets of those mahogany-faced Legionnaires, who on recovering from the concussion were now charging, yelling like fiends and burning to avenge their butchered comrades.

LEMUEL CAUGHT sight of a gaunt, tragic figure standing alone in the center of the field, and therewith felt a strange new strength rise within him.

No mistaking that thin, arrogant face, that snowy imperial; there stood Prince Alexander Michailov gazing with bitter, uncomprehending eyes upon the battle which had put a period to all his ambitions.

Perhaps it was as well he could not know that the ragged, broad-shouldered soldier who came tottering and swaying out of the pass was the one man to whom he owed his downfall. Lucky it was he could not read the thoughts of the bloodied sergeant, else the prince would have shot him without a second's delay.

As Lemuel strode up, his Indian face set in a rigid mask, the Russian made a stiff little bow which caused the decorations on his breast to glitter in the smoke-paled moonlight.

Like a man in a dream he turned to face the disheveled, blood-splashed Legionnaire.

"I surrender!" he cried disdainfully, throwing his automatic at Lemuel's feet.

But the sergeant evidently did not hear, for he did not even check his advance, but rolled up his sleeves as he came—a subconscious American gesture persisting even in this crowded hour of life and decidedly unmilitary as well.

"I have surrendered!" called Michailov, stepping back in alarm. "Did you hear me, Legionnaire?"

"Yeah," grunted Lemuel, and drew his weary frame together. "I heard you—but so did Reb Carver! Stand up, you butchering swine, and fight fer your life!"

SOME HALF an hour later a lean, gray-haired officer who wore on his cuffs the three *galons* of a captain in the Legion checked his horse at the entrance to the pass.

"Here's another *sacré* Russian, *mon capitaine*," called a man on foot. "*Nom de Dieu!* I am wrong; this man is a Legionnaire! See, sir—he still chokes a bearded Russian who has been dead a long time."

"*Dieu de Dieu!*" Captain Fontaine leaned low in his saddle. "Why it is *le sergeant*, Frost."

The Legionnaire, who was bending over Lemuel's unconscious frame, straightened.

"Yes, sir; 'tis the Sergeant Frost who rode from Um Wulad to send the warning. Close by the depot we found a little Englishman who was badly wounded, shamming dead. He swears 'twas the sergeant who planned the whole thing."

Now, Captain Fontaine was a Gaul and a man of strong impulses, so he thought nothing of leaping off his horse, of falling on his knees beside the gaunt American to feel for his heartbeats.

"Ah!" he sighed and smiled in sudden relief. *"Bon!* His heart beats like a Dahomey drum. Quick, Lefèvre—call the litter bearers! Here's a man to whom Madame La République owes more than she can ever give in honors and fame."

THE FETISH FIGHTERS

*Drums of war sound a tragic note as Lemuel
Frost and his fellow Legionnaires prepare to
stand between civilization and the unspeakable
tortures of a barbarous African empire*

CHAPTER I

A BLACK NATION ARMS

WHEN HE EMERGED from Captain Aristide Dunot's spotless but suffocating quarters in the Foreign Legion's *poste* at Kouande, there was a thoughtful look upon the face of Lemuel Zebulon Frost, a face that might once have been handsome. Although broken bones, scars and powder burns had rearranged its original contours, it was even now distinguished in a hard-bitten way.

Without gazing to the right or the left, he crossed the broad, sunlit courtyard toward the N.C.O.'s quarters with a long, loose-hipped stride and stalked into the inner gloom that reeked of chloride of lime—for the climate of Upper Dahomey breeds disease on the least excuse.

" 'Ello, look who's 'ere!" A small corporal with a red, round face sat up on his bunk. "W'at's the matter, Lem—didn't 'e promote you?"

"Yep!" Lem Frost's long dark head inclined and, for all his preoccupation, strong white teeth gleamed in a smile.

Corporal Harold Hackbutt sprang to his feet and extended an eager hand. "Bully for you, old rooster!"

"Félicitations," grinned Achille Gras, rat-faced corporal of the third squad.

"Thanks." Lem dropped heavily to the bunk he would occupy for the last time—sergeants sleep in separate quarters—and sat for a moment, elbows resting on knees, thoughtfully scratching his head with long, wiry fingers.

151

Harold eyed him with aggrieved disapproval. "W'at's the matter? 'Ere you've just been made a sergeant, but I don't 'ear no 'osannas of joy disturbin' them bats tip in the thatch." Harold pointed to half a dozen darkly indistinct objects hanging from the roof-tree like Indian clubs from a rack.

"Naw." The American's head swayed wearily from side to side. "I ain't cuttin' no capers o' joy. If you knew what I've learned, you'd go around with a face like a parson."

"W'at's that?" Both Harold and Corporal Achille Gras became acutely attentive, for rumors are the bread and wine of garrison life.

"We're in a bad way, son," Lemuel Frost said thoughtfully, as he commenced to unbutton his tunic. "Way up the creek, no paddle and a falls downstream—and I don't mean maybe."

"W'at's happened?"

"Old Glégle's bunch of native religious fanatics—his 'fetish fighters'—are puttin' on the war paint. And worse yet—them indecent Amazon females are gettin' up steam. They're the first prize scrappers in this part o' hell on earth, or so the cap'n said, and worth any two o' the Fulahs." Two deepset, steel-gray eyes that glittered bright in the rays of a smoky oil lamp fixed themselves on Harold's anxious, round little face. A moment of silence fell.

Corporal Achille whistled in pained surprise. "Those damned Amazons!"

"Yep. The whole border from Kintampo to Bambaga is stewin' like maggots in a carcass. A postal runner from up country allowed 'tain't but a question of hours."

SLOWLY PULLING off his heavy blue uniform coat, Lem flexed long arm's that were beautifully corded with muscles.

Harold looked doubtful. "Every other runner says that. It's orl a lot o' guff."

"Mebbe so: but have you noticed what's been happenin' in nigger-town?"

Lem shouted frantically to arouse the garrison.

"But yes," interrupted Corporal Achille with an astute gleam in his narrow black eyes; "of late there are many Fulahs and Hausas come into the native village. What does this mean?"

"Refugees." Harold's bald head with its fringe of reddish hair gleamed as he nodded wisely. "Refugees is w'at they is. Pore 'eathen Mohammedans what don't want to decorate old Glégle's fetish groves."

"Right, my boy!" Lemuel removed his trousers and sighed. "They don't want to be made chop-chop of, nohow. Don't blame them much, at that. There's pleasanter ways o' bumpin' off than makin' a basket lunch for a bunch o' the neighbors."

A gleam of apprehension crept into Corporal Achille's beady eyes. "*Dieu!*" he muttered. "And our battalion is down to seventy men!"

"Sixty-eight," corrected the big American. "Dropulous, the Greek first-class private, died at sundown of coast fever and Corporal Neelander stepped on an adder on his way to the well. Died in ten minutes; another burial detail. S'pose I'll have to go out with a party, bein' the newest sergeant."

"Jolly nice country, I *don't* fink!" sputtered Harold Hackbutt.

"What about those reënforcements we were promised?" asked Corporal Achille Gras, now definitely anxious, his thin, rodent-like face gleaming with sweat as he leaned forward. "Where are they?"

"God knows! Somewhere 'twixt here and Paraku. But they and them automatic rifles they're packin' along can't get here any too soon to please yours truly. I..." Lemuel broke off to snatch up a ponderous, hobnailed shoe in order to exterminate an orange-furred spider which, large as a cup's bottom, was leisurely ascending the head of his bunk.

"When's orl this rebellion due to begin?" Corporal Harold inquired, as he settled back once more and stared into the greenness of lush vegetation beyond the barred windows.

"Most any time."

"You're crazy!" snapped Corporal Achille, his face gone a pasty yellow. "Nothing 'll happen for..." Suddenly he paused, mouth yet half open in a grotesquely ludicrous expression of suspended animation.

AT THE same instant, as though attracted by some magnetic force, all three noncoms turned toward the small, barred window, listening in strained intensity. From the warm jungle without came a sound, a tiny vibrant sound so infinitesimal that it seemed to have been let in by a pin hole on the far and invisible horizon of Africa.

Lemuel's breath stopped dead as the sound came again:

Tunk, ta-ta, tunk! Tunk, ta-ta, tunk! Tunk, ta-ta, tunk!

Lemuel felt as though a rigid finger, cold as an arctic gale, was groping through his chest and toward his heart. Then nearer and louder:

Tunk, ta-ta, tunk! Tunk, ta-ta, tunk!

"Drums! Blime! It's the bloomin' fetish fighters a drummin'!" Harold's red little face had lost much of its color, his eyes were white and fixed, and his voice sounded as old and dried as an autumn leaf.

Tunk, ta-ta, tunk! From not half a kilometer behind the fort!

Corporal Achille Gras sprang wildly to his feet, staring about and uttering horrible curses.

Tunk, ta-ta, tunk! Below the fort. *Tunk, ta-ta, tunk!* Above the fort.

Achille Gras sought to drown out that ominous talking of the tom-toms by clasping horny, brown hands to his ears. *"Dieu!* Stop them! Stop them! We are lost. Listen! Do you hear? Drums everywhere!"

Along the parapet outside came the sound of hurried feet, the clatter of hobnails on stone, then clear and distinct over all noises rang the commands of Captain Dunot, calm, masterful and all-powerful. In exactly three minutes the *poste* at Kouande stood ready to repel attack.

Back in the shadow-ruled forest the drums talked faster, and here and there ominous smoke columns wandered lazily up the sky. Far away an elephant, annoyed at the clamor of the tom-toms, trumpeted angrily.

Sweating Legionnaires, with cartridge belts strapped over sweat-sodden undershirts, stood to arms at their battlements, peering anxiously and steadily out into the treacherous greenness of the forest where myriad butterflies in flight wove jewelled designs and the mists lay heavy over the sour-smelling earth. The drumming sounded on all sides, sometimes faint, sometimes loud; *throb, throb, throb,* to an infernal rhythm.

Lemuel could hear the hoarse, frightened cries of the Hausas and Fulahs in the village as, trembling at the threats of the drums, they assembled their spears, antiquated muskets and clubs, and prepared to sell their lives dearly. The discordant shrieks and wails of their women went ringing up eerily into the brazen expanse overhead in a great chord of deathly fear.

Like dark, indistinct pillars ranged at regular intervals against the whitish walls, Lemuel could see the company standing to arms.

The endless, ominous drumming slowly but surely was drawing their heat-tautened nerves tight as fiddle strings.

"Them tom-toms fair gives me the 'orrors," muttered Harold, for the fiftieth time wiping the sweat band of his *képi*. He felt he must talk, or the *cafard** would commence crawling in his brain. "Damn those bloody drums! 'Ow does it feel now to be an officer? Pretty swell, eh, w'at?"

THE LONG, dark figure of Sergeant Frost straightened deliberately as he spat resoundingly over the wall. " 'Tain't no novelty, son. I was a colonel once."

"A w'at?" Harold's tone was derisive to say the least.

"Yep. I was a full colonel; lock, stock and barr'l."

"Full was right, I'll bet. W'at army? In the Salvation Army?" Harold was aggrieved as a man is only when his intelligence has been insulted.

Lemuel Zebulon Frost sighed gustily and eased his Lebel rifle to the whitewashed mud parapet. "Listen, son, some day I'll jest nacherally spit on you and drown you and your wisecracks. I ain't givin' you no lie. Little Lemuel Zeb was a colonel in the army o' Guatecata. And I'm tellin' you, Harold, my boy, them was the days."

"Yes? Then 'ow's it 'appen you're nothin' but a sergeant now?"

In the blazing sunlight Lemuel's tall figure contracted and his great fists closed slowly. "All because of a woman and a rotten, stinkin', low-pressure, yellow-hearted, small-souled traitor I helped once."

"Love 'im, don't yer?"

"If I ever lay eye on that good-lookin', honey-tongued son of Satan. I—I..." Words failed and Lemuel lapsed into silence, breathing strongly through his nose.

"Who was 'e, matey?"

"A swell-lookin' palooka, the kind gals go nutty over, even if he was a breed. His paw was an English remittance man down in Brazil; his maw, well, she was half Indian, I guess. Anyways,

---

*   Literally "beetle," but in Legion slang it means madness.

that guy is to me what ratbane is to a rat. Poison, rank poison, son; and if ever Lemuel Z. lays eyes on that scaly-covered—"

"Hold on! What 'appened back in 'appy Guatecata?"

Lem choked and swallowed. "I'd fought through a tough revolution, backed the right general and got a cushy job down there. 'Twas for old General Andrada I fought, back in nineteen-four. As I said, our gang of black-and-tans won, and when Andrada became *presidente* he made me colonel in command o' the Household Cavalry. And I'm tellin' you, boy"—Lemuel's husky voice became charged with seriousness—"that was some cavalry regiment I run. I was slated for Minister o' War, or somethin' like that—"

"Yes," broke in Harold, "but where does this narsty bloke come in?"

"Keep your shirt on, I'm comin' to that. When everythin' was as happy as a bear in a honey tree this ornery guy, Fernando Daggett, shows up one day and asks for a job, claimin' to be white. Since he was English-speakin' and tolerable good-lookin', I commissioned him a captain in the Household Cavalry. Then one sad day he turns them Brigham Young lamps o' his on Mrs. President—Señora de Andrada—and there, son, was where the trouble begun."

"W'at did 'e do?"

"Three guesses. Soon's he found Sis Andrada was a pretty little bonbon—and I'll say she was!—that no-account hound plays it pretty for a while and begins makin' love to her."

"**AND THEN** w'at 'appened?" queried Harold breathlessly, the eternal drums momentarily forgotten.

"A heck of a lot. She ran away with dear little Daggett. Old Andrada loved her like mad, and committed suicide when he found what she'd done. Then Daggett joined the opposition, sold military secrets, and in two twinkles of a gnat's eye there was a humdinger of a revolution. I just skinned out of it with my life. That's where I got this." Lemuel laid a brown finger against a bluish smudge on his leathery left cheek.

"That powder burn?"

"Yep! Some of the *revolucionistas* took a pot shot at me as I sprinted out of the family entrance o' the palace. The bullet missed by a gnat's whisker. That's just part o' what I owe Fernando Daggett. It would 've been a great job if somebody'd got careless and drowned that handsome, yellow-souled cross-breed when he still sported nothin' but talcum powder and safety pins."

"Cross-breed, eh?" The little man's semi-bald head nodded wisely in the sunlight. "I've met a decent one 'ere and there, but the lot o' them ain't to be trusted wiv a 'ot penny. Dear Mr. Daggett must be a narsty cove, wiv morals none and manners shockin' bad."

Lemuel tilted back his head, allowing the pre-evening breeze to fan his craggy features. "Right!" he grunted. "Dear Fernando's about as *malo* an hombre as you'll meet in a month o' Sundays, and his Valentino mug just aids and abets. But he ain't all bad. I'll tickle your English vanity, son, by savin' his papa's blood makes little Fernando a mighty handy boy with his fists... You know, it'd be just like that rotter to turn up again some day."

"Like to see 'im again?" Harold's small eyes blinked sleepily; he was just prolonging conversation now, for the afternoon was heavy and sleep very difficult to deny.

Lemuel's square brown jaw shut with a click and he scowled out into the darkness.

"Bet your sweet life! I won't never forget how Pete Wilkins, my second in command in Guatecata, got lined up before a wall when those dirty *revolucionistas* o' Daggett's caught him." Lemuel's voice unconsciously softened. "You see, Pete Wilkins and I grew up together back in Adam's Falls, Vermont. Stole sugar out o' the same bar'l and got licked with the same switch. He was about the best friend I ever had." The expression on Lemuel's craggy face hardened once more.

Scarcely a hundred yards away a lion roared to greet the sunset. The men on the firing platforms shifted uneasily and stared with round, anxious eyes into the dark tangle of under-growth.

Meanwhile Glégle's deep-voiced war drums thundered and rumbled all up and down that great, hot valley. They were trying to say something, thought the weary Legionnaires, some oft-re-peated threat. "We'll kill you—kill you—*kill you*—if we can!"

"What a sacred cow of a country!" grunted Corporal Gras sullenly.

CHAPTER II

A TASTE OF SMOKE

BORNE ON THE heavy, fog-laden air of late afternoon came the faint sound of terrified shouts and howls and the spiteful crackle of rifle fire. In two swift bounds Captain Dunot emerged from his quarters, engaged in buckling on pistol and ammuni-tion pouches.

"Sergeant Frost!" he snapped as he slipped a clip into his auto-matic. "Order the bugler to sound the *alerte;* have the first and second platoons remain on the walls, take charge of the third and have it fall in for a rescue party. *Nom de Dieu!* Why haven't we those automatic rifles they've been promising us so long?"

During the next five minutes the *poste* at Kouande saw some rapid movement. At every other embrasure stood a dark-faced Legionnaire, rifle loaded and ready as he watched the courtyard gate swing open and a detail of thirty men trot out.

Clump! Clump! Clump! Out they went, hobnails grating the stone court paving. The long fixed bayonets twinkled blue-gray in the early evening light, heavy blue overcoats swayed in unison to the Legionnaires' stride and white neck cloths flut-tered damply out behind as they hurried down the road toward the tall, green wall of the forest from which came a scattering of shots.

"Rate of fire is falling; guess they've beat 'em off for a bit," mused Frost as, pistol in hand, he led the sally party, with the ammunition pouches jolting on his belt. His restless gray eyes flickered endlessly over the unhealthy green jungle. He halted. Something had glinted in there.

"Halt! Prepare for rapid fire!" As penetrating and martial as a bugle note, Lemuel's deep voice rang out. "Aim!"

Instantly the trotting Legionnaires came to an abrupt halt, faced the lacy tangle of jungle on either side, and swung their bayoneted rifles swiftly down to the horizontal. *Snap! Click! Clock!* Off went the safety catches, and flushed faces peered tensely into the tangled, multicolored brush. Panting and breathless, the blue and white column faced to the right and left of the trail, fingers on triggers tensely awaiting the word of command.

Perhaps half a minute they stood thus, a motionless line of alert and perfectly disciplined figures; then arose a wild, ear-rending shout, and a ragged fusillade crackled from among the scarlet and white blossoms lining the path.

"Fire!" shouted Lemuel, and set the example by firing full at a stalwart black with enormous gold earrings who, brandishing a wickedly ponderous *coup-coup*, magically appeared from a small clump of bushes like a rabbit from a top hat.

Crash! Crash! Two volleys thundered out, and as the Legionnaires fired, the leaves in front of them quivered and swayed with the concussion. Some were torn loose and drifted crazily earthward. Shrieks, howls, a few scattered shots came from the jungle.

Crash! Another volley blazed from the Legionnaires' guns. Groans followed; then headlong retreat.

"Cease firing!" Lemuel found time to look around.

Two Legionnaires were cursing and tying up wounds from which trickled or spurted bright blood. The others watched the bullet-torn jungle intently.

"And that's jolly well blinkin' that!" observed Corporal Harold

Hackbutt as he fed two more cartridges into the chamber of his Lebel. No one denied the fact.

Slumped in odd, lax positions in the long grass beside the edge of the jungle lay perhaps a dozen swarthy, evil-featured giants, clad in ragged loin cloths and belts of cartridges. Most of them yet clutched very modern magazine rifles. How bright their blood looked against the emerald grasses!

FROM FARTHER down the narrow trail came the sound of cheers, then, and the tread of many men advancing on the double quick—the reënforcing party.

Lemuel called his detachment to attention. "Attention! Forward! Double quick!" By no means must the reënforcements be allowed to think themselves a rescue force. The Seventh Company of the Legion needs no rescuers! Thus it was that Sergeant Lemuel Frost led his men at a long, pace-eating trot around a palm-shaded bend, and came face to face with the reënforcing column.

"Halt!" Lemuel held up a sinewy brown hand before advancing to welcome the officer in charge of the relief, evidently a sergeant.

"Hope he's an American," Lemuel was saying. But when the deep blue-black shadow under the strange sergeant's *képi* paled, Lemuel halted dead in his tracks, the smile of welcome fading into a thin, venomous snarl as he recognized the evilly handsome and faintly yellow features of a certain adventurer known as Fernando Daggett. The other grinned with consummate effrontery and halted also, his narrow brown eyes hardening and his hand dropping ever so carelessly over the butt of his gun.

"Hello, Lemuel," he said, and Harold marvelled; Daggett's voice and accent were those of an Englishman of good breeding. "Fancy meeting you here, old chap. A long way from Guatecata, eh, what?"

The bronzed skin seemed to tighten over Lemuel's Indian-like countenance, and his lips became a straight, bloodless line. Once he had been wholly deceived by that convincing air of frankness and *camaraderie,* but not again. There occurred to him the old Spanish proverb: "Fool me once, shame on you; fool me twice, shame on me."

He grinned mirthlessly and nodded, mimicked by his shadow. "A long way from Guatecata is right. I allow you'll wish it was longer before you leave this neck o' the woods."

An exceedingly unpleasant expression dominated Sergeant Daggett's handsome visage. "So, still on the warpath? Well, you're a damned fool, Frost—you always were. I've got twice the brains you'll ever hope to have."

The newcomer swaggered forward, his men silently watching. Harold studied the cross-breed. He was big, quite as big as Lemuel, but built on different lines. The wiry American was built like a capital V, broad shoulders, narrow hips and long straight, legs. Fernando Daggett, dark-haired and neatly mustached, was more like a capital H, wide shoulders, broad hips and heavy, powerful legs which gave him a decided advantage in weight.

Lemuel straightened himself, a gleam commencing to show in his blue-gray eye.

Fernando Daggett saw that gleam and halted. "All right, my lad," he stated with a faint sneer. "If you want fight, I'll give you fight—all you want of it; if you want peace, I'll leave you alone. It's up to you to make the first move."

"I'll make it, all right," promised Lemuel grimly. "I ain't forgot Pete Wilkins; but I'll give you more warnin' than you gave me that day in the *palacio* down in Guatecata, blast your treacherous hide!"

"At your service, Colonel Frost!" Sergeant Daggett laughed unpleasantly, and Harold realized with satisfaction that there was not the slightest trace of fear in his voice. It would be a grand fight when it came.

In a noisy, news-exchanging unit the consolidated forces made their way back to the *poste,* the newcomers sweating and cursing under the weight of four new automatic rifles and the ammunition for them.

"These guns, are they good?" Corporal Marnier inquired of a blue-jowled Spaniard in the reënforcing party. "Do they shoot well?"

"*Quién sabe?*" returned the other, slapping an over-inquisitive fly. "We don't know. They were issued to us just as we left Paraku. This precious sergeant of ours is the only one who understands them."

"A valuable man, this sergeant?" grunted the veteran.

"May the devil eat him!" The Spaniard spat viciously, expressively, drenching a delicate yellow orchid. "Valuable, yes, but only because he alone understands these new guns—for that reason only. Otherwise, he's a Portuguese pig with an English name that doesn't belong to him. *Dios!* What a march we've had from Paraku! The man's a beast, a savage!"

And with that opinion Sergeant Frost, striding stony-eyed at the head of the column, would have agreed.

UNEXPECTED DRAMA developed when the united column reached the *poste*. Corporal Achille Gras laid eyes on the newcomers and very promptly betook himself to the captain's office. Here was a chance for advancement, he reflected. What luck that long ago Corporal Gras had served in the Legion with this same Sergeant Daggett.

"Well, what is it?" Captain Dunot's tired eyes rested impatiently on the small, mean face before him.

"I have to report, *monsieur le capitaine,* that among the reënforcements is a deserter from the Legion."

"What?" Captain Dunot's clear blue eyes hardened.

Corporal Gras shrivelled a little. "But yes, *mon capitaine,* we served in the Fifth Company together in the great war. He deserted in the face of the enemy."

"The reason?"

"When on leave, he ran away with the wife of an artillery captain named Le Nellier. He was condemned to death by court-martial, but was never caught."

"Can you prove this?"

"Yes. *Mon capitaine* has but to communicate with Head-quarters."

A moment later an uneasy but defiant Sergeant Daggett, faced the implacable captain. "It's a lie!" he declared hotly; "or else this miserable creature is mistaken. I never served with the Foreign Legion before this enlistment."

Captain Dunot looked perplexed in spite of Corporal Gras's frantic insistence. "Very well, we shall make inquiry," he said. "But until we get further proof it is only a case of one man's word against another's."

Some one spoke; it was the grave-featured Corporal Marnier. He saluted sharply. *"Mon capitaine,* I will bear out what Corporal Gras has said." He spoke very quietly and with a certain reluctance. "I happen to know that this man Daggett did desert from the Fifth Company of the Foreign Legion."

"You are sure?" Captain Dunot seemed decided now. Marnier was a reliable man.

"Yes, *mon capitaine,* he is the one."

Cursing and livid with wrath, Daggett was disarmed and led off to the cells, there to wait transportation back to the coast and to a long-postponed court-martial.

With mixed feelings, Lemuel had witnessed the scene. "Ah, some of those stolen chickens coming home to roost," he muttered, and wondered all the more when Corporal Gras remarked:

"Now, how the devil did old Marnier know that Daggett had served with the Fifth? That old devil wasn't there when Daggett deserted. I wonder how he knew?"

And Lemuel wondered also, as he strode off to assign the new men to their quarters.

CHAPTER III

THE DARK TIDE POURS

LEMUEL FROST SLEPT badly that night. First of all, it was hot in the N.C.O.'s room: secondly, that devilish drumming kept up: third, he could not help pondering upon the strange but not wholly inexplicable reappearance of Fernando Daggett. What a good-looking devil he was—made Valentino look like a mud fence after a drought—but just as rotten as he was good-looking. Better be careful; Fernando was not the type to wait for attack. Lemuel wearily shifted his position when a tiny stream of perspiration commenced to trickle unbearably as it meandered over his chest.

Why the deuce couldn't he sleep? There was Schwartznagel, the big Alsatian; Hátvány Ferenc, the Hungarian, and the worthy Corporal Achille Gras, all plunged in the most profound of slumber. Alongside, Harold slept peacefully if audibly, his mouth open and several gold teeth clearly visible in the late moonlight.

From outside came the faintest imaginable *chink* of metal striking stone, followed by a sound as of a man drawing his breath to speak, but no sound followed.

The seconds ticked by. Lemuel, vaguely curious, sat up. Why hadn't that man spoken?

Because of chigres and other vermin he promptly thrust his feet into his hobnailed boots. No hookworm for that wily soldier!

Then, from the outer air, there reached his ear a soft noise like that of many hands being very gently clapped. Instinctively, Lemuel recognized the sound. Beginning at the base of his skull the hair commenced to rise on his powerful neck. Just one look the sergeant cast out of the barred windows toward the farthest wall, and he beheld a dark, stealthy tide pouring over the parapet. The moonlight gleamed frostily on a great many blades and rifle barrels and naked shoulders.

Simultaneously with Lemuel's frantic shout of *"Aux armes!"* came a hurried, scattering volley of rifle shots, fired as sentries at other points, their attention attracted to the threatened wall, beheld the calamity that had happened.

"Zan nyanyana!" Ten thousand demoniac voices seemed to split the night—truly "the night of death," as they were shouting.

Crack! Crack! Crack! Rifles snapped spitefully, desperately in the heavy, pre-dawn air.

The men of the Legion are used to emergencies; they are specially trained to meet them. But for all that, before the noncommissioned officers—whose sleeping room stood nearest to the courtyard—could do more than buckle on ammunition belts and bayonets and snatch rifles from the racks, the first of the howling invaders were charging in the door. Momentarily outlined by the moonlight the barbaric figures, terrifying in their savage regalia, stood tense with long spears, rifles and swords poised in mid-air. Then, with a cry like the chorus of Hades itself, they sprang in, followed by an indistinct swirl of maddened warriors.

Corporal Manco died instantly by his cot. Sergeant D'Ghiers, a lanky Algerian, uttered a long yell of *"Lah illaha il Allah!"* and bayonet in hand, charged with splendid courage into the mass of invaders which came pouring in the door like a murderous tide. *"Inna Mohammed an rasul..."* Sergeant D'Ghiers's voice ended in a bubbling gasp.

SOLDIERS TO their finger tips, the remaining N.C.O.'s had loaded their rifles and were forming in a ragged line across the lower end of the chamber. At short range they delivered a horribly effective volley, followed by another that dropped the howling blacks, choking and gasping, at the very muzzles of the Lebels.

"Now!" Unconsciously, Lemuel took command. "One more!"

Another shattering volley mowed down the screaming invaders in a shrieking, struggling windrow. To make the room a complete inferno, the bitter smell of burned powder billowed in the heavy air, almost blinding that thin line of corporals who, having ejected their spent cartridges and reloaded, now stood tense, peering blankly into the indescribable darkness.

"Quick, there's one!" Harold whipped up his rifle and fired. The brief flame lit up a slim, dark figure that seemed all eyes and screaming mouth. Harold missed, but another Legionnaire did not. It was Corporal Marnier—he who had known Fernando Daggett—who fired. The supple figure staggered, swayed and with a high shrill scream hurled the great sword he carried straight at the amazed rank of corporals.

"*Dieu!*" shouted Corporal Marnier, in a horrified voice. "This is no local rebellion. The Amazons of Dahomey have risen. God help us!"

An intangible thrill of horror shook those hairy, half-naked men. Not one of them but had heard of that ferocious, merciless corps of the Dahomey army known as the Faithful Followers of the Fetish. Every Legionnaire in the *poste* had heard of the insensate courage and fanatic devotion of those female warriors, with whose valor Danh, Gezo, and Glégle the First had reared the bloody Empire of Dahomey on the crumbled might of Whydah and Alladah. The Amazons of Dahomey! Theirs was the name to conjure with, from the jungles of the Ivory Coast to the steaming marshes of Loanda.

Lemuel felt a strange, sickish feeling in his throat. God above—he had been actually firing at women! He, Lemuel Zebulon Frost of Adam's Falls, Vermont, had undoubtedly killed two or three women! At the other end of the line, amid a tangle of heaped-up cots, he could hear Harold cursing softly. Then his eye detected more stealthy silhouettes hovering at the corpse-cluttered doorway.

"Bayonets!" he roared. Followed the brisk metallic *click, clock!* of the keen, three-edged bayonets being locked on. "Forward!"

Forward charged the N.C.O.'s, conscious that uproar inde-scribable reigned in the courtyard outside. Their place was out there. Forward they sprang, a grotesquely clad line, slipping in unexpected pools of blood, dodging murderously upthrust swords, pinning dark bodies that writhed, snake-like, to the floor with powerful lunges of their bayonets. Resistless, the corporals charged and fought the length of the N.C.O.'s quarters.

Lemuel, in the grip of a curious indecision, contented himself by directing the advance. Somehow, he could not bring himself to plunge that needle-like bayonet of his into the breast of a woman, even though that woman was a murderously inclined she-devil.

AT THE end of five minutes' furious fighting and mopping up the room was cleared, and Lemuel gained the outer door at the head of the grimly intent N.C.O.'s. Before them on the firing platform milled a dark mass of figures weirdly daubed with white clay; figures that uttered deep and not shrill shouts. Men, thank God! Lemuel felt the blood grow hot in his veins.

"Forward!" he shouted joyously. "There's some bucks out here."

"Hi yah!" The American sergeant uttered the famous charging yell of the Fourth Cavalry and launched himself like a thunderbolt of destruction among the six-foot blacks crowding the parapet, while the rest of the N.C.O.'s locked themselves in a desperate struggle with a detachment of Amazons advancing up the staircase leading to the courtyard.

Twice steel stung Lemuel, but he merely grunted, and catch-ing a vision of Harold gone berserk and whirling his Lebel by the barrel, he redoubled his efforts.

"Shucks!" he panted to Harold. "These here men ain't nigh so handy scrappers as them there gals. Come on, son!"

Slowly the two Legionnaires were brought to a standstill, sheer weight of numbers preventing a further advance. Snarl-ing and screaming like a pit full of fiends, the dark mass of Dahomeyans braced themselves, whereat the two—old soldiers of fortune that they were—gave back. Courage? Yes. But suicide? No, thank you!

By mutual consent the two half-naked Anglo-Saxons, grotesquely clad in unlaced ammunition boots, long-tailed shirts and cartridge belts, halted their onslaught to gulp the sour night wind into laboring lungs.

Meanwhile, Gléglé's male warriors on the firing platform remained where they were, nursing their wounds and content-ing themselves with shrieking promises of death and torture.

"Look at that!" Lemuel uttered a hoarse shout of amaze-ment and pointed a quivering forefinger to the wall across the courtyard.

Harold vented an incredulous shout, for there, clearly outlined in the effulgent moonlight, stood a strange, martial figure.

"A hen general!" choked Lemuel. "Well, may I be a long, tall son of a buzzard!"

An Amazon leader stood on the opposite wall, splendidly lithe and apparently all-seeing. She was shouting orders, gestic-ulating and directing the efforts of an apparently endless stream of attackers, who swung with catlike ease upon the walls, then dropped over into the courtyard, there to join in the savage struggle raging within. Crossed over the Amazon's superbly modelled naked breasts were two bandoliers of cartridges, and in her left hand she brandished a very modern and up-to-date Mannlicher carbine. As she pointed, yelled and motioned she seemed to the hard-pressed Legionnaires like some black heathen goddess of war.

"Schwartznagel! Gras! Neuboldt!" In tones like a trumpet's blast, Lemuel recalled three of the N.C.O.'s from the stairs which were now cleared. "Hold this firing platform!"

Their faces wild and bright with sweat, the three trotted up, needle-like bayonets dripping redly, while Harold and Lemuel dashed below. The hard-pressed Legionnaires in the courtyard, reënforced by the arrival of their N.C.O.'s, had become some-what steadier.

Captain Dunot, calm as most Frenchmen are in the face of real danger, directed the defense with cool and masterly intelligence. History began to repeat itself, and, as so many times before, sheer ferocity and weight of numbers completely failed to counterbalance the perfect discipline and coördinated efforts of a small garrison.

TIME AFTER time the screaming Amazons, mingling with their less hardy male companions, hurled themselves with futile fury on the thirsty bayonets of the Legion. These bayonets, fixed on the very long barrels of the Lebel rifles, reached out some six feet to form a steel hedge which could not be penetrated, slash and hack as the Amazons would.

As the battle reached a climax the uproar became deafening. As he thrust, fired, then thrust again, Lemuel could hear the hoarse, panting shouts of the Legionnaires, the guttural commands of the N.C.O.'s, mingled with the blood-freezing ululations of the attackers.

He got a glimpse of Hátvány, the Hungarian corporal, locked in a savage death struggle with a gigantic Amazon. To and fro the strangely contrasting fighters reeled, until suddenly the corporal uttered a shriek of pain when the gigantic Negress bit through his thin cotton shirt and sank her strong, filed teeth deep into his shoulder. Hátvány, panting a fierce Magyar oath, wrenched a knife from his assailant's belt and, grunting with the effort, drove the curved blade far into the Amazon's naked side. With a curious feeling of unreality, Lemuel watched the gleaming strip of steel shorten and disappear.

More shooting sounded from the walls. Riflemen detached by Captain Dunot from the rear of the line in the courtyard had been sent at headlong speed up to the watchtower and unassailed walls. Swiftly the firing increased. Many stabbing fingers of red, orange and yellow lit the night, and almost imperceptibly the fetish fighters began to give way.

At last the famed marksmanship of the Legion began to

count, and a whole section of the attacking force withered away like so many lead soldiers knocked over by the whim of a child.

"Now we got 'em. Come on, boys!" Gripping his rifle with renewed energy, Lemuel sensed a psychological moment. "Forward!" Lunge, thrust, stab, he fought as never before. He was not so fussy now; men and women alike were targets for his dripping *rosalie;* he had seen one she-devil in the act of cutting a wounded Legionnaire's throat. To his surprise he caught a passing glimpse of Fernando Daggett, freed in this hour of stress. He was fighting like a Trojan, using a clubbed rifle with terrific effect.

The right of the Legionnaire line surged forward; but the left fared not so well. For the leader of the attack, that brown girl who appeared to be the commanding spirit, had sprung down from the wall to lead a last charge in person. It proved to be all but irresistible. Some two or three hundred berserk Dahomey-ans hurled themselves forward regardless of the red bayonets that swerved to meet them.

"Help! Help!"

The left of the Legionnaire line was struggling desperately for life. The sergeants fought like devils to check the retreat. Suddenly the swarm of Dahomeyans broke through the line, cutting off a whole detachment of Legionnaires. A hurricane of shouts, yells and screams arose.

Then, by an access of ill fortune, a wandering cloudlet obscured the moon, plunging the whole scene in an indescrib-able darkness that was only faintly relieved by a gray promise of dawn on the horizon.

Suddenly blinded, the marksmen on the walls ceased firing, and though the wounded and dying kept up a heart-chilling outcry, a comparative silence fell.

Lemuel, wounded, blinded with sweat and badly winded, sensed a sudden relaxation of pressure. The enemy was giving back!

"Forward!" Again Lemuel's voice rose above the bedlam;

up whirled his rifle; a wedge of fighting Legionnaires hurled themselves after him, and suddenly the attackers broke and fled. Only their dead and dying remained to make a slippery, blood-splashed shambles of the *poste's* courtyard.

CHAPTER IV

SHAKEN MEN

IN THE MORNING an orange-hued sun, creeping up over the jade-green tops of the bombax, odun and baobab forest, lit a scene of breath-taking carnage and destruction at Madame La République's little *poste* at Kouande. True, from a staff atop the high watchtower the tricolor still cast its colors defiantly in the brief morning wind; but the inner courtyard resembled nothing so much as a slaughterhouse. With dreadful efficiency the whitewashed mud walls revealed ghastly red splashes and spots, where bullets had not scarred and pitted the surface.

Of the one hundred and fifty-odd Legionnaires who had lain down to sleep the night before, some thirty-five lay in a stiff, silent rank upon the dusty, blood-sprinkled flags. Tarpaulins covered the most terribly mangled: such sights are extremely bad for the morale of a besieged garrison. The other fallen lay staring at the gorgeously hued sky with fixed, unwinking gaze, as though held spellbound by flocks of ponderous-winged vultures and buzzards that wheeled over the little fort.

On the other side of the courtyard Lemuel superintended the collecting of a huge pile of half-naked black bodies that became indistinguishably entangled and interlocked. Savage, swart warriors and no less brutal Amazons lay in their last sleep, side by side, with their brief kilts of blue cloth horribly splashed and their garish trappings sadly bedraggled.

To one side of the fallen Dahomeyans was stacked a weird selection of captured firearms and ammunition as well as an interesting array of murderously sharp *coup-coups,* machetes, swords and daggers.

After calling the remaining garrison to attention, Adjutant Van Droon, a bloody rag twisted about the base of his stiff, blond hair, began to call the roll in a dry, unemotional voice.

Sergeant Frost stood like a man of bronze, jaw set and eyes dark and grim. For nowhere had trace been found of Fernando Daggett, Captain Dunot, nor some fifteen others whose bodies lay neither in the rank of dead nor in the overcrowded hospital room, where the medical orderlies labored endlessly amid clouds of persistent and voracious black flies.

Longer and longer grew the hard brown faces in the ranks, as man after man failed to report himself present and fit for duty. With a sense of dismay the garrison learned that seventy-seven men alone remained capable of bearing arms.

Experienced campaigner that he was, Lemuel realized that a complete annihilation of the *poste* was neither impossible nor improbable. Indeed, he and his comrades at Kouande now lived in the shadow of a death so terrible that he shuddered when he thought of it. Not for nothing was the torture of the Amazons feared in a country where death and suffering were commonplace.

What had become of Dunot, Daggett and the others captured? When the remnant of the garrison was dismissed, some to bury the dead, some to pitch the fallen Dahomeyans into the jungle and some to care for the wounded, Corporal Marnier lowered his voice—a rich, refined voice it was, too—and told him:

"Ah, the prisoners—" Marnier pulled his gray mustache thoughtfully. "God end their pain swiftly! Before now, most of the prisoners will be dead, terribly dead. I was with the expedition against Behanzin in '92; we surprised a camp of theirs once—" The veteran's bloodshot eyes wavered and he shuddered. "And what we found! *Dieu!* The worst nightmare you ever had, my dear Américain, could never be like that. Skinned alive were the lucky ones; others were boiled in oil, and others—*Nom de Dieu!* It was horrible, frightful!"

"No chances for the prisoners, then?"

"None. By now they have been sacrificed to the fetishes. They belong to the native idols."

"Guess it's orl up wiv your friendly enemy," said Harold as he unbuckled his cartridge belt. "W'at 'e deserved, I expect—"

"Shut up! You flap your mouth too damn much!" Lemuel's nerves were badly frayed. "No white man deserves a death like that."

A BUGLE blared, and the men dropped whatever they did to fall in once more. Lemuel, as he stood to the right of the line, felt his doubts arising afresh, for there was in Adjutant Van Droon's long, pale and restless features none of that alert decisiveness of Captain Dunot.

"A weak-looking sister," mused the American grimly. "It's a shame Lieutenant Foix had to get bumped off in the fracas last night, too."

On looking down the thin blue and white line he could read a distinct uneasiness on that double file of battered, brutal faces just visible beneath the *képi* visors. Faults and vices these Legionnaires had in superabundance, but timorousness was not among them. A few, like the good Corporal Achille Gras, would plot and plan during the quiet days of barrack life for the best means of preserving an unpunctured hide; but once the issue was squarely put up to them, they did not flinch. No man present had fought with greater courage than the little French corporal.

Corporal Hackbutt, standing a few paces away, ventured a low aside: "Old Van Droon's nerve is shook, Lem. Look at 'is fingers."

Lemuel nodded in silent disapproval and his frown deepened, for Adjutant Van Droon was a sight far from inspiring. The *poste's* new commander had small, pale-blue eyes which flickered nervously back and forth, resting unhappily on one rigid form after another. To make bad matters unconsciously worse and further diminish the garrison's scanty remnant of assurance, he attempted a little speech. Looking down his long white nose he studied the ground.

The situation, he announced, was bad—very bad indeed. Half of the garrison had been incapacitated. A numberless horde of savage natives were rising in rebellion, led on by a brutal king. In their obedience to the witch doctors they were fanatical.

"Heck!" growled Lemuel through locked teeth. "Why does that Dutch yellow-belly want to scare these poor devils more?"

The *poste*, continued Adjutant Van Droon with a dispirited shrug of his shoulders, would probably prove untenable; but perhaps a retreat could be effected to the larger and stronger fort at Paraku.

"W'at?" growled Harold, small eyes narrow with contempt. "Give up the *poste* and get slaughtered in the bush? 'E's balmy! 'Eck, we could 'old on 'ere for a bit wiv these new ortomatic rifles."

Adjutant Van Droon's little speech was about as disastrous to the garrison's morale as it could have been without a long preparation and a studied delivery. The Legionnaires, badly shaken by the events just past, stole sullen, covert glances at each other and perceptibly lost much of their soldierly rigidity, actually slouching in formation. Captain Dunot, keen to notice slackness, would have long since rapped out a sharp reprimand: but the unnerved Hollander let this dangerous symptom pass unchecked.

"Mark my words, son, this is goin' to be one fine party!" predicted Sergeant Frost as the garrison fell out to recommence its several tasks. "This bird's yellow as ocher; even that hound Daggett would be better. For all he's a cheatin', lyin', traitorous buzzard, at least he's got nerve."

A Legionnaire slouched up and saluted listlessly, whereat Sergeant Lemuel Frost drew himself erect; his face became a dull purple beneath his *képi's* visor.

"Stand up, you slack dog! Salute as you've been taught."

Like a man awakened from a bad dream the leather-faced

Legionnaire scowled, but clicked his heels together and repeated the salute with an entirely different manner.

"Well?"

"The adjutant wishes to see you at once, *mon sergent.*"

FILLED WITH trepidation, Lemuel made his way to the little room which had been Captain Dunot's headquarters. There he found Van Droon slumped over a desk with a bottle at his elbow and a downright frightened gleam in his small, watery eyes.

"Come in, come in, sergeant," the blond officer beckoned irritably, as he fanned flies from the blood clot visible on the bandage about his head. "Close the door, too, I—I don't want those big-eared louts of Legionnaires eavesdropping."

"And it's just as well, mebbe," was Lemuel's silent comment as he pushed to the heavy, steel-banded door.

"Well, *mon ajutant?*"

In nervous haste the big Dutchman got to his feel, moved from behind the desk and crossed the small, bare room to where a pair of the automatic rifles lay completely unassembled on a long table near by.

"Come here, sergeant. Do you know anything about this type of automatic rifle? That deserter took them apart to clean them when he first arrived; then he was sent to the cells. As you know, he was captured and carried off last night."

Without a word, Lemuel strode over to the oil-spotted table and felt his heart sink as he viewed a bewildering array of springs, bolts, screws, catches and other bits of mechanism. He had seen such a gun once before, but long ago.

"It's a German light machine gun, isn't it, *mon ajutant?*"

Van Droon's long blond head inclined, while the metal figure seven on his collar glinted softly in the early morning light. "Yes, it's one of that *sacré* intricate Madsen type. This and the others must have been surrendered to France at the time of the Armistice. This is the first I've ever been condemned to see... *Mon*

Dieu, sergeant! Do you realize that as they stand these guns are useless?"

Lines of anxiety were now graven deep in the adjutant's pale features: and the white bandage with its reddish-brown spot seemed only a shade or two lighter than his face.

"These guns must be put in order at once or we are doubly lost. Do you think you could reassemble them? You see the situation, eh?" Helplessly, Adjutant Van Droon spread hands that quivered a little. "We have only these four guns to help us, and there's not an unhung rascal in this *poste* who knows the first thing about them. Daggett, that miserable, worthless hound, was the only one to understand the mechanism. As you may know, he and these wretched guns joined the reënforcements in Paraku just before the column set out for here."

"I'll try," said Sergeant Frost. "There's enough parts scattered about here to make a flivver. But remember, I don't promise any results." Lemuel pushed the *képi* on the back of his dark hair, brushed two or three inquisitive flies from features that were already beginning to glisten with the day's heat, and bent over an amazing heap of grease and oil smeared parts that lay widely scattered over the food-stained boards of the table.

"Of course," he muttered bitterly, "I *would* have been an infantryman or a cavalryman all my misspent life." Nevertheless, he doggedly set to work while the adjutant paced restlessly back and forth, muttering endlessly to himself.

Lemuel's fingers were unusually nimble and his brain was as resourceful as the best of his race, but the hopeless intricacy of the parts, the apparent sameness of many pieces of mechanism proved utterly baffling. While his curses grew sultry and more picturesque, Adjutant Van Droon's weak, perspiring features fell into increasingly fearful lines.

"Keep on trying," he begged feverishly whenever the American straightened up. *"Dieu,* think of our fate if the *poste* falls!"

"Heck!" Lemuel stood up after an hour and a half's patient endeavor to reassemble the breech block. "I ain't a magician."

CHAPTER V

DREAD NEWS

COINCIDENTALLY THERE CAME a knock at the door, and a Legionnaire with white alarmed eyes reported the arrival of a runner from Gambaga.

A moment later there was led in a tall, muscular black with hideous tribal scars on face and forehead. Still gulping for breath, he stammered out the appalling news that Gléglé the Third was making a swift advance with three separate corps. Fear was written in every muscle of the runner's flat features as he informed the N.C.O.'s that the force which had assailed the *poste* was only the smallest and least important of the three divisions. The main body would certainly arrive at Kouande on the second day following.

"How many are his men?" stammered the adjutant, his pale eyes lowered.

"As the ants in a rotten log," replied the runner, licking blue-black lips and resettling the copper bracelets on his wrists and elbows; "as the locusts on the plains and the sands of the bitter water they are numbered."

"Nonsense!" snapped Lemuel. "Old man Gléglé's got mebbe two or three thousand hombres at the outside." He spoke as quickly as he could in an effort to dispel the adjutant's rising terror, but to no avail.

"All is lost! We must abandon the *poste* while there is yet time!" cried Van Droon, rushing to the desk. "Yes, sergeant, that is the only course!"

The Fulah runner rubbed the triple row of tribal scars on his chin and stared in amazement as the adjutant flung himself behind the desk and commenced to paw feverishly over a huge map of the territory.

"Look, sergeant!" Van Droon began to be calmer on having decided on a course. "This is the best route. We will take it."

Lemuel straightened his broad, blue-clad shoulders, and with more pity than wrath gazed upon the shaken Hollander. "Listen, Van Droon, you're still upset over last night or you wouldn't suggest it. We're not goin' to retreat. Once in the bush they'd massacre us. It'd be suicide to leave the *poste.* Our only chance is to hang on."

The watery blue eyes wavered up to Lemuel.

"True," conceded the adjutant, "but—*Dieu de Dieu,* sergeant!—it's also death to stay."

To all this the runner listened with deep interest. Simple savage though he was, he could read the stark, poignant fear in the Dutch N.C.O.'s eyes, and a crafty look crept into his ebon face.

Lemuel whirled about, jaw set and eyes alight. "What says head chief? Which way Gléglé come to make war?"

The Fulah hesitated, licked his lips and whined, "Toward Nilli, Banay and great, great river." The words fell easily from thick lips behind which teeth, filed to sharp points, glimmered like the fangs of a hungry wolf.

A long moment Lemuel narrowly studied the runner. Then, sensing a change of attitude, his hand shot out and as powerfully as a trap closed on the black man's naked shoulder.

"Aie! Aie!" The Fulah whined and cringed as the American's powerful fingers sank into his flesh.

"Tell me truth." Lemuel's blue-gray eyes were as menacing and trenchant as bayonet points. "Where Gléglé carry him war?"

"Let the poor devil be." Adjutant Van Droon's voice was sadly lacking in authority. "Let him be, or you'll have the Fulahs rising against us, too."

Lemuel ignored the command and merely tightened his grip. "Come on, you lyin' roustabout, sing out or I'll wring your blasted arm off!"

The runner fawned. "Gléglé him march first on Mangu, next

on Kouande, then down Ole River to Kanawee and so to the great bitter water."

Had the American been unhampered he might have learned more, but Van Droon, with all the smallness of a weak nature, decided to make a bid to restore his lost prestige.

"Silence, sergeant!" he shouted, pounding the desk. "How dare you disobey when I give an order? You'll do as I say at once. I am your superior!"

Thankful to have aroused even this small spark of spirit, Lemuel saluted, released the runner and stood at attention.

"Get out, you black devil!" The Dutchman waved the amazed Fulah from the room. Lemuel noted with anxiety the expression in the native's cunning black eyes. Very soon the news would reach old Gléglé that a coward was in command of the *poste* at Kouande and that dissension reigned among the officers. That *would* help matters!

ONCE THE runner had pattered off down the brick-floored passage. Van Droon's courage vanished like dew before the sun. "*Seigneur Dieu!*" he gasped, and buried his long face between his hands. "What are we to do? With the automatic rifles we might stand some chance of a successful defense; but—God in heaven!—the only man who understands them is either dead or a prisoner... Do you think Daggett might escape?" A wild and unreasoning hope burned in the adjutant's eyes.

"Small chance," grunted Lemuel, deep in thought. "If he does get loose, which ain't noways likely, you can bet your boots Fernando Daggett won't come back to this *poste*. What man would willin'ly give himself up to serve a term in the Zephyrs* or be shot for desertion? No, we'll never see Daggett again. Those black she-devils will have carved him into kybobs by now, unless... Now, I wonder?" Into his mind came the memory of Fernando Daggett's undeniable way with the ladies. It was not out of the question that such a splendid figure of a man might be spared. With that thought came the faint glimmer of an idea.

---

* The dreaded penal battalion of the French army.

"Mon ajutant!" A big blue figure, he leaned over the desk, towering above the crushed, sweat-bathed N.C.O. below. "There's a chance—only a chance, mind you—that this *poste* can be held."

"Speak!" It was terrible to see the return of hope in the adjutant's wan features. Spasmodically he clutched the edge of his desk. "Speak out, for God's sake! You were always a good soldier, sergeant. I—I—" He seemed to change his original thought. "We must protect the half million French citizens in this zone."

"Hold on a minute." Lemuel held up a warning hand. "Don't get all steamed up; I don't think there's a very big chance o' my findin' Daggett alive, and there's even less o' bringin' him back."

Even more swiftly than it had arrived, hope vanished from Adjutant Van Droon's long, sweating visage. "Are you mad?" he almost screamed. "You insult intelligence by thinking to find that rotter in the jungle. A needle in a haystack would be easier. Find Daggett? Such an idea is madness, sheer madness!"

"But it's our only chance." Sergeant Frost's voice became edged with contempt. "You know damn' well that if Glégle's force hits us as we are now, we'll be wiped out like an ant hill under an elephant's foot." The American's brown fist crashed down upon the table, making a bronze inkwell jump.

Feverishly the adjutant shook his bandaged, blond head. "No! You're of much more value here." Van Droon was almost chattering now. In the extremity of his alarm he caught Frost's blue cuff. *"Mon Dieu,* don't you understand? I must have you here. You are the most experienced soldier in the *poste*—you have fought all over the world. Help me or we are lost. I—I must have your advice."

"Well, I'm givin' it to you," declared Lemuel stonily. He began to wonder if the heat and his head wound had not upset the adjutant's equilibrium. What else could account for that feverish gleam in those weak blue eyes?

"Advice, yes. But not that! To try and find Daggett is madness! You could not go a hundred meters into that jungle out there before these *sacré* savages would cut you down. No! I will not throw live men after dead ones."

"But, adjutant—" A rising anxiety gripped Lemuel's being; too well he saw their absolute need of the automatic rifles to beat off the charge of Glégle's great horde of warriors and Amazons.

But with all the obstinacy of a weak nature Van Droon refused to listen. "No, never! I, your commanding officer, forbid you to make any such attempt." The Hollander glared up a little wildly. "Disobey, and I will have you instantly shot for insubordination in the face of the enemy!"

HAD NOT Lemuel Zebulon Frost been a soldier to his finger tips he might have openly defied that pitiful figure behind the desk; but long years of discipline had formed an unconscious barrier too great to be so easily overcome. Craftily, he adopted a new angle.

"Well, then," Lemuel spoke short and sharp, "I advise you to send out a reconnaissance party, to learn what's going on outside the *poste.*"

Van Droon considered. "Yes," he admitted, "you're right. You may take any ten men you want and an interpreter. Make a report on conditions in the native villages at Birni and Wangara. See if the revolt is spreading that way. But"—he raised a warning forefinger and his blue eyes became very hard—"move one meter off the trail from those two villages, and I give you my word I'll have you stood up against the wall and shot for insubordination in the face of the enemy. Now, sergeant, you may go and make your reconnaissance."

Lemuel hesitated on the verge of another appeal, but realizing he would only cause himself to be removed from the reconnaissance party, he merely raised his hand in salute and stalked out.

The buzzards and other carrion birds were very busy just outside the walls when ten anxious Legionnaires in light marching order, under the command of Sergeant Frost and Corporal Harold Hackbutt, tramped through the gate.

It was significant that the reconnaissance party marched with bayonets fixed, and that they took with them a corporal bugler.

"If we want help," Lemuel had instructed the sergeant of the guard, "you'll hear the bugle, as we'll never be farther than three kilometers from the *poste*."

"You'd better not," Sergeant Ormande growled. "This Dutchman's in a blue funk, but sure as Dunot's dead he'll shoot you if you disobey orders. Come, my friend"—he clapped the American a resounding blow on the shoulder—"forget about this Daggett creature. He's been killed. That's what Legionnaires are for."

Lemuel nodded, and, singularly grim, gave the order to advance.

"One, two, three, four—look alive, boys." The twelve disappeared down the narrow road.

"The main force went by 'ere," observed Harold, pointing to a blood-dimmed spear head that lay in the lush grass by the side of the track.

"Yes." In the shade of his *képi's* brim, Lemuel's steel-gray eyes darted continuously back and forth, endlessly probing the green undergrowth for hostile natives. The ten men behind him, who were fully alive to what might happen should they be surprised, looked likewise, their weapons ready.

CHAPTER VI

UNKNOWN PATHS

AMID AN UNNATURAL silence the reconnoissance party had proceeded in this fashion several hundred yards, when one of the foremost Legionnaires halted suddenly and uttered a grunt of alarm. Following the soldier's shaking forefinger, Lemuel glanced at the bole of a small camwood tree, and with a chill of horror beheld a severed hand, nailed to the silver-green bark with a clumsy dagger. It was a white man's hand, roughly hewed off at the wrist, and by some ghastly humor its index finger had been outstretched as though to say, "We went this way; follow if you dare."

Hardly had the reconnaissance party recovered from this first shock than Harold's restless, button-like blue eyes discovered the head of Captain Dunot. The thing swayed among a festoon of scarlet and white creepers, neatly impaled on the head of a pike. Mutilations had been done to that horrible trophy which made more than one war-hardened stomach writhe.

"God!" choked Harold. "It fair gives a bloke the 'orrors."

For a good kilometer the road to Wangara coincided with the line of the retreat of the raiders; it was unmistakably and liberally marked with dreadful tokens even worse than the first two.

Where the beaten road had been finally deserted, the black raiders had marked the spot where they had struck off into the jungle with an example of fiendish cruelty that made the stoutest heart turn glacial. They had thought it dead; but that red and white mass of agony which could not rightly be called either alive or dead, had *moved*. Lemuel, with a pitying oath, whipped out his pistol and shot the poor object through what remained of its head, then hastily led the blanched and shaken party on through the gay, green jungle where monkeys chattered and birds sang.

When at last the native villages were discovered, there was no need for an interpreter. The only inhabitants found by the Legionnaires were mangled corpses, on which great, green-bodied flies were already hungrily clustered. Though the others cursed and swore, Lemuel uttered no word. Soldier to his finger tips, he carried out the military details of his assignment with meticulous care, even going so far as to write out a report on the spot, which caused Harold no little surprise.

When the return march through the gorgeously beautiful forest was taken up, silence reigned until the reconnaissance

The Amazon stared at her yoked, rebellious captive.

party regained that spot where the retreating enemy had quitted the road.

"Here, Harold," said Lemuel suddenly, "just you mind this dispatch case for me a minute, will you?"

A shrewd suspicion crept into the little Englishman's ruddy face and his eyes narrowed as he readjusted the neck cloth on his blue-clad shoulder. "Yer ain't goin' to disobey orders, are yer, Lem?" he queried anxiously.

"Me?" Lemuel seemed deeply pained at the suspicion. "Heck, no! I'm just goin' to *pasear* along that trail a few yards—just want to see which way it goes."

Resentful at the delay, the ten Legionnaires grounded arms, nervously wiped the sweat from their faces and stared into the sweet-smelling jungle, thanking God that only a kilometer separated them from the security of the *poste*. They had not the least desire to share the fate of the prisoners. *Morbleu, non!*

"Listen 'ere, Lem, yer cawn't do this!" Harold snatched at the tall American's sleeve as he passed. "I know you're goin' arter Daggett. Come back, yer bloody fool! He's dead. W'at good'll it do to get yourself chopped into kybobs?"

"Oh, lay off! I'm comin' right back—I ain't goin' far." Lemuel lied valiantly and, by quitting the trail, laid an undeniable claim to the services of a firing squad at the fort. In his ears rang Adjutant Van Droon's spiteful warning: "Move a single meter off that trail and I'll have you shot for insubordination in the face of the enemy."

Have him shot, would he? Well, maybe. But first he'd make a stab to save the *poste*.

So, taking a fresh grip on his pistol butt, Sergeant Lemuel Zebulon Frost disappeared into the menacing jungle where the gay warblers vied with the orchids in creating a riot of color.

IT WAS quite easy at first to follow that trampled trail, for a line of crushed and bruised vegetation clearly marked the retreat of the raiders. It was hot in the jungle, and Lemuel found the exertion of stepping over tangled roots, wild snarls of creepers and boggy places in the trail enough to make him pant and gasp as he struggled on. He presently discarded his blue overcoat and ripped open his shirt at the neck.

"Somehow, I'm going to find that swine, Daggett," he repeated again and again. "I've got to. He's the only one knows how to work them new automatic rifles. Without him, old Gléglé 'll swamp us. Yep, it's up to me to locate that no-'count heart breaker."

Lemuel halted, staring blankly into the perfumed, emerald-green tangle ahead. Imperceptibly the trail had narrowed, and at the spot where he now stood the single clear path became three indistinct trails. He paused, uncertain, while the tropic sun beat mercilessly down and struck the exposed portions of his body with withering, feverish rays that burned like hot irons. From a near-by limb, a large yellow-brown snake sinuously uncoiled and vanished from sight.

"Whichever path I pick," he muttered aloud, "it 'll be the wrong one, o' course."

Down one of those three lanes the savage, ebony Amazons had taken Fernando Daggett. Which of the three should he follow?

He stood alert, but undecided, pistol in hand, for every clump of broad, shining leaves might conceal a lurking Dahomeyan. Then, recalling some of his tracking lore acquired long ago on the great plains of the West, Lemuel returned his pistol and squatting on his heels, commenced to study the ground narrowly.

"Must have been some prisoners go down this one," he muttered as he discovered in the spongy, brown soil the clear imprint of a square military boot-heel. "This must be the route to follow… What the heck?" He became increasingly confused as, on the second of the three trails, he also discovered a number of unmistakably clear boot-prints.

"Which one?" His bloodshot eyes scanned the ground anxiously. A mistake now would end all chance—slim as it was—of finding Fernando Daggett. He smiled wryly. How funny it was—here he was almost throwing away his life on the odd chance of saving a thorough rotter from a well-deserved death. Talk about ironies!

"Well," he concluded a moment later, "it's between these two trails." One large, sweaty hand crept into Lemuel's pocket; it found and withdrew a single copper coin.

"Heads, to the right—tails, to the left. If you got any drag with Lady Luck, Fernando Daggett, you'd better use it now!"

Balancing the coin on a broad, discolored thumb nail, Lemuel sent it flashing into the sky. It flickered an instant against the aching blueness overhead, glimmered down and landed tails up.

Lemuel wavered. There were many more boot-prints turning to the right than to the left, consequently his chance of finding the man he sought was greater in that direction. Still, Lady Luck had said "Turn to the left." Drawing his automatic, at the end of its stout lanyard, Lemuel warily pushed aside a clump of mango saplings and made his way forward, while a dozen varieties of jungle flies did their best to drive him to distraction.

On and on struggled the scarlet-faced sergeant, conscious that the twisting trail he followed would be very difficult to recognize on the return trip. Difficult? Why not face facts? It would be impossible.

Twice he halted, once as the crashing of a heavy body in the dense undergrowth sent his heart soaring to the roof of his mouth, and again when a cunning native deadfall nearly crushed the life from him.

CHAPTER VII

FLIRTING WITH DEATH

THEN, AS HE stood shaken by the narrowness of his escape, looking at the huge log which had fallen across his path, he heard a sound which halted the flow of blood in his veins. It was the soft rumble of drums not five hundred yards to the right of the trail.

Boom ta-ta boom! Boom ta-ta boom!

At the same time from behind him was raised a long, barbaric yell that reëchoed weirdly in the jungle, and the sound of feet crashing through the brush.

Knowing better than to hesitate longer, Lemuel gathered himself and would have darted off blindly into the jungle had not a gasping, barely recognizable, voice stopped him:

"Lem! It's 'Arold! Wait for me!"

The voice came from a patch of jungle just down the trail the American had been following. Gasping, choked with fatigue, it was none-the-less recognizable as the sturdy little cockney's voice.

Lemuel felt sick. Courageous, foolhardy little Harold!

"I oughta known," he grunted, "that half-pint o' hell 'd never stay behind." And though he swayed on the brink of an exceedingly painful death, Lemuel's heart went out to that rugged, gutter-bred little man who, for all his vulgarity and lack of breeding, yet unmistakably showed that indomitable spirit which had reared the mighty empire of Britain.

"Here, quick!" he called impulsively, though realizing that by so doing he threw away half his chances of escape.

The crashing of underbrush grew loud, then Harold burst into sight wild-eyed, bleeding from many thorn scratches and minus his *képi*.

"Quick!" he panted, casting a fearful look over his shoulder. "They're close behind. Sorry I brought 'em on yer, Lem. I was only tryin' to 'elp."

"O.K., Harold. Let's get a wiggle on."

Then desperately summoning to his aid all the craft of the frontier tracker, Lemuel led the way into the furnace-hot jungle where matted vines and tangled, treacherous roots made the going extremely difficult.

Not more than two hundred yards behind, came the Dahomeyans, fleet and unencumbered black shadows, following relentlessly on the plainly marked trail. It was then that both the harried fugitives learned that it is quite a difficult matter to force one's way through an equatorial jungle hampered by a canvas shirt, ammunition belt, gaiters, hobnail shoes and the rest of the Legionnaire's equipment.

On and on the two struggled, endlessly tearing aside the baffling, tentacle-like creepers with the strength of despair, for those blood-chilling yells from behind were growing louder.

"We've *got* to get away!" Lemuel kept telling himself as he wrenched apart the tough gaudy vines. "We've got to lose 'em! We've got to catch that swine Daggett—if he's still alive—and bring him back. The guns—guns—those guns have got to be assembled!"

On various occasions Lemuel had beheld the results of a slaving expedition's descent on a native village. There he had encountered sights which even yet disturbed his sleep. Now he pictured a far more awful scene—the whole of upper Dahomey ravaged and bathed in the blood of helpless blacks! The white settlements, too, widely scattered and incapable of aiding each other, would be blotted out in a murderous twinkle by Glégle's fanatic horde.

"THEY'RE GAININ'!" Harold's bloodshot blue eyes were very round, and his breath came in short, whistling gasps. " 'Ere, I'll 'old the bleedin' buzzards up a bit. You leg it, old bean." Harold actually stopped and drew a pistol he had acquired in some mysterious manner.

"Look!"

The two paused, spent and sweat-bathed on a slight ridge that traversed the jungle, affording a brief view over the waving elephant-grass tops.

Lemuel's heart sank, for plainly seen and not two hundred yards behind there twinkled a number of broad, blue-white spear heads—twenty-five, fifty, seventy-five of them! Crouched among the roots of a huge bombax, the hunted Legionnaires could even catch glimpses of black, gleaming skins, of gold earrings, and of blue and white loin cloths.

"Come on." Lemuel staggered to his feet once more. "Stick close. The bush is thin enough here—mebbe I can do some back-trackin'."

Streams of acrid, blinding sweat poured down the American sergeant's craggy face and stung where a thorn branch had drawn three parallel, bloody scratches across the bridge of his nose. From beneath the battered *képi*, dark hair hung dank over his bronzed forehead; in his deepest gray eyes was the desperate, intense calm of a man who knows that the sands of life are running very low.

Exactly like a wary old buck who hears the hounds dangerously near, Lemuel leaped to a long outcrop of black basalt that would leave no tracks and raced along for perhaps a hundred yards. Harold followed awkwardly as closely as he could, but for all his efforts his hobnails made faint gray scratches on the rock. At the sight of them Lemuel swore roundly.

"They'd stick out like electric signs to a Sioux or a Cheyenne," he gasped, "but maybe these dumb niggers ain't such good trackers."

Quitting the rock ridge at its terminus, Lemuel gathered himself and made as wide a broad jump as possible, landing far out in the yellow-green elephant-grass below. Good! No foot mark showed for at least ten feet.

Far behind, the puzzled Dahomeyans vented angry yells on encountering the basalt ridge.

"Come on! We ain't got all day!"

Harold braced himself but, in taking off, slipped and came tumbling down the smooth black rock, his bayonet scabbard scraping faint white streaks that seemed to the distracted sergeant as prominent as a boil on a man's nose.

Harold was very contrite. "Sorry, Lem," he gasped, as he got up and with a twig started cleaning the dirt from his pistol barrel. "You better leave me 'ere, I ain't no bloomin' long jumper."

"No. They've been fooled a minute. We've still got a ghost of a show."

From the far end of the rock ridge rose a savage, triumphant clamor. Lemuel darted off into the shoulder-high elephant-grass.

" 'Ere," objected Harold a moment later, "you're runnin' in a bloomin' circle."

"Know it," grunted Lemuel desperately, hurdling fallen logs, rocks and other obstacles with an ease that betrayed how much the shorter-limbed Englishman hampered him.

ALL AT once the powerful, low-flung branches of a camwood tree seemed to offer hope. Bracing himself, the long-bodied American sprang like a jaguar, caught the end of a moss-hung limb and deftly swung himself astride the branch. Then with the speed of thought he reached down to pluck Harold up beside him, just as from the far edge of the circle arose a series of triumphant yells announcing that the pursuers had discovered the betraying marks on the rocks.

"Climb as high as you can," fiercely whispered Lemuel. "Then, if you value your life, lie flat and lie quiet. Get me?"

Time was short, so the two could clamber up the tree but a painfully short distance, filling their eyes with particles of bark. The hunted Legionnaires had barely time to flatten themselves, Lemuel on a lower limb and Harold higher up, when the first of the pursuers came bounding eagerly along, small yellowish eyes fixed on that trampled trail. Like a black, disturbed current trickling through the jungle greenness, fully a hundred cruel-featured Dahomeyans appeared, their spear blades very bright and murderous-looking in the late afternoon sunlight. Others bore carbines of all makes and patterns ready in their powerful fists.

"Gosh—it's those Amazon gals again!" Although he stood within an ace of being cruelly snuffed out, Lemuel could not help a faint grin at the thought of Lem Frost of the Fighting Fourth Cavalry being chased by a gang of women—big, black women with manlike bodies and the eyes of tigresses! As on the night of the attack, the powerful limbs of these savage huntresses were hampered by nothing but weapons, a brace each of ammunition bandoliers, and short kilts of blue and white cotton. Their only attempt at uniformity was the wearing of a kind of white fez on which was stitched a crude blue crocodile.

With a singular absence of noise, the hunters sped past, all intent upon the ground. Presently the last spear point twinkled from sight, and after wiping some cold sweat from his forehead Lemuel heaved a faint sigh of relief.

"Gorn away!" Cautious but joyous was Harold's voice from above. "Yer fooled the blinkin' bounders."

Harold straightened up on his limb, but the American held up a fiercely restraining hand. "Down, you damn' fool!" he hissed. "The real danger ain't begun yet. In a minute these blacks will find they've been followin' a circle, and come back lookin' higher. Say your prayers, son."

Hardly were the words past his lips than an angry shout marked the discovery by the Dahomeyans that they were back again by the marked rock. Cursing and calling shrilly to each other, they appeared once more, this time running as a long line of skirmishers abreast, each some ten or fifteen feet from the next. With infinite patience and care the savages—men and women both—swept in a circle, their weird headdresses just visible among the grass tops.

With wildly beating heart Lemuel watched the half naked blacks searching, active as game dogs and probing every covert like hounds, while the sinking sun drew red splashes on their low, scarred foreheads. Would one of them, more experienced or more intelligent than his fellows, think to look up? If so, a certain sergeant's days of soldiering were over.

STEADILY THE barbaric array drew near, scanning every foot of the ground. A colossal warrior with a tuft of emerald-green parrot feathers in his kinky hair especially drew the breathless American's attention, for he was following the true trail, small amber-hued eyes flickering back and forth at waist height.

Nearer and nearer he came, working steadily this way and that like a well-trained setter. To either side marched a pair of Amazons, as cruel-looking females as Lemuel ever hoped to see. One of these able Boadiceas was carrying a heavy *coup-coup,* the other a Martini-Henry rifle. So close did they come that Lemuel, lying desperately flat and breathless on his limb, could watch the smooth play of muscles beneath their glossy skins. Would they look up? It was an eternal moment.

Ah! Now the two Amazons had passed, silent as shadows, and the rest of the searching party had also vanished in the jungle grass, their passage marked only by wild swaying of the grass tops.

The huge warrior with green topknot, however, seemed to have discovered something interesting. The hunted American's breath halted halfway to his lungs when the Dahomeyan dropped on one knee and narrowly eyed what must have been a boot-print. Then on hands and knees the fetish fighter crawled straight toward the camwood tree, with his *coup-coup* carefully spreading and flattening the verdant grasses for a clearer view of the earth.

Fascinated with dread, Lemuel peered through the tangle of foliage to watch and sensed the terror of an escaped convict who hears the deep baying of bloodhounds on his trail. Green feathers nodding and golden earrings a-sparkle, the huge black now rose slowly to his knees and, holding his *coup-coup* ready, moved stealthily farther under that very limb upon which the sergeant lay, every nerve tensed and jangling. Now the Dahomeyan was directly under the outer fringe of leaves on Lemuel's limb. So close was he that the American could see a double necklace of glittering cowrie shells twisted about the Negro's bull-like neck. A deep purple scar zigzagging across one shoulder was visible, too; evidently this warrior was a wily veteran.

Closer and closer came the hunter, treading very warily, he was directly under Lemuel, green feather-top now almost within reach. Would he look up? Lemuel gathered himself for a pumalike leap when the black man straightened, uttered a baffled grunt, took one backward step and then halted. Slowly his close-cropped woolly head tilted backward, as a gorgeous little yellow warbler trilled from a near-by bush, until he was looking up into that very clump of foliage which sheltered the agonized sergeant.

Gradually the outline of that kinky head-top changed and a strip of shiny, scarred forehead became visible. The black *was* going to look up! Back, back tilted the Dahomeyan's bullet-head. Then, for all the world like a cougar dropping on a bull elk, Lemuel silently launched his hundred and seventy pounds of bone and muscle on the huge savage beneath. His hands madly sought and found the warrior's throat, instantly cutting short a startled cry. Then commenced one of the great fights of Lemuel's turbulent career, for the Dahomeyan was slippery with palm oil, strong as a buffalo, and skilled in the art of wrestling.

In an instant the two crashed to earth, rolling over and over, crushing a dozen gorgeous blue and yellow blossoms beneath their writhing limbs. Two rending, sepia-hued fingers clawed for

Lemuel's eyes; but he wrenched his head desperately away, and thinking of the doomed men at the *poste*, squeezed his thumbs against that throbbing windpipe with the desperation of a man who fights for more than life. Yes, he was fighting for those men in the *poste* and countless thousands of blacks whose lives were at stake, he must hold on.

The strangling fetish fighter, in a final and terrific effort to break loose, brought his knee up sharply into the Legionnaire's stomach, almost driving the wind from Lemuel's body and creating a searing, indescribable pain that nearly made him let go in a faint. But just as the sergeant felt he must lose his cherished advantage, the black body, smelling of sweat and rancid palm oil, went slack. A dark and swollen tongue writhed between froth-flecked, purple-gray lips.

There was a sound of a falling body near by and Harold rushed up with pistol ready. " 'Ave you got 'im?"

Lemuel, as he held on for dear life, was too spent to answer.

" 'Ere," suggested Harold, ever practical, as he wrenched off his belt. "Use this strap to finish the blighter orf wiv—save your strength."

The two bent intently over the now unconscious warrior. Suddenly, a shadow flickered across the trampled elephant-grass, and Lemuel uttered a hoarse shout of warning. Swift as thought he sprang back, but it was too late. A savage ring of black figures was closing in. His eyes swept the array of assailants for a gap, and found none. He was definitely doomed, and the great game was lost beyond hope. With a roar of fury the American charged straight at the barbaric array as Harold, valiant to the last, snatched up the fallen warrior's *coup-coup* to make a few futile slashes before the black horde overwhelmed him and the tall American.

CHAPTER VIII

PRIMITIVE HOSTS

WHEN LEMUEL REGAINED consciousness it was to make the painful and unpleasant discovery that he lay securely bound with his right hand firmly lashed to the back of his neck. Moreover, his neck was thrust into a yoke made of the crotch of a forked, sawed-off tree, and secured there by a businesslike iron nut and bolt.

A few yards away Harold, dazed with the horror of the situation, crouched in an abandonment of misery. He was trussed in similar fashion, quite naked save for boots and uniform breeches that were no longer white.

"*I tá ea!*"

Lemuel's head still rang like a tuning fork and he felt very sick, but he realized that he was commanded to get up and walk. The sight of a burly Amazon advancing with a rhinoceros-hide whip in her hand urged him staggering to his feet. Nevertheless, that lady whirled up her whip and caught the reeling sergeant a hissing lash across the shoulder that felt like the touch of a red-hot bar.

"And here," thought the bruised and dizzied American, "is the end o' the trail." He wondered if he would meet his terrible fate with something of the fortitude with which certain of his ancestors had encountered death at the hands of Sitting Bull's torture squaws.

"*Dee wae zoo!*" rasped the nearest Dahomeyan, and enforced his order to move faster with the point of a spear.

Harold limped up alongside Lemuel, the trail of his slave yoke digging a little furrow in the unhealthy black soil.

"Too bad, Lem, old son," he muttered. "I guess it's a case o' Last Post for us—Taps, you'd call it, eh? But that were a great scrap yer put up. Guess we're slated for a little demonstration o' vi-vi-section, wiv 'orrid emphasis on the 'section.' Wonder w'at they'll do to us?"

"Plenty!" panted Lemuel, and swayed dizzily in his stride. "But don't go thinkin' 'bout it or you'll go off your nut."

With all the stubbornness of his race to admit defeat, Lemuel sought frantically for a means of escape, while the little column pushed on through the deepening sunset; but the more he thought the deeper grew his despair. His right arm had long since become numb, for the stout manila cord securing the wrist to the nape of his neck was distressingly thick and strong. But even granted he could get that loose, the ponderous slave yoke yet remained to hamper him. The future, Lemuel was forced to admit, was of an unrelieved blackness.

Staggering, gasping and struggling desperately to keep their footing, the two captives were driven pitilessly onward through the insect-ruled jungle. Did either Legionnaire lag the least bit, a keen spear point prodded him viciously to draw little runlets of blood on which a horde of stinging flies would settle greedily.

Gradually the nature of the ground changed. Enormous trees appeared, so shading the earth that the undergrowth grew thinner. Many of the warriors, who had been slashing a passage through the tough, tangled wall of green, now put away their *coup-coups*.

"Thank God! We must be getting near the home corral," panted Lemuel. "I couldn't last much longer. Smell the wood smoke?"

Harold's little snub nose crinkled. "Yus. But I smells somethin' else, too. Kind o' like an overdone chop."

A few yards farther on the odor grew stronger, and Lemuel wished he had strength to be sick. For the smell wafted to his nostrils was that of burning human flesh.

JUST AS the sun hovered over the horizon, the party entered what the half-dead American recognized as a fetish grove. In complete disregard for order, dozens of little huts of straw and mud had been erected to shelter quantities of small stone altars. On peering dazedly into the nearest, Lemuel recognized a typical assortment of those curious objects which the fetish worshiper adopts for his guardian angels.

Even while Lemuel stared at the odd collections of trinkets, one of the Amazons darted aside into a hut to prostrate herself on the ground before an altar of crudely carved wood on which stood nothing more nor less than an old-fashioned brass mariner's compass! In front of the compass had been set a huge offering bowl of nuts, alligator pears, bananas and other fruits; and as a further tribute, two freshly severed human heads dripped on the hard-packed earth.

On a larger altar to the right was perched a hideous, pot-bellied little god, carved of highly polished ebony. To the left stood a battered alarm clock, to which had been sacrificed three human heads. Two of them were black; but Lemuel realized with a thrill of horror that the third head was white!

"So 'elp us!" Harold gulped, and shivered. "Look at it! These murderin' swine! There's poor D'Ghiers's 'ead. Remember, Lem? 'Im w'at was corp'ral o' the second squad!"

In the dim, sightless eyes Lemuel read an expression of indescribable horror and agony. Brave though he was, he shuddered. Before very long, perhaps within the same hour, his own head would lie before some fetish. Poor D'Ghiers!

To his last hour, Lemuel never forgot that fetish grove. The withered corpses of many Legionnaires and black men were nailed to the various trees, some crucified upside down, and some minus various parts. Before an especially large shrine the horrified captives beheld a small pyramid of severed heads, crowned by no less than six heads of white men. In the sergeant's fevered imagination he saw many such pyramids grow. Pyramids that would arise after the *poste* at Kouande had been swept from existence in a torrent of blood. Poor devils! They'd die with the saving automatic rifles useless in their hands.

"Wonder if Daggett's represented here? He probably is…"

Dragging the ponderous slave yoke with him Lemuel marched through that grove of horror, forcing himself to examine closely each gruesome trophy. Many a familiar face he found, but nowhere could he discover any trace of the man he had thrown away his hope of life to find.

AFTER PASSING the outermost shrine where a surveyor's telescope, a clumsy clay model of an elephant, and a pair of shears served as fetishes, the column pressed on over the brow of a hill and soon came in sight of an apparently limitless encampment of Amazons.

Like giant jewels scattered among the dark tree trunks, at least a hundred watch fires flamed and flickered redly, around which dozens and dozens of weirdly armed and garbed warriors of both sexes squatted on their hams to tear with bestial impatience at the strips of half-cooked meat which formed their evening ration. As the triumphal procession passed, these dusky harpies sprang to their feet uttering guttural whoops of savage anticipation and came running over to prod and pinch the helpless captives.

Lemuel gritted his teeth and said nothing, but Harold cursed like a fiend and struck out as strongly as he could with his free left arm.

The prisoners were led straight toward a huge central fire, where half a dozen drums rumbled a sensual dance rhythm. Here a fresh group of Amazons assumed charge of the dispirited and exhausted Legionnaires, while the male warriors dropped aside at various camp fires, there to boast of their glorious conquest.

On the far side of the fire had been built a fairly spacious mud and wattle *chimbecque* or long hut, the outline of which Lemuel could just make out through tear-drawing billows of smoke. On guard by the door stood six fierce-eyed Amazons eagerly watching the approach of the raiding party. Then the drums became thunderous and a number of weirdly daubed and caparisoned witch-doctors—or so the American judged them to be—came prancing from the gloomy interior of the *chimbec-*

que. Capering like maniacs and springing high in the air they advanced, waved gourd rattles trimmed with bladders, feathers and knuckle bones, and yelled like madmen.

One particularly hideous doctor thrust a gargoylesque face within six inches of Lemuel's and spat, then dealt the stolid prisoner a stinging cuff and bounded away, a leopard's tail writhing grotesquely behind him. Back into the hut he whirled. The nearest Amazon roughly indicated to the bewildered prisoners that they might sink to the earth.

It was a grim, terrifying spot in which Lemuel and his companion in misery found themselves. All about, like columns in a Gothic cathedral, were the rough trunks of towering bombaxes, shining red-black in the fire light. Overhead their branches interlaced to form a shadowy natural vault roof.

To the right of the long hut was a white pile, erected before a more imposing fetish shelter. Lemuel strained his eyes a moment, then shut them hastily. What he saw was a rough altar of white stone whose whole surface was paved with glistening white skulls! Steadily the empty eye sockets transfixed him with a chilling, macabre regard.

Lemuel was still studying the grisly altar when there sounded a sudden shrill squalling of flageolets. Faster and faster sounded the death drums, then with one accord all the Amazons flung themselves flat on the earth, arms outstretched to lie as though they were dead.

Harold stirred uneasily. "Now, w'at the dickens?"

"*Nah-see!*" chorused the prostrate Amazons. "We are humble, O *Caboceer,* great general."

CHAPTER IX

A TIGRESS'S TOYS

THE TWO PRISONERS whirled about to face that large hut into which the witch-doctors had vanished. In the inner darkness there was a movement, then the faint glimmer of some metal ornament as there swaggered into the crimson firelight the most gorgeous creature Lemuel had ever beheld. He stared open-mouthed, like a yokel at a sideshow.

At first glance the sergeant knew that this lovely Amazon must have much white blood in her veins, for her smooth skin was no darker than that of many Latins and her well-shaped features were small and finely modeled. Her negroid blood was revealed only in her faintly golden complexion and the rather close curling of her jet-black hair, which tumbled back over her naked shoulders in glorious profusion.

"Strike me pink!" gasped the cockney, blinking incredulously.

"Sure is a good-lookin' gal," muttered Lemuel.

"Maybe," Harold sniffed; "but 'andsome is as 'andsome does, I'm thinkin'. She won't look so la-di-dah when she's runnin' our sacrifice."

With lithe, graceful steps, the Amazon *caboceer* strode forward, her kilt of leopard skin rippling smoothly in the firelight. The general was unarmed but for a beautifully shaped, gold-hilted dagger tucked in a rawhide belt. Two heavy bands of red gold were twisted in the guise of serpents about each arm and a double necklace of bright blue beads about her neck composed her sole ornamentation.

For all her undeniable beauty, the anxious Lemuel found something chillingly cruel, infinitely primordial about the Amazon *caboceer's* expression; and her large greenish eyes seemed to hold the clear and predatory brightness of a hawk's.

She halted perhaps ten feet from the fascinated American and gazed down upon his powerful, bound frame with an expression of infinite contempt upon her small scarlet lips.

Twisting his head in the yoke Lemuel grinned suddenly. "Howdy, sister," he said. "How are you goin' to serve us? Fried? Boiled? Or baked? Or maybe roasted whole with a yam in our mouths?"

Then a curious thing happened. The Amazon started, frowned and took a step backward, eyes wide.

"Oh!" she remarked in a rich melodious voice. "You English-mans?"

Lemuel blinked incredulously. Could this lovely savage actually be talking English? His hopes soared skyward.

"Sure," he replied; "at least Harold over there is. I'm an American."

The Amazon revealed white and regular teeth in a wolfish grin. "Zat very good. Taloya have never see American, Engleesh soldier."

"Well, here we are," grinned Lemuel. "Help yourself, sister, and take a good look."

The *caboceer* paused, fumbling with her ivory and gold dagger belt and apparently lost in thought. "Tell Taloya," she commanded, "Engleesh, American soldiers brave like French, German?"

"Ah!" joyously reflected Lemuel. "Here *is* a break! She's goin' to let us join the army." Then aloud: "Sure, brave as they come. Give us a workout, will you?"

Again that evil smile parted the Amazon's vivid lips. "Taloya no understand 'workout.' Captive dogs always get chance to show how brave. Taloya never see Engleesh, Americans die."

LEMUEL'S HOPES went out like a candle in a ninety-mile gale. "Listen," he pleaded, terribly conscious of all that depended on his freedom. "For the love of Mike be reasonable, Miss—

er—Taloya! Harold and me could be lots more use to you alive than dead. Let us—"

Taloya shook her lovely dark head imperiously. "No! Taloya curious. Taloya hurt you very much. Maybe Taloya make very brave Engleesh, American cry before dead? No? Chelata's fetish grow stronger if Taloya no sacrifice."

A frown of irritation creased the dusky girl's brow at the word. "Chelata." Lemuel, desperately intent, noted that the thought seemed to annoy her greatly. She spat resoundingly. "May Chelata rot in bellies of mudfish!"

"Beg pardon, miss," Harold was desperately anxious. " 'Ow about—"

"Be still!" Disdainfully Taloya beckoned half a dozen Amazons, who swiftly subdued the furiously struggling cockney. "Perhaps when American, Engleeshmans dead, then Taloya make fetish talk."

Lemuel wondered at her phrase. What did she mean by "talk"? He dismissed the question with the solution that her faulty English—no doubt picked up from some wandering English derelict—had caused a misuse of the word.

Then followed a nightmarish succession of events which convinced Lemuel that his death was now but a question of minutes. Half a dozen snarling witch-doctors dragged him and Harold to the skull altar, and after removing the slave yokes bound them upon it. Entirely divested of clothes the two lay, one at either side, so pinioned as to be utterly helpless.

The death drums increased their hollow throbbing until even the great bombax trees seemed to quiver with the thunderous reverberation. Like a dark tide the Dahomeyans deserted their outlying camp fires, crowding to see the white men perish for the greater power of the Amazon *caboceer's* fetish.

Abandoning all hope, the helpless Legionnaires' one thought was: How would they perish?

Very swiftly Lemuel learned. A crude wooden tripod was dragged above him and a long French bayonet, held erect by a pair of guiding rings, was poised with its needle-like point exactly over his wildly thudding heart. Lashed to the bayonet handle were two large gourds, one on either side. Above these gourds was suspended a goatskin of water, from which it would trickle into the receptacles on the bayonet handle.

The rows and rows of hideous dark faces chuckled, clucked and grunted. How very ingenious was their *caboceer!* With infinite pleasure they realized that water, trickling from the goatskin into the gourds, would increase the weight on the bayonet's haft with infinite delay, thus slowly—very slowly—urging the needle point downward into the prisoner's heart. Yes, fully half an hour should elapse before the trenchant point reached its target. They laughed like happy children—yes, there would be half an hour of agonized writhing and groaning to delight the audience. After that there still remained the smaller prisoner to be dealt with. Decidedly, the evening's program offered possibilities of genuine entertainment.

On the altar Lemuel lay gazing up into the purple-blue sky where stars as big as walnuts blazed with all that intensity they acquire in the tropics. He'd seen them blaze that way out in the Philippines, in Guatecata, and in South Africa. Well, he would never see them, again, that was a cinch. Lem Frost of the Fighting Fourth Cavalry was about to cash in his checks.

HIS SKIN involuntarily crept at the delicate contact of that needle point. It was going to be a terrible half hour, he knew it; but though the sweat had already broken out on his brow, he vowed to die as became a Legionnaire and an American. He looked about; everywhere were rows of dark, predatory faces; thick lips drawn back in anticipation. How those black bodies stank!

Then his gaze wandered to those two brown gourds on the bayonet handle; when filled with water those little calabashes would cause his death. Just above them dangled the damp and malodorous goatskin water bag—a black and brown goat it had been once. In a minute now one of those outlandishly clay-daubed witch-doctors would puncture it, and the fatal trickles of water would spring forth to make an excruciating end of Colonel Lemuel Z. Frost, late of the Guatecatan Army.

Wood smoke drifted over from the ceremonial fire and filled Lem's nostrils with a pleasant, familiar odor which recalled a thousand camp fires, bivouacs and hearths. Good-by to them all!

That beautiful she-devil Taloya was advancing now, her supple body gleaming like pale, polished bronze in the flickering firelight. Her eyes were hard and bright as that bayonet point poised over his heart.

One last revolt his spirit made against extinction. There *must* be a way to save the fort and all those it protected. But no; his hour had struck.

Taloya swept forward, placed a small, warm hand on his throat and commenced a high, barbaric chant, while the assembled Dahomeyans sank reverently on their faces.

"Layin' the corner stone, Harold," remarked Lemuel cheerfully. "Remember how the governor did it at Oran?"

"Blime!" gasped the other, invisible though a bare eight feet away. " 'Ow can yer joke, Lem?"

"Why not? No use givin' these damn' voodoo devils any more satisfaction than I have to."

As Taloya terminated her votive chant, she signaled a particularly hideous witch-doctor to her side, and with a pointed dagger he made a little incision in the goatskin bag. Instantly a tiny silver trickle of water pattered leisurely into the right hand gourd; and the icy hand of Death fumbled in Lemuel's brain.

It was the beginning of the end. Another nick with the dagger and a second driblet tinkled into the other gourd. Already the bayonet point felt a little heavier. How cold and sharp it was! That devil, Taloya!

For all his will power, Lemuel shuddered while the drops tinkled musically into the gourds. Then, bit by bit, the sting of steel grew sharper and he felt a warm trickle commence to run down his side. The skin of his chest had been pierced.

The evilly beautiful oval of Taloya's face loomed near, and for no explicable reason she suddenly kissed the parted lips of the doomed sergeant.

"Ze kiss of death!" she mocked. "Very poetic. No?"

"The poetry's all right, but the kiss was bum," commented Lemuel, fighting to contain himself. "Let me loose, sister, and I'll teach you what kissin' is really like. You're a rank amatoor. Too bad old Fernando ain't here. He'd open your eyes."

Tink! Tink! Tink! Drop after drop trickled into the gourd.

Cold sweat coursed down the American's cheeks. Harold wrenched futilely at his bonds and cursed the shapely belle with every vile name he could think of.

SUDDENLY TALOYA turned away, darted into the fetish hut and reappeared. A gasp of *"Ee mah ee voo doo koo ee!"* went up. "Worship the fetish!"

Lemuel knew that the Amazon was bringing forth her dread juju, some small object of great superstitious awe. Slowly she advanced, her hips swaying slightly.

"See, O little fetish!" she crooned. "A slave die for you. Speak to Taloya again."

Curiosity gripped the tortured sergeant even as fresh barbs of agony pierced his frame. "Might's well see what I'm being scragged for," he gasped, and turned his head.

When he beheld Taloya's terrible fetish, he burst into a peal of hysterical laughter that startled the forest and those hundreds of fierce two-legged beasts grouped about.

"W'at's so blinkin' funny?" demanded Harold wearily. "Why can't yer die quiet?"

But Lemuel laughed louder and louder with the realization that he and Harold were about to die as offerings to a rather dingy, fifty-cent, mechanical toy pig!

With a shrill snarl of rage, Taloya dropped her fetish, plucked her dagger from its sheath and bounded forward, green eyes murderously aflame.

"Hyena! Pig! Your eyes pay for insult!"

"No! No!" Lemuel cried out sharply. "Don't! If you do, your fetish will never speak again. For I, and I alone, can make it talk!"

"What?" The dagger point flickered a bare half inch from Lemuel's starting, blood-shot eyes. "What, you make Taloya fetish talk?"

"Bet your life." Lemuel was very earnest and emphatic. "I had a fetish like that myself once." He forbore to say that it had been when he was five years old. "I know that kind of fetish from A to Z. The one thing it don't like is white men's blood. No wonder it won't talk to you!" Lemuel was properly indignant.

Deeply suspicious, Taloya nevertheless wavered. "You make fetish talk again?"

"Surest thing you know, sister; only for heaven's sake stop that bayonet before it's too late. It's about got me speared."

Taloya dropped her dagger and with a low cry retrieved the toy, a cheap, tin object painted a glaring pink.

Lemuel felt the blade sink somewhat lower. Would she believe his desperate boast?

Abruptly Taloya sprang forward and wrenched aside the blade. "If American lie, and you no make juju talk," she promised vindictively, "Taloya make you dead three weeks long!"

"In that case," thought Sergeant Lemuel Frost, "I guess I'd better fix that damn' tin pig. Maybe it'll be simpler than those auto rifles at the *poste*."

CHAPTER X

TIN PIG PRIEST

DAWN FOUND LEMUEL still bending over the tin pig. In the still darkness Harold lay blue and shivering on the skull altar. A grim smile parted Lemuel's unshaven lips as, with the point of a dull knife, he tried the mechanism. A painful rattling sound ensued; the pig quivered as though afflicted with St. Vitus's dance, then jerkily opened a very red mouth and would have vented a series of shrill squeaks had not Lemuel abruptly stopped the mechanism. Too good a showman was he to give the play away prematurely.

Again and again he tested the clockwork machinery. Each time it functioned perfectly, thanks to an application of palm oil and the removal of several millimeters of thick red rust from sundry springs and ratchet wheels.

"And now," he thought, "for the big show. We're not out o' the woods by a long sight, but this ought to go a long way towards soothin' sister Taloya's gentle disposition. I wonder if she'll keep her word?"

So saying, Lemuel wiped grease-smeared hands on a discarded *haik,* and holding the rejuvenated pig before him in something the manner of a deacon passing a plate, he approached the doorway.

"Oyez! oyez! oyez!" Lemuel, once arrested as a tramp, had heard that word in court. He had not the least idea of what "oyez" meant, but the bailiff had used it that day and it sounded impressive.

As he made this proclamation several thousand dark eyes became intently fixed upon him; and the foremost were those feline green ones of the Amazon general Taloya.

A mother at the crisis in her child's sickness could not have been more concerned than the Amazon general, who stood, half smiling, half frightened, as Lemuel advanced.

He could feel Corporal Harold Hackbutt's anxious blue eyes upon him and a dreadful fear seared his brain. What if that fateful toy suddenly decided not to work? Supposing some cog slipped?

He looked at the waiting witch-doctors and shuddered; a nice gang of playmates! Yes they could take three weeks to torture a man. The spot where the bayonet had punctured his skin commenced to itch unbearably as he strode forward and, placing the fetish upon its altar, raised both hands to the scarlet, dawn-lit heavens and intoned like a station master calling trains:

"Hash-o-pup-e, tut-hash-i-sus, dud-a-mun-none, tut-hash-i-none-gug, wow-o-rur-kuk-sus!" Lemuel's eyes dreamily sought the tree tops while his deep voice sonorously rolled out the ridiculous incantation.

"W'at the 'eck?" grunted Harold. " 'E must be talkin' Injun."

Lemuel grinned to himself as the words of Tuttanee—that hog-Latin of the American schoolboy—recurred to him. It was all very simple; all he had said was in substance what he very fervently meant: "Hope this damn' thing works!"

It seemed utterly ridiculous that his life and those of several thousand other people depended upon such cheap theatricals. He *must* put over his foolish little fight for life. The effect on most of the audience was all that he had hoped it would be; but the witch-doctors remained lamentably unimpressed, eying him greedily, like hungry dogs.

With great solemnity Lem commenced making passes over the tin pig; then in the midst of a gesture he swiftly pressed a button, and his heart staggered in its beat. Like music sweeter than the sweetest symphony came the *whir-r-r* of clockwork, and the pig commenced to quiver and shiver. It shook more and more until it slid gently back and forth on the level stone top of the altar.

"Aie! Aie! Ee a wee naa koo ah!" A low, resounding moan arose from hundreds of throats. "The god lives!" Taloya stood as though transfixed, her great jade-colored eyes grown simply enormous.

Then, all at once, the lower jaw of the pig opened jerkily, *"Squaa-a-a! Squaa-a-a! Squaa-a-a!"* it squealed.

WITH THE instinct of a born impresario Lemuel at once clipped off the machinery, but the effect had already been obtained. Flat on their faces two thousand black fetish fighters lay shivering. For a long moment Taloya groveled on a level with Lemuel's ponderous Legionnaire's boots, then she sprang up with a rapturous cry and clutched the fetish to the cartridge belt on her shapely bosom; a fetish to which she had no doubt sacrificed several hundreds of human lives!

"Now," she chattered, like a woman who emerges triumphant from a bargain sale, "Taloya fetish greater than Chelata's. Taloya witch-general husban' soon be greater than Chelata white general!"

"What?" Lemuel was completely taken aback. Imagine being married to a little savage like that!

Still stretched naked on the altar, Harold laughed hysterically. "Name the first nipper arter me, won't yer, Lemuel?"

"Shut up!" snarled the sergeant viciously. "I'm damned if I'll... Well, if I'm goin' to be the he-coon of this wigwam, I ain't goin' to stand no impertinence." Lemuel avoided a bad mistake by changing his attitude. More tact and diplomacy were in order.

Suddenly the witch-doctors surged forward. Their faces, barely visible under weird headdress of feathers and monkey fur, were gray with professional jealousy and hatred. In an angry, noisy chorus they eddied about Taloya and the half-naked sergeant. In shrill fury they jabbered, pointing again and again into the white man's face. Lemuel's power over the fetish was evidently a very serious affront, if not an insult, to local talent. The sergeant shrewdly gathered they were insisting on a continuance of the rites so strangely interrupted.

A fairly large proportion of the silent onlookers seemed to incline to the side of the witch-doctors, for they drew to one side, fingering spears and carbines suggestively.

The flamboyant Taloya, however, was not to be daunted. In an access of royal wrath she sprang among the protesting witch-doctors, whirling with truly Amazonian fury a stick snatched from the ground.

"Go!" she panted, when they fled. "Taloya do what Taloya want." Then very tenderly she sidled up to the perplexed and embarrassed sergeant, her large eyes became infinitely soft. "When this war, she over, Taloya and Taloya man take for own upper Dahomey. If Taloya no give you to witch-doctor," she added mischievously, as a gentle reminder of her power of life and death.

Ever the diplomat, Lemuel silently agreed, but groped to find a way out of this tangle of savage intrigue. "If I only knew half as much about women as dear little Fernando's forgot," he mused, "I might be able to get out of this with a whole hide."

"Oh, yes," Taloya was saying dreamily, "after Taloya army take Dahomey, she sweep to sea. Ashanti and Nigeria after. Make big kingdom like zat." The queenly creature made a hoop of her delicately rounded but muscular arms and sighed not a little like Alexander as he dreamed of new worlds to conquer.

"SHE'S A doe Napoleon—some little go-getter," decided Lemuel. "Yep, a climber is little Taloya. A kingdom, eh? Always on the make... Wonder how we can use that ambition in our business?

"Listen, sister," he suggested aloud, "let's you and me mosey into the shanty yonder and have a good old heart-to-heart talk. If you and me are goin' into partnership business, we'll have to understand each other."

It was clear that Taloya did not catch all he had said, but the partnership idea she seized upon eagerly. An arch smile curved her full red lips and she unmistakably bridled as Lemuel strode to the door.

"You be Taloya general, no?"

"Sure!" grinned Lemuel. "O.K., but first—who's the hombre?"

"Hombre? No un'erstand."

"The boy your friend Chelata's got."

The fair face darkened at the name. "Taloya not know. Chelata—may spotted jackal tear her—she *caboceer* of Green Snake Division. Zat division attack *poste* last night. Me too far back." Taloya sighed and frowned regretfully.

Unmistakably she resented that she had not been able to join in the assault on the *poste*. "Chelata think Chelata beautiful, great fighter. No!" Taloya smote herself on the breast. "Taloya greater, Taloya she got fetish bigger!"

"Look a here, Susie," Lem suggested, with a slow smile on his haggard, unshaven features. "You say Chelata's fetish got stronger medicine than yours?"

"Was, but no more! Taloya's fetish talk again. Some day soon Chelata die—sacrifice, un'erstand?"

"Yep! But before you start lockin' horns, supposin' you let me see this white general o' Chelata's. Maybe my magic's got more kick than his, maybe not. Anyhow, you've got to see her if your two divisions are goin' to work together."

"Bah! For Chelata general Taloya cares zat!" The charming little lady pursed up her vivid lips and spat viciously and quite accurately through the doorway.

"O.K., Susie, but allee samee we really oughta drop over to Chelata's camp in the morning and take a look at this here hombre you was talkin' about."

Taloya frowned, hesitated, digging the earth with a pink big toe. Then her eyes fell on the rejuvenated fetish. "Taloya can do. Taloya general come too."

From outside came the rumble of many angry voices. Lemuel wondered greatly whether Taloya's strong will could offset the evil power of the jealous witch-doctors.

CHAPTER XI

TRAITOR

LEMUEL WAS AWAKENED long before dawn by the arrival of a brutal-featured messenger, who wore a white fez tastefully garnished with a blue elephant—emblem of the great Glégle's personal guard. Immediately Taloya sprang from the bare ground where she had unconcernedly stretched herself and, taking the runner by the arm, led him outside.

*"I'll have the whole outfit under my
thumb," the renegade informed him.*

"Your would-be bride don't trust yer much," sleepily grunted
Harold from the corner where he squatted upright and fought
off several varieties of voracious insects. "I thought 'usband and
wife 'ad no secrets."

The sergeant glared. "Thinkin' wrong, as usual. But you
couldn't expect her not to; she's too canny a gal. O' course that
runner's bringin' old Gléglé's instructions for the advance. God
help the boys at the *poste* if these divisions attack to-day! I
wonder where the gay and giddy Fernando is?—if he ain't been
scragged for the greater glory o' some nigger's fetish."

"You'll never find 'im." Despite the fact that, like Lemuel,
he had recovered his clothes, Harold felt very low. "W'at's your
little game, Lem? Do yer suppose yer could make a dicker wiv
this white general o' Chelata's? Wonder who 'e is?"

"Some Portuguese or Spanish renegade, most likely. At the
same time I got a queer hunch Br'er Daggett's still up and votin'.
He's the ornery kind of a snake that lives forever."

Harold sneezed as a gnat crawled into his nose, and his form,
clad in soiled white breeches and no less grimy undershirt,
looked very small in its corner.

"Wonder w'at's goin' to 'appen to us?"

"Plenty," promised Lemuel, "if we don't guess right. But I got a cute little idea I'm goin' to work on. It just might work."

"W'at is it?"

"You'll see, son, if you live long enough—which don't seem too likely with them witch-doctors snarlin' round the door."

"Garn! You're a nice cheerful bloke, ain't yer?"

DURING A brief march through the dew-soaked jungle toward Chelata's camp Lemuel proved himself an apt pupil of a certain Machiavelli, and cast all scruples overboard.

When the column was within five hundred yards of Chelata's camp, Lemuel suggested that he be given an escort and sent ahead as herald. This procedure, he skillfully pointed out, would enhance Taloya's prestige.

"No!" she cried, clinging to the gaunt sergeant's arm. "No. Zey kill."

"Don't worry, Susie, they won't kill little Lemuel. I'll just mosey in and see how the land lies."

"Quick, zen! King, him come zis morning."

At this bit of news Lemuel had a sense of shock. So Gléglé *was* coming on the scene, after all, and very soon! His arrival would stop all chances of carrying out Lemuel's elaborately evolved scheme. Still, there just might be time.

Armed with his own pistol and marching in the midst of a powerful escort of Taloya's Blue Crocodile Amazons, the American hailed the pickets of Chelata's Green Snake Division, and a few minutes later was ushered into the presence of another eagle-eyed *caboceer* of Amazons.

Chelata proved to be a savage-looking mulatto, several shades darker than her rival, and though far better-looking than the average of her followers, was by no means comparable with Taloya in either face or figure.

Scowling and ominously fingering a long-bladed *coup-coup*, she listened to a message from Taloya sent by word of mouth. One of Taloya's Amazon sub-officers repeated in verbatim.

With rising fury Chelata listened, a leopard skin flung over her powerful limbs quivering with the intensity of her indignation.

"Seems as 'ow it's bad news," remarked Harold. "We're about as welcome as a judge in Lime'ouse."

Chelata clapped her hands suddenly, and immediately from outside of the hut came the sound of many voices. Chelata's Amazons closed in together, whereat Lemuel, with the prompt dispatch of a man who lives by the trade of arms, instantly presented a pistol at Chelata's tumultuously heaving breast.

"None o' that," he growled, "We're ambassadors."

Although the lowering *caboceer* obviously understood not a word of English, yet the threat of Lemuel's presented pistol spoke in no uncertain terms. Sulkily and with her yellowish eyes angrily agleam, Chelata shouted an order through the door which sent her eager retainers back to their posts.

THEN SOMETHING happened which surprised the astute and watchful Lemuel far less than might have been expected. From the shadows of the adjoining room stalked a tall white man clad exactly like Lemuel and his small companion.

Fernando Daggett was thunderstruck to discover Sergeant Lemuel Frost standing in the *caboceer's* antechamber, armed and at the head of a detachment of exceedingly grim-looking Amazons. But he recovered his composure quickly and smiled.

"Well, if it isn't the Yank! Nice day, eh what?"

Lemuel choked down a stinging remark and nodded instead. Now was the time for diplomacy and lots of it. Death waited ready at his elbow. His first mistake would be his last.

"Does that gal understand English?" he inquired with a brief movement of his eyes in Chelata's direction.

Daggett's dark, shapely head indicated the negative. "No, only Portuguese, and third rate Portuguese at that." Daggett had been given a chance to wash, and looked almost debonair beside the battered two. "Fancy meeting you here, old thing. Have you gone native? I thought you were too good for that sort of thing."

A faint flush crept into Lemuel's cheek, but he managed a grin. "Same as yourself, it was a case of goin' native or bein' chopped. How do you like it here?"

Fernando Daggett pulled a black cigarette from the top of the *képi* he still retained. "Not so bad," he admitted smoothly. "This charming little lady here seems to have taken a fancy to me. Can't imagine why..." But for all his words, the worthy Daggett's tone implied that there was really nothing unusual in that. "Have a cigarette?"

"Thanks. You're lucky... Listen," Lemuel stepped close under pretext of taking a cigarette, "I suppose you know we're all one jump ahead o' the bone yard—and a mighty short jump at that?"

"Speak for yourself, my dear Colonel Frost. The charming Chelata and I get along beautifully. In fact, I'm rather beginning to fancy life here."

The unshaven, hollow-eyed sergeant struggled hard to contain himself. "What? You *like* livin' with all these damned, murderin' black Amazons?"

Daggett's dark eyes, insolently cool, met the American's. "Here I find plenty to eat, plenty to drink, plenty of amusement." His thumb indicated a compartment behind. "Back there are ten slaves who are ready to do anything I tell them. The Legion doesn't begin to offer such attractions, does it? Of course not, my dear fellow. Very shortly I'll have this whole outfit under my thumb. Then with a little well-regulated raiding here and there, and I'll be rich."

Black despair filled the American's soul; here was an angle he had not foreseen. He had expected to find Daggett eager to escape.

"Yes, I know," he objected, "but how about the boys back at the *poste?*"

Daggett's beautiful teeth shone briefly under his neat black mustache. "What do they mean to me?"

"Why, they're white men—your buddies, pals, *copains.*"

"Are they? A pack of mangy toughs, the scrapings of Europe's jails; to let them die is good riddance." Daggett's tone was utterly cool and matter-of-fact, as he puffed carelessly at his cigarette. "They're paid for risking their lives. Besides, what could I do to help them?"

"A lot." Desperately intent, Lemuel stepped closer. "Listen; you're the only man in this part of Africa who knows how to assemble those Madsen auto rifles. Without 'em our boys won't last as long as a snowball on a hot shovel, when this gang o' savages hits 'em."

"Too bad," grinned Fernando Daggett. "As I observed just now, Legionnaires are paid to get killed. Do you think I'm going to throw away my standing here and risk my life in getting back to Kouande to be court-martialled and perhaps shot for desertion? Come, now—back in Guatecata I saw signs of intelligence in you, my dear Colonel Frost. Please don't talk rot."

Lemuel stood in an unhappy daze. Colossal as had been the handicaps he had encountered up to this point, it needed just this final blow to make them quite overwhelming.

"But—but—" he stammered with outspread hands. "For God's sake listen, Daggett. You're white, and you're not goin' to let your buddies be butchered by this gang o' black devils, are you?"

The tall cross-breed blew a ring of smoke into the thatch just above his head. "I'm afraid so, my dear Lemuel. In this hard world every man has to look out for himself."

FIERCE FIRES blazed in the American's gray eyes; that any man with any pretensions to decency could so calmly contemplate the appealing massacre of fellow soldiers was unthinkable. But Daggett was clearly determined; so, deep in his shrewd Yankee brain, Lemuel plotted.

"Listen," he said hoarsely; "I'll promise that the charges against you at the *poste* will be dropped. If you come back, Van Droon 'll undoubtedly recommend you for the *Médaille* and promotion."

"The *Médaille?* A pretty piece of tinware worth five francs at the outside," sneered Daggett. "No, you're wasting your breath, Frost. If you'd the sense of a gnat you'd see we don't stand a ghost of a chance of getting back. Besides, I won't go back. You're crazy to think of it. Why should I go back?" he demanded. "I'm in soft here, with the pick of the Dahomeyan Amazons for my own. You saw her. A tidy wench, eh what?"

"Best-lookin'?" Lemuel's tone became honeyed.

"Yes. There's no one can hold a candle to my little Chelata."

"Yeah? I'll tell you right now, you're cock-eyed, Mister Daggett! There's a gal not five hundred yards from this spot who makes your little Miss Chelata look like a scrubwoman's stepchild."

The cigarette butt twitched between Daggett's well formed lips, and a new gleam, plainly sensual, crept into his large eyes.

"Indeed?"

"Just what I said. I got a better-lookin' gal who'll be here before long." Lemuel pulled off his *képi* and scratched his dark, tangled hair. "You're a brainy boy, Daggett... I been thinkin', and say—maybe you're right."

"About what?" demanded the big man suspiciously.

"About not goin' back to the *poste*." Lemuel sank onto a wooden bench and rested with elbows on knees. "I guess maybe you're right; we wouldn't stand much chance of ever reachin' Kouande."

"Beginning to see daylight, eh?" Daggett's voice lost some of its hostility. "Why, listen, you big idiot, the two of us with our knowledge of tactics and military science could control this part of the world like our own back yard. What do these bally creatures know about generalship, fighting and modern weapons?"

"Not a whole lot," admitted Lemuel a little doubtfully. "Still—"

"Still, nothing! I tell you, Frost, here's the chance of a lifetime!" Daggett's voice took on a persuasive, emphatic ring and he stepped closer. For all this callous willingness to let the Legionnaires at the *poste* perish, the thought of living a sole white man in a nation of blacks could not have been very appealing. "How about it?"

"There's somethin' in it," muttered Lemuel. "I'll think it over. Anyhow, I've got to report back to the outfit that captured me. Are you comin' along to give that gal the once-over? She'd make a lot of Ziegfeld's gals look like laundresses after a hard day at the tubs."

Chelata, still frowning and suspicious, reappeared at that moment, and Daggett explained to her in hurried Portuguese that out of courtesy he himself would escort the visiting *caboceer* into camp. For a moment Lemuel thought that a harsh refusal would follow, but he underestimated Daggett's already powerful influence with his tigerish captor.

After a perfunctory protest Chelata weakened, then nodded. A liquid softness was in her amber-hued eyes and she heaved an entirely feminine sigh when Daggett saluted carelessly and sauntered off, his wide shoulders swaying beneath the ragged remnants of what had once been a shirt.

CHAPTER XII

A KING IS HERALDED

TOGETHER, THE THREE Legionnaires started back to that spot where Taloya would be waiting with ill-concealed impatience. Lemuel suddenly noticed that Harold had not spoken in a long time.

"What's eatin' you, son?"

"Ah, shut up!" snarled the little Englishman furiously, and his scanty hair gleamed red in the morning sun. "You're a lily-livered turncoat." The small blue eyes fairly blazed contempt, and Harold spat copiously. "Turning native, are yer? You and Daggett."

Lemuel's sunburned body stiffened and his huge tattooed

fists balled themselves omniously. "You damned little squirt!" he snarled. "You ought to thank me for gettin' you out o' that death-trap of a *poste!*"

"Thank yer for nothin', Mister Traitor!" rasped the cockney. "A fine specimen of American gentleman yer are, goin' back on yer mates!"

"Don't be a fool." The big sergeant's tone was icy. "What chance would we stand o' gettin' back to Kouande? What if we did? Glégle's got twenty thousand men"—Lemuel chose the figure at random—"and he'll just nacherally swamp that mud fort."

Harold, true to his lights, refused to be mollified. "All right!" he snapped. "Say w'at yer wants to, but 'Arold 'Ackbutt's only 'ere because 'e's a prisoner. I'm tellin' yer both—yer dirty renegades! First chance I gets I'm goin' to escape!"

Daggett threw back his big handsome head and laughed pityingly. "Go ahead, my dear Hackbutt, by all means run away—and see how far you get! I shouldn't be surprised but some ignorant native could use that head of yours, ugly as it is, in front of his fetish hut."

Growling, but far too practical to buck a situation which was overwhelmingly against him, the small Legionnaire tramped onward through the jungle, glowering straight ahead while the vivid vines and blossoms parted about his narrow shoulders like so many huge butterflies.

Presently the three Legionnaires, surrounded by Taloya's escort, reappeared in the glade where Lemuel had left the *caboceer* of the Blue Crocodile corps.

By some theatrical whim of nature it chanced that a sunbeam, piercing the thick tangle of bombax leaves, came streaking through the gloom of the forest like a golden shaft to illume the supple, ivory-tinted form of Taloya, delicately emphasizing every graceful curve and giving to her tawny skin a strange golden radiance. The *caboceer* stood with shapely legs braced apart, a slender, ivory-hilted scimitar in her hand. She was testing the quality of the steel as a fencing master tests a foil. Finding the blade of good quality, Taloya threw back her head and laughed just as the embassy, with Daggett at its head, came into sight.

"*Dios!*" The big deserter halted as though a bullet had hit him. Struck dumb, he stood in a curious gesture of arrested motion, one hand grasping a scarlet creeper, the other hand extended toward the pagan beauty.

Then the chatter of the Amazon guards arose loudly, attracting the superb creature's attention. Taloya looked upward, and for the first time her eyes met the dark, glowing ones of Fernando Daggett. Something seemed to pass between them on that glance; they stared a long minute quite motionless, oblivious of all save each other.

With grim satisfaction Lemuel watched Daggett, confident, powerful and easy-motioned as a champion boxer, stride boldly forward into the patch of sunlight which pierced Taloya's barbaric and martial array like a finger of gold.

"What a swell-lookin' guy that rotter is," muttered the American. "No wonder the gals fall for him!"

WITH HIS *képi* set at an insolent cant on curling, blue-black hair, Fernando Daggett advanced straight toward the *caboceer* as though mesmerized by that strange Amazon's appeal. Halting some five feet away, he raised his hand in salute.

"You Chelata general?" demanded the Amazon with a curious quaver in her slightly husky voice.

"Yes—for the present." Daggett's full, well-formed lips parted in a winning, trust-inspiring smile. His tone, thought Lemuel, clearly implied that although he was Chelata's general now, he might very readily become Taloya's.

"Well, here goes." Realizing that he was delivering himself into his enemy's power, the big bronzed American then did a peculiar thing. He stalked forward into the glade and, dropping awkwardly on one knee, seized the renegade Daggett's hand and humbly kissed it, hiding his writhing grimace.

Harold, in the background, uttered a strangled oath. "Strike me pink if Lemuel ain't 'eaded for the funny farm! W'at for does he want to do that? Now 'e's ruined 'imself proper!"

Deliberately Lemuel rose and addressed Taloya: "Here, O Taloya, is a general whose power is greater than mine. With this general to help you, Taloya's fetish will become the strongest in all Africa. Any other fetish"—he paused significantly on the word—"will be like dust before it."

"I say, Frost..." Daggett seemed vaguely alarmed; he by no means knew what lay back of Lemuel's surprising admission of defeat. What was this Yankee's game? He left the question unanswered as he realized that the American had surrendered whatever influence he'd had with this dashed good-looking *caboceer*. The poor fool! Frost had publicly admitted that Daggett's influence was greater than his own! Well, he'd need Frost a while, but after this campaign was over he'd dispose of him and that quaint little cockney by the lifting of a finger. Daggett grinned. What a fool the American was!

Lemuel stood silent a moment, wondering whether his play had failed or not. At last he caught a calculating gleam in Taloya's eyes as she held forth her hand to Daggett and said:

"You help Taloya?"

"Charmed, my dear lady." Yielding to the theatrical sense of his mother's people. Fernando Daggett executed a bow that would have done credit to a Seventeenth Century gallant and swept the twigs at Taloya's small bare feet with his heavy Legionnaire's *képi*.

Taloya looked about joyfully. "Now we go see Chelata—may vultures crack her bones!" Then, as her eye lit upon Lemuel, her lip curled cruelly. "You get back there, slave man. Maybe witch-doctor get you now. How you like?"

There was nothing subtle about the Amazon's methods. This new white man was more powerful than the one who had breathed new life into her fetish. Had the first one not acknowledged the fact himself? Of a truth her fetish was working potently once more. Turning, Taloya cast a loving eye on the tin pig, while the witch-doctor who carried it glowered speculatively on Lemuel as though to say, "Pretty soon we'll get you."

TWENTY MINUTES later Lemuel's heart was beating quicker; the fatal hour of crisis was very near at hand. Glaring balefully at each other, Chelata and Taloya were standing face to face. Between them panted a messenger from Gléglé, announcing his immediate approach.

With this news the American's breath stopped. Damn! If Gléglé appeared, he'd ruin everything. In quick action lay the only chance of saving Kouande! Deliberately Lemuel molded the situation to a swift climax.

Her breast ornaments heaving tumultuously, Chelata stood gazing furiously upon her more lovely rival. At first glance she had understood the catastrophe which had befallen her. She had lost Daggett. Chelata's tawny eyes glittered in their rage like those of an animal seen by the light of a camp fire.

Taloya, insolent in her ascendancy, stepped forward with her small, bare feet moving noiselessly over the brilliant green carpet of the primeval African forest.

Daggett stood on the alert. He knew enough of womankind to realize that a savage clash impended, and shivered with the thought that at that instant Chelata or Chelata's followers would gladly have slaughtered him. There was no help for him if Taloya lost the battle!

Quick action! Lemuel, spying Chelata's fetish a few yards in the rear, sprang forward.

"Listen, Taloya, I put life in your fetish; and since you've treated us so well, I'll kill Chelata's. You'll be the boss then."

His ragged shirt fluttering, Lemuel sprang past the startled Taloya, caught up a glowing ball of red glass which was Chelata's fetish, and dashed it violently to earth.

A deep, horrified groan went up to the lofty branches as the gaudy bit of glass shattered into a thousand winking pieces. Chelata swayed and turned as pale as her complexion permitted, while the Mannlicher carbine slipped from her nerveless fingers, partially burying its barrel in the rich, black soil at her feet.

From the Amazons of her Green Snake Division arose a terrible shriek of mingled fear and rage. Even Taloya seemed stunned and taken aback, and when a dozen spears and rifles were raised to kill the American she hesitated for an appreciable moment.

Lemuel's face was hard as granite. Would she let him be killed? He could see Daggett grinning faintly as though to say, "This Yankee fool must want to commit suicide."

BUT TALOYA, swift as the leopardess whose skin she wore, leaped forward, small hand imperiously pointed between her rival's eyes. "Down!" she commanded in a strident voice that was as harsh as a peacock's cry. "Down! Chelata fetish dead! Taloya juju alive. Down on ground before Taloya."

Such was the might of superstition that instant obedience followed, and Chelata flung herself, sobbing with fear and hate, at the feet of her rival.

With cold, unutterable contempt Taloya eyed the writhing woman, then stooped and with a vicious jerk snatched the bandolier of cartridges from her rival's shoulders.

"Go!" she hissed. "You no more man.* Go back to villages and make children. You *woman.* Go!"

It was a terrific moment. The Amazons of both divisions, as Lemuel had astutely calculated they would, stood eying each other askance and poised to do battle. He fully realized that everything depended on Chelata's reaction to this overwhelming insult; one word from her and the second division, two thousand strong, would hurl itself forward to wash out the affront in blood.

Racked by uncertainty Lemuel watched, carefully measuring the distance to that spot where Daggett stood. From the tail of his eye he caught Harold's attention and winked desperately.

The breathless seconds continued. With savage delight

---

* The Dahomeyan Amazons believed they had changed their sex.

Taloya spurned her fallen rival with a small brown foot while Daggett stood nervously to one side, his pistol half drawn. The witch-doctors of both sides eyed each other like jackals.

When Taloya's heel ground her face into the dirt, Chelata stiffened. Lemuel braced himself for the crash of musketry. Eternal seconds dragged by. He riveted his eyes on Chelata as she half rose, a terrible expression on her face. Success? Perhaps! Lemuel hovered between hope and despair; then Chelata's streaming eyes fell upon the shattered remains of her fetish, and to defeat Lem's purpose completely, relaxed once more with a hollow groan.

"Heck! That female ain't got a mite o' spunk," growled the American wrathfully. "That's torn it for fair! I ought to 'a' known superstition 'd lick her."

He felt sick, utterly discouraged. The outburst he had counted on had failed to materialize, and the events he had heretofore controlled began to slip through his fingers like quicksilver.

Who'd have thought that a woman who would fight as Chelata had during the surprise attack on the *poste*, would curl up and quit like a whipped kitten because a Christmas tree ornament of red glass had been broken? It was fantastic, incredible! Yet it was so.

With increasing alarm, Lemuel realized the gravity of his position. He had earned the enmity of Taloya's witch-doctors by restoring life to the tin pig. He had gained the undying hatred of Chelata's partisans by ruthlessly destroying her fetish. And to cap it all, he had deliberately set up his old enemy Daggett in a dominant position. Even Harold hated him for a renegade.

"As a diplomat," he concluded bitterly, "I make a fine gas fitter!"

In swift succession further ghastly results of his awkward plotting presented themselves. The *poste* at Kouande was now doubly doomed! United under one head, the Amazon divisions would be just twice as powerful and effective. At any moment now Gléglé would arrive and the entire Dahomeyan force would sweep forward, eager for the massacre to commence. More white heads for the fetish groves!

Like a man helpless in the grip of a rapid and nearing a fatal whirlpool, Lemuel's shrewd New England brain struggled madly to evolve some scheme, some means of thwarting the awful disaster.

CHAPTER XIII

STORM BREAKS

DEEP IN THE jungle there arose a dull, insistent rumble, and a fresh pang of despair seized the sergeant's heart. They were the war drums of Gléglé!

He sighed; the game was up. Exasperating especially, because some moments back he had noted a familiar face among the few female warriors present. It belonged to a half-breed Fulah who, in normal times, dwelt in the mud and thatch village outside the *poste*. Nomeh was the rascal's name, if Lemuel remembered accurately. At the point of a gun Nomeh might have been persuaded to show the way back to Kouande. Now, bitterly mused the American, there would be no need of the half-breed's services.

"W'at for did yer wink at me?" Harold had sidled quietly through the crowd of palm-oil-anointed Amazons.

It was the spur Lemuel needed: Never say die! How he'd manage to carry on he'd no idea—but he must!

"I want you to catch a buck black over there," he whispered from the side of his mouth. "Remember that Nomeh boy who lived in the hut next to the head man at Kouande?"

"Yes."

"Well, he's yonder; keep an eye on him."

Then, with the amazing suddenness and brilliance of a star shell bursting on a stormy night, came an inspiration; but

Lemuel shivered at the thought of what would happen should he fail.

"Watch that man Nomeh, Harold," he snapped. "When the ruckus starts take him into the bush to that big ebony yonder." The American's bloodshot, anxious eyes flitted to a stately tree some fifty yards distant, towering above the surrounding vegetation like a grenadier above a congregation of dwarfs.

"There's agoin' to be a rumpus. As soon as the first gun cracks you catch that Nomeh. It 'll be your neck and a terrible death if you lose him."

Harold's golden teeth glimmered in the steady, tight little smile. "Count on me, Lem, 'e'll be there! And, Lem, I'm sorry I mistook yer back there."

But Lemuel, his tattered garments fluttering weirdly, was already at Taloya's side. "Listen, Susie," he suggested with infinite guile, "you've got Chelata's gang on the run. All you need now to get her division roped, branded and hog-tied is to give 'em a little demonstration o' your fetish. Let it talk turkey to 'em; then *you'll* be the ward boss o' this neck o' the woods, and no mistake!"

"Righto!" smiled Daggett. "The bally Yank is right. Give the Green Snakes a knockout punch while they're still groggy."

Lemuel's lean head inclined and his eyes were very quiet and bright beneath the *képi's* scratched visor. "All right, Daggett, you come along, and be the presidin' officer. You'd better, since you're the old he-coon of this outfit now. Do some hocus-pocus and look handsome, while I wind up this toy."

AT THE opening of the ceremony, Taloya spoke briefly in Ewe—the Dahomeyan language—no doubt extolling the might and beauty of her fetish; while her witch-doctors, though green with envy, dutifully shook their gourd rattles and muttered curious little bird-like chirrups.

It was not by chance that as he strode to the altar Lemuel quietly unbuttoned the flap of the holster of his pistol, which

Taloya had considerately returned to him before he fell into disrepute.

A deep, awed silence fell upon the hundreds of fierce-eyed Amazons crowding the little glade. Thousands of eyes followed Lemuel and Daggett when, straight as though on parade, they marched to the little portable altar upon which rested Taloya's apparently invincible fetish.

"Now make this stagy," instructed Lemuel in an undertone. "See that little button under the pig's belly? Press that; it sets the mechanism goin'. I'll have to wind it up first. When I slip it to you, put your hand over it and say some kind of hocus-pocus gibberish—understand?"

"Right-o!" Fernando's expressive dark eyes were agleam with pleasure. Decidedly things were going better than he ever dared hope. What a blundering genius this idiot of an American was!

"Talk to 'em," snapped Lemuel. "Keep 'em busy a minute!"

His fingers closed on the winding key and tested the cool little strip of metal. Funny! It almost made him laugh to think that on that key depended the life or death of ten thousand human beings. He turned the key once, felt the spring tighten. He turned it again, his fingers whitening to meet the increased resistance. Then he drew a deep breath and cast his life into the scales of Fate. He gave the winding spring one more turn and deliberately *broke the main spring*.

"That damn' thing will never run again," he reflected, as he signalled Daggett back.

The big deserter made a wide theatrical gesture with his powerful arms while Lemuel stepped back a pace or two, eyes narrowed to mere slits and hand creeping to his pistol butt. Carefully, the sergeant measured the distance to that dense thicket.

"All right," he muttered hoarsely. "Let her go, Daggett."

Daggett leaned forward, every eye in the glade upon him. Taloya stood to one side, barbaric, lovely and triumphant.

Stripped of her arms was Chelata, cowering on her knees to one side.

SLOWLY DAGGETT'S fingers groped toward the catch. He pressed it. The pig gave a starting shudder! Lemuel's heart bounded. What if that accursed thing worked, after all? An icy rivulet coursed down his spine. But beyond that preliminary tremble, the tin pig remained motionless, staring on the sea of savage dark faces with stupid, glassy eyes.

"Make fetish speak!" hissed Taloya, her eyes enormous with a sudden fear.

Daggett pressed the button frantically, but the pig remained quite silent and motionless.

Chelata was watching, a murderous light in her eyes. So, perhaps Taloya's fetish was not so potent after all! She gathered herself.

Like the first whisper of a storm among the leaves of a forest came an ominous growl from the Amazons of the Green Snake Division. Even if the power of Chelata's fetish was broken, it now appeared that Taloya's was no better! Muscular hands crept tighter about spear hafts, and the soft click of many gun hammers being drawn back sounded clearly in the glade. Murder trembled in the sultry air.

As Daggett shook the pig in frantic desperation, Lemuel tensed himself like a sprinter waiting the gun. Taloya stood like one transfixed, a stunned expression upon her face as Chelata, venting the shriek of a furious jungle cat, sprang to her feet and snatched a *coup-coup* from the nearest of her retainers.

Then the storm broke. A gale of shrill shouts split the air, rifles barked and spears flickered like rays of light, while the *zwe-e-e-e-p* of swiftly drawn daggers and swords promised sudden death.

"This way! Quick, Daggett! For your life!"

Lemuel gripped the dumfounded cross-breed by the arm, and lashing out savagely with his pistol butt, forced a way through the disconcerted struggling mass of Blue Crocodile Amazons now rallying to protect Taloya.

Terrible were the cries that rose as the two divisions became locked in a grim, furious struggle. As though possessed of demons, Chelata was urging her fierce partisans on, with the memory of the theft of Daggett rankling like liquid fire. Taloya was fighting desperately to regain her lost ascendancy.

The two Legionnaires were terribly hard pressed, for a swarm of witch-doctors, unerringly detecting the source of the quarrel, came charging up, screaming like demons.

"Shoot!" panted Lemuel, firing full at a howling demoniac figure that brandished a gleaming scimitar. *Crack!* Up flew the sorcerer's arms as he pitched forward coughing blood.

Daggett's pistol barked again and again; while the American, delivering his shots to best advantage, dropped three or four foolhardy witch-doctors who tried to cut off his retreat into the friendly thicket. *Crack! Crack!* White-daubed black bodies dropped convulsively.

A way was almost clear now through the seething mass of combatants. Five yards more! Lemuel had fired five shots and Daggett as many, if Lemuel had counted aright. From behind arose an indescribable pandemonium and the thunder of many kettledrums. Gléglé with his warriors was arriving upon the scene!

Like a vision in a nightmare Lemuel beheld a huge, frothing witch-doctor come racing forward. "Shoot him!" panted the American. Daggett instantly obeyed, and thus quite emptied his pistol of cartridges while Lemuel, with admirable fore-sight, retained one last shot for the possible benefit of a certain deserter called Fernando Daggett.

Even as the ragged Legionnaires plunged into the sheltering thickness of the jungle, the uproar of conflict commenced to wane perceptibly. Lemuel shrewdly guessed that Gléglé's forces were now engaged in beating the infuriated Amazons apart.

"Come!" he snapped. "If they catch us now, we'll die by inches."

"Hell, no! I'm going back. We can't get away—our only

chance is to bluff!" Daggett hesitated; but promptly the muzzle of the American's pistol was jammed between his ribs.

"Come on, you swine! You're goin' back to the *poste* or die on the way. Git!"

And Fernando Daggett got, as a man must when the barrel of a pistol held by a determined hand bores into the small of his back.

Breathless, Lemuel and his prisoner arrived at the base of the great ebony tree, there to find Harold wild-eyed and menacing an exceedingly pained and surprised native. The native was Nomeh, the man who probably knew his way back to Kouande.

THE HEADLONG, death-dogged flight through the jungle that ensued remained forever fixed as a hideous nightmare in Lemuel's memory. The former one was as nothing compared to it, for now he and his companions were wanted as escaped prisoners, fetish defilers, and tricksters of the king's *caboceers.* Their fate, if they were captured, passed imagining.

First of all ran Nomeh, a black wraith fearfully picking a path through swamps, lowlands and tangled forests with Harold, grimly intent, levelling a pistol at his back. Daggett followed, cold with fury, wild-eyed and clad in the tatters of his uniform. Last of all ran Lemuel, ever peering anxiously back over his scratched and thorn-torn shoulder, listening intently to the fiendish yells and shouts echoing in the jungle behind.

Twice he gained precious time by confusing the trails with elaborate loops and figure eights, but always the ebony fetish fighters found the right track again and bounded on with renewed speed and fury.

Spent, cruelly lacerated by thorns and brambles, the three white men and their unwilling guide were puzzled after two hours' flight to hear the sounds of pursuit abruptly die away.

"Why?" sternly demanded Lemuel of the gasping and wide-eyed Nomeh.

"Fort near."

It appeared on further inquiry that the *poste* was now but

a scant half kilometer away, invisible of course because of the overwhelming denseness of the jungle.

"Safe!" gasped Harold joyously, displaying all his golden teeth.

"Safe, heck!" Daggett's dark, sweat-streamed countenance contorted itself into a furious scarlet mask. "Safe, nothing! That *poste* can't possibly be held even if your crazy American friend does think so. Seventy or eighty men and four automatic rifles hold out against ten or twelve thousand fanatics? He's mad. We'll go under at the first attack, and then—" his large dark eyes, smoldering with hatred, came to rest on Lemuel's gaunt visage; "and then this bright boy's clever plotting will get us the death a yellow dog doesn't deserve! I'm going to shoot myself when the *poste* falls."

"Yeah?" Green flames shone in Lemuel's eyes. "That ain't a bad idea. But before you shoot yourself, Mr. Renegade, you're goin' to put them automatic rifles together, if I have to use hot irons to make you do it!"

Daggett started to his feet, quivering hands outstretched. He hesitated when Lemuel made no motion to raise his pistol, but squatted, gazing up from beneath his tangled hair.

"Go ahead!" he invited between heavy breaths. "Go back to your black friends and see what kind of reception you'll get."

Daggett swayed uncertain, a blank look in his eye. "You're not so dumb, Yank, I'm beginning to think."

There came a derisive snort from the cockney. "Oh, yer just found that out, eh? Just wait—Lem 'll fix those she-devils up for good and all."

Daggett spat contemptuously and wiped his brow with the remains of his shirt sleeve. "Listen, you silly little cockney fool; Napoleon himself couldn't win against fighters like Gléglé's. They're one hundred to one against us. Get one thing through your silly little head: these are born and bred fighters, the best in all West Africa. The wildest Fuzzy Wuzzys you've ever heard of are like lambs compared to 'em."

And Lemuel, wiping the sweat from his forehead, had to

admit that the charming Mr. Daggett was quite right in one respect. The fort was dreadfully far from secure, even now. He'd never imagined Glégle had such a numerous, well-equipped army. Maybe Van Droon had been right, after all, and it would be best to abandon the fort.

Wouldn't old Van Droon be surprised to see 'em back again! Then for the first time he remembered the adjutant's promise; he wondered if the Dutchman would be small-souled enough to carry out his threat of punishment for Lem's disobeying his command to stay on the trail.

"Well, we'll see," he muttered, as the four rose to scramble through the last jungle barrier separating them from Kouande.

CHAPTER XIV

A COMPANY WITHOUT HOPE

OF FINDING THE garrison cheerful, Sergeant Lemuel Frost had not the least expectation; but he was totally unprepared to meet the deep and hopeless dejection in which the remnant of the Legionnaires were plunged.

Van Droon, he learned, had become delirious from his head wound soon after the reconnaissance party had left, and was now dying by inches of a combination of fever and blood-poisoning. Poor devil! That would account for his wild behavior on assuming command.

"Thank God, you have returned," sighed Corporal Marnier on whose shoulders had fallen the unwelcome responsibility of command. "No sergeants, no good corporals, the morale hopelessly undermined—I'm at my wit's end, I'll admit it. Every hour come fresh reports of Glégle's overwhelming power and numbers. Three poor fools deserted during the night; their bodies, or rather parts of their bodies, were thrown over the gate at dawn. Yes, *mon cher sergent,* Antoine Marnier is glad you are back."

Lemuel heaved a deep sigh. His long bruised body as well as his brain and his nerve was weary to the point of breaking. Iron-limbed and lion-hearted though he was, the fearful strain of the past twenty-four hours had been terrific; yet he merely nodded and beckoned to two Legionnaires.

"Dominguez and Tezloff! Throw some starch into your worthless backs and report here. Quick!"

Sullenly, the two Legionnaires shuffled near, their eyes furtive and rebellious.

"Why annoy us, sergeant?" grumbled the foremost, a battered giant of a Russian. "This is no time to be a martinet. We've got to die—we're doomed, we know it. Go to the devil! We're going to enjoy—"

Lemuel's hard fist smacked into the Russian's sullen countenance. "Doomed? You damned yellow-belly! I'll show you if we're doomed or not. Get up! Now, damn your eyes, find Corporal Gras and send him to me! And you, Corporal Marnier—" he broke off, conscious that the grizzled, gentle-mannered senior corporal was gazing with peculiar interest on Fernando Daggett.

"Quit star-gazin' and take the prisoner into the captain's room. If those auto guns aren't assembled and in perfect working order in half an hour, take that deserter out and hang him."

Daggett smiled wryly as Marnier very willingly drew his pistol. "My hat's off to you, Frost. I'm beginning to think you're a good soldier and what's more, that you've got brains."

"Thanks for the compliment. But remember you've got just half an hour to get those Madsen guns together. After that I'll give you another half hour to instruct certain men I'll send you in the art o' firin' them. If you do both of these things, I give you my word court-martial proceedin's against you will be dropped. But after this row's over we'll settle our private fight. Pete Wilkins's ghost ain't been laid yet—you treacherous scum!"

To cut short a stream of protestations from Daggett that no

man could perform such miracles in an hour, Lemuel turned his
back and signalled the two guards to hustle away their prisoner.

FORCING HIS exhausted body to obedience the hollow-
eyed, scarecrow-like American next went into the garrison, to
find that only sixty-five men were ready for active duty. Those
sixty-five were men whose self-confidence was badly, almost
hopelessly shaken.

In brisk, hope-instilling accents he addressed them briefly;
told them that their only chance of survival lay in strict obedience to orders. Each man must fight like a stack of black cats,
he put it; otherwise they would meet unspeakable death. They
understood the situation? Good! There was a small chance that
if every Legionnaire did as he was told the *poste* might be saved.
Were there any ex-machine gunners among them? Six, eight?
Good! He would speak with them later.

Meanwhile the rest of them would distribute water and
ammunition around the firing platforms. When the bugle blew
the *"alerte"* they were all to go to their stations, prepared to fight
like Legionnaires of the Seventh Company. He, Sergeant Frost,
would shoot the first man who moved without orders. They
understood that, did they? Good!

There ensued a period of feverish activities. Lemuel paused
in the N.C.O.'s quarters just long enough to wipe the accumu-
lation of blood, sweat and dirt from his leathern features. Then
he pulled on a fresh tunic, reloaded his pistol clips, and appro-
priating Van Droon's *képi*—the Hollander wouldn't be needing
it any more—he sallied forth to evolve some plan whereby the
might of Gléglé and the avenging fury of the Amazons might
possibly be beaten off.

Shortly after the sun had commenced to descend, the thunder
of drums in the jungle grew ominously loud, and the Legionnaires toiled like sailors who seek to complete their tasks before
a hurricane breaks. Those of the sick and wounded who were
capable of loading or handling rifles emerged from the hospital

room, and limping up to firing steps, sank pale-faced on chairs prepared for them.

"Boom! Boom! Boom!" roared the drums. "Kill! Kill! Kill!"

The sinewy American sergeant was everywhere, speaking an encouraging word here, and spurring some laggard there. At the foot of the watchtower he passed Harold as the little cockney staggered up from the subterranean magazine with a blue-banded box of ammunition on his shoulder.

"'Ark to them drums!" he panted. "Them gals must be fair ravin' mad; and w'at Misses Taloya, Chelata & Co. won't do to yer, Mr. Lemuel Frost, if they catches yer alive!"

"They won't," promised Lemuel grimly.

Harold gazed about. "I say, mate, I only see two o' them automatic guns o' yours. Where are the other two?"

Lemuel found time to wink solemnly. "Don't you wish you knew? Don't worry, son, they'll speak their piece after a bit."

"Orl right," grunted Harold spitefully; "but yer might tell me."

Sergeant Frost grinned and glanced up at the watchtower, a white pillar against the darkening sky. Up yonder was a small red flag that should flutter up when he blew his whistle thrice. "Nothin' else I could do," he murmured. "With only forty rounds to the magazine of those blasted Madsens, I'll have to reckon on surprise to break 'em up. Weight of fire would never stop 'em— the drums would empty too soon."

PRESENTLY, WHEN the hollow rumble of Gléglé's war drums grew deafening, heart-shaking, the bugle sounded defiantly and the little garrison stood to arms. Apparently scorning any effort at surprise, the black king was advancing straight through the forest intending to wipe out that little white fort in passing.

Thus it was that the anxious sergeant had a little time to marshal his handful of cursing, shaken Legionnaires carefully on the walls. With the practiced eye of an old soldier of fortune, he sensed those points which would sustain the heaviest assault, and there sent the largest numbers of blue and white clad Legionnaires with bandoliers of ammunition dangling from their hard, tattooed fists.

For a reserve he was forced to content himself with but five men. One of the precious automatic rifles he posted in the watchtower under Marnier's command; the other, with Daggett in charge, he emplaced in a slightly elevated position above the main gate where it would most efficiently enfilade the probable line of the Amazons' attack.

All at once a great silence fell as the drums in the jungle abruptly stopped. It was as though they had never existed. In that unexpected stillness the nerves of the sixty-odd Europeans in the *poste* snapped and quivered in the height of the afternoon heat.

"Our precious commander is crazy as a loon," growled Corporal Gras as he carefully disposed his rifle clips within reach. "Why has the fool mounted only two of the machine rifles?"

Harold pulled his *képi* lower. "Stow your gab, Frenchie, Lemuel ain't nobody's fool. I could tell you a few things. Some'ow, some way, them guns is goin' to come in useful. Look at Daggett, will yer?"

The big cross-breed was busying himself above the main gate in piling the bright circular drums of ammunition in convenient locations. As Harold noted with surprise, the pardoned deserter was in full uniform now.

" 'E's a bleedin' bounder and a narsty cad," observed Harold in grudging admiration, "but 'e ain't the least bit frightened. Look at 'im larf as 'e works."

CHAPTER XV

AN INCIDENT IS CLOSED

WITH THE SUDDENNESS of a tropic squall breaking, Glégle's attack materialized from the west. One instant only the still, treacherously beautiful jungle was in sight; the next a deep terrifying roar arose, as from the screening green underbrush sprang a swift black tide that dashed with headlong fury across the hundred yards of clear area straight at the low bullet-pitted walls of the *poste.*

"Attention!" Lemuel's whistle and command rang out clear-sounding above the barbaric howls without. It betrayed none of the poignant fears he felt for the fate of the garrison and for the helpless souls down-country. "Aim!"

The sixty pairs of wide-strained eyes peered over rifle sights covering that vast, multicolored horde. There were hundreds, many hundreds of howling blacks clad in fantastic rags, parts of uniforms and cartridge belts. Weird war emblems made of stuffed crocodiles, hawks and vultures floated crazily above the Dahomeyans' thick-packed ranks. In the center swayed the dread skull flag of Gléglé himself. To the shaken handful on the walls the charge was a blood-chilling sight, as tossing their weapons in the air until the whole array flashed like a wave of death the Dahomeyans raced closer and closer, now fifty yards away, twenty yards! Lemuel waited until details of their equipment were clearly distinguishable.

His whistle shrilled: "Fire!" The command was lost in a great, rolling crash that sounded not unlike the noise a giant might make in ripping apart a huge strip of linen.

As the Legionnaires' volley struck, the foremost ranks of Dahomeyans performed curious antics; some threw their arms skyward to plunge heavily forward on their faces with flat, black noses pressed into the steaming earth; others twisted violently sidewise; others sprang spasmodically into the air, then fell; still others seemed to lose sense of direction and ran amuck among their fellows apparently crazed by the violence of the Legionnaires' response to the attack.

Crash! Crash! In steady, murderous volleys the scattered rifles of the Legionnaires mowed down the foremost attackers in a howling, shrieking windrow. But the effect was only momentary, for the whole cleared space in the center of which stood the fort was now alive with yelling, charging figures.

Firing as fast as he could from above the gate, Lemuel recognized the two corps of Amazons. He even got a glimpse of Taloya, frenzied with rage, leading the attack like a dusky Joan of Arc. At her ferocious expression he shuddered. A houri before, she was now a veritable demon.

Crash! Crash!

The long Lebels delivered their fire faithfully, but for all that the seething black tide swept on up to the walls, seemingly irresistible.

Crash! Crash!

The rifle magazines were empty and Death's shadow lay dark over Kouande. But following Lemuel's orders the two automatic rifles commenced to chatter like gigantic, murderous typewriters as soon as the rifle fire waned.

Rat-tat-tat-tat-tat! So the Madsens took up the burden of defense, while haste-frenzied fingers crammed more cool brass clips into the reeking magazines of the Lebels.

With no little skill two detachments of Amazons fell out and, taking cover, commenced to snipe at the walls of the *poste*. Reports, shouts, groans, cheers and the frantic roar of the war drums united to make the uproar utterly deafening. Cool and all-seeing, Lemuel was pleased to note that the machine gunners obeyed orders and only fired while the rifles were being reloaded.

SUDDENLY, JUST as the screaming Dahomeyans were about to scale the walls, an inexplicable panic seized the foremost and Glégle's whole army dashed away back to shelter at the base of two great umbrella-shaped bombax trees which marked the trail to the westward.

"Taught the bleedin' swine a lesson," coolly remarked Harold, passing a wet rag over the heat-shimmering barrel of his rifle. He heard the water sizzle as it encountered the hot metal. Then he glanced around and felt his heart sink; two, four, ten—fifteen or more Legionnaires lay either sprawled on the firing step or crumpled lifeless in the courtyard below. Beside each embrasure was a litter of empty cartridge cases and torn pasteboard boxes. Here and there a bandage gleamed white in the sun's pitiless glare.

Corporal Achille Gras significantly detached a bullet from a clip, and setting it apart on the firing platform, raised his *képi* to it with a macabre laugh.

"Isn't she pretty?" he demanded of his hollow-eyed companions. "My little ticket of escape. Oh, no, *mes amis;* Achille Gras becomes just a dead pincushion for the brats."

During this brief breathing space the grim, hawk-faced sergeant ordered the dead and wounded to be collected and fresh ammunition to be given out. This done, he cast a shrewd, searching look at the watchtower. Up there Corporal Marnier cautiously raised his head, met the sergeant's eye, nodded.

Lemuel addressed the scarlet-faced men about him: "This time, my bright lads, comes the main attack—beat 'em off and we've won."

The weary, death-haunted Legionnaires nodded shaggy heads. *Bien!* So much the better! Knowing that, they would fight until the breath left their bodies, for not a soul in the fort dared think of victory.

Then all at once the king's grand assault began in force. In close-packed ranks Gléglé's main body, supported by the crack Amazon corps, emerged from the shelter of the forest and, protected by a sharp fire from the jungle, advanced on the walls, gradually gathering momentum as they went.

Again the Legionnaire rifles mowed them down amid a brief, bitter-smelling fog of smoke; but there were not so many Lebels to speak. With sharp dismay Lemuel realized that the black tide seemed not to be checked as before. Gaunt, almost naked riflemen were actually taking up positions only a few feet below the walls, to fire point-blank at any Legionnaire who dared to show himself in an embrasure.

"Lead us, O Gléglé!" roared the black horde.

Experienced as he was, the tall American felt his heart drop. He sensed that this rush could not be stayed. A Polish Legionnaire beside him clapped both hands to a scarlet-dyed chest, rose to full height, tottered drunkenly, then plunged over the firing platform into the screaming throng below.

Instantly a stalwart Amazon warrior cut off his head. Lemuel, in a desperate attempt to stem the tide of death, blew a blast on his whistle, and at once both automatic rifles opened fire before the Lebel magazines were empty. Chattering in staccato fury, they added their efforts, seeking to crumple up Glégl's terrific onslaught with a withering blast of lead.

Lemuel knew that the magazine of his Lebel would be empty after the next round, and so would those of other Legionnaires. Worse yet, the ammunition drums on the auto rifles could not last much longer without changing.

Up, up surged the black wave, defying a rain of bullets; shrieking Amazons leaped up to catch a handhold on the walls, then fell back singed, bleeding and shattered as some hard-pressed Legionnaire fired at point-blank range.

The reserve Legionnaires had long since been flung in as Lem made a hopeless effort to stem the tide of catastrophe; but their rate of fire was dropping steadily, fatally. A few cool veterans did manage to reload, but the majority were now thrusting, stabbing desperately with their bayonets to keep those lithe hell-cats, the Amazons, from gaining a real foothold on the wall. Nearer and nearer fluttered Glégl's black and white skull banner.

"Can't wait any longer!" thought Lemuel, as the rifle butt recoiled with his last shot. He snatched up the whistle that dangled from its lanyard and blew three short imperative blasts which rang clear even above the violent tumult all about. His eyes flickered to the watchtower. Where was that red flag? Hell! Was Marnier dead or asleep?

LIKE A diver who loses his balance before he intends to take off and so wavers on the brink of a fall, the battle swayed. In another minute Glégl's black horde must sweep triumphantly

over the whitewashed walls, in a trice blotting out the handful
of white men within.

Again the three despairing, insistent notes sped from
Lemuel's whistle, but still no red flag fluttered from the tower
top.

Horrified at the delay, the cursing sergeant waited no longer,
but risking a broken leg he sprang from the firing platform to
the court, hurdled five or six dead and dying Legionnaires lying
in his path and sprang with frantic haste up the staircase. In an
instant more he had reached the tower top.

The Amazons were on the wall! Ignoring two limp bodies
stretched at his feet, Lemuel snatched up a square of red cloth
fastened to a short stick and commenced to wave it in frantic
circles about his head.

Then a miracle happened. From somewhere in the forest
behind the horde of fetish fighters sounded the dry rattle of
automatic rifles firing! The Dahomeyan rear ranks melted into
kicking, blood-bathed heaps.

Rat-tat-tat-tar-r-r-r!

Then Glégé's grisly skull banner rocked uncertainly, as the
king's followers paused on the very brink of triumph, bewildered
at this sudden murderous attack from the rear. From where did
it come? In that deafening uproar they could not distinguish the
direction of the reports. The gunners and guns seemed invisible.
By tens, twenties and thirties the fetish fighters fell.

Lemuel, fearful of this uncertain moment, pushed aside the
limp body of Corporal Marnier, to snatch up the Madsen in the
tower top. Finding its magazine half full, he trained the slender
steel tube on the thickest swarm below and sent a deadly spray
of lead full into a mass of gleaming, sable bodies.

"Good boys!" raved Lemuel as the hidden machine gunners
mowed down Glégé's bodyguard. "They certainly are pickin' 'em
right."

An instant his eye wavered toward the tops of those two giant bombax trees, and with satisfaction noted that from the foliage near the top of each sprouted tiny plumes of white smoke.

An endless minute more the battle swayed uncertainly; then the Legionnaires, having found time to reload their rifles, recommenced fire—those of them that were left. Hemmed in front and rear by a murderous rain of bullets, Gléglé's decimated forces were seized with sudden fear. The magic of those invisible gunners in their rear was too much!

"Guess old Gléglé knows how we felt in the Argonne when them Kraut machine gunners in the trees opened up on our rear," commented Lemuel. "All over but—"

A bullet sang in through the embrasure and clipped Lemuel's skull, so that he slumped forward over the hot, oily barrel of the Madsen, and so saw nothing of the headlong, despairing retreat of those overwhelming hordes defeated with Yankee ingenuity.

Below, Harold, who knew nothing of Lemuel's fate, chuckled joyously and nudged Corporal Gras. "Didn't I say 'e were a wise bird? Who else would 'ave thought o' riggin' M.G. nests in them there bombaxes? I tell yer, Gras—like Napoleon said once, there ain't nothin' so bad for the morale as unexpected fire from the rear."

MUCH TOO spent and too shaken by their narrow escape to think of pursuit, the surviving Legionnaires remained in their embrasures, gazing with incredulous eyes on the appalling scene of carnage without—all save ex-sergeant Fernando Daggett.

Very unostentatiously he quitted the gun he had served so efficiently, descended from the firing platform, and pistol in hand walked carelessly in the direction of the watchtower. He alone of the garrison had seen Lemuel plunge forward on his face, and with a very wise smile decided that the occurrence might be used to the advantage of one Fernando Daggett.

Up the stairs he clambered, making surprisingly little noise for all his heavy, hobnailed boots, and when his handsome head emerged into the sunlight through the trapdoor it wore a satisfied grin. He beheld the three slumped figures: Frost, a machine gunner, and Marnier.

"A clean sweep—got the old guy, too. Wonder who the devil is that bird Marnier? Evidently knew me in the old days—wish I could remember."

Bent well over lest he be seen from the firing platforms, Fernando Daggett crept forward, dark eyes intent on Lemuel's aquiline visage. It appeared that the American was either dead or very gravely wounded, for the left side of his brown face was completely dyed with blood.

"Might as well make sure, though. We'll settle that Wilkins matter now."

With an evil grin on his lips the cross-breed crept forward, picked up the sergeant's limp, brown wrist and tested it. Then his smile faded. Lemuel's pulse was not only beating, but beating strongly.

A fresh volley of shots broke out from the firing steps as a number of Dahomeyans, after having successfully shammed dead, arose and made a futile bid for escape.

The rifles crackled briefly and loudly, causing the gray-faced Marnier to open dimming eyes in time to see Fernando Daggett in the act of poising a slender, gleaming bayonet over the unconscious American's heart.

Swiftly and silently Captain Antoine de Nellier, late of the Artillery, and otherwise Corporal Marnier of the Seventh Company, expended the last of his strength in whipping out his pistol. He sighted carefully; then his hand flew up with the recoil as he shot Fernando Daggett through the heart.

"And there—dog!" choked Captain Antoine de Nellier, with a ghastly smile. "At last you—have paid—for—my wife's—for Françoise de Nellier's damnation!"

So saying, Captain de Nellier, late of the Artillery, sank back while the smoking pistol clattered to the tower floor; then he folded his worn hands, and with a smile of infinite satisfaction drifted off into the endless sleep.

The next morning Sergeant Lemuel Zebulon Frost bent a bandaged head over his morning report and wrote with a firm hand: "Enemy repulsed yesterday with a loss of thirty-five men and noncommissioned officers. This day, *poste* routine as usual."

THE TWENTY WICKED PEOPLE

*If the enemy didn't get him, his own Legion
cutthroats would, Sergeant Jake Miller knew*

CHAPTER I

FOOL—OR SCHEMER?

JAKE MILLER, SERGEANT of the VIième Compagnie, Foreign Legion, brought the heels of his hobnailed shoes together with a click, and stood at rigid attention before the rough whitewashed door of the commandant's office at Bunbaki.

"He might give a guy time to wash up," he muttered, as he realized that the marks of travel through a country hot as a stoke hold in the Red Sea were unmistakably evident. His green-epauletted blue overcoat collar was dark with sweat, his hands were grimy, red and swollen and slashed with thorns from the tropical jungle through which he and his platoon had been forcing their way ever since they had left Libreville some ten days previous. He recalled the brief but significant conversation he had had with Commandant Marais, when the platoon was ready to pull out.

"Mon enfant," the grizzled old veteran had said, "when you reach Bunbaki, keep your eyes open. There's something wrong up there, for where an officer doesn't want to leave a pest hole like Bunbaki at the end of his tour of duty, he must be either a fool or a rogue. It's up to you to find out, very unofficially, which the local commander is. It's a chance, *mon enfant,* and your brains, which are not of the ordinary, will be all you have to help you. If you make mistakes, you can expect no help from me."

Commandant Marais had held out a long pale-blue envelope which bore no superscription.

"This," the commandant had said, "is an order recalling that

jungle-loving individual at Bunbaki. If you get proof, definite proof, mind you, that things are not as they should be, you may give Lieutenant von Krass this envelope; but God help your miserable soul if you make a mistake! *Allez.*"

Sweat now poured down Jake's bronzed and hollow cheeks, picking a leisurely course among the reddish bristles sprouting on his unshaven chin. While waiting he automatically ran his hand over his buttons. Good, they were all in place except the one which had been torn off in a thorn tangle not five kilometers below that *poste* at Bunbaki.

From the other side of the door sounded a footstep, and he drew himself up, prepared to report to his new commanding officer, Lieutenant von Krass, the man who wanted to stay at Bunbaki. What sort of a man was he?

"Come in," called one of the deepest voices Jake bad ever heard. The sergeant went inside, his short but powerful body far from filling the door frame. In the plain whitewashed room before him stood a rough table, upon which were stacked neat piles of documents, and behind this table was seated a huge blond man who wore the uniform of a lieutenant. At first glance

Miller planted a bullet in the
Venezuelan's merderous heart.

Sergeant Jake Miller knew he would find no bed of roses in the *poste* at Bunbaki.

SITTING STIFFLY behind the desk was the most typical Teuton Jake had seen since the great war. Fixed upon him were two small, very blue eyes, the whites of which were discolored by bright red networks of veins. All the while Lieutenant von Krass tugged at a heavy yellow-white mustache.

Having arrived before the desk, the new arrival saluted sharply.

"Sergeant Miller of the Sixth Company reports for duty, sir, with twenty-five Legionnaires."

Having said this, he fell silent and began to flush under the glassy scrutiny of the lieutenant who, sitting quite motionless, permitted his shrewd blue eyes to travel deliberately from Jake's thorn-slashed boots to puttees, and on up until his china-blue eyes met the American's gray ones.

Silence continued, broken only by the drone of huge bluebottle flies that circled like a tormenting halo about the heads of the two men. What a mean mouth that Boche lieutenant had!

"So?" Lieutenant von Krass's thin lips curled. "This is what they send me from Libreville. *Gott verdammt mich!* and I asked for a soldier."

By his sides Jake's large insect-bitten hands tightened, and it occurred to him that they would just meet comfortably around that thick red neck. What a hell of a way to treat a man at the end of a perilous, exhausting march!

"So you are a sergeant, eh?" Lieutenant von Krass glared down his long high-bridged nose.

"Yes, sir."

"Well, unless I'm much mistaken, you won't be one long. It takes men to man this *poste* at Bunbaki."

Jake deliberately fixed his eyes on the fly-blown map just behind Lieutenant von Krass's narrow, short-clipped head. That heavy black line indicating the river Bonny made a convenient thing to concentrate on.

"Why did they pick you? Was the rest of the scum so bad?"

"No, sir; I asked to be sent."

"Oh, one of these ambitious soldiers, eh?"

The sneer would have made a jack-rabbit sit up and fight, but Jake had not been a soldier fifteen years without learning self-control.

"Yes, sir," be said. God, how hot and tired he was!

"Well, you've come to the wrong place. When I choose men for sergeants, I don't pick half-pints that imagine they're soldiers because they've campaigned against some frightened Arabs in Morocco."

JAKE SWALLOWED and said nothing. What a fool he had been not to have learned more about this forgotten *poste* among the evilly beautiful and festering jungles of the French Congo before applying for duty there! Still, it had seemed the best bet for action, and Commandant Marais had his eye on him since the skirmish at Ain Argoula.

Furthermore, there was that English girl back in Marseilles

who, though she had freely confessed her love for him, declared she would marry no less than a gentleman and a commissioned officer.

Yes, Mazie was well worth it—a fine, strong girl that would raise him a brood of stalwart little Jakes who would resurrect the glory of a family gone to grass amid the shiftlessness of a Mississippi bayou.

"Du lieber Gott!" Lieutenant von Krass's bass voice filled the room like the boom of a gong. "How dare you appear before me dressed like some wretched *bleu?*"

"But, sir, I've only been in the *poste* fifteen minutes."

"Silence!" Up from his chair the Prussian reared his long body, narrow face quivering. "I teach you to come tramping into my headquarters looking like some Apache dragged from the slums."

He halted, leaning forward, hands on the desk, eyes ever probing the sergeant's hard brown face. "So you want promotion, eh? Well, first you'll have to prove to me that you're worthy of the rank some besotted idiot's given you. How an unsoldierly baboon like you got past private *deuxième classe* amazes me."

There was a sinking sensation in Sergeant Jake Miller's being. One would think he was a blue-gilled *pékin* fresh from the Marseilles recruiting station, instead of a veteran of two campaigns in Indo-China, the Philippines and many small colonial wars.

A red mist commenced to descend over his eyes—it was not right, his *dossier* at Sidi bore nothing but favorable entries, no court martial, nothing but promotions and citations.

"Don't look so damned sullen," barked the Prussian suddenly. "I'll not have it. Now listen to me, sergeant—" What a world of sarcasm he put in that word! "I have decided to let you keep your rank for twenty-four hours, just so my N.C.O.'s can have a good laugh. Stand to attention!"

The red-haired sergeant's craggy features turned a furious scarlet and his short body contracted, whereupon the Prussian smiled bleakly and his hand wandered toward the pistol he wore belted outside his tunic. It was that smile which saved the outraged sergeant. No use to play this devil's game of Von Krass's and get himself shot down like a clay pipe in a gallery.

"Thought better of it, eh?" jeered the lieutenant and he seemed a little more wary, as though he had learned a little respect for the new sergeant.

MURDER, MAYHEM and violent assault were the least of the impulses milling in Jake's brain when he saluted, executed a sharp about-face and, inwardly seething, stalked off along the dim whitewashed corridor leading to the courtyard.

Ever stronger grew the conviction that there was something back of the Prussian's effort to make him lose his temper. Well, he had gained his stripes from using his head for something other than a *képi* rack, in fact, he had risen in two short years with the Legion from *soldat deuxième classe* to sergeant, a feat seldom accomplished.

Unreasonable martinet and rogue the gigantic Von Krass might be, but there was nothing slipshod about his soldiery; that Jake appreciated when he emerged once more into the Turkish bath atmosphere of the *poste's* courtyard. With an experienced eye he noted that everything was *klimbin,* from the wooden-faced Legionnaire pacing before the great hardwood gate to the whitewashed spotlessness of the courtyard wall.

Squatting and lying about in the bluish shade of the courtyard wall he found his reliable stalwarts of the VIième Compagnie, mostly Danes, Germans and a sprinkling of White Russians, sturdy chaps not much given to nerves.

"What happened, *mon sergent?*" Borst, corporal of the first squad, looked up from digging a jigger from beneath his thumb nail. He waited, knife clasp still open, peering up into Jake's red and quivering features.

"Oh," he said, "another Sobeloff?"

To a man, the reënforcements looked up, for Adjutant Sobeloff was of evil memory.

"Another Soboleff! Another Soboleff!" The name flickered down the squatting rank of hollow-eyed, insect-gnawed Legionnaires.

"Don't kid yourselves," was all Jake said. "This squarehead is a different breed of cats from Soboleff. He's ornery as a rutting moose and a toe-tied Igorot put together, but unless I miss my guess he's a wise hombre, so don't make any breaks."

SERGEANT MILLER was at the point of ordering his men into the stifling ovenlike barracks of whitewashed mud brick, when staggering up the little hill to the gate of the *poste* came a topknotted Zandeh boy. He gasped a few broken words, while the left side of his throat emitted a bloody froth and his brown-black visage was contorted with pain.

As one man the reënforcements groaned, as one man the hard-featured, malaria-blighted regulars of the garrison uttered a cry of joy.

"Active duty, *grâce à Dieu!*" cried one hulking rascal as he ran toward the barracks. "Thank God!"

Speculating on what effect this event would have on his own particular problem, Jake frowningly watched the fainting runner being half led, half carried into the *poste* proper. A little trail of red spots followed.

"Nicely carved up," he observed to Corporal Borst. "Even a Jebel Bani couldn't do better."

And Jake Miller's heart rose as he gazed at the twenty-five stalwarts behind him. With these under his command he might be able to learn why Von Krass wished to remain lost in the depths of the jungle and at the same time keep his stripes.

"Wait here," he commanded. "I'll find out where you bunk."

Wary-eyed, hot and ready for trouble, he strode into the officers' quarters, and on looking about found small room for encouragement. Two other sergeants, men he would not have trusted with a red-hot penny, glowered at him in silence, and a single corporal, black as the ace of spades, went placidly on tattooing a design on his left forearm. At length he turned around, scratched the fuzz on his skull, and looked up.

"*Bong joor, avez vous* any Americans in *les* reënforcements?"

A warm trickle entered Jake Miller's heart. In spite of the heavy hobnail shoes, in spite of the thin putteed shanks, the white canvas trousers and pale blue belly band, "Georgia coon" was out all over the speaker.

"Why, yes, corporal," Jake said in English, "we've got one—I'm it."

Down clattered the Negro's tattooing needle and he leaped forward, extending a sable hand that was as big as a ham.

"Fo' de lan's sake!" and an ivory expanse loomed in the sable garden of the corporal's face. "Boy, you sure is welcome—like a quart of whisky at a funeral! Put 'er there!"

Instantly Sergeant Miller's figure stiffened, and for the first time in years he relapsed into that soft drawl which is spoken in his native Mississippi.

"Who you callin' 'boy'? I'm Sergeant Miller to you."

The Negro drew back, a furious scowl on his face and his huge body stiffened. For a moment it appeared that he would risk court martial by striking a man who still wore the green chevrons of a sergeant. Suddenly:

"Yas, suh, yas, suh, it sho' am good to hear one of de quality folk talkin' again. Excuse me, suh, Corporal Amby Dextrous is sho'ly glad to see some of de real quality agin."

"Glad to hear that, Dextrous."

At once Jake held out his hand and, their basis of relationship having been definitely established, he proceeded to take the sable corporal into confidence in that inimitable way of Southerners.

The other N.C.O.'s, however, regarded with pained disapproval this child, a mere puling infant, who wore the stripes of a sergeant.

"*Bigre!* Observe, my dear Ibañez," grunted a scarred, snaggletoothed veteran, with the scaly head of a marabout stork, "here is the new nursemaid for the Twenty Wicked People."

JAKE RAISED inquisitive eyes at "Little Amby," as the colored corporal begged to be addressed. Just then came the sound of running feet ringing through the humid air, like the strokes of doom, and outside a bugle commenced to fling the brazen notes of the *alerte* against the ever encroaching green wall of jungle surrounding the *poste*.

"N.C.O.'s report to headquarters."

The American found himself standing in single rank before the now familiar desk. Back of it Lieutenant von Krass sat very stiff-backed, pink as to face and harsh as to expression. Already Jake noted he was completely accoutered for a jungle expedition, from scarf-lined *képi* to jigger-proof boots.

"So," he rasped, without looking up, "you're here at last! What have I done to be afflicted with such a lot of clubfooted baboons for officers?"

Panting slightly the seven men stood in silence while Lieutenant von Krass stood and spun to face the map that Jake had previously noticed.

"Listen," said he, "there is much to do. Word has come that that old devil Labastida, whom you all know by the name of El Cocodrilo, is reported to have crossed the Rio Muñi border and is descending the Ikembe River for a slave raid on the Oshebas. Twice he has escaped us, but this time he has crossed the Spanish border once too often."

It occurred to the silent American sergeant the same man did not usually escape the Legion twice—evidently El Cocodrilo was a wily bird. There were a number of questions he wanted to ask.

"I notice by the map, lieutenant, that the Ikembe River forks just below the Rio Muñi border. I was—"

Down crashed the butt of Lieutenant von Krass's pistol, and his cold blue eyes blazed.

"Silence!" he roared. "Who gave you leave to notice things? In Bunbaki I do all the thinking."

And Jake, on looking at the stolid, unemotional countenances of his fellow N.C.O.'s felt disposed to agree.

The soldier in him revolted. Why the devil should the big-boned lieutenant trust so implicitly the word of a Zandeh boy, when it was a well-known fact that no bush Negroes could be accurate even on the rare occasions when they wanted to? Zandeh? He suppressed an involuntary exclamation. His eyes narrowed, following the details of the yellowed map on the wall. He wanted to ask questions. Why would not that second fork in the Tembo River serve just as well as the first, for a sudden descent on Bunbaki?

However, it stood to reason that Von Krass knew his business.

VON KRASS, with jaw thrust out, whirled and snapped:

"Sergeant Ibañez, take the first platoon and proceed to Bikuki. Sergeant Renoire, you will take the second platoon and occupy the forks of the Ikembe. According to orders you will receive by runners. Now give me your close attention."

The Prussian took quick, brief steps back and forth, stabbing the map with his blunt forefinger and occasionally speaking over his immensely wide shoulder as he planned as neat an ambuscade as Jake had ever seen. Yes, the Prussian was a soldier, every inch of him; but increasingly his own disquiet grew for when the plan of campaign came to an end his name had not once been mentioned; moreover, the platoon of reënforcements had been taken over by the lieutenant himself.

"They will need watching," he remarked. "Doubtless a pack of hare-hearted yellow bellies out of the VIième."

Chill as the breath of an iceberg was Von Krass's manner when at last he turned and fixed a baleful eye upon the dismayed American.

"And now as to you, my promotion-hungry hero, I aim to give you a chance."

Jake's heart leaped. Perhaps the Prussian was not such an unbooted swine after all.

"Yes, sir?"

"To you, I will assign two squads of garrison that are known as the Twenty Wicked People." Von Krass's slash of a mouth parted in a mirthless grin. "I wish you joy of them, and them of you."

"Thank you, sir," said Jake and he wondered.

"You're too quick with your thanks, you tin soldier. I am bestowing upon you the very dregs of the Legion—depraved rascals who were originally sent out here to be killed and who have so far been so unreasonable as to remain alive. Inside half an hour you will march them out of this *poste*. You will march to the fords of Talato and there observe the crocodiles disporting themselves on the banks of the Tembo River."

"The Tembo River, sir?" Jake's face flushed to the roots of his red hair and the crisscross scar burned deep scarlet. "But that's nowhere near the scene of action."

"Indeed?" observed Lieutenant von Krass, slipping the ammunition clips into the carriers about his gleaming leather belt. "I couldn't trust you in a real fight. To me you are a nuisance; as are also the Twenty Wicked People." He shrugged, making the ornaments on his red collar blink briefly. "You see what a clever fellow I am?"

How intense were those blue eyes as they searched his face, thought Jake.

"I stand nothing to lose if you kill some of them or if they kill you. Should you," the amiable lieutenant paused in the act of pouring some permaganate of potash crystals into the small glass vial which every soldier must carry in that land of numerous and treacherous snakes, "come back alive and with the Twenty Wicked People completely under your control, I might—I do not say I will—I might let you keep your rank. *Verstehen?*"

CHAPTER II

THE CUTTHROAT ARMY

IT WAS WHEN the doors of the *poste's* lockup were flung open that the red-haired sergeant appreciated the magnitude of the task before him, for there stepped out into the humid orange-yellow sunlight such a collection of evil-featured, shifty-eyed rascals as he had never before seen. Of all races and of all degrees of intelligence were the Twenty Wicked People. A couple of Greeks, three or four Serbs, two or three Latin-Americans and, worst of all, half a dozen or more of that dreadful species of man called the Paris Apache. Of the twenty there were not three to whom he would willingly have presented his back on a dark night.

It was only then that he appreciated the true cunning of Lieutenant von Krass. There would be no troublesome courts-martial, no inquiries, merely an automatic removal of a man who, for reasons of his own, he did not want around. The only redeeming ray of light was the fact that Corporal Amby Dextrous was assigned to help him handle this poisonous crew.

Being thoroughly experienced in the ways of the wicked, the new sergeant proceeded to institute a search of the person of each of the Twenty Wicked People, especially those who happened not to be in the cells at that moment.

"Nice gang of thugs," he remarked as from the cursing, furious suspects he amassed an amazing collection of dirks, brass knuckles, knives and other interesting cutlery.

"Not authorized by the Ordnance Department," observed Jake grimly. "Wipe off that frown, you verminous dog. And now," his gray eyes swept that lowering, sullen rank, "since we're going to campaign together, you'd better understand one thing. I want and will have prompt and unquestioning obedience, and any man who doesn't give it, is going to be badly hurt."

Along that unshaved line more than one pair of lips drew back from uneven and discolored teeth in a derisive smile. *Dios,* why this sergeant was not of even average height! There were a dozen men among the Twenty Wicked People who could have broken him into little pieces—like they had that *sacré* Englishman six months back.

With the quick, short stride of a game cock, Sergeant Miller strode along the rank, chill gray eyes veiled with disapproval.

"At present," he announced, "you offend both the eye and the nose. You are a disgrace to the Legion, you look like the tramps, thieves and porch climbers you once were. When we come back from the Tembo I'm going to have you looking like soldiers or know the reason why."

Down the line some one made a noise which is known in the United States as the Bronx cheer. And to make matters worse an N.C.O. of the VIième strolling by, uttered a hoarse guffaw and nudged his companion.

"Look at these brave lads, how they smile in the face of death!"

IT WAS a harrowing half hour while the half platoon was being rationed and equipped for a five-day expedition. Jake, inwardly seething, was drawing ammunition when Lieutenant von Krass, straight as a ramrod and powerful in his build as a young buffalo, appeared in the doorway. The Prussian's expression was thoughtful when he noted the thoroughness of Jake's preparations.

"How many rounds per man, *mon sergent?*" inquired the supply sergeant.

"Forty rounds per man," ordered Jake as he checked over a supply of hand grenades, "and if you value your greasy hide, issue me clean clips. I want no clogged cartridges."

"Forty rounds per man?" cut in Von Krass's deep decisive tones. "*Gott im Himmel,* what do you intend to do with all that? Hold a Saint Bartholomew of crocodiles?"

"No, sir," replied Sergeant Miller, springing to attention. "Forty rounds is not too much for an expedition to carry; slave raiders occasionally change their plans and surprises are possible in thick country like this."

"The only surprises you are likely to get will be from the Twenty Wicked People. Sergeant, issue the half platoon twenty-five rounds per man."

"But, sir," protested Miller angrily, "regulations call for a minimum of thirty rounds—"

"Oh, so you're an army lawyer?" Von Krass's teeth glinted in the pink-angularity of his features. "Well, I make the regulations for this *poste*. Make it twenty rounds, sergeant. Any more talk out of you, my clever Amerikander, and I'll send you out with a single clip apiece. How would you like that?"

Breathing hard, and realizing that events were getting away from him, Jake managed to control himself. Didn't the fool know it was suicide to march around this part of the French Congo with only twenty rounds per man? What if he stumbled on a column of gunners, on a war party of Gabrons? Of course Von Krass knew—and the frown on the sunburned forehead of Sergeant Jacob Jackson Miller grew ever deeper.

EXACTLY ONE hour from the time that the bleeding Zandeh boy had rushed in, the *poste* commenced to disgorge orderly little columns of blue and white clad men who, with N.C.O.'s at their heads, plunged silently off into the tangled forests where baobabs, cotton silk trees and a hundred varieties of palm formed a dense screen that shut off all air and shut in all the humid heat.

It was with a heavy heart that Jake beheld his sturdy comrades of the VIième swinging off behind the soldierly, quick-stepping figure of Lieutenant von Krass.

But he had little time to consider more than his own troubles. Already he had been forced to knock obedience and several front teeth into an evil and gigantic Greek named Dropulous who had openly defied him. Furthermore, his knuckles still ached from their impact on the jaw of Le Bœuf D'Or, as a singularly sinister Marseillais Apache called himself.

Consequently Jake was very much on the alert when, amid

the jeers of the men who would probably see action, he marched his half platoon off down a narrow trail which wound like a dark serpent through the mango and lemon-tree thickets. Bright-ly-colored parrots, shrieks and warblers of infinite variety flit-ted back and forth. Monkeys, gray and brown, chattered and screeched at the Legionnaires who tramped onward, cursing the heat, continually brushing from their hands and necks multi-tudes of leeches that fell like rain from the adjacent foliage.

With care, Sergeant Miller posted the most obviously treach-erous men in the point of the advance, so that if *coup-coups* suddenly flashed, his loss would not be past bearing. He followed them, not for fear of ambush, but as a pure matter of self-pres-ervation. Next marched the main body, if the men could so be dignified, and last of all came Corporal Amby Dextrous.

Presently the trail narrowed, so perforce, the detachment marched in single file.

All at once the trail took a sharp right turn and automat-ically Jake studied the men ahead of him. Dropulous was in the lead, then a blear-eyed, stiletto-scarred Venezuelan called Orteaga, behind him the enormous Bœuf D'Or, pushing aside the tangling creepers with vicious thrusts, and immediately in front of the watchful sergeant plodded the hulking Dane who was reported to have a penchant for strangling women with his bare tattooed hands.

Dropulous vanished around the gorgeous hibiscus bush forming the corner, then Orteaga. Now the long barrel of Le Bœuf D'Or's Lebel was swinging around that cluster of red and while blossoms.

" *'Cré nom de Dieu,* but it's hot!" The Dane shifted the rifle to his other shoulder and, just as he neared the hibiscus, he sprang off the trail to the left, and with startling abruptness Jake found himself facing a trail which was empty save for Dropulous and Orteaga. These had dropped on one knee, raised their Lebels, and were sighting at him with the unmistakable intention of supplying a vacancy in the ranks of the N.C.O.'s of the Legion.

THE WICKED plot had been neatly prepared, and had these two of the Wicked People to deal with any one but the warwise Jake, they would undoubtedly have succeeded in their scheme, but even as the Dane leaped aside a very capable automatic seemed to sprout in the red-haired sergeant's broad brown hand. Sergeant Jake Miller lost no time in planting a bullet square in the Venezuelan's evil heart, and so disturbed the aim of Legionnaire Dropulous that the Greek shot and, unluckily for him, missed.

As the N.C.O.'s pistol barked a second time, Dropulous jerked forward like the blade of a shutting jackknife and fell forward on his face, while his rifle spun crazily through the air to fall in a bed of yellow orchids.

Nor did the sergeant cease his endeavors at that point. Quite ignoring the two dead men, he spun rapidly on his heels, reached into the tangle on the left, jerked the Dane out by his collar and drove a fist squarely into that startled individual's bloated and unlovely countenance. Then he turned and, speaking to the wall of the forest, said:

"I see you, Bœuf. If you don't instantly come out of there with your hands up, I'll drill you."

And after that Sergeant Miller had practically no trouble for a while, save that Corporal Dextrous was afforded an opportunity to "take 'part" a blue-jowled Bulgarian who thought he would hide in the jungle and quit the hard service of Madame la République.

"Yes, Mistah Miller," apologized the sable corporal, "Ah expects Ah got a little severe with this boy." And Miller, viewing the breathless Bulgarian's blackened eyes and split lips, agreed.

A BRAZEN ball of sun was hovering over the tops of the forest when, during a cigarette pause, Corporal Dextrous came up alongside, parting the jungle with the ease of an elephant.

"Boss," said he, "we-all's fixin' to pass right by a place where some of our folks met plenty trouble last yeah. Ol' Cocodrilo, he cornered 'em and what he didn't kill he took home."

An inner instinct warned Jake that it might be wise to see what he could see, for the more he thought, the more he came to the conclusion that Lieutenant von Krass was a man of more than ordinary intelligence. Rather neat the way he'd sent him out half-ammunitioned with a gang of murderers.

The battlefield proved interesting.

"No survivors, eh?"

"No, sah. Ol' Mistah Cocodrilo, he just naturally massacreed them boys."

With his foot, Jake thoughtfully turned over a split skull from which sprouted a gorgeous red trumpet blossom. There were more all about.

"Halt!" Jake directed the sweating, sullen Legionnaires. "Cigarette pause."

With one accord the eighteen Wicked People eased their packs and lay down to light and drag at that villainous black tobacco which Madame la République issues to her armed sons.

"I don't understand it, Amby," remarked Jake. "Why wasn't there more shooting? I don't see any cartridge cases around these bones."

"Oh, but there was a lot of shootin'. Heard it clean down to the *poste*."

"Then where are the cartridge cases?"

Corporal Dextrous's pawlike hand crept up to remove sweat from his broad black nose.

"Boss, I don't know, but I expects them cases must be hereabout."

Some hundred yards nearer the forest the frowning American came upon what he sought, several little piles of verdigris-greened Lebel cartridge cases.

"H'm," he remarked, "only two or three men fell here." Deep in thought he tramped into the forest and there, behind certain trees he discovered a very plentiful supply of Mauser cartridges, evidently fired by El Cocodrilo's men. Deeper grew his perplexity and his uneasiness. There seemed to be an ominous parallel between his situation and that of Sergeant Harris save that El Cocodrilo was nowhere near. But was he sure of that?

Why, he asked himself, were there neither Lebel nor Mauser cartridge cases where the Legionnaires' bones lay?

"H'm," was all he said as he filed the men in and set off again toward the distant Tembo River with his eighteen Legionnaires cursing him in nearly as many languages.

LONG AFTER the eighteen Wicked People had laid down and had apparently gone to sleep, Jake remained silent, lost in thought and gradually piecing together a very ugly realization.

When the fire had died down he quickly removed his overcoat, rolled it into a man-like figure, placed his *képi* at the head and then retired to the shelter of a hibiscus thicket.

"So," he decided, "there were two separate attacks on that detachment and a third which caught them by surprise. Now where did that successful attack come from?"

His meditations were interrupted by the sight of one Mohammed Hassan, the Arab representative among the Wicked People, picking his way among his sleeping companions with amazing soundlessness. Pleasantly he nodded to the Legionnaire on guard and then crept on toward those blankets which contained Jake Miller's overcoat.

A yard away he halted, produced something that reflected the dull glow of the coals and drew near that sprawled figure. Unfortunately for the plans of the worthy Mohammed, a bullet came smacking out of the hibiscus thicket and pierced his left arm through the fleshy part. After that the red-haired sergeant appeared, put away his revolver and proceeded to beat up the would-be murderer with a thoroughness that commanded the respect of painfully disappointed Wicked People.

CHAPTER III

DESPERATE MANEUVERS

NOON OF THE next day found the detachment in a position covering the fords of the Tembo. And such was the grip of Sergeant Jake Miller on his protégés now that only once that day did his command try to kill him.

"This," said Jake to Corporal Dextrous, as they cooked their noon meal, "is not going to be so bad. If I was only sure that El Cocodrilo really was off to the east and playing tag with the Oshebas—"

"Well, sah," Amby shook his shaved head, "we ain't back to the *poste* yet. And them boys is powerful ornery. I was thinkin'—"

He paused suddenly, for somewhere in the hazy, sour-smelling jungle to the north a drum commenced to sound, throbbing through the moist hot air with reiterating emphasis. Another commenced and Corporal Dextrous sat up very straight and attentive, the whites of his eyes very prominent.

"Zandeh drums," he pronounced. "That *ta-ta dum, ta-ta dum* means bad news; that's the danger signal for these here trifling Zandehs. They drums like that when there's a raid on. Many is the time I's heard it."

A brief consultation with his map brought home two salient facts to Jake. First, in all probability, the wily El Cocodrilo had done the unexpected and was advancing down the Tembo and not the Ikembe fork; the second was that any reënforcements worth mentioning were a good seventy-five kilometers away. And then he remembered—twenty rounds per man.

Through his agile brain flashed a number of unpleasant realizations. For example, Lieutenant von Krass had very deliberately sent him and the now eighteen Wicked People there. Yes, it was a very neat trap. If he did the only sensible thing and retreated from the ford he had been ordered to hold, Von Krass would have excellent grounds for a court-martial.

Twenty rounds per man. Even with the famed marksmanship of the Legion, four hundred shots would not go very far toward holding up the advance of a well-armed marauder like El Cocodrilo.

"Boss," observed Corporal Dextrous, with an anxious frown, "us has got to retire. We ain't got bullets enough."

"On the contrary," said Jake grimly, "us are not going to retire. I happen to have orders to hold this ford. However, on looking over the terrain I've an idea we just might be able to hold this ford. Now go and rout out those bums in uniform and we'll make 'em sweat a little for the glory of France."

FROM NOON until far in the afternoon the vicinity of the ford became the scene of frenzied effort, for when it was borne in on the eighteen Wicked People that they were thus neatly trapped they fell to work. They knew Von Krass, and were also coming to respect this hard-fisted, quick-witted sergeant who drove them unmercifully.

"*Entrañas de Dios!*" panted Legionnaire Gonzales as, stripped to his shirt and wielding a razor-edged *coup-coup*, he did certain interesting things to a young bamboo tree sprouting amid the papyrus on a wide tree stretch back of the ford. "This Americano is a very serpent for wisdom."

"No!" spat Kolchof, the Bulgarian. "He is mad. Why arrange all these defenses in an open space like this?"

"Hush yo' fuss." Corporal Dextrous bent a somber eye on the speaker. "Come on, you little boys with strong backs an' weak minds, hump yo'selves. Git them stakes sharp!"

However, the Wicked People needed no urging, for ever the thunder of the alarm drums drew closer, and not one of them but was familiar with the quaint amusements indulged in by El Cocodrilo. For example, that saddle-colored renegade thought it very funny to hang a Legionnaire by his hands from the limb of a tree, so that his naked feet cleared the surface of the river by a good foot or so. Indeed, Señor Labastida found it very amusing to watch the ugly, mud plastered crocodiles rear up out of the water and snap at the victim's legs until the wretch, wholly exhausted, could struggle no more. A droll fellow was El Cocodrilo.

When the attack commenced toward sundown, five of the Wicked People commanded by Corporal Dextrous were neatly ensconced on a bowlder-crowned hillock which overlooked the ford. About them *képis* set on sticks gave the impression that there were many more. Anxiously they regarded the river curving sharply away to the right, leaving a wide, treeless area which was thickly grown with papyrus and elephant grass.

To the left at a distance of some hundred yards, the vine-grown forest presented an admirable jumping-off place for an attacking party, and it was to face this menace that most commanders would have deployed their men. Mightily the Legionnaires grumbled when Sergeant Miller left but six of his tiny command among those rocks facing the forest. It was a gamble, he knew, but the memory of those lonely bones back in the forest was strong in his mind.

With the remaining *képi*-less thirteen, Jake occupied a small dried gully which enfiladed the wide papyrus meadow and also commanded an excellent view of the coffee-colored river.

It was going to be a nasty affair at best, Jake realized and, having only twenty rounds per man, the battle, no matter what its outcome, would be short.

Gripping that Lebel which had been the property of Legionnaire Orteaga, late of the Twenty Wicked People, Sergeant Miller viewed the line of disheveled, sweating Legionnaires who, following instructions, lay perfectly motionless beneath the fan palm fronds.

BEGINNING WITH the suddenness of the first drops of a thunder shower, a crackle of rifle fire sounded from beyond the knoll. The hidden men could see the rock splinters flying from the stones above Corporal Dextrous and his five fellows. Louder grew the fusillade and ricochets commenced to moan by.

"*Peste!*" one of the Legionnaires not far from Miller spat. "Why are we doomed to have such a fool for a leader? If we were all on that knoll we might stand a chance. As it is, the slavers will chop us to ribbons with their *yataghans.*"

"And I will shoot you in a minute if you don't keep quiet," warned Jake, venomously.

Louder grew the crackle of musketry and bullets commenced to sever twigs and branches which drifted earthward like shot birds.

"They'll attack from the woods in a minute," whispered Gonzales. "See if they don't—"

But just then a new and very noisy detachment of the enemy opened fire from the flank, enfilading the rocky knoll from two angles.

"No, you fool," a gigantic Russian with smallpox-ravaged features shook his head, "the real attack is beginning now. That first was only a feint."

However, the Russian was as wrong as his friend and with it was deep amazement as the ambushed Legionnaires beheld off to their right the first glimmer of white *jellabias* among the yellow-green elephant grass.

Up above, Corporal Dextrous and his men were following orders and were shooting off their rounds as fast as possible and certainly giving the impression that there were more than six thoroughly unhappy Legionnaires up yonder.

In the breathless, rigid silence, the fourteen men in the gully watched the progress of El Cocodrilo's main body through the elephant grass. Nearer and nearer they came, passed right by the ambuscade and went on, dark, small-featured faces savagely intent.

Soon they would be in the shorter papyrus where the bamboo sprouted in bright emerald clumps. Louder grew the fire in the forest, and the answering shots of the Legionnaires came twice as frequent; in fact the forest rang to the reports and multitudes of terrified birds rocketed up into the green-blue sky.

"Steady," cautioned Jake, as he beheld the dark mass of his enemies gathered at the edge of the elephant grass. In a minute would come that rush from that supposedly unsuspected quarter, that rush which had heretofore always brought victory. Well, El Cocodrilo might learn a few things about jungle fighting.

"*Yah-il-il-Allah!*" That heart-shaking shout of the charging Arabs arose and, led by a man in olive-green shooting clothes, there sprang from the elephant grass a mob of perhaps fifty men of all colors and bearing a weird miscellany of arms, ranging from Mauser carbines to plessors of a type as old as war itself. Yelling exultantly they started across that open patch of papyrus which seemed exposed, so thoroughly improbable for a route of attack that an ordinary commander would never have thought of attempting to defend it.

ALL AT once things began to happen out there. Agonized shrieks and yells arose as the slavers' bare feet came in contact with the sharp bamboo stakes the Legionnaires had planted there under Jake's expert direction. Lao foot barbs had their uses.

Since the needle-pointed spikes were practically invisible amid the bushy papyrus, the attackers knew not which way to step and a moment later they began to drop as Igorot man traps, sprung by the hurrying feet of the attackers, flickered upward. As Jake and any one who knows the festive Igorot can tell you, if a young bamboo be split, carefully trimmed and sharpened along the edges and then bent back, it will inflict a serious if not fatal wound when released to fly upward.

Like so many hacking blades the sprung man traps slashed at the legs and bodies of the bewildered attackers. Losing their balance or springing aside to avoid the trenchant wooden blades, many of the discomfited Arabs and half breeds skewered themselves on wooden lance points cunningly hidden amid the thick blue-green papyrus leaves.

In short, the attackers were having a wholly wretched time of it when Sergeant Jake Miller piled Ossa on Pelion and blew his whistle. Forthwith the rifles of the Wicked People commenced to crackle and fling nickel jacketed Lebel bullets into the struggling mass of slavers.

"Shoot, you devils!" roared Jake, red head agleam. "Shoot! You butter-fingered baboons, now's your chance! Yell!"

And the band of Wicked People who, for all their faults, could shoot when called upon, delivered steady, well-controlled volleys at the brown and white clad throng that came struggling back out of the papyrus.

Some few of the slavers did have sense enough to halt, take aim and fire at the ditch that spouted smoke and flame. But these, happily, were a minority. El Cocodrilo, screaming curses in mingled Spanish and Arabic, rallied his men and, on seeing how few were the Legionnaires, attempted to lead a charge. This was his second mistake of the day, for there is nothing a Legionnaire likes so much as to find a charging foe over his front sights.

It was a pretty little bicker while it lasted and a few desperate slavers did gain the ditch, there to make their *yataghans* flash like windmills of steel and so dispatch some eight more of the Wicked People for that place which was especially intended for bad Legionnaires. The rest of the attackers simply melted back into the forest from which they had come, leaving Jake and his men to remove from the bodies of their fellows such trinkets as might appeal to them.

The fight, as Jake had foreseen, was over in very short order and save for the mangled bodies in the papyrus, and the bayoneted corpses in the ditch, forest and glade seemed as they were half an hour ago. Of the men on the knoll three appeared; Corporal Dextrous, brown-black and very solemn because of a ragged hole through his left ear, and two others appeared to join the seven survivors below. Then after nothing more was heard of the leaderless, thoroughly discomfited raiders, there followed a short and bloody interlude in which the wounded slavers were disposed of as painlessly as possible.

BUT THE greatest surprise of the day was yet in store for the hollow-eyed, red-haired sergeant, whose thoughts were turning grimly to Lieutenant von Krass. On the malodorous and unprepossessing body of him who had been known as El Cocodrilo, Jake discovered a worn leather dispatch case. In it was a neatly folded letter addressed to Señor Labastida, which said:

> Better raid the Zandehs this time, but make a feint toward the Oshebas. Am sending half platoon against you. Fight it or go around it. First payment received, expect second when you recross Tembo.

For signature appeared the significant initials, "V.K."

"The dirty swine! No wonder the square-head likes Bunbaki," Jake said, fingering the letter. "Shouldn't wonder but he's made quite a good thing of it. But let's make sure." And so Sergeant Miller held the paper toward the sunset-reddened sky and was very much interested to discover that on the paper the French Government water mark appeared unmistakably clear.

"The sly son of a hyena," he muttered to himself. "No wonder he wants nothing but dumb-bells around him—thought he'd make a bluff of standing off old Cocodrilo and get rid of me at the same time."

Carefully he folded away that fatal bit of evidence in his blouse.

"What you got there, boss?" asked Corporal Dextrous curiously.

Jake patted his pocket.

"A piece of paper, Amby," he explained, "which may be worth a lieutenant's commission to me, or a lead bullet."

CHAPTER IV

MARKED FOR DEATH

A GRIM SMILE decked the insect-bitten and unshaved countenance of Sergeant Miller when, through the screen of baobab and mango, he beheld a glimmer marking the white walls of the *poste* of Bunbaki.

Was the other expedition back yet? If it was there would very likely ensue a pretty serious half hour when he and Lieutenant von Krass met once more. His sweaty hand crept up to touch the bosom of his thick blue blouse and to test the outline of that envelope containing Commandant Marais's order recalling Von Krass to Libreville. Would the Prussian size up the situation aright?

"Wonder what that *mal hombre* will do?" Jake asked himself. "H'm, it'll be one nasty fix I'll be in—can't draw a gun on him less it's in self-defense, and that squarehead'll take damn good care I won't get a chance. Still, if he's stupid enough to put things like that letter in writing, he may not tumble."

Thinking furiously he strode on through the green and gold wilderness with the boots of the now thoroughly chastened Wicked People crunching on the mold under foot. He glanced over his shoulder, for now he had no misgivings about marching in front of the Wicked People.

The nine survivors of that *corps d'élite* were behind him in more senses than one. It had penetrated even their thick skulls that Lieutenant von Krass's intentions toward them had not been of the kindliest, and, furthermore, that one Jake Miller was a leader such as few men are favored to serve under. Yes, their expressions were satisfactory now, their evil, bronzed faces were set and they strode along like soldiers proud of having successfully carried out a difficult assignment.

It was perfectly reasonable that Jake's heart should commence to thump under his heavy overcoat as they drew near the iron-studded gate and beheld a brace of sentries staring down at him as on a ghost.

"Get down off there. *Schnell!* Get a move on, you sow-mothered worm casts, and unbar the gate!"

Very straight and alert was Sergeant Miller when he led his decimated detachment into the drill yard and heard the walls reverberate to the tread of the hobnails of the Wicked People.

"Halte! Sacs à terre!" he snapped. "At ease."

He eyed them a moment and noted the thin-featured Arab who had tried to murder him. Legionnaire Hassan was looking very thoughtful—and besides, he was quick in his movements.

"Legionnaire Mohammed Hassan, front and center, follow me."

Leaving the other eight Wicked People to glower malevolently at the Legionnaires who appeared from *chambrée* and mess hall, Jake marched across the white-hot sunlit court, heading straight toward that portal which led to the inner sanctums.

"Dieu!" he heard the comment going around. "That sacred coward of an American retreated without orders."

"Well, well, there'll be a little shooting practice to-morrow morning. *Pam! Pam!* and another grave dug."

Under his four days' beard Sergeant Miller's lips tightened, his fingers crept upward, undid the catch of the heavy leather holster in which he kept his automatic. No use taking chances.

In the furnacelike gloom of the *poste* he cast a look over his shoulder. Behind him Legionnaire Mohammed Hassan tramped along with his small supple hands hanging loose from his wrists and with a look of bland happiness on his saddle-feed visage.

AT LAST Jake arrived before that door which held nothing but unpleasant associations and his breath came a little quicker as he rapped on it with an insect-bitten knuckle.

"Come in!"

Von Krass was in there all right, Jake realized, and he drew himself up to full height as his hand closed on the hot iron of the latch. He stepped briskly inside and saluted, all in one motion.

"Du lieber Gott!"

Startled, Von Krass spoke in his native tongue and his hands, which were on the desk before him, stiffened quite perceptibly.

The Prussian was a little redder due to exposure to the sun during his recent expedition, but otherwise he was the same stiff-backed, blond-haired giant he had previously been. His small, china-blue eyes were very direct as he returned the American sergeant's salute.

"Well?"

"Sergeant Miller, sir, reporting with ten men." Queer how his voice seemed to fill that hot little room.

Von Krass simply glared a moment, wetted his sun-cracked lips, then said:

"Where are the rest?"

"Dead, sir."

"So you retreated, eh? Didn't carry out your assignment. You know what that means."

How deadly was the glare of the seated officer! Jake tried to read the expression behind those staring blue eyes. Was there a hint of fear in them? No, decidedly not.

"Mission completed, sir. We held the ford and destroyed the force of El Cocodrilo—inflicted casualties amounting to fifty-four men. There were no prisoners."

An expression of disgust swept over Von Krass's narrow features.

"Fifty-four men? The slave raider wiped out? Bah! Don't insult my intelligence. You couldn't have done that with twenty men and only twenty rounds per man."

Jake's inner soul boiled. There was no doubt of it now, Von Krass had deliberately doomed him and the Twenty Wicked

People to death. He wondered if the worthy Mohammed Hassan—he who was given to rapid thinking and whose motions were quick—caught the significance of that last statement. There was no way of telling.

Jake heard his own voice saying, "I'm not lying, sir. El Cocodrilo is wiped out. I have in my pocket," he tried to keep his voice steady, "papers taken from his body."

For a moment the face of the seated officer lit.

"So? You really killed him," he said slowly, as though the words were wrenched from his mouth. "If what you say is true, there is no doubt that you are a magnificent soldier. But," he snapped, "I think you are lying, nevertheless."

"I'm not lying, sir." And forthwith Jake described his tactics, eyes riveted on the sweat-beaded red features of the officer before him and, as he went further into his narrative, he beheld the birth of suspicion, of alarm and then of uneasiness on the narrow face of Lieutenant von Krass.

"You!" he snapped to Legionnaire Mohammed Hassan. "Speak up, you Arab ape. Tell me the story as you saw it."

STUMBLINGLY AND in a weird mixture of Arabic and Legion French, the Wicked Person gave his version of the affair, and so occupied a certain amount of time in which Jake guessed that Lieutenant von Krass was coming to some rapid and unpleasant conclusions. But what chiefly attracted Jake's attention was the large automatic which lay before the blue-coated lieutenant on some papers.

As the Arab continued his rambling account, Lieutenant von Krass casually, oh, very casually, picked up the automatic and commenced to finger it, giving a beautiful counterfeit of absentmindedness.

"*Ach*, so!" commented Von Krass when the account drew to a close. "Then it is my duty to commend you, sergeant."

"A minute, sir," broke in Jake suddenly. "I—I've been careless, very careless, sir, about a certain matter."

Suspicion darted into the Prussian's face as a fish darts into a pool and he sat just a little straighter as he said:

"How so?"

"When I reported, sir, I forgot to give you a letter from the Commandant at Libreville," explained Jake, his eyes riveted on the German's long, thin fingers.

A fraction of a moment previous Von Krass's thumb had come in contact with the safety catch and now suddenly it had been pushed clear.

With the precise, correct movements of a robot, Jake pulled out the letter, now wrinkled, sweat-dampened and out of shape and, stepping forward, laid it on the desk before his superior.

"That, sir, is a message the commandant sent to you by me. I'm very sorry, sir, I forgot it before."

For a long, tense moment the big officer sat quite still, his eyes fixed on Jake's, probing their depths like lance points; but Jake assumed a poker face and stood to attention, busily gauging the amount of time necessary to flip up the holster cover and draw the automatic beneath.

"This is inexcusable!" barked Von Krass as he picked up the envelope and tore the end off with a brief, irritable motion. "I was going to make you a corporal, but a man who cannot remember to deliver a message is not fit to be a *soldat première classe.*"

ALL THE while the Arab looked on and moved one of his feet while his soft brown eyes fixed themselves meditatively on the map just above the stiff bristles on Lieutenant von Krass's head.

The lieutenant picked up the letter and began to read, and the muscles of Jake's body gradually tensed themselves as he watched a tide of scarlet well into Von Krass's cheeks and dye his whole visage a brilliant scarlet.

"Look out!" shrieked a dozen inner voices. "He's going to kill you—"

Slowly the Prussian's eyes swept upward and in them was a look of complete understanding. Suddenly he stiffened.

"Name of God!" he barked. "Who ever told you you were a soldier? Look at your uniform—pockets unbuttoned, holster unbuttoned. Police yourself!"

His life, Jake realized, now hung by a very slender thread. If he should obey orders and button his holster flap, he stood not the ghost of a show of reaching his gun in time to defend himself.

His fingers seemed very thick and awkward as he slipped the metal uniform buttons through their holes, neglecting the holster flap. He dropped his hands, but his hope was cut short.

"You've forgotten to fasten your holster flap," reminded Von Krass coldly. "What a slovenly dog you are. *Schnell!* Do as I say."

There was no doubt that Von Krass was going to try to kill him, that Jake realized; but equally well was he aware that to disobey orders would be equally fatal.

The blood roared in his ears as he pushed the heavy leather over the bronze stud. His only chance now lay in the possibility that Von Krass might miss, or that his own tortured brain might be able to work out some trick.

He had no time to conjecture further when the Prussian, who was toying once more with that automatic before him, leaned forward, teeth gleaming white in the sunlight.

"You said, sergeant, that you found certain papers on the body of El Cocodrilo?"

"Yes, sir."

"Let me have them."

Jake reached to the side pocket beside the pistol holster and commenced to fumble in its depths when, from the tail of his eye, he saw the muzzle of the Prussian's automatic flash upward, sidewise. There sounded a deafening report—or was it two reports?—that filled the little room like the roar of a field piece. Acrid fumes filled the air.

Jake, wrenching to free the holster flap, wondered why he did not seem to be hit. The gun was out and he was about to shoot when he suddenly became aware that Von Krass was standing quite motionless, rigid, the smoking automatic still in his hand and staring before him bewilderedly.

So he remained a long fraction of a minute, then a single drop of bright blood appeared on his lips, fell free and spattered on the recall orders. All at once Von Krass collapsed forward on the desk, upsetting a bottle of ink which, wandering over the papers with the other color, gave the effect of the national colors of the dead man.

"*Kelb ibn kelb!*" remarked Legionnaire Mohammed Hassan— he who thought fast and who was quick in his movements. "Once I would have stolen your life, *sidi,* and now I have given it back to you. *Allahu Akbar!*"

And so saying, Legionnaire Mohammed Hassan sank to his ragged knees, dropped the cheap pistol he had stolen from some raider's body, and then collapsed on his face, quite dead, for officers of the Legion seldom miss.

Sergeant Jake Miller who, in his own quiet way was quite a judge of human nature, nodded once to himself and then turned on his heel to call the guard.

ABOUT THE AUTHOR

WORLD TRAVELER, ADVEN-TURER, Harvard graduate, and onetime liaison officer in the "A.E.F. is F.V.W. Mason.

F.V.W. Mason

He comes from a family of soldiers, a family steeped in martial tradition from the time they settled in this country three hundred years ago. When the Civil War broke over the nation seventeen of the Masons answered the call to arms. Two of them returned.

F.V.W. Mason began to read intensively in books of history and adventure when he was a small boy set back by a childhood disease. He started his travels early, in the days before the World War. His grandfather was a consul-general in Paris and Berlin and his family moved around Europe. When he was not travel-ing, he and his brother were in the woods hunting.

It was with his brother that he tried to get into the French Army when the Germans began their invasion. But both boys were 'way below the age limit. F.V.W. Mason waited two years and then managed to get overseas, first with the French and then as a lieutenant in the Interpreters' Corps of the American

Army, in the capacity of a liaison officer. And he went through, over there, considerable action.

He came home after the war to get a degree at Harvard University. His summers he spent making land cruises from Marblehead to British Columbia and down the Pacific Coast to Mexico in a dilapidated flivver.

For a while after college he drifted—Central America and the Antilles, Hungary, Roumania and the other Eastern European countries.

It was the suggestion of a former instructor in English at Harvard that put him into writing. The instructor told him that stories he had written in college had always looked promising, and Mason decided to try his hand professionally. And he has been doing it ever since, with success that has borne out the teacher's prophecy.

1. GENIUS JONES by Lester Dent
2. WHEN TIGERS ARE HUNTING: THE COMPLETE ADVENTURES OF CORDIE, SOLDIER OF FORTUNE, VOLUME 1 by W. Wirt
3. THE SWORDSMAN OF MARS by Otis Adelbert Kline
4. THE SHERLOCK OF SAGELAND: THE COMPLETE TALES OF SHERIFF HENRY, VOLUME 1 by W.C. Tuttle
5. GONE NORTH by Charles Alden Seltzer
6. THE MASKED MASTER MIND by George F. Worts
7. BALATA by Fred MacIsaac
8. BRETWALDA by Philip Ketchum
9. DRAFT OF ETERNITY by Victor Rousseau
10. FOUR CORNERS, VOLUME 1 by Theodore Roscoe
11. CHAMPION OF LOST CAUSES by Max Brand
12. THE SCARLET BLADE: THE RAKEHELLY ADVENTURES OF CLEVE AND D'ENTREVILLE, VOLUME 1 by Murray R. Montgomery
13. DOAN AND CARSTAIRS: THEIR COMPLETE CASES by Norbert Davis
14. THE KING WHO CAME BACK by Fred MacIsaac
15. BLOOD RITUAL: THE ADVENTURES OF SCARLET AND BRADSHAW, VOLUME 1 by Theodore Roscoe
16. THE CITY OF STOLEN LIVES: THE ADVENTURES OF PETER THE BRAZEN, VOLUME 1 by Loring Brent
17. THE RADIO GUN-RUNNERS by Ralph Milne Farley
18. SABOTAGE by Cleve F. Adams
19. THE COMPLETE CABALISTIC CASES OF SEMI DUAL, THE OCCULT DETECTOR, VOLUME 2: 1912–13 by J.U. Giesy and Junius B. Smith
20. SOUTH OF FIFTY-THREE by Jack Bechdolt
21. TARZAN AND THE JEWELS OF OPAR by Edgar Rice Burroughs
22. CLOVELLY by Max Brand
23. WAR LORD OF MANY SWORDSMEN: THE ADVENTURES OF NORCOSS, VOLUME 1 by W. Wirt
24. ALIAS THE NIGHT WIND by Varick Vanardy
25. THE BLUE FIRE PEARL: THE COMPLETE ADVENTURES OF SINGAPORE SAMMY, VOLUME 1 by George F. Worts

26. THE MOON POOL & THE CONQUEST OF THE MOON POOL by Abraham Merritt

27. THE GUN-BRAND by James B. Hendryx

28. JAN OF THE JUNGLE by Otis Adelbert Kline

29. MINIONS OF THE MOON by William Grey Beyer

30. DRINK WE DEEP by Arthur Leo Zagat

31. THE VENGEANCE OF THE WAH FU TONG: THE COMPLETE CASES OF JIGGER MASTERS, VOLUME 1 by Anthony M. Rud

32. THE RUBY OF SURATAN SINGH: THE ADVENTURES OF SCARLET AND BRADSHAW, VOLUME 2 by Theodore Roscoe

33. THE SHERIFF OF TONTO TOWN: THE COMPLETE TALES OF SHERIFF HENRY, VOLUME 2 by W.C. Tuttle

34. THE DARKNESS AT WINDON MANOR by Max Brand

35. THE FLYING LEGION by George Allan England

36. THE GOLDEN CAT: THE ADVENTURES OF PETER THE BRAZEN, VOLUME 3 by Loring Brent

37. THE RADIO MENACE by Ralph Milne Farley

38. THE APES OF DEVIL'S ISLAND by John Cunningham

39. THE OPPOSING VENUS: THE COMPLETE CABALISTIC CASES OF SEMI DUAL, THE OCCULT DETECTOR by J.U. Giesy and Junius B. Smith

40. THE EXPLOITS OF BEAU QUICKSILVER by Florence M. Pettee

41. ERIC OF THE STRONG HEART by Victor Rousseau

42. MURDER ON THE HIGH SEAS AND THE DIAMOND BULLET: THE COMPLETE CASES OF GILLIAN HAZELTINE by George F. Worts

43. THE WOMAN OF THE PYRAMID AND OTHER TALES: THE PERLEY POORE SHEEHAN OMNIBUS, VOLUME 1 by Perley Poore Sheehan

44. A COLUMBUS OF SPACE AND THE MOON METAL: THE GARRETT P. SERVISS OMNIBUS, VOLUME 1 by Garrett P. Serviss

45. THE BLACK TIDE: THE COMPLETE ADVENTURES OF BELLOW BILL WILLIAMS, VOLUME 1 by Ralph R. Perry

46. THE NINE RED GODS DECIDE: THE COMPLETE ADVENTURES OF CORDIE, SOLDIER OF FORTUNE, VOLUME 2 by W. Wirt

47. A GRAVE MUST BE DEEP! by Theodore Roscoe

48. THE AMERICAN by Max Brand
49. THE COMPLETE ADVENTURES OF KOYALA, VOLUME 1 by John Charles Beecham
50. THE CULT MURDERS by Alan Forsyth
51. THE COMPLETE CASES OF THE MONGOOSE by Johnston McCulley
52. THE GIRL AND THE PEOPLE OF THE GOLDEN ATOM by Ray Cummings
53. THE GRAY DRAGON: THE ADVENTURES OF PETER THE BRAZEN, VOLUME 2
    by Loring Brent
54. THE GOLDEN CITY by Ralph Milne Farley
55. THE HOUSE OF INVISIBLE BONDAGE: THE COMPLETE CABALISTIC CASES OF
    SEMI DUAL, THE OCCULT DETECTOR by J.U. Giesy and Junius B. Smith
56. THE SCRAP OF LACE: THE COMPLETE CASES OF MADAME STOREY, VOLUME 1
    by Hulbert Footner
57. TOWER OF DEATH: THE ADVENTURES OF SCARLET AND BRADSHAW, VOLUME 3
    by Theodore Roscoe
58. THE DEVIL-TREE OF EL DORADO by Frank Aubrey
59. THE FIREBRAND: THE COMPLETE ADVENTURES OF TIZZO, VOLUME 1
    by Max Brand
60. MARCHING SANDS AND THE CARAVAN OF THE DEAD: THE HAROLD LAMB
    OMNIBUS by Harold Lamb
61. KINGDOM COME by Martin McCall
62. HENRY RIDES THE DANGER TRAIL: THE COMPLETE TALES OF SHERIFF HENRY,
    VOLUME 3 by W.C. Tuttle
63. Z IS FOR ZOMBIE by Theodore Roscoe
64. THE BAIT AND THE TRAP: THE COMPLETE ADVENTURES OF TIZZO, VOLUME 2
    by Max Brand
65. MINIONS OF MARS by William Gray Beyer
66. SWORDS IN EXILE: THE RAKEHELLY ADVENTURES OF CLEVE AND D'ENTREVILLE,
    VOLUME 2 by Murray R. Montgomery
67. MEN WITH NO MASTER: THE COMPLETE ADVENTURES OF ROBIN THE
    BOMBARDIER by Roy de S. Horn
68. THE TORCH by Jack Bechdolt
69. KING OF CHAOS AND OTHER ADVENTURES: THE JOHNSTON MCCULLEY
    OMNIBUS by Johnston McCulley

70. THE BLIND SPOT by Austin Hall & Homer Eon Flint
71. SATAN'S VENGEANCE by Carroll John Daly
72. THE VIPER: THE COMPLETE CASES OF MADAME STOREY, VOLUME 2 by Hulbert Footner
73. THE SAPPHIRE SMILE: THE ADVENTURES OF PETER THE BRAZEN, VOLUME 4 by Loring Brent
74. THE CURSE OF CAPISTRANO AND OTHER ADVENTURES: THE JOHNSTON MCCULLEY OMNIBUS, VOLUME 2 by Johnston McCulley
75. THE MAN WHO MASTERED TIME AND OTHER ADVENTURES: THE RAY CUMMINGS OMNIBUS by Ray Cummings
76. THE GUNS OF THE AMERICAN: THE ADVENTURES OF NORCROSS, VOLUME 2 by W. Wirt
77. TRAILIN' by Max Brand
78. WAR DECLARED! by Theodore Roscoe
79. THE RETURN OF THE NIGHT WIND by Varick Vanardy
80. THE FETISH FIGHTERS AND OTHER ADVENTURES: THE F.V.W. MASON FOREIGN LEGION STORIES OMNIBUS by F.V.W. Mason
81. THE PYTHON PIT: THE COMPLETE ADVENTURES OF SINGAPORE SAMMY, VOLUME 2 by George F. Worts
82. A QUEEN OF ATLANTIS by Frank Aubrey
83. FOUR CORNERS, VOLUME 2 by Theodore Roscoe
84. THE STUFF OF EMPIRE: THE COMPLETE ADVENTURES OF BELLOW BILL WILLIAMS, VOLUME 2 by Ralph R. Perry
85. GALLOPING GOLD: THE COMPLETE TALES OF SHERIFF HENRY, VOLUME 4 by W.C. Tuttle
86. JADES AND AFGHANS: THE COMPLETE ADVENTURES OF CORDIE, SOLDIER OF FORTUNE, VOLUME 3 by W. Wirt
87. THE LEDGER OF LIFE: THE COMPLETE CABALISTIC CASES OF SEMI DUAL, THE OCCULT DETECTOR by J.U. Giesy and Junius B. Smith
88. MINIONS OF MERCURY by William Gray Beyer
89. WHITE HEATHER WEATHER by John Frederick
90. THE FIRE FLOWER AND OTHER ADVENTURES: THE JACKSON GREGORY OMNIBUS by Jackson Gregory